GOING HOME

C. C. AVRAM

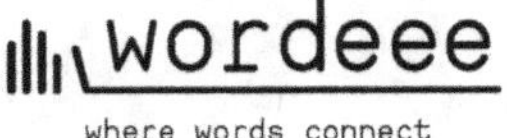

GOING HOME

ISBN: 978-1-946274-93-9 (Print)
ISBN: 978-1-946274-94-6 (eBook)

Library of Congress Control Number: 2022947819

Jacket Design: Okomata
Interior Design: Amit Dey
Editor: Winsome Hudson

Website: www.wordeee.com
Twitter.com/wordeeeupdates
Facebook: facebook.com/wordeee/
e-mail: contact@wordeee.com
Published by Wordeee in the United States, Beacon, New York 2022

Printed in the USA

CHAPTER ONE

"HOLD UP DERE NICE LADY," a strapping man, skin the color of prune, matted hair flapping in the wind, jumped from his perch, and rushed toward the woman walking briskly along the water's edge. She wore Sportos, a see-through lime green sarong knotted over a black bikini. Her curly, pony-tailed red hair bounced from side to side.

He had to jog to catch up with her.

"What kind of hurry yu in this h'erly morning?" The man wheezed.

The woman turned to look at him—possibly through him, and then smiled. It wasn't the controlled smile that warned he might be intruding, but one that said he'd interrupted her deep concentration; one that hinted that at the very moment of his interruption she was about to solve a complicated problem.

"No hurry." April Summers's tentative smile reached its fullness.

"You need a guide to 'elp yu slow down and appreciate paradise?" he asked.

"Not today," April said, her pace unchanged.

Her admirer regarded her with deference. *Any woman brave enough to be walking alone at dawn on a foreign beach was tallawa.* "Yu, sure now?" her suitor persisted.

"Couldn't be surer. Only time for a quick dip this morning."

"Awright." The man's face crumpled. "But mi hafi tell you one thing before mi leave yu though. Yu is one fine specimen." A wide, toothless grin spread across his unwrinkled face as he fell in stride next to her. The sweat-drenched odor of his well-worn clothes filled April's nostrils, blocking out the sweet smell of the purple sea grape trees on the banks of the beach.

"Is that so?" April couldn't help but smile.

"Eh-eh. Why mi a go tell yu if it no go so? Yes, mon, it definitely so."

Determined to find a reason to lag behind her uninvited companion, April abruptly halted to inspect a large, pink seashell wedged into the sand. Instead of picking up the conch shell, she tried to unearth it with the tip of her Sporto and stumbled.

"No bother mash-up that beautiful face till me look at it again." The man was beside her in a second. Grabbing her arm, he hoisted her up, breaking a potentially nasty fall.

"That's stuck in there, huh?" April braced herself against his torso. "Thanks for your help."

"No problem, mon. Mi here fi protect yu." Her companion yanked the shell clean from the stubborn sand in a swift and expert move, handing it to her.

"Thanks again." April smiled, taking the shell, and putting it to her ear. She listened. Nothing. She listened harder. Still nothing. All she heard was the wussssh of the sea rushing in to meet her. April pushed the shell closer to her ear and silenced her breath. Was it still possible to hear the distant echo of spirit warriors? Or, as legend has it, the last cry of Sanju, the slave woman who, after swathing her baby to her breast, threw herself overboard a Zong slave ship. She listened too for the beating of the Sankofa wings, or for the wail of suffering that had taken place upon the shores of Jamaica, an important port in the evil triangle. Still, she heard nothing but endless silence. Not even more recent ancestors like Grandpa Addison spoke a word., though for good reason as he probably had no interest in coming near his tiresome daughter Josephine.

"The sea loud, nuh?" Her new best friend asked.

"But it's not giving up any secrets today. I was hoping to hear our ancestors; learn a bit of our history from the waves."

"Them days long gone mon, plus Jamaican duppy don't travel over water. Dem prefer dry land. Most of them probably drown the moment them backside touch water, you nuh. But listen again, listen real good; you might just hear the suffering of the people today. Even in paradise, we suffering now."

No longer attuned to her "real self," April felt alienated from the sounds and traditions of her forbearers. Diluted blood, ivy-league brainwashing, willing consent, and assimilation, thrown into a cauldron and mixed into a new constitution, prevented her from being a part of those still privileged to remember. The intentional erasure of memory; the beginning of the death of her people, had embraced her. If only she had memory. April tossed the muted shell back onto the sand. The echoes of the sea, she decided, were reserved for those with the keenest of sensibilities, who were allowed to hear, to remember, to record. Sam, a proud Black man not willing to give up his identity, she was sure, would have heard them.

"All right, Miss Pretty Lady, I have to leave yu here for now."

As her companion strode off to one of the many hotels dotting the shoreline, his big feet imprinted the sand as his silhouette in the early morning followed the shore, "but if yu change yu mind about a guide," he called back, "I'll be right here."

April waved goodbye to her suitor. Stretching her neck, she turned eastward, the sea breeze caressing her face as the incredible, pale glow of the rising orb warmed every freckle dotting her nose. Dawn, in its discontent, was barely clinging to the horizon. Confident of its win, the sun waited patiently for the moon to give up its reign. For millions of years, every morning, it had played the same trick on its partner, laughing as the night's globe, broken and grumpy, reluctantly crept out of sight. Oh, how well aware April was that the sun and moon couldn't occupy the sky at the same time. It was like her and Sam. He was eclipsing her sun, and she, his moon.

The beach was empty. The crystal water of the Caribbean Sea ebbed warm and welcoming, but it had not always been that way. April removed two large towels from her bag, flapped one with deftness and spread it on the sand. The other she rolled and placed under her head. The shock of reddish- hair, curly because of her ancestral legacy rested comfortably against the make-shift pillow. Under the pale orange of the rising sun, her hair shone like a beacon. The neon green sarong against her tanned skin added a new shade of green to the verdant flora. In anticipation of the rays to come, April coated her body with sunscreen. Five days in the brutal sun had turned her pale skin an angry red, forcing her, except at dawn, to take refuge under shady trees. April closed her eyes and perked her ear again, just in case a snippet of old news wanted to reach her. Maybe Nancy Tumi would remember her and tell her a secret that might help solve the awful state of her relationship with her husband, Sam. Or any news at all that might make the waters separating their shared heritage thinner than the blood that bound their shared history. Nothing. All she heard were the little waves breaking against the shore.

The breathtaking view was limitless. Foliage of great variety, way beyond her vision, swayed and rustled in the gentle breeze. Bamboo and almond trees bowed politely, welcoming plumed friends. Fish darted just beyond the shore, and land crabs burrowed deep into sandy culverts, making their way to safety before daybreak. She felt at peace. Her beach friend was right. She was indeed in paradise, a land full of color and promise. And she wished it would never end.

Jamaica had been a good decision. Only last evening, while resting in Sam's arms, their eyes had locked in hope. He'd declared this the best vacation he'd ever had, and it had been encouraging to see the laugh lines in his face relax and to hear his voice softly calling her name. If only she could freeze time. She loved Sam desperately, but she was a woman who needed her own life and to make her own decisions. April allowed her lids to flutter as she shielded her eyes from the rising sun. If only Sam could get it. She had dreams. Big dreams. And a life she loved. A career she loved. Why would she want to mess up a good thing? Surely, she loved babies—other people's. April was keenly aware being in paradise was not enough to solve her marital problems. She rose onto her elbows and, for a moment, rested in child pose. Jumping to her feet, she kicked off her Sporto and ran to the water's edge. Scooping a handful of seashells, sieving the sand through her fingers, she pelted them one at a time, watching with delight as they skipped over the water. She was happy to be "home."

Forty minutes of peace and abandon, floating carefree on the turquoise water, swimming laps out to the bobbing orange buoys, and occasionally donning snorkeling gear to look at life below was sheer bliss. April's fluttering feet picked up their tempo, and like the beating wings of a bird flying south, she made her way back to the shore. She removed her goggles and sighed audibly.

"Mek yu a sigh so. Nobody should sigh like that in a place like this. Yu in heaven, you know." The dreadlocked man was walking back toward her.

"I believe that" April said. "I really do." She glanced over to the cottages. There were a few more people on the beach now.

Women scaling fish and roasting breadfruit; fishermen with nets and fresh catch.

"Trevor." One of the women called.

"So yu husband can take care of that sigh?"

April did not answer the insolent man.

"Trevor," the woman repeated.

April assumed Trevor was not going to answer.

"Trevor, wah wrong with you this morning. You no hear mi a call you?" The woman persisted. "No bodder wid no hoity-toity this morning. Mi need you to come here right now."

Lights now turning on, one after the other, signaled the start of another leisure day. Inside her rented cottage, the kitchen light glowed. Miss Muriel was getting ready to prepare another mouth-watering breakfast. "Hunger calls," she smiled at her admirer, allowing him to gracefully obey the woman who looked like she'd beat him with the fish she was scaling if he tarried one more minute. "See you later, perhaps," she turned in the direction of the bungalow.

"Yu have a great day, yu hear, pretty lady," the man said, showing his one brown tooth. "Lawdy, Lawdy. Yu sure is one beautiful woman. Mi name is Trevor. If you come down and me not here later on, just ask for Trevor. Everybody 'round here know me, just say Trevor, and I'll be dere."

"Deal," April said, wrapping her body in her sarong and wet hair with a matching turban. "I'll send my husband if he wants a tour?"

"Yah, mon. But make sure yu come with him."

"Mornin' Miss," the helper said as April came through the door. The aroma of fresh coffee filled the room. The spacious cottage with its lattice French doors opening onto an encircling red brick patio was shrouded by the garden's perfusion wafting bouquets of roses, tiger lilies, and bougainvillea surrounding its perimeter. Star-apple, coconut and mango trees secluded and protected the house from gawkers. Beyond the tennis courts, the golf course's spectacular rolling green proved a highlight for Sam.

"Morning, Miss Muriel. Is Mr. Summers up yet?"

"Me don't hear him yet, Ma'am. *Lazy brute.* "You have anything special in mind for breakfast this morning?"

"How about ackee and saltfish? No, make that bammy and fry fish. Mr. Summers needs to experience everything Jamaican before he leaves the island. You remember our deal, right? No bacon or eggs for our entire visit, even if he begs you," April said.

"Bacon and heggs. No sah, not in this 'ere house. When in Jamaica, be a Jamaican. And later, a *goin* mek him some sweet curry goat." The woman sucked at her teeth. *The lazy brute this woman call her husband should tek him backside down to h'erly mornin' sea to see sunrise. If he want to be Jamaican, him would haul his dead ass outta da bed before blazin' sunshine come through window. Why a good Jamaican woman would pick up with a useless American man?*

"Good." April's eyes crinkled from a broad smile.

"Don't worry. Mi'll take care of 'im. When mi done feed him, he ain't going back to 'Merica."

"How about a cup of that great smelling coffee?"

"Coming right, hup."

"This has to be the best coffee in the world," April said, inhaling deeply, out of habit, checking her iPhone.

"Haperently. The Queen tink so too," Miss Muriel said proudly. "You want condensed or cow's milk?"

"Condensed." April loved the gooey milk Caribbean people seemed to relish. Taking a sip of her delectable coffee, April said. "I'm going to get Mr. Summers up now. Is half-hour good for you, Miss Muriel?"

"Anytime. Mi 'ere till four o'clock," she deadpanned as if to say, why the backside you don't shut-you mouth and gwaan bout yu business. The curt, tongue-in-cheek attitude of the locals was no longer a bother to April; she'd spent many a summer with the haughtiness of a local maid.

April stood quietly, looking down at her husband, a handsome man. His face was now a healthy Nutella brown. He was snoring lightly, more like a gust of wind ruffling leaves. She wanted to breathe softly against his lips like she imagined a kiss from God, but something stopped her. April padded to the bathroom, a deep sigh escaping her lips. Her early morning companion's words replayed; "No one should sigh like that in a place like this." That man is filled with wisdom, April thought as she stepped into the cool running water.

"Wake up, sleepyhead," April flapped her towel at a stirring Sam as she came back into the room.

"I could live like this forever," Sam said between yawns. "Waking up to the smell of delicious food, and then the first thing I see is a beautiful, half-naked woman near my bed. Come here," he reached for her. "Tell me this is heaven."

"It's close, isn't it?" April said, toweling her hair vigorously. "I'm all wet, honey."

"I like wet," he grinned.

"Some life, huh?" April sidled up to the bed.

"All I can say is this is the life, Miss April."

"And to top it off, you're in for a culinary experience this morning. A national specialty," she kissed him on the lips. They were cushiony and welcoming.

"Come here, woman." His eyes hazed over. "Did I tell you how much you take my breath away," he said, unable to ignore the discussion below his waist.

"Tell me again."

"April, you're the most beautiful woman in the world to me."

She touched his face. "You're pretty special too, you know."

"I am, huh?" he glanced down at his body. "Since I'm so special, how about fixing me up with a specialty appetizer before our special breakfast, then? This weather might be good to make babies."

April stiffened and then decided to play along. "Appetizer? Too fattening," she giggled like a schoolgirl, unable to take her eyes off her husband's rising attraction.

"Who says?"

"Uhuh?" She mulled over the invitation. "Not I." Unwrapping her towel, she covered him with her warm, still moist body. She had nothing to worry about. She was on the pill.

"Now that's what I call, muuummmm, muuummm good."

CHAPTER TWO

IT WAS WITH WELCOME relief Melody dressed for work. Another insufferable day off because of the confounded holiday season would've turned her life from unpleasant into agonizing. Melody looped earrings through her lobes, her thoughts laser-focused on April Summers, the cocky Jamaican financier on her merger deal. April gave her a headache. Melody wanted to start her year with a bang, and she just hoped the woman had her deal numbers this morning.

It was the dead of winter in Chicago. The weatherman was droning on, "The skies are sunny, but today promises to bring another blisteringly cold day. Last night's five inches bring the snowfall this winter to nearly twenty inches, and it's only the beginning of the inclement weather for the week."

Glancing at the TV, Melody wondered how on earth the weatherman's statement could be true when through the window, the sun's rays splayed prismatic colors on the bathroom walls, and the temperature was blistering in her home. "For Pete's sake," Melody hissed, opening the window a crack before pulling down canvas shades. It wasn't with indifference that she blocked out the sun.

"Miss Melody, it's already at sixty-eight degrees in here."

"Then turn it to sixty. It's too hot in this bathroom." Melody cursed her internal thermostat, which appeared to have taken a leave of absence.

"Yes, Miss." The housekeeper buttoned her sweater.

"Have you made coffee yet?"

"Doin' it now, Miss."

Melody Adams, lips drawn tightly, had the determined look of a warrior. Attractive from a distance or up close, with makeup or not, she hovered in front of the wall-to-wall mirror, desperately trying to apply her eye pencil in a straight line. She arched her perfectly shaped eyebrows, putting more distance between brows and lids. Her hands were shaking something terribly. Two days in a row now. What was going on with her? A month before, December second, to be exact, Melody had turned thirty-seven. Before that, she'd been perfectly fine. Then, *wham*, without warning, she fell apart; lightheadedness, trembling hands, palpitating heart; symptoms her best friend Veronica said were classic of menopausal mid-life crisis. Poppycock! Straight up hogwash if she had ever heard it. Who has menopause at thirty-seven!

Scrubbing her face clean again, Melody grabbed the hand mirror, turned it to the magnifying side, sat on the chaise under the window and tried her artistry once more. If she failed this time, her face would remain *au naturel*. Wiping away the last residue of a crooked line with a glycerin-drenched swab, she carefully applied new eyeliner. The diffused light from this angle was good, very good. Somewhat like the proverbial north light an artist prays for in a moment of inspiration.

Successful, at last, with her eye makeup, Melody reached for the natural bristle brush on her dresser and stroked her thick, nape-length, raven black hair. One hundred strokes until her hair gleamed brilliantly—just as her mother used to do every night before she went to bed, *'Girl, you got the best head a hair in the world. Just like your Grandma Bernice.'* No! Melody said firmly. *No way am I going there this morning.* Memories were dangerous, and there were no charm or sweet sensations in her childhood to trick the mind into fantasy. "Next, Sweet Pea," she said in the mirror. *Sweet Pea.* That's what her brother had nick-named her because she loved the gentle green giant in a can, which was sometimes all they could afford.

"Stockings. Yes, that's it." Melody said loudly, riffling through the chest's bottom drawer to find an un-laddered pair. All thirty pairs, in various colors, were snaked in wash-ing machine tangle. Melody pulled out all the jet blacks and pushed a hand in each contorted leg to check for runs. "Bingo!" she said, tugging on a wholesome pair. Straightening to her full height, five feet five inches, she dabbed her lips with a touch of powder, outlined them with a burnished pencil, applied frosty orange lipstick and stepped back to survey her reflection in the mirror.

"Effie, how do I look this morning?"

"Lovely. Very Lovely, Miss Melody." The housekeeper came running. "Mighty fine."

"Does it feel a little cold in here, now?" Melody asked, twirl-ing this way and that between parallel mirrors. Effie gladly turned up the heat.

She looked dapper. Stately but not boring. The burnt orange suit, deftly toned down with a scoop-neck, piqué, white princess top, matched the shade of her lipstick. The reflection of colors turned the hammered gold tortoise earrings into agates. Yes indeed. She had that look. The indefinable elegance, perfect but uncontrived of the well-born. Just the right amount of shine in her hair, color on her lips and assuredness in her step.

Melody, who absolutely and resolutely believed image was everything, had orchestrated her entire life around the concept *perception is reality.* Pleased with her impeccable appearance, a dimpled smile puckered her face. Her brother used to tease her about the deep dimples, insisting they were a birth defect. "Very nice, huh?" she said. For a second time, Melody looked for reassurance. Effie nodded enthusiastically.

Ready and eager to get back to her life, Melody padded to the stark white kitchen, with its stark white Krupps coffeemaker, white Starbucks coffee grinder, white sub-zero double-sided refrigerator, and white GE toaster into which she popped a raisin bagel, after slicing it open on the white resin cutting board. She poured a cup of coffee into a white, oversized mug.

"Jesus, Effie, where did you get this god-awful coffee?"

"It was on special this week."

"How many times do I have to remind you, you get what you pay for? Believe me, dear, nothing good comes cheap or easy. Can you understand that?" Disgusted with the coffee and Effie's lack of interest in her lecture, Melody gave up on the idea of breakfast. Impatiently she pressed the intercom to the garage. "Bernie, I'm on my way down," she said with resignation, neurotically brushing crumbs from the countertop. "Effie don't forget to dust the picture frames today. You forgot last week. I almost died from dust inhalation."

The housekeeper, used to finicky Melody Adams, said, "Remember I'm leaving this morning. My sister is coming into town. You said it was all right when I asked you last week."

Melody scoffed. Wasting time as usual. People like Effie always waste time. That's why they cleaned other people's houses. "Yes, I remember, but make sure you wash the tub before leaving. You know I hate a dirty tub."

Effie nodded. The woman was such a pain in the ass. Mean as hell when she wanted to be.

The elevator light blinked on the twenty-fifth floor, indicating a short wait. Still, Melody impatiently tapped black-pump-clad feet.

"Good morning," she said to an elderly woman and her care-giver as she got on the elevator. Moving further to the corner, the woman smiled at her. The relic reeked of wealth.

"It's cold out today," Melody said.

The woman nodded, casting her eyes to the floor. The condo, inhabited almost exclusively by whites, was a fashion-able address in Chicago. Not long ago, and maybe even today, entrance to the likes of her would have been denied, except she was a Chicago powerbroker. As the elevator descended, feeling a bit light-headed, Melody leaned against the cabin. It wasn't just a physical sickness; it was deeper than that. There were changes in her body: increasing clumsiness, hot and cold sweats, and foggi-ness. Veronica had said her hormones were adjusting. Adjusting to what! People don't usually go into menopause at thirty-seven! "Have a great day," Melody said to her cabin companions as she stepped briskly off the elevator. Her midnight blue Lexus was idling at the front door.

"Good morning, Miss Adams." The uniformed car attendant smiled, opening the door.

Melody pulled her shearling close to her body and recipro-cated with a smile. She threw her briefcase onto the back seat and slid into the car. She rested the manila folder tucked under her arm on the camel brown-leather passenger seat. Her com-plexion, the folder and the seat blended.

CHAPTER THREE

HYDE PARK, CHICAGO, was quiet and covered in a blanket of snow. Randolph Whittaker dug his hands deep into the pockets of his sweater and stared out the window of his guest bedroom. Remnants of the night's festivities, revelry, and feting; tasseled hats, empty beer cans and discarded garland half-buried under the overnight snowfall littered the street from bringing in the New Year. It was already 2013. Where had time gone? Randolph glanced at his watch. Six-ten a.m. The street-sweepers would soon be by to return the exclusive Chicago neighborhood to its pristine condition. What a pity they couldn't mop up the tsunami that'd devastated his life last night, washing away his reality in its wake. Randolph Whittaker turned on his heels and walked to his children's bedrooms. They were asleep. What would he tell them? How could he tell them? Only God knows, he thought as he walked toward the master bedroom.

The room was dark. Visually it looked as it always had. Veronica, practical as always, had furnished the house elegantly, but to withstand two growing children. Theirs was a home that felt lived-in and welcoming. Randolph felt his body constrict. He knelt by the bed, bringing his face within inches of his wife's. He peered closely at her. Head resting on the pillow, nothing seemed out of the ordinary. Repositioning his body to better study her expression, he wondered how he could have missed the signs. Veronica's face was tense and showed signs of fatigue and strain. Knitted brows in the center of her forehead spoke of her displeasure. Her long lashes barely covered eyeliner smudges, which implied she had been crying. Full lips still showing a tinge of color reminded she had become a stranger to him. Before last night, Randolph had never wondered why his plain wife Veronica had suddenly started wearing makeup or dressing up. He'd chalked up the reddish-gold color of her cheeks, the thick black eyeliner, and the deep cranberry lipstick as her way of hiding the ever-increasing tiredness beginning to settle in her body. How could he have been so damn unsuspecting?

Veronica rolled onto her side. Opening her eyes, she came face-to-face with her husband's burning gaze. Immediately she registered the look of pain and heart-wrenching disappointment and quickly turned away.

"What's the matter with you?" She bolted upright, throwing back the covers.

"Do I have to answer that?"

"I suppose not," she pushed past him and got out of bed.

"Veronica," Randolph caught her by the arm. "We need to talk."

"Not now. I have rounds this morning." She wriggled from his grip. Stuffing her feet into fluffy white slippers, she pulled a floral robe around her body and disappeared into the bathroom.

Who was this woman in his bed? Randolph felt his heart muscles constrict and anger surge through his body. While she had been sleeping, he should have closed his hands around her pretty little neck, wringing the very life he held so dear out of her. How could she do this to him? Betray his love. Images of his torture flashed before him vividly. *Hands getting tighter and tighter. She begging for him to spare her life. He tightening his grip until he felt her body go limp.*

Despite fervent pep talks about being logical and rational, Randolph's pained expression, instead of inspiring empathy in Veronica, left her angry. Relieved to have found the courage to speak her thoughts, there was no way she'd retract her confession. But he didn't deserve her vitriol. She knew that. If he hadn't insisted on her spending more time at home, she might have been able to hide her feelings longer. How was she to do that as the only breadwinner in the family? Sweeping into the bathroom, Veronica turned on the shower. She had to be crazy. How could she be so cruel to a man with whom she'd spent a lifetime? Had two beautiful children? Stepping into the scalding water and jumping back from the heat, she spun the dial to tepid, squeezed gel onto her bath cloth and inhaled deeply. Her mind pushed past Randolph's pain and right back into her pleasure. *Lilac on a summer day. Jasmine in June. The scent of a woman. That's how I'll announce my presence to Tony this morning*; she lathered her body with scented body wash. If she saw Tony. She the laughed out loud at her imaginary affair. All her obsession was motivated by a Tony who had no clue she was tripping about him!

Where do you suppose we should go from here?" Randolph was still in the room when she re-entered. Dead eyes, half-masked to hide the pain, watched his wife dart around the room. His eyes drew helplessly to her pointed, brown nipples as they disappeared behind lacy fabric. This morning Veronica's tall, well-endowed body no longer stirred him. Eighteen years! How could eighteen years have come to an end like this without warning?

"Did I say I was going anywhere? Randolph, all I said was, I'm drowning in this marriage. That I need some air. A little time to sort myself out."

"And that you have stopped loving me," he reminded her.

"I didn't say that. I simply said I need some space."

Veronica," his voice was grave, "where will you go to get that space? The guest room? The hospital? A new home?"

"For God's sake, don't make this a fiasco."

"Fiasco? What exactly do you think it is?" Randolph asked.

"Look. I'm juggling too many balls. I don't know what I feel. I need some space. Is that too much to ask?" Veronica said.

"We had *that* conversation last night. What I'm asking *now* is, what will happen to our family? Are you moving out? What do we tell the children?"

"Stop!" Veronica threw her hands up in exasperation. Randolph had the ability to be practical and calm in any situation. Like the night in senior high when they'd cut through the alley after seeing a movie. Some troublesome kids had pulled a gun on them. They might have been hurt if it had not been for Randolph's gift of gab and calm. How rational he had been. How she had swooned at his calmness. It was that very calmness that now drove her crazy. "Which part of I *am* not going anywhere, don't you get? I *said*, and I repeat, I'm not going anywhere. The only reason we're having this conversation is because you keep badgering me. Distance this and distance that is all you ever talk about anymore. I thought you should at least know how I'm feeling, but I'm sorry I said a friggin' word. It's obvious you can't handle the truth you asked for."

"Truth?"

"Randolph," Veronica shouted, "back off. You're getting on my very last nerve."

"Vee, to be frank, I don't give a hill of beans about your nerves," Randolph said, his voice barely above a whisper, "I'll keep asking questions until I get an answer."

"An answer, or the answer you want. There is no such answer. The one you want is no longer possible."

"Try again. Every problem has an answer," Randolph said calmly.

"Shut the hell up, damn it! You're such a jerk. How I stood you this long is the real question here that needs an answer!"

"I'm simply trying to understand what brought all this on."

"Why are you allways trying to screw with everybody else's head except your own? Isn't it tiring to figure out what makes people tick and tock and go mad? Have you given one thought to the fact that your goddamn perfect, dot-to-dot living could drive a person crazy?"

"Preciseness is not neurosis. What has my preciseness cost us?"

"Are you kidding? Let me suggest a few things. Our marriage. Our love. And that's only for starters. If you miss psychoanalyzing people feel free to take your dead ass back to work. Get the real basket cases to take up some of your free time and give me a break. Look," Veronica softened her tone a bit, "a few weeks. At most, a few months to sort myself out. That's all I'm asking."

"Please, Vee. I can help you get through this." Randolph was stroking her arm.

"Stop it, damn it," Veronica screamed, violently brushing his hand off her arm. "No, you can't! I don't need any help. I don't need smothering. I don't need fixing. I don't need you. Time. That's what I need. Some goddamn time. Why can't you just accept that and let it be?"

"So that's it, huh? Our marriage is over just like that?" Randolph snapped his finger across her face. "Vee, you disappoint me. Never in a million years would I've believed you'd leave your family at the first sign of glitter."

"Fuck you, Randall." Veronica yanked the yellow dress over her head. "If you're going to resort to guilt, then go right ahead. Why don't you try snapping your fingers again and watch me disappear?"

"Mom. Why are you shouting?" Jenny, their six-year-old daughter, was standing in the doorway.

"I'm not, sweetie. Just talking loudly. Go back to bed." Veronica knelt before her daughter, "I'll explain later."

Still looking curiously at her parents, Jenny went back to her room. They were not a loud talking family. Then again, maybe her mother was kinda.

"You'll break the kids' hearts," Randolph said sadly.

Veronica pushed past him and left the house in a huff.

CHAPTER FOUR

BREAKFAST WAS interrupted by a surprise.

"By God, woman, you have grown beautiful." The smoky, dreamy upscale voice, now completely transformed from an island lilt to one of a cosmopolitan woman, reached April through space. Sophie entered the room, handing a bottle of Cristal to Miss. Muriel.

April squinted at the woman moving toward her. An apparition floating in a halo of light. "Sophie?" April's mouth gaped in surprise. "Is it you?"

"Mother told me you were here," Sophie said. Sleek, slender, exercised, and drop-dead beautiful, Sophie hurled herself into April's arms. Wrapped up in each other, they rocked back and forth until the space between them ceased to exist.

"It's really you. I can't believe it. Sophie, I thought you'd never come back to this place," April said.

"I thought you'd be the one who never came back," Sophie said. "Not after those awful summers with mom."

"I could always leave. I can't imagine I'd ever come back if I were you."

"Time, darling. It heals all."

For just a split second, Sophie's eyes, dark as coal, slipped into that place where the dead transitions, then suddenly crinkled into a warm smile. Nothing had changed about those eyes.

The dark, brooding eyes which had felt the pain of discrimination and withstood the denial of her ancestors still drew people deep into their sticky pool. April observed the bottomlessness of the eyes that seemed infinite and more lethal.

Since the age of twelve, Sophie, April's aggrieved cousin, had perfected the art of using her exotic eyes as lure. Enchanted, men willingly jumped into their abyss only to find themselves sucked into the quicksand behind them. They would spiral into a wild, corkscrew ride of unchained love or madness. "Shine Eye Gal is a trouble to a man;" the rhyme they sang about Sophie popped into her head.

Sam instinctively cupped his nape, feeling a rush of wind around his neck. Unlike April's pale complexion, this woman was a deep, burnt sugar. Tall with incredible eyes, voluptuous lips, and hypnotic beauty, she threw Sam into a trance. Struggling back from the magnetic pull into the vortex of her iris, past the optic nerve and down into the watery belly of her vitreous humour, Sam forced himself to sit still as she glided into the room. He was silently singing "Jamaican Woman Sugar and Spice" before he caught himself and shushed his mind.

Graceful, with movements honed from years of dance instructions, the woman's classic look exuded a regal yet unstuffy image in an era of kitsch and vulgar self-expression. As a child everyone thought Sophie beautiful, except Aunt Josephine who over-cooked in Anglo-Saxon values, always felt ashamed of her daughter's too obvious genetic reminders. Who wanted to be reminded day in and day out of a boat loaded with uncivilized Ashanti and Mandingo landing on the shores of Jamaica? Certainly not Aunt Josephine, the octoroon offspring of Lance McInroy from Sheffield, England, who had married a man the color of midnight. Sophie, therefore, had to regularly listen to her mother's daily reminders to use a skin lightener and to pin the bridge of her nose with a clothes pin every night.

"God, Sophie, you look terrific. Really great! How long has it been? Sixteen. Seventeen years?"

"More like eighteen."

"Never! It couldn't be that long." April's eyes turned upward in mental calculation.

"1995. Remember we cried rivers into the sea?"

"Boy, did we ever. Time can be so deceptive."

"As can all things," Sophie said ruefully.

As her mind traveled through time, remorsefully April remembered how adamantly she'd vowed never to return to the island. As a teenager, she had spent many summers in Port Antonio with her Aunt Josephine. "It's good," her mother would say as she'd put her on a plane island-bound, "to understand your culture and your origin. Roots are important." Dressed in a charcoal suit, even to go to the airport, lips crimson and shiny and hair in a perfect chignon, her mother, a woman of gentile upbringing, was undaunted by April's whimpering.

Port Antonio, a harrowing two-hour drive from Jamaica's capital, Kingston, was incredibly beautiful with its varying scenery and splendid grottos. Though convinced it was the Garden of Eden, April had come to despise the place. Not even its complex mixture of lush vegetation, rolling mountains, azure skies, stars that twinkled brighter than anywhere else on earth, or the luminous blue-green waters could placate April's anger towards Aunt Josephine.

"I simply can't believe you're standing in front of me," April shook her head.

"It's me, sweetie. Really me. Look." Sophie pointed to the little heart-shaped mole on the spot just above her lip.

"A marker if I ever saw one. Please, please," April begged, "say you are here to spend the day."

"I wish I…."

"Com'on Sophie, for old time's sake. We'll get in bed and turn off all the lights. Catch up on the years. I bet there's a lot to tell. I'll have Miss Muriel fix us the best snack, and at midnight we'll drink a fabu bottle of champagne."

"You're still so sweet." Sophie cupped her cousin's chin. "How on earth did you escape the influences of this crazy world?"

"Believe me, I haven't. So, what's your answer?"

"There is nothing more I'd like to do, but sweetie, I can't. I have to be on the set at four. My driver is picking me up at one o'clock."

"Shoot. I'm dying to hear how Aunt Josephine enjoyed her crow when you came back. I can't imagine her eating it without complaining bitterly."

"She almost choked on the feathers. I had to think twice if I wanted to do CPR." Sophie's eyes crinkled. "But I'll be damned if I came all this way to talk about Mommie today. Let's save her for another day. Miss…," Sophie gestured in the direction of the helper.

"Muriel, Ma'am."

"Miss Muriel. Serve the bubbly with whatever you're cooking. It smells to die for."

Sophie glanced at Sam, who had not said a word but was rooted in his chair. Her eyes sent out beams of glitter like a sparkler in the dark on the night of July 4th.

"Oh, forgive me," April slapped her forehead. "Sam, this is my cousin Sophie. Sophie, this is my husband, Sam."

"Sam. The man. I like green eggs and ham, Sam."

"As you should," Sam rose from the chair. He was wearing a white tank top and bathing trunks. His imposing figure reminded

Sophie of the linebacker she'd dated on the UCLA football team. She remembered what those powerful muscles, broad shoulders and narrow hips had done to her. And this Sam was, as they say, all that and more. Then a deeply suppressed knee-jerk reaction kicked in. Sophie wanted to take something away from April. All the years of comparison with April who'd won the colonial lotto of good hair and light complexion, which earned her preferential treatment made her want what April had.

"I'll open the champagne," Sam offered, seeing the worried look on Miss Muriel's face.

Narrowing, Sophie's eyes flickered over Sam as he headed to the kitchen. What worried her was her nose had flared at the corners, which was a bad sign. *Whoa, baby,* she caught her thoughts, flushing a little as she turned to face April. "I'll stay for breakfast," she smiled, inconspicuously running her tongue inside her bee-stung lips.

"Miss Muriel set another place at the table, will you?" Sam's voice betrayed no bewitchment.

April pulled a chair closer to hers and patted the seat. "Tell me," she begged, "just a tiny bit about Aunt Josephine's reaction to your coming back. Just a teeny, tiny bit."

"Let's just say some things never change. Would you believe she told me to change my dress to meet one of her friend's sons?" Sophie slid gracefully into the chair.

"Can I?" April rose to open the shutters. Even in the tropics, the seasons obeyed divine order. Russet and green leaves from almond trees had fallen around trees' roots splaying the sun's rays in patterns across the sand. "Believe me," April reiterated, "I can."

Fed up with her mother's badgering and the unhealthy colonized minds of too many Jamaicans, Sophie had simply disappeared after high school, the final straw—her mother's stupidity.

To Aunt Josephine's disappointment, Sophie had gotten into the second-best film school in the U.S.A, not the first. "Huh," Aunt Josephine had gruffed. "Who cares about seconds? Second is nothing but the first-place loser." Needless to say, Aunt Josephine didn't quite know why a girl of Sophie's ordinary looks bothered to think of a career in film. "What about medicine, where brains were more valued than looks?" It suddenly dawned on April it was not Jamaica or Jamaican culture she'd hated all those years; it was Aunt Josephine.

"So," April said, retaking her seat next to Sophie, not pressing the subject of Aunt Josephine further, "life's been good then?"

"Absolutely superb. But that's enough about me. What about you? It seems life's been good to you too, April." Sophie's lips curled into a brilliant half-crooked smile. "Do you have coffee, darling?" She turned her smile on Miss Muriel before unconsciously allowing it to rest on Sam.

"Honly the best. Blue Mountain. Right from the tip top."

"The Queen's favorite," April added.

"Marvelous." Sophie pushed back her chair and reached for her bag, retrieving a gold lighter and cigarette case from her Prada tote. She tapped a cigarette lightly against the table before lighting it, "So darling, tell me, when did you get over your phobia of the island?"

"Only last week. What about you?"

"I haven't. It hasn't changed much, has it?"

"Yes and no." April hesitated, looking out toward the sea's rising tide, "but mostly yes," she said tentatively, unable to totally deny her newfound love for the island, yet careful not to betray her childhood camaraderie with Sophie.

"I suppose I'll find out." Sophie's voice took on a breathy haze.

April looked sadly at Sophie, covering her hand in a tender touch. "I should have kept in touch."

"Me too, but hey, it's all good. Anyway, for a while there, I dropped outta life. Had to do the psychiatrist thing to get over mom, you know." The pain was still there, pushing up at the edges of her hard-found contentment. April could see her reaching for the spiritual Novocain. "Don't worry," Sophie reassured, dragging deeply on her cigarette, "we'll see a lot of each other soon. After this movie, I'll be back in America for good. Thank God too, for I've had it up to here," her hand shot up five inches over her head, "with the Europeans. They are as slow as molasses."

"You'll be in LA?"

"Yes. It's a pill, but it's where I must be for now."

"Despite Aunt Josephine, make sure you enjoy the island while you're here. Make sure you get in lots of sunshine since, as you know, of course, there's not much of that in LA, unless you're fond of filtered smog."

"You're still pretty funny, chickadee," Sophie chuckled, thinking she did prefer filtered smog. There was still no love lost between her and the sun. "I have to tell you; it's a downright hoot seeing you like this. Married and all."

April rested her head on Sophie's shoulders. "What about you?" she said. "Are you married?"

"Darling, *please*. Of course not! No noose around this pretty neck."

"And pretty it is too," Sam smiled, returning to the table with four glasses and the champagne bucket on a tray. "One for you," his eyes lingered as he handed Sophie a glass, "and for you, dar-ling," he kissed his wife tenderly and out of guilt. "And for you," Sam handed Miss Muriel a glass.

"I don't drink, yu know, sah."

"Aaaah. Come on. It's New Year's Eve Day. One swig won't hurt," Sam insisted, lifting his glass. "A Happy New Year to all when it comes," he said generously, sipping his bubbly. Before he could replace the bottle in the bucket, Miss Muriel had drained her glass.

"Ditto," Sophie said, tipping her glass to her lips.

"Ditto, ditto," April said, laughing at the charming way Sophie had responded.

Sam sat between April and Sophie. Excited by new taste buds to be activated, and with Sophie on his left, he was glad to dig into his culinary experience as a distraction, if nothing else.

April salivating at the memory of ackee and salted fish, johnnycake and callaloo, fried plantains, bammy, mackerel and onions, dished generous portions of food onto her plate. Sophie dished a smidgen of the mouth-watering morsels onto her plate, chain-smoked throughout breakfast, hardly touching her food, preferring to drink several glasses of bubbly.

"Uh, uh, uh, Miss Muriel." Sam shook his head. "As they say back home, you put your foot in this food."

"A so, sah? Jamaican food sweet fi true."

"Yes, Man. The food sweet, sweet bad," Sophie lilted in patois, though nothing seemed to have disappeared from her plate.

Somewhere close by, April's cell phone trilled to the tune of *Auld Lange Syne*.

"Yes, hello."

"April. Happy New Year and all that when it comes?"

"Who is this?"

"Martin.'"

"Martin who?" April barked. She hated people who didn't identify themselves on the phone like she should ask twenty questions or something.

"Martin Spiro. From the office." Martin bristled she didn't recognize his voice.

"Martin, it's New Year's Eve Day. Why are you calling me?"

"Kusak's been fired, but I suppose you suspected that. Eastman is calling an emergency meeting, and you'll need to be in town by January 2nd, 8 a.m. sharp. He wants to meet the woman who uncovered Kusak's scheme. I was asked to call."

"Martin, I'm on vacation. I have no plans to come back to Chicago until a week from Sunday. Tell Frank Easton just that. I'll see you a week from Monday morning."

"They want me back in Chicago," April said to Sam and Sophie, pushing the 'end' button on the phone. The CFO has been fired."

"And?" Sophie inquired.

"I'm the one who cracked his crooked scheme."

"You!" Sophie said. "A brain drain schizoid money professional? Never thought! I was so sure you'd be a doctor like your parents, or some super-duper social superwoman waging war against the injustices of children in third world countries."

"Me too, but I am a card-carrying member of capitalist greed and yuppiedom. That's what I've turned out to be."

Sam looked distressingly at April.

April heaved a sigh. What bad timing. How would she ever broach the subject that her dream might finally come to fruition? *Sam, darling, can you believe I'm going to be the next CFO of S&G.* No, that wouldn't do! Better to do it after he was loaded up on killer rum punch. *Sam, I don't know if I told you, but I'm being considered....* No, that wouldn't do either. Maybe tonight, after three or four glasses of rum punch and fantastic sex. *Sam, darling, you were incredible tonight. This place sure helps our sex life, doesn't it? Wouldn't it be wonderful to have a home like this on the island? You know, if I get that CFO job, we could easily afford it. Not like that timeshare stuff but ours, outright.* If Sam weren't sufficiently intoxicated with Jamaica or the over-proof rum and, for that matter, the fantastic sex, regardless of how carefully she'd planned seductive manipulations, leaving the island would spell a death blow to their marriage.

"Sam hates my job," April said to Sophie. "He wants me to do women's work."

"Such as?"

"Change diapers. Right, my sweets?"

Sam was mute. His jaws tightened.

"That sounds awfully romantic to me," Sophie said. "I'd certainly give up this hullabaloo if I had such an option."

The phone rang again.

Martin tried to sound authoritative. "April. I think you need to come back."

"I'll get back to you, but Martin, don't call me again, or I'll definitely not come." April powered off the phone.

Compelled to get on a plane, April picked up the outdated black phone (faster than the internet), flipped through curled ear telephone pages and dialed the airport. Within minutes, she booked a seat on Delta flight 251 to Miami, connecting to O'Hare on United 935. The flight, on New Year's Day hours away, would force her to hurriedly and regrettably pack. April looked pleadingly at her husband. "Why don't you stay down here? We still have seven more days all paid for, right, Miss. Muriel?" The helper nodded enthusiastically. "I'm sure Sophie will be a dear and show you around in her spare time. I bet the island practically eats out of her hands now she's a big Kahuna."

There was going to be an argument. She could tell by the tightening of Sam's jaw. "You wouldn't mind, would you, Sophie? I'll be back as soon as I can if I can."

"Of course not. My schedule isn't ridiculous until next week. You'll find the set fun, Sam." She slapped him playfully on the shoulder, leaving her hand on his back a second too long. "Don't worry," she said reassuringly, "We'll find lots to do."

"You two have a lot more in common than you know. Sam's an entertainment attorney. Who knows, you guys could be good for each other."

"I'm sure of it." Sophie's eyes smiled as she dragged deeply on yet another cigarette. She picked up a luscious mango and bit into it.

CHAPTER FIVE

OUTSIDE THE HEATED Lake Shore garage, life on the Chicago roadway was a downright deathtrap. Nothing but piled up snow and stalled vehicles. Melody inched her car along the road, slipping and sliding this way and that. She had to let go of the steering wheel several times to correct a skid. Twenty years in Chicago made her an expert driver; still, she could, without a doubt, live *sans* driving on snow and ice. This morning, to make matters worse, visibility was now almost zero. Gone was the sun that had poured through her window barely two hours before. It was now snowing hard, snowdrifts splattering across her windshield.

Traffic, at barely a crawl, was a challenge for Melody. Abhorrent of wasting time, she balanced the manila folder holding the proposed merger between Comtech and Microtech on her steering wheel. Opening it to the financial page, she ran a finger down columns of numbers. Why hadn't she highlighted the row in question? Engrossed in examining the page, she had not moved the requisite half-inch in time, and the car behind her honked.

In the spring and summer, Melody sometimes trekked it to Comtech to meet ever-mounting weekly commitments—two or three out-of-office meetings, speeches to women's groups, schools, and high-profile social functions, which were now impossible.

The company insisted she use her driver, but Melody always had a backup plan. Who knows when a driver would oversleep or have a flat tire? To compromise, she drove to and from the office. During the day, the driver tooled her around the city. Nothing was left up to the "whatever universe." There was no "whatever" or "leave it up to God in Melody's world." Action was what got results. And precise action—perfection.

The upcoming acquisition of Microtech, a deal spearheaded by her, had proven to be an exceptional idea and a fantastic opportunity. It had cemented her position at Comtech as much as it would strengthen Comtech's position in the telecommunication industry, allowing it to compete in a booming, cutting-edge technology marketplace. Not that Comtech wasn't a powerhouse. The high-tech company, just twenty-two years old, had staggering sales figures *and* was changing the game. This merger unquestionably clenched her nomination as the next CEO of Comtech. Melody's dream was to be the first black businesswoman in Chicago, not counting Oprah, to make the Forbes 400. Nothing now would prevent her from joining the small, prestigious cadre of women CEOs, or the even smaller group in technology and the minuscule number of Black women CEOs.

Melody Adams punched out the number for April Summers. It was an easy number to remember as it formed a diamond on the keypad.

"Ms. Summers' office."

April Summers, God forbid, as there was nothing sunshiny about the woman's personality remotely suggesting summer, was the investment banker on the Comtech deal. One of the best and brightest women execs she'd met, Summers, was Black. Black financiers were rare, and Melody had been elated to meet April for exactly one minute.

"Melody Adams. Comtech."

"Ms. Adams. How are you?"

"Fine. And you?"

"A bit over the top. How may I help you this morning?" Melody could hear the trilling of a phone.

"Do you need to get that?"

"I do. Would you mind holding a moment, please?" The pretentious hold music came on, and then she was back. "How may I help you, Miss Adams?"

"Is Ms. Summers in? I need to verify some numbers before I go into a meeting."

"I'm so sorry, Ms. Summers is on vacation."

"When will she be back?"

"Well, to be frank, I'm not sure. I believe she is scheduled to come back next week, but I could check and call you back. If you have a problem with the numbers, I can put you through to her assistant, Sydney. I believe he's been assigned to the deal."

"That would be great." *What kind of secretary doesn't know her boss's schedule!* Melody thought in disgust.

"Sydney Rambolt." The voice was dead cold.

"Melody Adams. I need an explanation on the numbers April sent over."

"Really?" the tone suggested she was intellectually inferior? "Let me try to help. If you'd like, I'll send them over again."

The condescending snob. "That won't be necessary. I have them right here. Just answer a few questions."

After the conversation, Melody hung up the phone. People like April Summers and her cronies from S&G, all Ivy League grads, made her prickly. Mildly chaotic. A bit uncertain. As her insecurity clamored for attention, she impatiently pulled the car out of the main artery of traffic and onto a side street. By the time she'd calmed her ego, she'd long passed the alternate route to the office. "Shucks," she banged the steering wheel, quickly hanging a hard right. The car spun out of control and did a one-eighty. Luckily, there was no oncoming traffic. Shaking, Melody gripped the steering wheel hard until she regained her composure. Shifting into low gear, she inched along six back streets, sliding past stalled cars and several accidents. To her chagrin, she was on some convoluted road in a rough part of town. Nice and shabby. So, characteristic of Chicago. You are in the ritziest of neighborhoods for one block, and then two chains down the road were scabby slums with decay and rot all around. That was especially clear in Hyde Park, where Veronica lived. Melody hated the ghetto and would traverse Chicago to avoid it.

Overhead the EL groaned. Melody, forced to brake to miss clipping a boy sauntering across traffic, his pants almost down to his knees in the dead of winter, was in a state of utter frustration. "Loser," she was tempted to shout out the window, but realizing the foolhardiness, kept looking straight ahead. According to her creed being homeless, jobless, addicted, and barefoot in the projects was the choice of people who preferred to stay in a life of hopelessness, waiting for their God or the Government to come. Huh! Religion. Savior or opiate of the people? Politics! The subjugation of the collective world. Today, she had little patience for apathy, religion, or politics.

Inching the car across two lanes, Melody crawled down a one-way street. Ahead she saw the Sears Tower and kept going east. Blessed with a good sense of direction, she was back on track after a few more twists and turns. Melody pulled into her designated parking spot, two spaces from the door of the impressive building that housed Comtech. The sign that read reserved for CEO would soon bear her name. Her pride swelled every morning as she pulled up to the building her efforts helped erect. "Losers," Melody said for the second time noting piled-up snow the removal crew had scooped into open parking lot spaces and walkways. Flipping down the rearview mirror, Melody glanced at herself to ensure the distressful morning had not ruined her look. For a moment, she sat in the car, trying to muster the courage to step into knee-deep snow with half-boots. Grabbing her briefcase and draping her ankle-length shearling over her arm, Melody reached for the door handle and yanked it open, ready to make a mad dash to the lobby only inches away. Though everything irritated her these days, slipping and sliding in knee-deep snow, dealing with April's guard dog, almost killing herself and others on the streets of Chicago hadn't helped matters. She slammed the car door with hostility.

Moving swiftly toward the building, she didn't get far before she was yanked backward. Her skirt was caught in the door. Snatching open the door, Melody released herself and sprinted to the lobby. Body shaking and teeth chattering, she was about to put on her coat when she noticed an unsightly rip in her brand-new skirt. What was she supposed to do now? Her meeting, in less than fifteen minutes, left no time to go home and change. The obvious rip, too close to her rear end to go parading into an executive meeting, caused her pause. Under no circumstance would she step into any meeting less than perfect, even if it were with the motley group of techs who made up Comtech's executive team. She scanned her brain to see what clothes hung in her office closet. Nothing appropriate for this historic day.

Melody felt like crying, and her self-pity was at its peak. Compelled, she began climbing the stairs leading to the executive floors but stopped suddenly. Her usual sprint up the first ten flights of stairs before taking the elevator to her office on the thirty-fifth floor held no appeal but for the sudden nauseousness she'd have done it anyway. Even the enormity of her responsibility couldn't make Melody go up those stairs and into a room full of men, disheveled. To hell with the meeting and Comtech, the thought exploded in her head. Melody pulled on her coat and returned to her car instead of going up the steps. Plunking herself back into the heated leather seat, she cranked up the engine and swung out of the lot. Surprised at the forcefulness of her decision, a devilish smile spread across her face as she turned down Wabash, her intention, to go directly to bed. This was some midlife crisis for sure!

Pushing button five on the dash player, *Weber's The Phantom of the Opera* filled the car. Impatiently, Melody flicked the dial to FM. A deep pulsating beat grabbed her emotions, and Melody found her body gyrating to Reggaeton Cuban artist, Pitbul's, *I Know You Want Me.* Now that, as Veronica would say, was a jam. Melody sang at the top of her lungs, though she hated the misogynistic song. *You'll never get me,* she substituted the words, turning the volume way up from a button on the steering wheel. For the first time in her life, since she'd been five years old, to be exact, she was going to do what she wanted instead of what she must. Her head bobbed as the music's drum tempo became hypnotic. Melody jigged as the car inched along the avenue. Lowering the volume, she dialed her office.

"Ms. Adam's office, Angel, Melody's executive secretary, answered the phone at once. Angel was efficient beyond words, always predicting her every move, always one step ahead, and never too familiar.

"Angel, I'm not coming in today."

"Excuse me, Ms. Adams?"

"Which part of that didn't you understand?" Melody spoke like a mute who'd learned language.

"I'm sorry, Miss Adams. It isn't something eh…serious, is it?"

"Serious as a heart attack."

"Oh, my God! Who should I call?" Angel was flustered.

"Angel! Melody laughed loudly, a surprise even to herself, "I'm not really having a heart attack. It's just a saying."

"So, what's wrong?"

"Mid-life crisis."

Angel chuckled nervously. She couldn't tell if her boss was being serious or joking. Melody never joked. In fact, she was downright severe, sometimes to the point of cruelty. Lately, she was downright awful. "I'm not here to be liked, loved, or cherished. I'm here to deliver the goods, and that I do well. Any arguments?" She often spewed, making many grown men cry.

"Ms. Adams, your meeting with operations begins in two minutes, and at noon you have lunch with the men from Microtech. The merger. You know?"

"I know all that, but I'm not coming in today."

"I guess we can try to reschedule the Microtech people, but they're from out of town." Angel tried her best to change Melody's mind.

"So? Aren't we the ones interested in buying them?"

"Yes, Ma'am, but…."

"Angel, never buts, you know I hate that. And for the record, Angel, we can do whatever the hell we want. Reschedule them.

Angel, and indeed Melody, was astounded at the ease with which the mild profanity fell from her lips. Never had she used questionable words in public and certainly not in the office. Not even to herself, except with Veronica, who brought out the worst in her. Not she, who'd spent her free time studying the Webster dictionary for entertainment. Profanity was an unfortunate bromide in language.

"Well, okay. But what do you want me to say to them?" Angel asked. Her surprise was evident.

"Call the hotel and tell the boys to reschedule for Monday because I'm unexpectedly unavailable. If their company can't afford to put them up for a weekend, then we don't want to buy them now, do we? However, offer to cover their accommodations if it comes up. Give them a few local attractions to visit to fill up time if they are brave enough to broach this weather! And, while you're at it, tell the people upstairs, I'm sick. Since this is a first, they'll send flowers. Make sure of it." Melody's formality was back.

"Whatever you say, Ms. Adams."

"Whatever is a poor word choice," Melody said.

Melody hung up and smiled with smug satisfaction. Knob firmly gripped between index finger and thumb; she turned the stereo volume to full blast. What she'd done, including cursing, felt good. It'd probably cost her later, but she was beginning to like this new menopause, Melody Adams. It was hard always to be on all the time. To forever live up to other peoples' expectations. To always live up to her own expectations. Today it felt really good to be Melody Adams, uncontrived. *I know you want it.*

CHAPTER SIX

"ONE, TWO, THREE, RIGHT JAB." The instructor's toned body contorted as if it were on a spring. Beads of perspiration glistened on her skin; her measured breath tapped rhythmically through the microphone. April fixed her gaze on the woman's back. *How could anyone be that fit?* Eve's body was cut. Washboard abs and tight tush contoured to retain the femininity of a siren.

"Use those legs," Eve, whose name April knew only from the class roster, shouted and April felt a kinship with the authority of her voice. Just like her mother's. April Summers concentrated, trying as hard as she could to pivot her body into a fighter's jab, but there was no way in hell her brain would obey the command. Not this morning. The flight had worn her out. Maybe if she concentrated on her presentation to Frank Easton later that morning, she could muster enough hostility to land a jab at her opponent or opponents at S&G.

"Don't try so hard," Eve was standing behind her, pulling her arm back into position. "Find your own edge. Don't go over it."

Class over, an exasperated April grabbed a towel and headed to the women's locker room along with all the other overdriven, corporate ladder climbers. Everyone these days needed an adrenaline rush to start pressure cooker days. Discarding her exercise clothes, April donned a white towel, wedged her feet into plastic baggies before putting on her rubber sandals and headed to the shower. Moments later, she entered the sauna, spreading out to take up as much space as possible. Over and over, she rehearsed the speech she'd be delivering. Frankly, it narked her to no end she'd felt compelled to return to Chicago, cutting her vacation short. She should've had the guts to say no and let them fire her if they wanted. She was tired of proving herself at S&G without proper recognition. Worse, she hated being used as a black statistic, especially if, the truth be told, she was the brightest and most qualified to take over Kusak's position as CFO. Why didn't she make Frank Easton wait instead of her husband? After all, she'd been waiting for eight years to be promoted.

On the slat, lying prone, April found her mind straying to the last few months. Hers and Sam's life together had been intense. Screaming, slamming doors, raging threats, and squealing brakes had brought them to a halt. Little cracks in the armor of their marriage were widened by differences in their backgrounds, culture, and class. Cracks now opened up at the seams. April's reluctance about going to Jamaica and her hesitation to push off the Microtech deal to Stanley had made matters worse but paled in comparison to her desperation to save her six-year-old marriage. If they'd continued as they had been, they were headed for the scrap heap marked "irreconcilable differences." Now here she was, throwing it all away for a job.

You are thirty-two, Sam had bellowed, *when do you think that the idea of starting a family will occur to you? What will it take to get family on your priority list?*

April's body had been covered in 'duck skin' as the argument that jettisoned them to the island replayed itself inside her head. Unbeknownst to Sam, there was not a shred of thought about children in April's near future. She'd made sure of that thanks to Primavera.

She loved her husband, but why couldn't he understand her? She was willing to sacrifice having a child to have a career for the time being. The Jamaica trip was to see if she would change her mind. What did he expect her to do? Could she do it? She was about to have the greatest career win of her life—becoming a C-level player at a major bank at the respectable age of thirty-two. It was a big deal and an accomplishment in anyone's book, so why couldn't he be happy for her? For a woman, a Black woman especially, it would be a coup and one not to be taken lightly. April thought Sam would at least be pleased it would avenge black subjugation of four hundred years.

The door creaked, but April did not open her eyes.

"Hey, there, killer." Came a soothing voice. "You did pretty well in there, you know. Don't try so hard next time, and don't be so hard on yourself. You've got to train the body into flexibility."

April squinted, twisting her head toward the voice. It was Eve. "Easy for you to say. You didn't feel what my body was feeling."

"You shouldn't feel any pain. That's my point."

"I had other things on my mind. I guess that spurred me on a bit. How on earth did you get so fit, anyway?"

"Try fifteen years of training."

"I'm not sure I have enough time left to command my body into this kind of submission."

"Wanna bet? Get a personal trainer. Your body is in great physical shape. A few concentrated exercises in all the right places, and you'll see."

"Are you a trainer?"

"Nah, couldn't find the time. My job keeps me busy enough. I teach so I can force myself to keep in shape. If I didn't do this, I wouldn't have enough energy to keep up with my husband, kids, or clients, plus I don't get to pay the exorbitant club fee you guys do"

"What do you do besides teaching Cardio box?"

"I'm a psychiatrist, but I function mostly as an Executive Coach for women."

"Executive Coach? What do they do differently from a shrink?"

"It's just a different approach to helping people bring balance to their hectic lifestyles."

"So, how to better handle super-womanhood, huh?"

"Nowhere close. Anyway, she's dead. Haven't you read Shriver's book?"

"No, I haven't."

"Well, do."

"Hope it's convincing. I have no clue how women like us can have balance in this day and age?"

"It's because of this day and age why we must try. Too much going on every single day. I started coaching because I needed to look at my life from a holistic point of view. It's not easy, but it's possible. Today I'm totally in balance. I don't want anything more than the other. I can stop anything I'm doing and feel fulfilled."

"You have to tell me your secret. Let's have coffee sometime, and I'll clue you in. My office is in the Sears Tower." Eve went prone on the wooden slats stretching to complete relaxation. The women drank in the crackling heat of the room in relative silence.

"I'd better get out of here before I become a prune," April said. "See you next time. Coffee, right?"

"You bet, Eve said without moving a muscle. "My office is on the fifth floor." Years of training made her suspect April Summers could use some therapy.

April dressed quickly and left the sports club. It was only seven a.m.. She could tell the day was going to be one of those days. Balance indeed! What a dream! Her usual five-minute drive took twenty. She checked her email, making sure nothing pressing came over the wire. An email from Sam. She'd read it later. While firing up her computer, April was still thinking of Eve. Executive Coach, indeed. In April's high-stressed world, everyone knew coach was a code word for the psychos who help overstressed, high-strung executives limit their intake of too many "tranquilizing" substances before their habit had them put away for good. In April's opinion, people who had to see a person like Eve were "defects." Mental weakness or illness was God's error and could never be righted.

No one in April's family talked about mental illness. Mental illness was a mistake, a part of the human experience need not acknowledged. Damnable nuisance that vilified the lives of prodigies. Julian, a budding genius and beloved brother of Gabriella Dixon, April's mother, had been hospitalized at eighteen, never to be sane again. It was a family secret heavily guarded. April had overheard a quarrel between her mother and her Aunt Josephine about whose responsibility it was to take care of her uncle Julian, or she would never have known. "Ah, who cares," April said, logging into the computer system. The market opened at nine thirty a.m. EST; eight thirty her time. Before meeting Frank Easton, she wanted to get a jumpstart on the day, not to talk about being informed. April Summers managed billions in assets for S&G clients and made a handsome living. As CFO, her life would calm down, though she suspected she'd spend more time traveling. That would certainly not bode well with Sam, who was becoming more hostile with each baby conversation. She shuddered. That man was acting irrationally as though her refusal to have a child was a betrayal of some sacred trust between them. April walked over to the built-in cabinet and poured herself a glass of orange juice. Balance and one's daily dose of Vitamin C. The beep in her ear signaled a call. How far away Jamaica seemed.

"Yes."

"April, Martin here. This morning's meeting has been rescheduled. Frank has been called away on a family emergency."

"Sonofabitch. Sodding hell. Blankety, blank! Damn it, Martin! I canceled my pissing vacation for this shit. My family emergency was put on hold. I should have known better than to be so damn agreeable."

"I'm sorry, April. There is no rescheduled time yet," Martin continued, nonplused by April's outbursts.

"Why doesn't that surprise me? Where the hell are you, anyway?"

"I was just leaving home when I got the call."

"It figures," April said sarcastically. The man was such a lump. Martin couldn't get his fat ass anywhere on time. How he'd amounted to this much was a mystery to her. "Screw this. I'm outta here," April snarled, dropping the phone receiver into the cradle. After a few minutes, Martin was still trying to unclog his ear.

April was furious. At least twenty times, she'd practiced her casual "why you should make me CFO of S&G" speech and was in a great frame of mind to deliver it with verve. This morning was her time to subliminally condition the old geyser, Frank Easton, about her superior qualification while deriding Kusak's ineptitude. "Bloody hell!"April's eyes caught the paper on which she'd scribbled Eve's information. She flipped through the phone book for an exact address. "Why not?" she said aloud, snatching it up. "Today feels like a day for balance." Grabbing her coat, she left her office in complete fluster, determined to take the day off after all. Hell, she needed a lifetime to recover from the stress of S&G.

CHAPTER SEVEN

AT THE MEDICAL SCHOOL, Veronica detoured to the cafeteria for a cup of coffee, hoping to calm her rattling nerves. Her behavior this morning was deplorable. She was so damn tired of everything; physically tired, emotionally tired, and tired of living life by the book. Still, Randolph didn't deserve her vitriol.

The drab corridors of the hospital did nothing to lift her spirits.

"Coffee, please. The large cup. No sugar, lots of cream," she heard herself say to the waitress when it was her turn in line.

"Dollar fiddy." The woman, hair covered with a black hairnet, didn't bother to smile.

Veronica counted out six quarters from her change purse, dropped them into the woman's hand, and headed to her lab. *Were she in Randolph's shoes, she would've been a little shellshocked at the suddenness of such a confession. But hell, it's not like people don't separate every day. The divorce rate in America was fast climbing towards sixty percent, in other words, people split up more often than they stayed married. Eighteen years of marriage, in today's world, was two or three lifetimes. And she had tried. Hadn't she? She was not going to give into Randolph's guilt trip. What else could he want from her? He'd had the best of her prime. It was his own damn fault anyway. He, of all people, a psychology major in college, should know distress when he saw it.*

And didn't he realize that when a woman holds down the fort for too many years, it does serious damage to her psyche? No matter what women say, they wanted a take-charge man as their mate. Randolph hadn't been that in years.

"Are you having an affair?" Randolph had asked her, and she didn't have an answer.

Was she? Was obsessing over some kid she knew absolutely nothing about having an affair? Yet, obsessing about Tony had taken on alarming proportions during the holidays, so much so, she was at a point of total dysfunction. A few days before, Veronica had walked down the hall to Eve's fifth-floor office to buy some sense.

"It's crazy. What's going on with me is crazy, but I don't know how to stop."

"Try yoga. Meditate on your decision," Eve had said.

So, she did—chakra yoga. When Ravi Singh had said breathe in *Sut* and out *Nam*, she had found herself breathing in Tony Reifenburg instead; and inside her, he had stayed. Physiologically and intellectually, Veronica understood the dance of dopamine and the state of limerence; still, lust consumed her. Emotionally, however, they were daring her to take the challenge and risk everything for her freedom. Despite her ire, as Veronica neared the lab, she knew the quickening of her pulse had nothing to do with anger but rather with the anticipation of seeing Tony.

"Mornin' Dr. Whittaker. One cold day, ain't it."

"Morning." Veronica nodded to a lab technician. "But you made it in, as usual, Solomon."

"Got to." The man said.

As she wove her way past trolleys and orderlies, Veronica tried to understand the genesis of her obsession with Dr. Tony

Reifenburg. Trained at John's Hopkins, Reifenburg was a star physician ten years her junior, another good reason to heed caution! Unfortunately, Tony Reifenburg was a hard man to ignore. Four months ago, Veronica became excruciatingly aware her admiration of him had turned into something else. Skillfully she had applied thought control techniques, succeeding to a large extent, in suppressing her attraction. If the man had simply stopped smiling at her every day for Christ's sake, she might've battled temptation to the death! Habitually, and it seemed purposefully on rounds, Dr. Reifenburg would stand behind her bristling her neck with his warm, peppermint breath. After weeks of wringing her wrist, Veronica had finally solved the problem. She'd wait until the good doctor had settled before placing herself opposite to where he stood. Try as she did, however, ignoring him was impossible. Now she was going on unnecessary rounds just to catch a glimpse of him.

"Dr. Whittaker," he'd cornered her one day after rounds, "I was wondering if you'd entertain the idea of my helping out on your research project. I worked on a similar study before coming here and believe I can contribute to your work."

Veronica had jumped at his offer to help for more reasons than she would now admit to herself. She needed the intellectual stimulation and a new eye to ferret out her research oversights. With Tony, her equal in every way, unlike other residents, and regrettably sometimes her husband, she didn't have to tiptoe around her potent brain. Leveling her gifts for fear of hurting the feelings of those less gifted was not on her top ten list of things to do. Moreover, after too many years of living a dot-to-dot existence, Veronica appreciated Tony's offhanded philosophy on life—let things happen without too many plans and foresight. "Live in the now," he always said. She hadn't ever believed in *Que Sera*. Couldn't have, or she'd still be on the south side of Chicago, eking out the little life had destined for her. It was control, belief in changing a destiny, planning and hard work that had gotten her to this point in her life.

Before entering the lab, Veronica clasped her hands in prayer. *Please, Lord, please, don't let him be there.* Contradictory feelings surfaced; the part of her that desperately wanted him to be there said, *Please, please, please, Lord, let him be there.* Keenly aware she had neither a level head nor a calm heart to resist Tony's charm today, she prayed harder. *Please, Lord,* she tightened her hands around the coffee cup. *I know I'm a little rusty on Christianity. Maybe I haven't earned a conversation with you lately but try hard to hear my prayer. Show me that spending every Sunday morning in church for twenty years counts for something. I've tried to live a decent, aspiring, and honest life. Why are you testing me beyond my limits? If Tony is in that lab this morning, God, I don't know what I'll do. Today I need a rock to lean on, so please let that be you.*

Tony would probably laugh her to scorn if he knew the nonsense she'd been conjuring up in her fantasy world. It was incredulous and ridiculous, even to her, she'd missed him so much, and that warm thoughts of him were what kept her sane and smiling at a husband to whom she could no longer connect. *Veronica Whittaker!* She cringed at the thoughts that were steamrolling her. *You need to get a grip. Where do you think you're going with this? The man doesn't even know you're alive. Please, please, Lord,"* She clasped hands again. *"I beg of you. Please don't let him be there this minute. Any electricity between us today would spark a blaze that could engulf everything in my life. Today I feel powerless to stop it. I am weak, but I know that you are strong.*

Excuse me, Miss, a voice thundered in her head. *Are you talking to me? About lust and adultery? Tenets of my Commandments?*

When Veronica finally approached the lab door, it was with conflicting feelings for and against Tony being there. She touched the knob, but the door flew open before she could push on it, and a breathtakingly handsome Tony stood smiling at her.

"I can tell the sound of your walk from a mile away." He smiled broadly.

Spellbound, she drank in every detail of the man—his strong jaw, the upturned corners of his lips, the little mole at the side of his nose, the deep cleft in his chin, the long, slender fingers of a brilliant surgeon, the slight gray at his temples for one so young, the tight, tight body she yearned for and.... Exhausted from her thoughts, Veronica ran a hand across her face hoping to side-step a total body flush. *He was too perfect! No one should be that perfect. He had to have a flaw.* But there was none she could see. Chiseled, saddle-brown and molded, Dr. Tony Reifenburg was perfect!

"Good morning, Dr. Reifenburg."

"I know you better than that now. Why won't you call me Tony? Without a doubt, if I can tell, the click of your heels and know your favorite coffee, a grande skim latte that has to qualify us to call each other by our first names." Tony's smile towered over her by four or five inches.

Veronica drew in a sharp, deep breath to quiet her heart which was galloping on a racetrack all by itself. It sounded like a damn mambo in her chest.

"If you choose to drink the dishwater in your hand, you'll still have to pay for the latte. Five dollars, please." Tony put out his left hand, his right hand holding the latte above his head. "Come on," he prodded. "Pay up."

"Put it on my tab," Veronica grabbed at the latte he waved in front of her. *Would she drink from this cup of sorrow?*

"I'd be happy to start a tab for you if you can prove you pay your debts on time?"

"Doesn't everyone?" Veronica said, and he could tell from the tone in her voice she was sincere. At the bill-paying desk in Randolph's office, not only was every bill noted with a date ten days before it was due, but they were also dutifully logged into the computer after they'd been paid. It had been so easy to find the proof she needed when Neiman Marcus had misapplied her payment. There were some benefits to dot-to-dot living.

"I could retire if I stopped paying late charges." He handed her the Latte. "But then again, I'm not disciplined."

As she reached for the cup, her hand, trembling ever so lightly, brushed against Tony's. "Thanks," Veronica said hurriedly, hoping her emotional spiral was not obvious. "Thanks for saving my taste buds." Quickly turning away before the deep purple crept up her back and reached her face, Veronica walked to her locker and stashed her purse. Bargaining for more time to regain emotional balance, she went to the sink and dumped the cafeteria brew. Tony's eyes were following her. She could feel them in the small of her back. More composed, she turned to face him. "Why are you here today, anyway? Don't you have a life?" Veronica acted calm but inside quivered like a wilting plant. That improv class she'd taken with Melody proved to be a blessing! "I was so sure you'd still be away for the holidays."

"Why? I have no wife or children—only my work. Work makes me happier than most things. What about you? Why are you here? Shouldn't *you* be making plans and setting goals you swear you'll keep this year?"

"We already broke them at 12:02."

"We?" He flashed perfect teeth.

"Well, my daughter ate enough candy for the year already. My son backtalked his father at the stroke of midnight, and my husband is still going over his list of goals for the tenth time, crossing t's and dotting i's. He's very precise."

"Uh-huh."

"So," Veronica shifted the focus of the conversation from her life. "Are you saying there's no one in your life who you'd rather spend New Year's with other than Miss Curvaceous Test Tube?"

"Just old beaver here." He rattled the cage of the animal.

"Well, I hope this shows my appreciation." Veronica dug into her bag for a few minutes before nervously handing him the Christmas gift she'd agonized over giving him.

"For me! How nice! Can I open it?"

"It's yours."

"This is nice and functional. No tie, cologne, or socks. I'm excited." He scribbled on the scratchpad with his Waterford pen.

"You never have a pen on rounds," she said.

"Consider that oversight a thing of the past. I have something for you too," he put a wad of paper into her hands, pecking her cheek innocently as gratitude for the once stylishly wrapped gift. "I hope these results are enough of a gift."

He hadn't gotten her anything personal. Hadn't thought it proper. She'd never once been overly friendly with him—all business. Until today, he had no idea she had two children. He supposed he could've figured out the marriage part from the simple gold band on her finger. There were, indeed, more women than he could handle vying for his time for New Year's, but somehow, he wanted to find a way to please Veronica. That's why he'd spent the entire holiday break with old beaver.

"Oh, my God!" Veronica embraced the man at her side. "Tony! You didn't. Jesus, look at these results. They're… they're …oh my god, do you see what I see?"

"Do you see what I see? Sounds like a Christmas song. Tis the season."

"Oh, stop!" Veronica laughed up into his eyes. "Tony, this is fantastic. Superb! Did you work all through the holidays?"

"Yes, I did. I was onto something and couldn't break the rhythm," his voice was excited from reliving the breakthrough. "I can't tell you the high I had. I can't imagine anything would've been more gratifying. My family understood." He said, catching his excitement. He didn't want to seem like a heartless cad. But to be frank, work was everything to him. It was his purpose. "I'll go out to visit with my family later in the month." He added.

"Tony, this is truly wonderful!"

"That I worked all through the holidays, am committed to my work or the results?"

"Silly, the results. You're amazing. Truly amazing. Why didn't you call me?"

"And miss the look on your face? Never! But it was just a matter of time. You knew you were onto something here." Tony tightened his grip around her waist to a squeeze. "With the LAMBER Award and now this, you'll be quite sought after, Dr. Whittaker."

"*We* are on to something. *We* will be sought after," Veronica said softly, feeling every digit of his hand against her plump hip. "I couldn't have done this without you, Tony. How can I ever thank you? When this gets published in the *New England Journal of Medicine,* we'll be asked to speak at every university. We'll be in demand."

For different reasons, desire coursed through the veins of Veronica Whittaker and Tony Reifenburg. The win was what bound them. It was their purpose. A shared vision. Tony's attraction to Veronica was unusual but clearly there. Definitely out of character for him. She wasn't his type. Then again, he never stayed long enough with women to appreciate their types. Veronica intrigued him. Her brain dazzled him. All that had fueled a desire in him to know her totally, to fuse not only their brains but their bodies as well. Attractive in an authentic way, plain and straightforward, Veronica hid behind no mask, unlike most women. And Tony, getting to that age where realness was far better than form, found himself desperately seeking her professional approval. If he could get that, the rest would come. Cautioned, perhaps because he sensed Veronica wasn't the type of woman to entertain the idea of an affair, and frankly, he respected her too much to try to bamboozle her with his usual smooth-talking; he loosened his grip on her. "It would be quite an honor being on the road with you, Veronica," Tony said finally, his eyes admiring the sheer honesty of her face.

"Ditto, for me too, Tony," Veronica's eyes expressed deep gratitude. "Thanks for all your objective opinions, hard work and analytical skills… just plain thanks." Veronica reached up to brush his cheek. Her lips, lingering there a moment too long, electrified her body. God knows she hadn't planned this moment, but she realized she'd wanted to kiss Tony the moment he'd walked into her life. A madness came over her. Moments later, Tony's eager, waiting, and willing lips met hers. She poured all of her into the kiss feeling her body go weak. With absolute conviction, they had moved as though choreographed to the next level of passion Veronica felt intense, non-suppressible emotions colliding into a deep need to remember her marriage vows. How could she so easily have forgotten them? But this passion was re-validating her life. She was floating though her feet were still on the ground. In this kiss was freedom and the release from bondage. In this kiss were planted the seeds of good and evil.

"Tony…."

"Shush." He moved her backward toward the laboratory door, bolting it from the inside. "We deserve this. We deserve this," he kept murmuring, his passion fueled by their joint accomplishment—a reward for work well done.

"Please," Veronica said out of obligation, half-heartedly trying to move out of his embrace. "I can't… do this. What about…."

"Your husband?"

"Yes."

"What about him? You tell me."

Veronica's world collapsed. Sinking rapidly into the belly of delirium and intoxication, her body, seething with pure desire, nullified her superhuman effort to walk away. Her feet were planted, rooted to the spot while her soul, now fully released from gravity, soared into the vast open universe. Answering the aching from the ecstasy that seemed to rise from inside and out-side of her was the only thing that mattered. Veronica knew then she would never answer the question he asked. This kiss, this kiss was pivotal…centrifugal motion.

CHAPTER EIGHT

MELODY ADAMS, packaged, controlled and literate, was the epitome of well-bred America. Distinguished and solidly in place among the power elite was no luxury she took for granted. That she, a prodigy, an exception, an experiment, might one day smash the belief of Black intellectual inferiority was still a notion in the larger world. Far from being a stereotype, Melody had so deeply assimilated she no longer seemed a threat. Consequently, she was forced to listen to men rip women apart for merely being female and to colleagues who believed Blacks were shiftless, lazy and America's worst nightmare. She had listened to more than she had bargained for when she chose to become invisible. Indeed, Melody had singularly earned her peers' respect, but that didn't stop them from thinking of Black women as hoochie mamas and their rightful whores, and Black folks' excellence as an aberration.

Melody looked at her watch, eight-fifteen. What exactly would she do with an entire day? There was but one friend to call. With more jobs than a new Jamaican immigrant, Veronica would have little time to socialize, much less to spend an entire day consoling Melody. *Anyway*, Melody thought, *I don't feel much like burdening her.* The truth was closer to Veronica's mounting marital discontent being center stage in all their recent interactions, and to be frank, trouble in paradise conversations were burning up her ears. Women, men, love, and its' accompanying issues. What a colossal bore!

It was true, men found no comfort in Melody Adam's achievements. And if they were able to overcome their fright, none would be able to live up to Melody's pathological need for perfection, or her need to control everything within states of her. Yes, states such as Wisconsin, Michigan, Ohio, Pittsburgh, and Philadelphia, too. But Melody Adams would argue vehemently that behaviors such as perfection and control were simply the by-products of successful lives; two of the *Seven Habits of Highly Effective People*. Even with her idiosyncratic foibles, many a man had tried to get close to Melody, but her underlying lens that filtered and distrusted everyone, eventually delivered a lethal punch, TKOing anything that looked, felt, or smelled like love. Love was a waste of time. The mushy, unwarranted feeling was a killer of drive and achievement. That was her perspective on life, and as any fool knows, perspective creates and cements reality.

Rush hour winding down, Melody could move more steadily on the road. *What would her life have been like had she married Carlton Reiner?* Thinking of the past, melancholy began creeping through Melody. Symbolically she shrugged her shoulders, casting off any thoughts before they rooted in her mind. Her life was in the now, the past, long forgotten. Melody thought fleetingly of going to the gym or to a day spa where some handsome Swedish masseuse would give her a sensuous massage from a...*Sensuous! What a laugh!* She had no idea what the word meant. She, a woman of great and rising importance, had no one with whom she could laugh. If it were true that a well-lived life boiled down to the single experience of belonging, she, without question, had failed miserably. A single tear threatened, escaped, and then cradled itself at the corner of her eye. *God,* Melody snapped. *I'm having a really, really bad day. I should go and see Eve*, Melody thought as she brought the car to a halt at a stoplight.

It was never too late. Suddenly Melody felt dizzy, and a blinding headache shifted her vision out of focus. The red light became a diffused haze, and a strange tremor shook her body. Sweat was pouring down her back and her stomach felt queasy. As a jagged light flashed across her face, she gripped the steering wheel, trying to focus. Her temples throbbed, and an excruciating headache was spreading across her cranium moment by moment. Melody's first thought was to get the car to safety. Anyone else, sweating, shaking and in agonizing pain, without explanation, would've panicked, but not Melody Adams. As the light turned, she pulled the car safely onto the curb. Pressing the emergency button on the phone, she wiped a hand across her forehead and waited. Her vision was still hazy, and things kept moving in and out of focus. What was wrong with her? She couldn't be reacting this violently to anger, anguish, frustration, burnout, or loneliness! Could she? *Oh boy,* she rubbed the back of her neck; the car was hot. Maybe the heat was too high but realized it was set at seventy when glancing at the dial. Depressing the sunroof button, she tried to regulate her breathing as bitterly cold air filled her car. Just as quickly as the shaking began, however, it stopped.

"Hello. Hello caller," someone was shouting on the other end of the line

"Oh, Hello," Melody said calmly. "I dialed your number by accident. Thank you."

Well, Melody, now shivering, closed the sunroof and started the car, *this is some mid-life crisis.* In moments, she felt perfectly normal. Maybe she should make a doctor's appointment today. The question was, with whom, an internist or a psychiatrist! Eve was who she needed to see today.

The beeper in Veronica's coat went off, and reality rushed in and demanded answers. What had she done? Oh, no God, what had she done? "I've gotta go." She jumped to her feet, fumbling with the beeper in her coat pocket. "My office," she lied, looking at the number registered home. *How could Randolph know!* Flushed with embarrassment, she grabbed her bag and ran to the door. "Bolt the door after I leave," she insisted, furtively looking up and down the hall for spies. Why was she so nervous? For Christ sakes, she shared the lab with Tony! "I won't be making rounds this morning," she said, quickly pulling the door behind her. Guilt weighed on Veronica like a vice. Feelings of betrayal escalated as she thundered down the corridor. In the stairwell, she took the stairs two at a time. What on earth had she just done? "It was a mistake," Veronica said, charging forward. "You are allowed one mistake." "*Sut Nam.*" She said, inhaling deeply. "I'm allowed one mistake."

Buried under responsibilities since the age of twelve, Veronica's life had been a grand pantomime of sacrifice. Giving sometimes what wasn't hers to give. Through sheer determination, Veronica Whittaker had broken the fetters of life in the projects. Even today, she was held up as the poster child who'd successfully unshackled mental slavery. Committed never to failing those who depended on her, Veronica, well beyond what was good for her, continued to give more than she could emotionally afford. Along the way, she'd expired and, unbeknownst to her, had entered the world of the living dead. For the first time in her life, she'd taken something she wanted, something she needed, and now the guilt was unbearable. Which was better, life or death?

By the time Veronica made it to her office, her waiting room was crowded. The work overload would be a relief.

"Good morning, Sybil," she glanced quickly at her reflection in the wall mirror. Did she look like an unfaithful woman? A Hussy? A Charlatan? Lady Chatterley?

"Oh, good morning, Dr. Whittaker. Your husband has been trying to reach you all morning. He sounds anxious."

"Thanks. I'll call him while you prepare the exam room."

While her practice was in its infancy, Veronica had continued in the research position she'd held through medical school to help pay the bills. The offer for a teaching position at the medical school came later. Honored, she was hard-pressed to turn it down. Convinced she was close to proving a new theory on infertility, she'd refused to abandon her academic research. Now, fifteen years later, there was a break-though. A discovery that could change lives. But biological justice for the infertile was hardly what was on her mind this morning. The memory of Tony sucking her life out through her lips was the dominant thought. Digging into her bag, Veronica stuffed six tic-tacs into her mouth before walking into the first patient room. After so much self-sacrifice and self-restraint, why on earth was she willing to destroy her carefully planned life? Living her young life in the margins of existence had prepared Veronica for a lot, but it hadn't prepared her for desire's uncontrollable madness.

"Josephine," Veronica said flatly. "How are you this morning?"

"No spotting at all last week." The patient looked expectantly at Veronica.

Ten patients later, Veronica could still not make herself dial the number to home. Tapping her fingers nervously against her desk, she ordered herself to call. *Call. Call.* It could be about the children. Could Randolph know! He always knew everything, she thought! Finally, picking up the phone, Veronica punched up a number. Tony's voice answered, and she slammed down the phone; why she didn't know because they had caller id. Dear

God! Was she so on the edge of insanity? A few minutes later, she grabbed her purse and headed toward the door. She could blame not calling home on an emergency.

"Sybil, where's Marlene?"

"Dr. Marlene is in with patients."

"Would you ask her to see as many of my patients as she can fit in? Cancel the rest of my day. Maybe I'll be back, but I can't be sure. I'll call. Slight emergency at home."

"Dr. Whittaker, are you all right?" Sybil inquired with a worried look on her face. *Could something awful have happened at home?* It was not her place to ask.

"I'm fine. Really, I am."

CHAPTER NINE

THE WOMAN BEHIND the desk looked like a grown-up Annie. April stood in the waiting room, wondering if she had been too impulsive.

"Good morning," the woman's voice was as chirpy as her hairdo. "I haven't seen you around before. Your name, please?"

"I'm not a client," April squeezed her bag close to her body. "I'm April Summers. Is Eve available?"

"She should be finishing up with someone. Why don't you wait here a second, and I'll check? You can hang your coat in here if you'd like."

Curls disappeared down a corridor, leaving April to observe the tastefully decorated waiting room. It didn't look anything like a room for loonies.

"Morning," a husky but silky voice interrupted April.

"Hi." April nodded, automatically looking up to see who owned the distinctive voice. A woman in a doctor's coat stood smiling at her. Whoever she was, she should consider doing commercials. Her face, bare except for a dab of blush and cranberry lip-gloss, seemed familiar, but from where she hadn't a clue. The woman, unfortunately, was a fashion disaster, a ghastly sight to behold. Yellow in winter. Unforgivable!

"Where's Ruby this morning?" The doctor's head jerked toward the reception desk.

"If you mean the receptionist, she just bobbed down the hall."

The doctor's throaty laugh filled the room. "That she does, doesn't she? It's genetic. You should see her family. All red curls. Like you."

The door opened again.

"Veronica, April?" Melody looked incredulously from one woman to the other. "Melody?" The women echoed.

"You know each other?" Veronica asked.

"Yes. April is on my Comtech merger deal."

"What?" Veronica said.

"The project I was telling you about."

"Veronica is your basic non-businesswoman type. She thinks 401K is a race," Melody said, to April, and by the way," she rested her gym bag on the floor, "I thought you were on vacation." The women eyed each other.

"And what about my being here suggests I'm not on vacation?" April said.

"Didn't know S&G paid for Dr. Luz," Melody snapped. She couldn't stand April Summers. The woman had such an air of entitlement it nauseated her.

April was unaffected by Melody. From time to time, she got a hunch the woman was an imposter, yet it wasn't enough of a curiosity to cost her any brain cell activity. Every time their paths crossed, for the fun of it, April found herself trying to find the one incongruence that would confirm her suspicion about Melody. The wrong scarf. The wrong jewelry. The wrong shade of pantyhose. Anything. Until today, she hadn't succeeded. From the Prada shoes to the Yurman jewelry, the woman was always flawlessly put together, but today, by God, was a day that would go down in infamy. Melody Adams was wearing casual wear with heels! A Saint John's jumpsuit, mind you, but a jumpsuit nonetheless!

"Ladies. Ladies." Veronica intervened as she saw talons appearing. "I suspect we're stressed out and all that, but please, why add to the chaos in our lives?"

"Chaos? Vee, what exactly is tumultuous about your life? Anyway, what are you doing here?" Melody was genuinely surprised to see Veronica in Eve's office. With her back to April, Melody made no move to include her in the conversation.

"I thought I'd pay for some enlightenment from Dr. Luz, as you so aptly put it a minute ago, especially since my "friend" is getting tired of my constant barrage. Reckon I'd use up a bit of professional courtesy. Eve is a patient of mine, not to mention the convenience of having her so close. Just trying to keep this life of mine real. Right now, at this very moment, it's in pretty bad shape."

"I'm sorry I didn't return your call *immediately*." Melody couldn't dodge the dig. "You can't imagine how hectic it's been. Tell her, April." It was expedient to call on the annoying woman for support.

"Tell her what?" April's very proper accent annoyed Melody to no end.

Melody sucked in her breath. *That's what I get relying on people.*

"Don't paint yourself into a corner, missy," Veronica said, seating herself on a sofa. "What do you think? That you are my only friend? Anyway, what are you doing here?"

"I've been seeing Eve for months. It's a job requirement before I take over as CEO. She trains all the senior execs at Comtech." Melody, after a month, had found her sessions with Eve liberating. Now she'd come to think of her as her success compass.

"Sure," April said, coyly turning toward Veronica. "It was nice meeting you, Dr. Whittaker." She read the embroidered name on the white coat. "Melody, I'll be in the office tomorrow if you still need me, but I've got to go right now. Leave Chicago's B&B to your moments of continued inspiration and enlightenment? God, look at these nails," April exclaimed. "Now there is a productive way to spend some of the mornings, especially since it appears Eve won't be available for coffee." She got up to leave.

"B&B's?" Veronica's eyes expressed curiosity. "I hope it doesn't mean what I think."

"New word in Corporate America. Best and Brightest." Melody volunteered.

"As if I really care." Veronica quipped. "Seems to me it should mean Black and Bitchy!"

"Then why did you ask?" Melody let out an exasperated sigh.

April watched the women, who appeared to be long-time friends, with some scorn and envy. Friends were not painted on her tableau. April found friendships quite taxing and somewhat appalling. Without question, she couldn't bear it when people felt the need to unburden their lives on her and, worse, when they invited themselves into her life. Surprisingly, April found herself liking the woman with the husky voice, wishing she could chat with her a little longer.

"Dr. Whittaker." The bobbing receptionist re-appeared. "I wasn't expecting you this morning."

"Well, being in balance demands attention when you least expect it. How are you, Ruby?"

"Pretty darn good today." The receptionist smiled jovially.

"When will Eve be free?"

"Tough day today, but she'll be out in a minute."

Well, I'll be a monkey's uncle. April looked more closely at the woman in the lab coat as recognition registered. This was "The" Veronica Whittaker! The hotshot researcher whose work was making waves. Now April could firmly place the face of the woman.

"Well," April said, outstretching her hand to Veronica. "Congratulations on your award. My parents were quite impressed with your write-up in the Journal. They are both neurologists at Northwestern."

Veronica Whittaker, who had recently been recognized with the prestigious Lamber Award, had been pictured on every Chicago paper's front page. Veronica Whittaker was also, on several occasions, the subject of her parents' dinner conversations. Little discussions which were probably meant to remind April she wasn't doing anything meaningful with her life.

"What's your name again?"

"April Summers."

"I think I know of your parents and all about their work, but we've never met. Do thank them for thinking so highly of me. It's an honor."

Too bad I'll never conceive. April felt suddenly solemn. "I'll be sure to do that."

Yada. Melody thought. "My dear," she turned to the bubbly redhead receptionist and repeated Veronica's question. "So, when will Eve, be free?"

"About five minutes, but she has a client right after. And Miss Summit," she glanced over at April.

"Mrs. Summers," April said. "Like the weather."

"Mrs. Summers is here to see her." The receptionist smiled apologetically.

"I'm not here to *see* her, *dear.* I'm here to take her to coffee." April flouted.

Veronica, who had absolutely nothing to laugh about, did. Here she was drowning in the guilt of a harlot, an adulterer, a fallen woman, yet she couldn't help laughing at April's ridiculous and pointless vanity. Veronica stared openly at the beautiful, defensive woman who paced impatiently. Even her pacing was done with confident precision. What would someone like her have to be so defensive about? It seemed the Almighty had given her every advantage, for April Summers was uncommon in her beauty, obviously successful and wellborn. Veronica could see Melody's point. April Summers not only exuded an air that could never be schooled, but she was also the kind of woman who inspired poets to write lines such as *"in her wake, the breeze stirred restlessly."*

April fixed her gaze on Veronica—direct, challenging, and bordering on a leer. "What on earth is the matter with you?" Her haughty eyes traveled scornfully over Veronica's attire. "Do you think everyone in the world is a basket case?" She said, whirling in defiance.

"No, I don't believe all people are loco, but I have this sneaky suspicion you are."

"What? What did you just say?" April said.

"Com'on tell the truth for once." Veronica reached for April's hand, intentionally examining the well-manicured nails. "Success is a bitch, ain't it, dear? It takes all prisoners."

"Whatever." April waved a dismissive hand.

"I'm just keeping it, real girlfriend. We are all here to talk to Eve about over-demanding lives."

"Keeping it real!" Melody hissed. "That's an annoying phrase."

"Excuse me?" Veronica turned on Melody. "Since when did they make you the slang po-lice? I'll say any annoying phrase I damn well, please. Just keeping it real. It says so much, doesn't it, girlfriend?"

Melody rolled her eyes and glanced at her watch.

"It's the age, forty," Veronica said in explanation to April. "It gives me the freedom to be real."

"Reality has a price," April said.

"True. True. But I'm willing to bet breakfast that if we were all being honest, we'd admit reality is why we're all here. And that, on the other side of our success, is a tremendous loss. It's not what it's cracked up to be, is it? This success?"

April stared again. Her stare was neither warm nor cold.

"If we," Veronica waved a hand which included April and Melody, "aren't proof of people who've overdosed on success, I don't know who would be. Tell me truthfully, women, is it just an accident that Chicago's Black Trinity are gathered in an Executive Coach's office looking for balance?"

"What a catastrophe it would be if it ever gets out." Melody tugged a straying hair back into a twist at her nape. "I can just see the headlines: The new corporate breed: Executive Coaches, AKA new age gurus with names like Ragbaniswanna, take corporate top guns by storm."

"As I said," April could not make peace with her spirit, "I *am* here to take Eve to coffee. She's my Cardio Boxing instructor." She frowned anew at the idea of struggle.

"As wound up as you're, Missy, I wouldn't drink any coffee. I suppose you want us to believe you're not here to get your dose of Zoloft, eh?" Veronica asked.

April's jaw dropped. She took a step backward, studying the women intensely, a distasteful scowl on her face. The look she'd perfected to make mere mortals quiver had no effect on Veronica Whittaker. Veronica, wearing a loose yellow shift, flat black shoes, a colorless pair of stockings, her virgin hair pulled back into a single braid, didn't flinch. Obviously, this was not a woman of convention or one burdened by the tenets of the status quo. April, though agog, appreciated Veronica's authenticity. With a presumption of knowledge, she knew they would become friends. She and Dr. Veronica Whittaker.

Not one compelled to engage in blurb talk, Melody prepared to leave.

"Right or wrong?" Veronica sought reconciliation.

"Look, *dearie*, and do pardon the expression, but I know misery loves company, but I am not… how shall we say, suffering from any anxiety," April said flatly.

"To what do I owe *all* this pleasure?" Eve said, coming down the hallway, and Melody waited.

"Swinging pendulums that won't stay in the middle. Otherwise known as stress." Veronica piped up. "And since you're the best EC in the Midwest, *voilá*, here comes Chicago's B&B's."

Eve's eyebrows shot up.

"Black and Bold or something like that," Veronica said, stifling a grin.

"I was in the neighborhood and thought I'd take you up on that coffee offer," April disassociated completely from the explanation of psychological stress, "but I'll call, and we'll reschedule."

"Well," Melody piped up. "I ripped the hell out of my brand-new Rena Lange skirt, changed into these sweats in my car in broad daylight and had a mid-life episode on my way home. So, here I am to get some damn herbal tea, but Valium will do too."

Veronica and April's heads snapped to attention. Was that Melody speaking, or did some alien invade her body? They couldn't help but burst into laughter. Melody, usually humorless, was on form and poised to do battle.

"I'm so sorry, ladies," Eve stifled a grin, "but I have a chock-full schedule today. Let's plan to meet soon, though. Ruby will rearrange the schedule for tomorrow." Eve disappeared back into her office.

"I have an idea." Veronica offered. "Has anyone had breakfast?"

"Breakfast?" April looked at her watch. It was nine-forty-five.

"Yes, breakfast. What time do you have breakfast?"

"I never have breakfast," April said brusquely.

"That could be a part of your problem."

April opened her mouth but shut it as the incorrigible Veronica Whittaker said "Blah, blah, blah. So how about a new experience? Breakfast at Melody's."

"Not! Melody said vehemently. "You don't mean at my house, do you?"

"Yep. That's what I mean," said Veronica akimbo.

"Really, I *mean*, you don't *mean* my house." Melody nailed the option shut. "And it's Breakfast at Tiffany's anyway."

"No to Tiffany's, but how about that little restaurant up the street. What's it called again?" Veronica asked.

"Angelo's. They have the best egg white omelets."

"I thought you didn't have breakfast?" Veronica eyed April suspiciously.

"Lunch. Thanks for the offer. I'd love to join you, but I'm on my way to the office." April danced around the commitment of spending a morning with Plain Jane and Uptight Suzzie.

"To do what? You're on vacation, remember? Let me further remind you, you were about to spend it in a psychiatrist's office." Veronica said with smug satisfaction.

"Executive Coach. Two different functions." Melody said.

"Regardless, we are all here because we're overworked, out of sort, not in harmony, right?" Veronica pushed the elevator button. "Maybe we can help each other out—a sistah solidarity kind of thing. Form a coaching group of our own so top-of-their game sistahs like us can let our hair down and keep it real. Who can we afford to show our vulnerability to except each other? I bet we can help each other better than …"She looked around and lowered her voice, "Eve. Cultural nuances and stuff."

"Really. I'm sure you're probably right, but I've some stock review stuff to do. Be sure to invite me over for the next girl talk, though," April said cynically.

"Don't you have a Smartphone?" Melody seemed aghast.

"And if I don't?"

"I can get you one cheap. My company helped pioneer the technology." Melody was gloating.

"Sure, it doesn't follow the dot.com fate?"

"We pioneered the technology. Did you miss that?"

"Shut up. Shut up." Veronica pleaded. "Can't you two be civil? What's all this hostility? It's so unattractive and so programmed in us women."

"Hostility? Disagreement," April corrected.

"Mine and Melody's agitation is pre-menopausal." Veronica said to April, ushering her onto the elevator, "At your age, what could make you so disagreeable?"

"I don't know what you're talking about." April snapped.

"Don't worry. I'll figure out your malady before long. Not enough sex, probably. I can tell from the splotches on your face. I can give you something for that too. In a few weeks, you'll be a pussycat." Veronica said. "If that fails, I'll try Prozac, Lithium, friendship? Don't worry; by lunchtime, I'll have you diagnosed and treated."

Angelo's was Angelo's. An establishment that had occupied the same corner for as long as Chicago has been and christened with very little change to the décor since then. What made Angelo's special was, it understood about culinary diversity long before it was *de rigueur*. April had egg white omelet, Melody Melba toast and Nova Lox, and Veronica hometown grits and scrambled eggs with a side of bacon. Though the conversation remained light, the women indeed had something in common. Extraordinary success.

"Now tell me that this wasn't fun. Why don't we meet once a month? What do you say?" Veronica drained her teacup. They hadn't exhaled, but the women had found, if tentatively, camaraderie.

"I hate to admit it, but this felt rejuvenating. Let's take turns hosting the meetings. I'll do the next one." April offered.

"Let's not." Melody put ten dollars on the table. *What's with this flake? All of a sudden, she's into camaraderie!*

"Let's." Veronica insisted on paying the bill. "We'll call our group the Trinity. The Holy Trinity. I like that." Her eyes, though saddened, genuinely smiled.

"No need to get holy," Melody said, finally following the majority rule. To be honest, she really liked Veronica.

CHAPTER TEN

F RIDAY, VERONICA'S OFFICE was unusually hectic. Exhausted from work and from trying to quell thoughts of Tony, she didn't collapse at her desk until well into the evening. Too much was happening in her life, and she needed to decide what was important. Veronica shuffled the charts to be notated. Charting was the last thing in the world she felt like doing. Clicking on the recorder, she began dictating. In this world of technology, she shouldn't be doing this shit!

The knock at her door was a steady tap. The cleaning crew already? If a light appeared under the door, their habit was to knock before using their master key.

"I'm still here," Veronica shouted, "but come on in. You can clean around me."

A few minutes later, the knock came again. Veronica wearily dragged herself to the door and yanked it open. Tony was leaning against the doorframe, as handsome as anyone could be, holding beautiful peach roses.

"Hi there." He smiled.

Blood gushed from her heart into her cheeks. "Tony!" Veronica said, the burn traveling from face to neck, then shoulders. "I've… I've been meaning to call you. It's been a hectic couple of weeks, and I haven't been able to make it into the lab or general rounds. How are things with the students?"

"Things are fine."

"I'll be in tomorrow. I figured we had a little time before we told anyone about our new find."

"The research or us?" His eyes never strayed from her.

"You know, I'm glad you're here. We need to talk, but this is a busy delivery time for me."

"How well I know the drill. Today, I had eight surgical cases and a waiting room full of pregnant patients. I'm used to long days and sleepless nights. The sleepless nights have been killing me lately, but it hasn't been from overwork."

"We must've been crazy going into private practice." She said, avoiding his eyes. She knew what he was intimating with his double talk.

"You can always give it up and be a full-time researcher. NSF would love to give you grants."

"Uh-uh. That's a thought. So," she eyed the flowers, "are you visiting someone in the hospital?"

"No. These are for you."

"You know Tony; we really should talk. When are you available?"

"Right now." Why haven't you answered any of my pages, emails, texts, or calls? I've figured I'd made you mad, so I'm here to make up for a fight I didn't even know I had," he handed her the flowers.

Veronica took the flowers. "Thanks. Tony, I have to get home tonight, but I want to talk."

"I want to talk now." Tony insisted, pushing further inside the door. "Are you going to invite me in, or will we talk in the hall?"

"Sorry. I'm a female doctor. Can't be with a male patient without an attendant. As you can see, I'm home alone. So, no. Anyway….," Veronica could not stop herself from rambling.

"I'm not a patient. I'm a doctor. We can discuss a case if you'd like to make it official. But how could you be home alone when a man like me is standing in front of you?" He ignored her plea for an escape.

"You're an illusion. Not real. Can't be real. Please….go away."

"I brought roses! Feel the prickles. They are real."

"But you are not. Tony! I'm a married woman. What happened between us was a mistake. A confluence of things in your life and mine made us misbehave. An error in judgment. Situational. Friends. That's all we can be."

"Look, Veronica. It was just a kiss! I'm not pressuring you, but I'm willing, capable, and able to be all that I can be. A friend, a colleague or a…."

Despite herself, Veronica laughed. "Come in, Tony. There is no need to audition for the army," she stepped aside, fidgeting with the roses to keep her eyes off the man making her heart flutter. "Let me put these in water." She went to the office kitchen to find a vase. "I should cut these stems."

"No need. They were just trimmed."

"Do you want anything to drink?"

"No."

Tony was making no effort to be discreet about staring flirtatiously at Veronica. Today she was wearing a flared, rocket red dress that stopped just above the knee. Trendy black pumps graced her feet. He'd never seen her more beautiful. Tony glanced around the office. The setting screamed success. The place was exquisite, from the Lalique hall table to the expensive rug. A beautiful bronze statue caught Tony's eyes as he followed Veronica to her office. It captivated him, and he went over to take a closer look. *Defiance,* the bronze plaque read. It was a remarkable and telling piece of art. "This statue is amazing. Where did you find it?"

"Which?" Veronica turned. "Oh, *Defiance*. Isn't it marvelous? It tells a powerful story of pride and dignity, doesn't it? Look at that face. From the slave's proud and defiant expression, you couldn't imagine the excruciating pain she must have been in from her whipping. Look," she spun the statue around to show the whip marks captured in bronze by the broken flesh on her back, "look at her gripped toes. It's the only sign she's in distress. Such bravery. Such resilience. Not even the brutality of slavery could break her spirit. I saw it out West. On a ski trip. It called to me. My sister gave it to me as a surprise."

Tony noticed a passion in Veronica as she talked about the survival of *Defiance*. She, he was sure, identified with the story a great deal.

"So, you ski, huh? That's my favorite sport."

"Really?" Veronica hurled past the point.

"We should go together sometime."

"No can do. Tony. Look…."

"Veronica, you can defy things sure enough, but you don't have to feel pain by choice. *Defiance* felt pain at the hand of a slave master. Where does your pain come from? I know where mine does."

"What happened between us was wrong. You know that too. Let it pass. Let it die. I'm sorry, Tony, but I must ask you to leave."

"Tell me you don't want to be with me. Tell me now, and I will leave and never return." Tony took her by the shoulder, turning her to face him.

Veronica stood still, not moving a muscle. She knew what she was supposed to say, but no words left her lips.

"Veronica," Tony pleaded. "Do you want me to go away? Do you?" He pulled her to him, the warmth of his breath against her face. She met his penetrating eyes that were desperately asking permission to go further. Inside his eyes, she saw love. She saw hope. She saw salvation. He was going to kiss her again, and she wasn't sure what she'd do. Tony's touch moved down her back, his fingers lighting a fire through her dress. Her body trembled as he brought his hand to rest on her hips.

"Go now." She pleaded.

"I can't."

Taking him by the hand, Veronica led him around her office. "All this," she waved a trembling arm, "I've worked very hard for. How can I give it up for a moment of lust?"

"Why do you have to give it up?" You could double it."

"Tell that to Randolph. I'm not going to stand here and deny you've opened up something in me. Neither can I deny I haven't dreamed of the formidable force you and I could be in medicine. I can't even deny what havoc you play with my heart, but I am a married woman with two children. Committed and secure."

"Are you?" His gaze dared her to lie.

"What do you want from me? To finish what we started with a big bang? If I slept with you tonight, would you be able to move on with your life and forget me? Can you promise never to discuss this again? Can I get you to promise me that?"

"Why are you so afraid to live?"

"We should go." She pulled out of his embrace, knowing the time had ended in her fairytale world. Did she want to live? How could he ask her that as if she were dead!

"Do you want me to go?"

"Yes I do. You must."

"A pity." He began unbuttoning her white coat. "After tonight, I promise," he said. "Just one night in your arms."

Veronica moved out of his embrace. "let's give this time. It will all go away," she said, ushering him out the door.

After Tony left, Veronica quickly gathered her belongings. She needed the familiarity of home tonight: her children and her husband. Tony was leaning against Veronica's car in the parking lot when she descended the steps.

"You are one hard-headed man." Veronica walked around him to the driver's side of her car, pressing the unlock button. In plain view, though no one was around, Tony pulled her close to him his lips inches from hers Pulling back, he rested his head against hers and softly sang, "I'm ready to learn all about love." And by God, he was on key. "Come away with me for the weekend, Veronica. Let me help you decide on not just stolen moments."

"I can't."

"Yes, you can. Just say yes. Please."

"I'll think about it. Okay?" She hurriedly got into her truck.

It was well past midnight when Veronica tiptoed up the stairs. Randolph had taken to sleeping in the guestroom, so she didn't worry about waking him. Confused and in need of old realities, Veronica walked down the hall and pushed open her son's room door. There, on the bed, were three bodies in contorted positions. Gerald at the foot of the bed, Jennie's foot across her father's chest, and Randolph, his body half hanging over the bed, a book still on his chest. Veronica felt small. How could she? She shook her head and began backing out of the room. She was married to one helluva man. Why was that not enough? How could she even think of cheating on him?

"Is this a scene from the burning bed?" Randolph's deep voice reached across the room.

The man had such an imagination. His vivid imagination had helped her see her future so clearly and made him such a brilliant writer. Momentarily, Veronica felt a longing to be in his arms. "You ought to be quiet before you wake the children. And quit being so smart. Because I want a little space doesn't mean I want to murder you!"

"You are murdering me, Veronica," He gingerly rearranged the children before getting out of bed and following her into the hallway. "If you turned out like Lorena Bobbitt because of something horrible I did to you, I'd accept my punishment." Sadness weighed heavily in his voice. "But for loving you? I can't go on this way."

She couldn't see his face but the pain in his voice crossed the distance between them.

"Randolph, please. Stop talking like that. I couldn't hurt you that way."

They continued to their bedroom. Veronica closed the door. If an ugly argument got the better of them, they wouldn't disturb the children. She sat on the side of the bed.

"Being made a eunuch would be an easier hurt, and I would at least understand the reason."

"Randy, we've lost our way," Veronica said solemnly. "I'm tired. Tired of three a.m. calls followed by nine a.m. office followed by more delivery calls. I don't see the kids. I don't see you. I don't even see myself. I want the choice to slow down, but how can I? I haven't given up on your dream, but I'm beginning to doubt your dream will ever come true. You're a great writer, an even better father, and you're still the best man I know, but it's not enough anymore."

"What is, Veronica? What is?"

"I didn't expect to climb this high. You know the saying the higher monkey climbs. People are looking at me now; people in the streets know who I am. My face is recognizable to people other than those in the hospital. My life is under a microscope, and I'm…."

"Ashamed of me. I suppose I can't blame you. Success is what society values. Integrity and commitment mean nothing nowadays. People behind masks are far more interesting."

"Stop making things up. I'm not ashamed of you."

"Where were you tonight, Veronica?"

"At the office. Eighteen years and you've never asked me that. Do you have a reason to question me this way? This alone shows we've lost our way."

"People in love do and think desperate things." His voice was apologetic.

"Are you saying you love me? Is this how you show love? By making me feel I'm betraying our family by asking for some space. What kind of love is that?"

"Love, by its very nature, is irrational. It defies logic, society, and compromise. It just is. People like you and I need love, Veronica. It was love that gave us the fire to get out of the projects. It was love that gave us two beautiful children. And maybe it's only love that can help us find our way back. I should tell you I have no reason to ask but a feeling. After eighteen years, it's unfortunate to ask such a question."

CHAPTER ELEVEN

F RIDAY MORNING, Martin Spiro, always a last-minute riser, was up earlier than he imagined possible. He was standing in front of the mirror, putting his tie around a neck creased over his collar. Finally, the meeting had been rescheduled for this morning. He was a little agitated. *Frank Easton was a prick.* Martin thought angrily, struggling with the top button of his white shirt. *Call an emergency meeting and then disappear for two weeks.* Martin Spiro wanted the CFO position at S&G, but his "loyalty" to the establishment wouldn't be enough to secure the job. Realizing he had little to no chance of competing against April Summers, he'd spent the past two weeks racking his brain on a strategy to improve his position.

S&G was a conservative firm. Though Black brilliant, fierce, unapologetic, unforgiving, and ruthless, it was April's blackness Martin felt was his one ace. S&G was too conservative, staid, and traditional a firm to consider a woman as CFO. And a Black woman CFO, not a chance! Martin was committed to playing the race card to his advantage if that's what it took. For Martin, however, there was a more pressing and essential reason to become the CFO of S&G. Getting the damnable job for which he had no passion was to disprove his father's opinion that he was a spineless clod. Without question, this was far more important than April Summers's advancement or diversity quotas.

Turning over the brown envelope in his hand, he licked the flap, pressing the moist adhesive in place. Certainly, it couldn't hurt to legitimize April's disqualification with a bit of bad news while solidifying his reputation as a company man. What he had to do was nothing personal, only business. Martin moved with heavy strides through the room. He felt like a slug. He pulled on the dark blue socks and was so out of breath from the minor activity he was hyperventilating. He had to do something about his weight. Momentarily he felt bad about his plan. He'd learned a lot from April over the years, and he really liked her. In fact, he'd always found her downright attractive and erudite, but a woman like her would never give him the time of day. Martin dropped the envelope in his briefcase, walked to the kitchen, stuffed a glazed donut between his teeth, then headed out the door of his condo.

The air in the boardroom was as thick as dense fog. Everyone, totaling ten, tried to make small talk. It was clear nerves were on edge. This was going to be a very delicate situation. The only two people yet to arrive were April Summers and Frank Easton. Moments later, April strode into the room, her steps firm and confident. She made no effort to smile or distract herself with coffee or formalities. Instead, she took her seat at the table and waited until everyone who'd stood at her arrival, were again seated. She was in command of the room. Silence reigned, and there was a sigh of relief when Frank Easton finally arrived.

"Good morning, gentlemen and lady," Frank unbuttoned his jacket and sat in the reserved seat, pouring himself a glass of water. He did not hurry. When he was good and ready, he looked around the room before fixing his eyes intensely on April Summers. An unattractive man, merely five feet ten, though the power he wheeled made him Goliath, Frank's penetrating, squinty green eyes met hers. He smiled, showing a row of uneven teeth peeking through thin lips. Frank was getting on in age now. April clocked him at about sixty-eight, maybe even seventy though he looked considerably younger. Distinguished and confident, despite his physicality, his supple skin showed little evidence of aging, and his modest erect frame could make him fool people that he was in his early fifties. Ugly or old, the man's reputation was legendary, and at S&G, Frank Easton was Master of the Universe.

Mechanical responses resounded through the room.

"Are we ready, gentlemen?" April inquired, her palm pressed firmly against the cherry conference table leaned further in, her steely brown gaze piercing the faces of the mostly gray-haired white men across from her. She brought her unflinching eyes to once again rest on Frank Easton.

"Go ahead, Ms. Eh…, Frank Easton looked down at the paper in front of him. Summers."

April did not stand up. She felt powerful. In control. Her voice barely above a whisper, she began. "Ronald Kusak is a man whom you've all trusted. And trust had allowed him to embezzle almost one hundred million dollars from this firm. I don't care that he was the CFO. I don't care that he's from Wharton. I don't care that his father is a leading Chicago businessman or a friend of many people here on this Board; S&G must uphold the values this institution stand for and be irreproachable to our shareholders. We cannot reward wrongdoing. Ronald Kusak stole, and he must pay the price. His toying around has cost each of you handsomely.

Tell me how many of you have been sleeping peacefully, knowing Kusak's need for excitement has substantially impacted your personal wealth. Worse, if there's a scandal, then what will you do? How will you, the Board, justify your oversight? Kusak didn't need money. He didn't need power. To him, it was just a game—a game that could affect our shareholders adversely and our reputation irreversibly if we don't handle it right away. For once, he's gone too far. I," April's voice lowered to a mere whisper, "not only ask that you remove him permanently from S&G but that his license to be in investment banking be revoked for life."

"How did you come to discover this irregularity?" Frank Easton rocked back in his chair, his eyes never leaving April's face.

"I stumbled upon something irregular with the books a few years ago, but I could not verify it. Looking back, I should probably have said something then, but I'm not so unprofessional as to levy accusations without proof. It was by accident, quite frankly, that I got the proof. Kusak was spending more and more time away from the office—on the golf course, at lengthy lunches and left me to oversee day-to-day operations. An important decision needed to be made, and we couldn't find Kusak anywhere. So, I had to get on with the business of running S&G. As I was reconstructing things, I happened upon a pattern in trading. The scheme was clever, I must say, but obvious to those better trained than Kusak." April made no apologies for her blatant reference to her own Ivy League education.

"Can you show us some of this evidence?" Frank seemed eager to get to the details.

After two hours of examination, which still bamboozled Frank and most of the Board, Frank Easton finally said, "And Ms. Summers, you feel prepared to take over the helm of S&G Financials?"

"Sir, I have been ready. I stand here before you today as committed as the day I walked into this firm eight years ago. I have proven," she paused dramatically, her voice lowering further, delivering the message more forcefully than if she'd been shouting, "that I *am* ready and capable of becoming the CFO of S&G."

The room was silent. April, buttoning her Persian violet and sage silk jacket walked over to the carafe. If Kusak were a Black man, they would have strung him up by the balls. However, as the son of a well-respected, powerful white businessman and politician, all these men, she could tell from their faces, were willing to keep this debacle quiet. April rarely thought in terms of color before she'd married, but it seems she was becoming more and more paranoid with each passing day. "Coffee, anyone?" April poured herself a coffee, holding up the carafe.

Frank Easton, whom April had met on only a few occasions before, flinched uncomfortably in his chair. Easton, it was rumored, rarely showed emotions, but today there was a fissure in his years of reserved calm. It'd probably just dawned on him his lead investment banker and Executive Vice President was a Black woman, and for the first time, he understood the fight ahead. How the hell did that happen?

April watched Frank closely. Reading his mind, she had to do everything in her powers to stifle the grin forming at the corner of her lips. Any gloating could kill her future at S&G. One small inappropriate move, and her dreams would go up in smoke. Pouf!

"Ms. Summers," Frank spoke. The bass voice as commanding as his presence. "How long did you say you've been with the bank?"

"Eight years, Sir."

"And you realize the enormous responsibility of the job you're applying for?"

"Sir. I don't mean to be presumptuous, but who do you think has been running this department for the past five years?"

Papers shuffled as people moved nervously in their chairs, picking up anything they could find to distract their eyes. Frank Easton leaned backward in his chair. His transparent green eyes held April's, and then he turned to his right-hand man to make an inquiry in an inaudible voice before turning back to April.

"Very well, Ms. Summers. Thank you for your take on this situation and your savvy in this case. We ask until the bank decides what to do about this, you exercise top management's judgment as you must realize, having been so privy to the bank's position, there is a multitude of considerations before S&G can decide how best to handle this matter, or make a final decision about a replacement. The one thing we can tell you is, Kusak will be replaced. Once we have successfully quelled any scandal, we'll schedule another meeting. Paramount right now is that we must preserve the image and culture of S&G at all costs." Frank Easton rose to indicate the end of the meeting. Buttoning his jacket, he stood gracefully. "Ms. Summers, I look forward to meeting you again soon, and thank you" He could definitely understand Kusak's comfort in leaving April to run his business. It was obvious the woman was on time all the time. Damn the fool, Kusak. What a waste of talent. Frank had never thought much of the over-educated buffoon anyway. Too soft in the underbelly of luxury.

"I look forward to it, Sir." April's handshake was firm and, in her mind, conclusive. "And thank you!"

Frank's grip was as firm as hers. He couldn't believe this woman had uncovered the carefully hidden evidence of Kusak's embezzlement. Not only was it an embarrassment to the establishment, but it could prove menacing to the very culture and climate of the good old boys' network. Could she know how far the deception went?

Outside the "inquisition' room," at the end of what she termed "the first day of deliberation," April allowed her lips to curl into a cynical and wide grin. It was her turn.

"Brava, Brava," Martin Spiro, her contender, boomed, pumping a hand still looming at her side. She was neither in the mood to play games nor to act cordial. She didn't have to and quickly withdrew her hand from the blubber's clammy, cold grip.

"I heard you've made yourself the most powerful woman at S&G, maybe even in Chicago, and" he paused, "probably the most hated. It's being touted you did a great job, my dear, great job. What you did today should put America to shame for submerging a mind like yours for four hundred years. A mind," he grinned at his stupidity, "is a terrible thing to waste."

"Martin, you are one of a kind. After so many years of education, all you can do is spout advertising lines?" April rubbed her hand on the side of her silk skirt to get rid of his sweaty palm's remnants. How does one get through life being so stupid? Martin was the kind of guy who told "knock, knock jokes" and recited his interactions with people of color. Inside, he was probably seething because, by seniority, he was next in line for Kusak's job. Of course, the problem was Martin's job was a favor, and Martin was a dunce.

"John said you sure piped up in there. He said the look on Frank's face made for a Kodak moment."

"Where were you, Martin, in John's pocket?"

An idiotic grin spread across Martin's face. He was slow to understand everything, including, he'd been insulted.

"Well, I'll dare say they didn't expect this thing to get so sticky. You surprised everyone, I'm sure. If it's been years that these shenanigans have been going on, then not even the accountants were able to crack Kusak's mathematical genius of a scheme. Shame, shame, shame, wouldn't you say?"

Kusak was, indeed, a mathematical genius, a wunderkind. The brightest there was at S&G. Kusak, who was handsomely compensated and from blueblood oligarchy, had little need for money. What he needed were challenges to occupy his brilliant mind. April felt a jolt of remorse. Kusak had been her mentor, and she'd hoped her work would prove to be as credible as his one day. Kusak's many years of outstanding, flawless work was likely why the accounts had stamped their names to his reports without scrutinizing them. Her work now needed to be more flawless than Kusak's.

If this scandal got out, heads would roll. The powerful men in S&G's employ had missed out. That their sole minority female executive had discovered this debacle would be an embarrassment. Frankly, none of it mattered to April. If they didn't give her the job, she'd bring the establishment down, lawyers, accounts, and CEO. To put it briefly, it would piss her off maximally. And they'd better not offer her women's pay either! Now she knew the bundle Kusak made, beaucoup, beaucoup dollars, she wouldn't take a penny less than they'd paid the winged-tipped, power-tie-wearing thief. April could use this to her advantage, but that's not how she wanted to earn her promotion. Threatening to go public would paralyze the organization and embarrass the head honchos. Not only that. Now she needed to behave like a "company man."

"Of course, you didn't hear this from me." Martin was still talking when she registered him still in front of her. "Well, may the best man…person win." He grinned. "Either way, you or me, S&G wins. What about a drink to celebrate?"

"That would be a little presumptuous, don't you think? Who knows? They may bring someone in from outside the bank."

"Huh, never thought of that." Martin passed a hand over his forehead as if that would help him think. "Nah, I doubt it. Look, I gotta go, but after meeting with the sharks," he looked at his watch, "let's celebrate anyway."

"I'm going home to celebrate with my *husband.*" April flinched. Martin was such a snake in the grass. His oversized panda-like body, sweaty palms, and bushy eyebrows made him look like a swarthy, always-over-tanned Brezhnev nauseated her. "Maybe another time," she lied, "I want to get home, so Martin, you'll have to excuse me."

"Another time then," Martin was saying as she turned her back on him.

Martin watched as April disappeared down the hall, his eyes fixed on the muscles in her calves which pumped with each strident step. Cold, professional, calculating, ambitious, and he'd surely add breathtakingly beautiful to the list of words that came to mind when he thought of April Summers. Her angelic oval-shaped face, framed with a stylish off-the-face hairdo, and her jet-black eyes were quite haunting. Martin shrugged. Turning toward the boardroom, he thundered down the hall, the floorboards squeaking under his weight. Never in a million years would she notice him, anyway. He wasn't exactly Mr. Powerhouse. He thought he should lose some weight as the floorboards made a racket as he walked. First thing in the morning, he'd sign up at the gym. But right now, there were more important matters to which to attend. No matter how cute Miss Jada Pinkett's knockoff was, he wasn't about to roll over and play dead to some affirmative action chickee. War was inevitable. And April Summers was capable of the bloodiest of wars, but so was he.

Martin collared Frank in the hallway. "Frank," Martin boomed. "So good to see you in these parts. Do you have a minute?"

"Martin, my boy. You look well? How much of a minute do you need? I'm in a hurry, but for you," Frank put his arm around Martin as they walked together down the hall.

"Not much time at all." Martin patted his folder. "I think the future of S&G deserves a little time, right."

"Uhhhhuuum." Frank led the way to his private office.

CHAPTER TWELVE

MELODY NEEDED fortification before going to the Trinity meeting, so she kept her appointment with Eve. It proved convenient as the women were meeting in the lobby at six p.m.

"Let's talk more about your childhood," Eve said as soon as she sat. "Clearing away the challenges of the past will further your success. Something in your past gave you a driving spirit."

"Uhuh? That's funny for a girl who was taunted for reading the dictionary for fun! But it's all I have."

"Meaning you had no friends? So, how did you deal with that?"

"I didn't. My mom forbade me from "hanging out" with the undesirables, as she called them. 'Them chillen,' she'd say, 'ain't going no place but to an early grave.' That was my mother's answer every time I complained about being lonely or bullied. My only friends were on the pages of books and my siblings. That didn't last too long because one by one, they fell prey to the streets."

"How long since you've seen your family?"

"Twenty-years. There's no turning back now. I had to. I had to for my mom's sake as much as mine."

"We'll pick up here next time. I think you have an appointment now, right?"

How did Eve know? She bet from motor mouth Veronica.

"Great. Next week then."

Melody was just rounding the corner to the meeting spot when she ran into Veronica.

"You're on time. How's all the free time treating you?" Veronica asked.

Melody, who had been ordered to take time off, said, "Painfully. I'm not sure which is worse, the tiredness or the idleness. I don't know what to do with myself. It's taken me the entire week to learn to sit still." *Idle, of course, was a death sentence for people in the throes of denial and avoidance.*

"Hello, ladies," April said, bouncing up. "Sorry, I'm late. I stopped to get a frappe. Can't do without my stimulant."

"You don't need it," Veronica said.

Melody smiled tentatively.

"So, how long do you have to take off?" Veronica again turned to Melody.

"What's going on?" April looked puzzled.

"I'm on mandatory leave for two weeks. Doctor's orders. Said something about Chronic Fatigue. I don't believe any of it."

"Oh, that. Your secretary did call me. I've been so busy getting insulted at work I haven't had much time to monitor the deal's progress. Some ass told me the other day, my mind was a terrible thing to waste! What's going on with the merger, anyway? Sydney is doing okay on the deal, isn't he?" April rested her frappe on a ledge and put on her coat.

"Yes, everything is fine." The woman, Melody thought, was an unsympathetic moron.

"So, did you decide if we're meeting at the restaurant or your house?" Veronica asked. It had been April's turn to host the Trinity's get-together, but because of the distance and their schedules, the women decided to meet in the Sears Towers' lobby to finalize plans with their schedules.

"I can't understand why you'd refuse," April said when Melody huffed and hawed. "Your place is central. Just right around the corner, so why sit in a restaurant for four hours? Any good businessperson wouldn't let us anyway."

Finally, they convinced Melody to supply the venue.

"So, where are you parked?" April asked.

"Over there." Melody jerked her head in the direction of the doorman. "Joseph is my new best friend, and I suspect he'll be as long as I keep the cash coming."

"That's pretty funny." April broke stride with the group. "I'll get my car and follow you. I'm just down the block."

"How far down?" Veronica asked.

"Few blocks."

"Get in. We'll give you a ride to your car."

Outside, the women piled into Melody's Lexus.

"This is pretty asinine," Melody put on her blinker to merge into traffic. "I can't believe we're acting like schoolgirls with this Trinity nonsense?" The truth was, she was glad to have company, even the company of fools meant she wouldn't be alone.

"What's wrong with schoolgirls? Too often, we grow up too fast for our own good. Hell. If I'd known how I got to be forty, I'd have preferred to remain a schoolgirl!" Veronica said, cracking the window. "Forty," she said, laughing.

Because of a sudden flash, Melody, who under normal circumstances would be aghast at dismantling her seventy-dollar hairdo, welcomed the brisk wintry breeze, tousling her thick hair. She loved her hair, though she was not quite as bad as Louisiana women who were often missing at the poll if it rained; but she was close.

"Do you know it's thirty degrees outside?"

"These last few months, I feel like I'm in the Sahara," Melody said, fanning herself with her hand.

"Let's hurry if we have to endure winter inside the car. I know this wonderful gourmet store close to here," April said, ignoring the middle-aged body-possessed woman and loving every moment of her ridiculous, uncharacteristic behavior. She needed this. "Oh stop … stop. Pullover, I'm right here." April pulled her coat close around her neck as she click the unlock button to her car.

"Girl, don't you know how to give calm directions to a driver?" Veronica said.

"Sorry." April jumped from the back seat as soon as the car stopped. She clicked open a midnight blue Beemer. "I won't be able to get out," she said, waving Melody backward.

The two blue cars clipped down Michigan Avenue only to stop about five minutes later, pulling into the store's parking lot.

"I'm petrified of mid-life crisis." April fell in stride, picking up the conversation from earlier.

"You should be. It sucks," Veronica said. "How old are you anyway? Twenty-eight, nine?"

"Thirty-two," April said, pleased with the youthful number Veronica chose.

"Thirty-two! A babe in the woods. And no babies! Do you know your eggs came with an expiration date?" Veronica said incredulously.

"Not you, too." April groaned.

"Your husband? Baby-wise, you're getting as old as mud, so he's right. The women hurried their steps to reach the warmth of the store.

April filled her basket with caviar, champagne, orange juice, nuts, Brie, water crackers and anchovies. "What else do we need?" She asked.

Veronica examined the basket. "What the hell is this stuff?" Veronica picked up a can and read the label. "How do you plan to feed Black women with Caviar? Anchovies! Girl, where are you from? This shit is too salty. It's not good for Black women. We die from hypertension. And who wants to do that before we have time to cry in our soup? Excuse me" Veronica got her own basket, "I'll just get some hearty food."

Melody didn't lift a finger, since against her wishes, she was supplying the venue. How on earth did she end up doing that for April's get-together? Because Missy lived in a mansion an hour outside the city and Veronica's house was filled with kids she got saddled with unwanted guests!

"Ready." Veronica pulled at the sleeve of Melody's blouse.

"Been ready." Melody snapped.

"God. Give me strength." Veronica looked up to the heavens. "You're one foul person."

"Where to?" April said jovially. She had no explanation for why she was happy to be going to a Trinity meeting.

"I'm not far from here. Next light, make a left. Lake Shore Towers." Melody informed.

"How did you get in there?" April asked in surprise. "I hear the waiting list is two years long."

"Affirmative Action. Isn't it how we all *get there*?" Melody said sarcastically.

"Speak for yourself." April was ready with her brand of barb.

"I'll drive with April and direct her." Veronica rolled her eyes. Melody had a cinder block on her shoulders this evening.

Behind, buildings receded. No way was Melody going down Michigan Avenue at this hour to get caught in bumper-to-bumper rush hour traffic. Looking up and down the street for the men in blue, she waited until the traffic was light, quickly made a U-turn in a no U-turn zone, and zipped along with ease looking behind to see if April had made the same decision. April was a nose away. Why didn't that surprise her? April Summers felt she owned the world. A catchy tune came over Spotify but Melody not in the mood even for music clicked off the app from her dash.

Melody stared at the frozen lake. How she wished she had someone to go sailing with this summer. She'd settle for someone to have dinner with, go to the movies with, or for crying out loud, go rollerblading. Someone to ask the answers to the Sunday crossword puzzle would do just fine too. Anything would be better than kibitzing with two frustrated women or being alone. She was truly tired of being alone.

CHAPTER THIRTEEN

PARKING WAS CEREMONIOUS and indeed a power play. Melody waved a hand at the porter and made both cars disappear. She hoped April choked on that. Melody's twenty-third-floor apartment could only be reached by inserting a special key into the elevator. Fiddling with the key, her hands were shaking ridiculously. It took a minute to get the elevator moving. Veronica steadily gazed at her friend, a worried look knitting her brows, but decided to say nothing.

"My nerves." Melody noticed her stare before yanking the key from the slot. "It's not usual that I have a hen party in my home." The entire exchange was lost on April, who was singing and tapping her feet to music on her iPhone.

With great apprehension, Melody opened the door to her condo. "Please, make yourselves at home. I have to go to the bathroom. Part of that quote-unquote mid-life crisis business I don't believe in." Melody waved her friends into the condo. Apart from her housekeeper, no one had ever been to her home except Veronica, especially no one like April Summers. She wondered, with much anguish, if April would spot her careful deception. People like April, born into gentry, had nothing to strive for but power. A mere condo on Lake Shore would hardly incite anything but curiosity. The girl was already nosing around.

Melody understood the void that fueled her hunger for money, status, glamour, and the need to be at the top of the corporate ladder. Poverty. Money validated her paltry beginnings, but she didn't want to be subjected to scrutiny by the likes of April Summers. *Ah, shut the hell up and stop with this tomfoolery. How long does it have to be before you accept this life as real? It's not a make-belief world. This is your reality, and you have worked damn hard to make it real! You belong here. This is your home.* As she closed the bathroom door, Melody unbuttoned her skirt, stepping out of it with great haste. From nowhere, with such urgency, she had to pee. That was another thing changing about her body. When she was a kid, she could hold her pee for hours. Now, the minute the sensation hit her brain; she was squirming around like a snake. If she didn't make it to the bathroom in seconds, oh well. She'd taken to wearing those ultra-thin panty liners, which saved her La Perlas when she coughed. Veronica had called it stress incontinence when Melody had mentioned her bladder concern on one of their morning powerwalks. If memory served her right, it had only gotten her a bit of leveling sarcasm.

"Yeah? So, what do you want from me, a second opinion? Girl listen, we're all getting as old as mud. Can't have everything working properly like when we were little chickadees."

"For crying out loud. Why do I even bother?" Melody had been unable to suppress her laughter.

"To be honest I am a bit concerned. I am going to give you a referral to a great doc because I won't treat friends. House rules." Since they had become friends, Veronica had, to her word, fired her as a patient. "Tony, my colleague, will hook you up."

Melody had rolled her eyes and just kept walking.

The Spanish terrazzo-tiled floor of the bathroom, cool under her feet, sharply contrasted with the inferno inside her body.

Relief, at last, Melody toyed with the idea of just lying on her divan, begging off from a migraine headache.

"Shush, April, I'm getting on the phone for a sec." Veronica's voice reached Melody through the bathroom door.

"Okay. I've got a few emails to answer," April said, still looking around at the painstakingly clean apartment. The apartment was as impeccable as Melody, but there was a formality which could have belonged to anyone. No real person. Everything was too perfect. She sighed, earning her a look from Veronica.

"What's wrong?"

"This place is too perfect. How are we supposed to relax here? I feel like I'm in a museum." April looked distressed.

Although she lived alone, Melody insisted her housekeeper report to work daily, and there was no mistaking it in the spotless, disinfected, sterile, fastidious, museum-decorated apartment. Boasting hand-woven rugs, hand-blown glass lamps, exquisite modern furnishing, and silk-lined walls on which hung original oils and numbered lithographs, the enviable condo was a decorator's showpiece. She'd paid a pretty penny to the interior designer to ensure her success was reflected in the best quality, name-brand furnishings. Aubusson Stark rugs! She'd never heard of it before Betsy Clark solidified her tastemaker image. Naturally, one had to live up to their accomplishments, and without question, she had been transformed from head to toe, not even a trace of her Watts accent remained.

"You'll get used to it. Don't worry. Just throw a pillow here and there. That'll be enough to put Melody into a catatonic state and then we can do what we want." Veronica chuckled.

Inside the bathroom, Melody lamented, patting the yellow and blue divan with regret. Resigned to the fact that spending a good part of this meeting in her bathroom, basking in the glorious light beneath her east window, was out of the question, she made her way back to the living room, straightening things the women had moved. "Who's preparing the food?" Melody said with forced brightness.

"Melody, you can't cook, and April, I get this sneaky suspicion it would be a challenge for you too, so I suppose it's me."

"Did I proclaim domesticity?" April asked. "To this day, my mother won't let me into her kitchen. She always tells me I have better things to do with my time than slave over a hot stove. Things like conquering the world. But I can fix the caviar." The women headed toward the kitchen.

"So, your mother is a great cook, huh?" Veronica said, opening drawers to find a wine opener.

"Third drawer down." Melody informed her.

"Heavens, no! We've had cooks as far back as I can remember."

"What color were these cooks?" Veronica looked aghast, bumping the drawer shut with her hips.

"What do you mean?" April seemed genuinely at a loss for the direction of the conversation.

"I need wine more than ever." Veronica dug into the shopping bag for a bottle of *vin rouge*. "It seems so wrong. So very wrong. Especially since we were mammies; it's so politically incorrect."

"It's more than politically incorrect. It's downright stupid and insensitive." Melody chimed, adding a bit of fuel to the argument.

"To have a cook?" April said in utter astonishment.

"No, to have a "Black" cook."

"Who said anything about color? And even if I did have a Black cook, why are you both being so intellectually dishonest? Melody, don't you have a housekeeper? If not, pray tell, who keeps this place so antiseptically clean?"

"Yes. I have a cleaning person."

"Is she or he Black?"

"Yes, but that's different. She comes in a few hours a day. That's all."

"Daaahh. And that makes it okay? My bad. Melody, didn't you tell me you were educated at Stanford and Northwestern?"

"April, where are you going with this?" Melody demanded.

"I'm trying to find the logic. Please, I need someone to explain where my line of thinking is off here."

"Having Molly Maid is a far cry from the way people in Jamaica have servants," Melody said indignantly.

"It's a job that pays and keeps the economy going. But does anyone here know I'm an American?" April asked

"I thought you were Jamaican. Your accent…." Melody began.

"Stereotyping. There you go stereotyping. My parents are Jamaicans. You wouldn't call my accent Jamaican if you had an ear for accents. If it makes your argument any more logical, my mother's live-in housekeeper is Italian, and mine is straight-up blond."

"An Italian cook! A blond housekeeper! Oh, Lawd! You know, Melody, that wine sounds delicious right now." Veronica was holding her head.

"So, what's taking you so long to get the cork out?" Melody squawked, completely flabbergasted by the conversation.

"You know what. I'm not going there right now. Why don't you make yourself useful and get some glasses? You'll probably feel far more accomplished than arguing with Miss Harvard Debate Team over here."

"I went to Stanford."

"Hardly Harvard." Veronica deadpanned. "Just keeping it real."

Melody sliced her in two with her eyes. "Glasses are in the cupboard, above your head."

Veronica put three glasses on the table.

"Those are water goblets," Melody said sarcastically, looking distastefully at the crystal.

"And? They hold liquid, don't they? You have a problem with that?"

"Veronica, a woman of your position, should have more panache. Just keeping it real."

"No! You mean someone other than you "should" know the acceptable protocol. Damn, sometimes you sound like Randolph. Always living life as though you're drawing a connecting dot picture."

"Better than living life in circles." Melody deadpanned.

"Or in a triangle. A fine geometric figure, however. The basis of all great mysteries such as the Pyramids." April smiled. "On second thought, I believe circles are better. They seem more expansive. More congruent to life. The everything turn, turn kinda thing, you know."

"What are you two fools talking about," Veronica spooned chicken salad into a bowl.

"Life needs to be confined, or it will lead to chaos. And chaos leads to total anarchy." Melody ignored Veronica.

"The way of the world, my dear Melody, is one of chaos. Entropy. Some law of thermodynamics, I believe. Humans are the ones who try to make order out of chaos. No wonder we're so screwed up." April snapped the cashew nut tin top, pouring a few nuts into her hand before emptying them into a bowl.

"April. Why don't you shut up with the philosophizing, science lecture or whatever? I didn't come here for proper etiquette or a chemistry lecture, so *pa-lease* spare me. Just..."

"Veronica, don't. Not today. No way are you going to drive me crazy with that nonsense saying. What exactly are you keeping real?" Melody said.

"I was about to say. Just let's move on. But you've got to presume you knew what I was going to say. Pour the damn wine and shut up. Yes, damn it, pour it into the goblets." Veronica commanded.

"Now, you're talking." April intentionally took a glass and began a ceremonious wine protocol; the sniff, swirl, and swig intended to let pretentious people feel like connoisseurs. Hell, half the people she saw sniffing wine wouldn't know a wine bouquet from a bouquet of flowers! She relished watching Melody cringe. "This is fine wine. More than pretty good." April smiled warmly, showing an unexpected fissure in an otherwise caustic personality.

"This is so crazy." Melody rolled her eyes.

"Why? Because what we did today was not planned? Life should not always be by the book. It needs to be shaken up a little sometimes. Take it by the tail and swing it around." April whirled a throw around her head."

Melody was appalled at the woman trashing around her thousand-dollar Pashmina throw as though it was some rag. "Plus," April let the throw fly, "I hate dot-to-dot living too. Let's break out by starting with water goblets as wine glasses. Who's to say they aren't anyway? Maybe I'm an incredibly, unbearable snob, but today I am going to be a goblet wine drinker."

Veronica poured more Shiraz. The girl was crazy.

Melody retrieved her throw and arranged it gingerly on the sofa.

"To goblets." Melody couldn't help having the last word as she lifted the glass, examining the sparse legs of the wine. Throwing daggers was in her nature. But the daggers had nothing to do with wit but with her compelling need to deflect bad manners; should, by heavens, such crass behavior be mistaken as her ineptitude or inability to know right from wrong.

If she wasn't sure before, April was now more convinced than ever Melody was a poser. The girl showed obvious traits of insecurity. She was educated but spiritually vapid. Materialism had defined her entire soul. But who's to judge. Whatever delusions she needed to tackle this life had served her well. Melody Adams was making waves in Corporate America.

"Well? How is it?" Veronica asked.

"Honestly, not bad." Melody conceded.

"Melody, this is not what you think. For you, I brought a special brand of venom. Concentrated. Will kill on the spot. No antidote. Just like the Alligator man from Australia in that FedEx commercial. You won't feel a thing. This will take you out of your misery once and for all."

"You know what. This was a bad idea. A really bad idea." Melody put her glass on the counter. "Maybe we can do this another time. Like never! All of a sudden, I'm not feeling so well." Melody's voice took on a clawing edge.

"What's pulling your chain today, girl?" Veronica rested her glass and moved closer to Melody. The girl did not look well.

"We missed our coaching session." April offered. "It's the root of our discontent. But alas, the vicissitudes of life…."

"The what? What's with the big vocabulary? I'm from 43rd Street, so give me a big break. What the hell is viss… viss…hell. What the hell is the meaning of that Vee word you just used. If it ain't Vagina or Veronica, I don't know it. Never heard it."

"Look it up. That's how we all learn." Melody interjected.

"Smartass Melody Adams. You should know. Isn't reading the dictionary your hobby? Your life?"

"What harm did it do? I'm going to be the next Black female fortune 500 CEO in America. Seems to me more people should read the dictionary." Finally, and permanently, Melody intended to shed the stereotypes Blacks leave behind on their way up the corporate ladder as they became invisible powers, sidelined to jobs with big titles but no power. When it came to savvy in Corporate America, Melody Adams was no fake. She was for real—a warrior in solid gold, shining armor. "It would be quite awesome if we all took our destinies into our own hands, wouldn't you agree, April?" Melody asked.

"Yeah. But that's easier said than done. It's easy sitting here debating the point with goblets of wine. Extolling the nonsense theories of the virtues of the American Dream. Believe me, there's no hope for most people in the ghetto." Veronica vehemently disagreed.

"Veronica, I want to make sure I've heard you clearly. Are you saying people from the ghetto can't change their reality? What about you?" April was truly curious.

"An anomaly. You couldn't possibly understand. You and Melody grew up in rich, if not rich, middle-class homes. You're expected to make it. Me? I'm the exception to the rule—the mistake. I lucked up and somehow believed my own press just enough to make me succeed. Many people don't get that chance, April. Sometimes we don't get what we deserve."

"But you succeeded." April was insistent.

"Things might appear changed on the outside, but the seeds of doubt still live within me on the inside. They are still there. That's what spurs me on. Fear of going back to where I came from, of waking up from this dream. I didn't change. I don't believe people ever do. Maybe when they come back as dogs or men."

"That's pessimistic. Almost vile." April cringed at the thought of total hopelessness. "You can't believe that? You are a prime example of life's guarantees. You worked hard. You did the work. You got an education, and you got whatever was promised to you!"

"Guarantees? Did you say guarantees? Girl, get real. If you want a guarantee, buy an appliance with your Amex card. You can get double the coverage when you're ready to claim. That's if you can find the receipt. That's all the lifetime guarantees available in this world, my friend. Life is so simple. Get with the program and understand that poverty is a bitch, and only very few make it out of the darkness." Veronica shook her head. "My friend, you've been living in a fabled world."

Moment by moment, Melody was becoming more agitated. Inside, a rage welled, sweat beaded her upper lip, and her mouth thinned. Her eyes seem to fix themselves on the past, and almost unconsciously, duty-bound, she joined the argument. Her voice was pained. "Tell me seriously, April, have you ever been to the ghetto? Have you ever seen a mother's strung-out child with a needle in her arm or a face rearranged by a pimp? Have you ever smelled the stench of a crack house or seen innocent babies die from stray bullets? Have you ever seen, April, how the ghetto grows rich with the ruins of people's lives it uses as fertilizer? Why don't you ask those people about the realities of the ghetto? No, *mea culpa* can't prevent reality, no matter to whom we pray. These atrocities April, have been happening for centuries, with very little hope for change. Why don't *you*," there were tears in her eyes, "ask them about changes and guarantees? You see, April, when one escapes the ghetto, it's a damn miracle."

"Hey," Veronica was gently rubbing Melody's arm. "Hey, girl. Where did you go?"

"What do you mean?" Melody jerked back to lucidity; her face composed.

"How do you know so much about the ghetto?"

"I worked on a social work project in school." Melody recovered, sipping her wine generously. "Anyway, why are we having this conversation?" Inside she was panicking. She'd almost slipped! Middle class indeed. If Veronica only knew. "What folks like us should do is stop talking about the plight of the disenfranchised and invest our money in causes that matter. Who knows, maybe we can change our world? The market is booming today. Isn't it April?"

But inside her reality, Melody understood more than anyone else in the room. Why would anyone who watched their brother die on the sidewalk leave anything up to God? And how can anyone say "whatever" when they watched their sister's body racked in tremors from heroin addiction. Lessons of survival, exacting its great emotional price, had taught Melody that "whatever" was a word to be stricken from the dictionary and that wise people rely *only* on "can do," "must do," and themselves, but still she knew only few with an iron will made it.

As a sophomore at Stanford, Melody had fallen in love with Carlton Reiner. Carlton Reiner was elegant and from an established San Francisco family. Melody's insecurities had weighed in heavily, playing havoc with her self-esteem. So instead of risking self-disclosure, she'd walked away from her first real love. That was when she consciously registered the potency of her iron will. It was then she knew she could do anything she put her mind to. As she grew older, the reasons for not having relationships changed. Excelling in school required dedication, and so did her career. At the end of her steep climb, Melody realized, not only had she climbed farther than most, but she had also set new standards and records.

"So, what do you suggest we buy to change the world for Black folks, Miss April? More cars? More houses? More Tommy Hillnigger? More crack cocaine from suburban drug lords?" Veronica said sarcastically.

"Okay. Let's change the subject." April backed away from the race conversation. She had enough of it in her home with her husband, Sam, Mr. Black Panther himself. Plus, as she had veri-fied in Jamaica, she was no longer able to hear the wails of the sea or the beating wings of the Sankofa bird.

"Good. Now, since I made a hefty investment in this here food, I'll be damned if I'm not going to get my monies worth before Melody's finicky ass kicks us out. Let's table this conversation and have some grub." Veronica brought the conversation to an end. Three bottles of wine later, the Trinity had mellowed, and the idealism for changing the world was but a notion.

CHAPTER FOURTEEN

AFTER KUSAK'S DEPARTURE, six S&G old-timers took early retirement. Something about the chain of events made Martin curious. In desperation, and to prevent being passed over for the CFO job, Martin Spiro did desperate things. While working with April on the Kusak cleanup, he'd copied some confidential information. Now he fancied himself some kind of detective, which wasn't a bad idea, as sleuthing was probably his next profession if his plans failed. Martin felt a right Uriah Heap, but, alas, everyone must use their talents the best way they know how. His big driving force, facing his father with pride. Daily his mission grew more clandestine. He thundered his way to the interim CFO's office. Martin, aware he wasn't the world's most attractive man, knew power was an aphrodisiac that obscured and forgave a lot. After all, look at Onassis and The Donald!

"Muriel." Martin had taken to visiting the executive offices when the acting CFO was out. It seemed he had the same weakness as Kusak. Golf. But unlike dumb-butt Kusak, he had the operations under lock and key. His only mistake, the key, was with his trusted assistant, who would be far too undereducated to understand any matters of finance. And unbeknownst to Martin, he had reasons to leave the key as a few senior-level execs were charged with removing Kusak's theft evidence.

"Why, Mr. Spiro. How are you this morning?" Muriel blushed purple.

"Better for having seen you," he handed her a dozen donuts.

Muriel, two hundred and fifty pounds, or better, of solid fat needed more than Slim Fast to budge a pound. A gastric bypass was her only hope, so a few doughnuts were inconsequential. On the other hand, Martin believed he could exercise and diet to shed his unwanted seventy-five pounds!

Not used to male attention, it wouldn't have mattered to Muriel if Martin Spiro were, in fact, Shamu the whale.

"Do you have a moment for coffee this morning, my dear?"

"Sure, Sir." She'd blushed, as she always did when he came into the office.

"Now, how can you have coffee with someone you call, Sir? Please, he allowed his hand to linger, "Call me Martin."

"Yes, Sir." Her eyes fluttered.

It had taken exactly four months to get the goods. Some goods were better than others. Martin pressed his lips together in memory. Muriel, to his surprise, was nowhere as shy as she pretended. No wonder men left their wives for what others called fat, unattractive secretaries. *How could they be with a woman like that?* He'd often heard. Now he knew.

"Hey, honey. I'm home." April rested her briefcase in a corner and went to find Sam.

"Hi." He didn't look up at her through the mirror. In the bathroom, with his face covered in shaving cream, he looked ridiculously akin to Santa. A cigarette burned between his lips.

"What's eating Gilbert Grape?" April paused at his gruffness, "And why exactly are you shaving at night?" April loosened her jacket, sat on the bed, and pulled off her shoe. She flopped across the bed, raising her arms overhead before clasping them behind her head.

"I'm going out."

"With whom? Some of the guys at work?"

"Nope," he volunteered no more information.

She eyed him. "Chicken skin" warned of impending danger. April ran her hands up and down her arms, trying to rub heat back into her body. She knew. She knew what had to be done but instead did what came naturally. "Sam, you can't *still* be mad about Jamaica?" Boy, was he ever turning into a nag, testing her reserve soon to be past empty! Since they'd returned from Jamaica, the man had been quite trying.

"Don't flatter yourself." he barked.

"Are you mad at me about something?" April pressed, sitting up to look more closely at her husband.

"Hey, I'm not in the mood for all the who, what and why, all right."

"Okay, so how about the where. Where are you going?"

"I'm going out, and that's that," Sam snapped.

"Fine. You're grown. You can go anywhere you want."

"Damn straight."

"It wasn't a crooked sentence." April snapped back.

"Shut the hell up, April. I'm not in the mood for this."

"I won't do this. Do you hear me? I won't. I've had a hard day. If you're looking for an argument, you'll have to argue with yourself."

"Go on," he prodded. "Go on. Go back to where you normally bury your reality."

"Damn it, Sam. Why do you do that? What do you want from me? Blood? I'm not...."

"Ah, get off your mighty horse and see someone else's point of view for once."

"Point of view? The same point of view you've been nagging me about for over a year? Even a blind man could see it."

"Time to change the subject?" The razor flew across the bathroom counter.

"Great idea. I'll tell you about my very trying day. Maybe you can offer some constructive opinion instead of always finding fault with everything."

"Why? Your Mother wasn't home?"

Sam was being cruel. April folded her arms around her to block out the attack. Her mother was her Achilles heel. Even as a woman of great strength, she would lose confidence in her mother's presence, her esteem leaking out like a balloon slowly losing helium. April could never bear the look of disappointment in her mother's eyes, or the secret that bound them for eternity and beyond.

"Oh, Jesus, Sam. Don't…."

"What do you mean, oh, Jesus? Tell me, since when does my opinion rate? You should be telling your mother about your big, trying day. Then again, what am I talking about? You probably called her from the car. I can't imagine why you don't share your—little drinking problem with her."

"I don't have a goddamn drinking problem. Why can't you understand that? Millions of people drink to relax. For Christ's sake, Europeans drink at lunch, dinner and for dessert. It's their culture. If you'd pull yourself out of this decrepit country more often, you might become more than just book educated. Give up on this *erroneous* perception you have of me. I'm not your father, so don't give me his problems. For the last time, and the very last *Sam*, I don't have a drinking problem."

"Tell that to the birds."

"You know, you're testing my tolerance and really testing my reserve. This drinking nonsense you're forcing on me is nothing more than an excuse to air your issues. Why don't you be honest about your real feelings once and for all? Do whatever but quit taking out your frustrations on me."

"My frustrations? They are beyond that. I don't know what you want anymore. The only thing we talk about these days is your job. For Christ's sake, you're thirty-two. When do you think you might consider having a baby?"

"What about the CFO position. I have a shot at it. We can try in a year." It wasn't true, but it sounded good to April.

"One thing I do know April is, I can't be in bed with three people. This entire notion of having you, your job and me is a turn off. That'll take care of the baby issue, won't it?"

"Try Viagra," April snapped.

"You bitch." Sam raised his hand

"Sam! Don't you dare! Don't you dare!"

"You're the one who started it."

"I'm over this." April left the room, banging the door so hard it gave way at the top hinge. "Bastard."

In the kitchen, April quickly drank a glass of wine. She counted to ten, took four deep breaths and then gulped another. Heading back to the bedroom. She was determined to de-escalate this argument. Having had no lunch, the wine shot straight to her head. Maybe it was time to tell Sam her story. Perhaps he would understand her fear. Why not just try and see what happened? And what if she had a baby? Everyone in the world had nannies. Why couldn't she? It was not a physical problem that kept her uterus almost virgin, it was the deep psychological scar yet to be excised. That much she knew.

"Let's do it." April returned, ripping off her blouse and throwing it at Sam. "Let's make babies."

Sam, ignoring her, squeezed pomade into his palm, dabbed his hair and then vigorously brushed it to a shine.

"What's the matter?" April stood in front of him, forcing him to notice her.

He stepped around her, pulled a navy and white striped shirt from his closet and slipped his muscular arms through each sleeve.

"Sam," April's stepped in front of him again. "I thought you wanted to make a baby."

Sidestepping her again, he loosened his pant belt and tucked his shirt into navy pants.

"All talk, huh? You've always loved to hear yourself talk." April sneered, lowering herself to the floor.

Sam grabbed her by the hand, yanking her to her feet. "You want to make a drunk baby!" He roughly pushed her aside, catching a whiff of the wine. "Straighten up your act, April, or we're through."

At six feet three, Sam Summers was imposing and commanding. His body rippled from years of playing ball. April often said country folks could launder clothes on his washboard abs. He wasn't a light or airy man. He was heavy, purposeful, and his commitment steadfast. That'd been April's attraction to him in the first place. Now she wished he had a better sense of humor. April watched Sam through the mirrored bathroom wall, a troubled look contorting her face. She didn't know whether to laugh or cry. The granite set of his jaw suggested something colder than usual. In the years since they'd been married, she'd never seen such a look of defeat in his expressive brown eyes. After splashing aftershave on his face, he pocketed his wallet, buttoned his checkered sports jacket, and headed for the bedroom door.

"You're going to walk out on me? Can't take the heat, huh? Go right ahead. Good riddance, too, because you're no prize husband. You bitch and moan and nag just like Mummy. Why you complain so much about her is beyond me. You two are exactly alike."

"Shut up, damn it! Why can't you just shut up?" Sam took two long strides and stood over April, who was on her knees picking up discarded clothes.

"Make me." April dared.

Sam spun her around to face him. His head was spinning, his emotions negatively galvanized. It felt like a dream, totally surreal when he heard the impact of his hand coming down hard across April's face. The blow knocked her to the floor. With disbelief spreading across her face like melting plastic, April brought her hand up to cover the burning spot. Sam dragged her into their bedroom and pushed her face first into the pillow with swift movements. "You need to know who is in charge here," Sam bellowed, struggling to loosen his belt. April struggled, but Sam was too strong for her. "Why do you make me have to do this to you?" He growled.

April's arms flailed. Everything from the nightstand went flying to the floor. As Sam collapsed on her back, she felt his grip loosen and hurled her body backward. Off guard, he tumbled to the floor. April, tears falling on his shirt, pounded him with her fist. "How dare you. How dare you," she screamed, sliding to the floor.

The look on Sam's face was of bewilderment. My God, in his anger, he had slipped away to another world—had become another person. His loss of control was frightening as he crawled on his knees over to where April wept. "I'm so sorry. So very sorry." He moved to gather her from the floor.

"Don't …don't touch me, you crazy bastard." April thrashed her arms around, swinging wildly, landing a blow to Sam's chin. His head snapped back. "Have you gone crazy?" April screamed.

"You really want to hurt me?" The bitter reality sunk like a rock into her stomach. "How could you, Sam? How could you?"

Sam felt insane. What had come over him? How could he have done that? Deep regret registered in his eyes, and his shame was great. Grabbing his keys from the dresser, he hobbled to his feet and left the bedroom without another word.

CHAPTER FIFTEEN

THE CONFERENCE WAS in Phoenix. Because Tony would be there, Veronica debated whether or not to go. She'd erred, and she wasn't about to do it again, no matter what she'd promised. It would be too tempting to be in his presence which she had avoided like the plague since their mishap. Forbidden love was not worth the price.

Dr. Whittaker, the Department head, wishes to see you." Her assistant poked her head around the door.

"Now?"

"Yup. Now."

"But I'm in private practice. He can't summon me at will."

Still, to keep relations at his hospital and her operating privileges in good standing, she made her way to his office. He simply wanted to confirm her attendance at the conference, something he could have done by phone.

On Friday night, Veronica landed in Arizona. Her talk on behalf of her host hospital was Saturday morning, and she intended to take a night flight out right after. On the evening of her presentation, before her flight, she decided to have a few drinks with the OBGYN group at the conference, which included Tony. She had one too many drinks and instead of ending up at the airport, she was in Tony's room!

"Just give me a sec to compose myself and I'll go down and get a room." Veronica sat on the sofa.

"The hotel is booked."

"I'm sure they'll find something." She watched as Tony removed her shoes.

"Go lie on the bed. I'll sleep on the sofa. How do you feel now?"

"Really drunk."

"Is this real, or is it Memorex?"

"It feels real," Veronica said, watching the flames of a votive candle dance with ominous shadows. "No, it feels like a dream," she recanted. *It could only be a dream,* Veronica thought. In real life, there was a lot more to relationships than between the sheets. There were mealtimes where Randolph would say the ceremonial grace before everyone grabbed their favorite piece of fried chicken, deep-fried catfish, and greens. On Sundays, they always had pot roast and black-eye peas, or smothered pork chops with cornbread, and they would linger for their weekly catch-up sessions before the family outing to the movies. Veronica had sat through *Game of Thrones* and then had to listen to Jenny talk incessantly about going into battle. On the other hand, Gerald sat in the back row so no one could see how excited he got about such a stupid movie! Memories.

"It can be a real dream Veronica. If you just give it a chance it can be. Let me make it more real to you."

"Dreams don't last. And I'm afraid this one may have already played itself out." Passion was no stranger to Veronica. Randolph had taught her that years before. They were childhood sweethearts. "And Tony, what happens when we wake up?"

"We don't have to."

I will not commit adultery."

Tony went to the refrigerator and pulled open the well-stocked bar. "Catholics, they made that up. I don't believe in the Bible. "Scotch, Vodka, something smoother?" Tony moved unhurriedly to retrieve the glasses.

No answer.

Going back over to the bed, Veronica had fallen asleep. Tony sat on the bed and looked at the beautiful woman. "Sometimes God can make a mistake. I think he made a mistake with us," he said to the wind. He'd never felt this way about a woman in his life. His nights and days were restless. He'd tried to honor her request, but her pull was too great. He would drop by her office after work to show her new reports. He'd have her latte and old-fashioned crumb cake on her lab desk in the mornings, Even though she'd made sure her schedule was opposite his. Finally, she'd figured out a way to avoid him all together and he missed her so much. He leaned in to kiss her, but he was not a man who took advantage of a woman. He would win her over. What Veronica needed was more than passion. She needed reassurance. Reassurance she could have it all and no one would get hurt.

Veronica woke with a nasty headache. Tony was sleeping on the sofa. Her heart jolted and her respect for him shot way up. In the shower she could not tamp down the feeling of passion she felt for this man. Would one betrayal doom her to death? Could she? Okay," Veronica thought. Just one time.

Softly, she sat next to him. She studied his face and was about to get up when he grabbed her by the wrist. "Don't walk away from me." Tony's pulled her into him.

In the darkened room with flickering shadows, an inferno burned, fountains gushed, rivers broke through dams, and Veronica had cried out into the dark in rapture ascending to a place reserved for only those who saw the light of love and returned to tell the story in music, art, literature, and science.

CHAPTER SIXTEEN

MELODY ROLLED over onto her back and stared at the ceiling. She felt great. She was going back to work. The only thing missing from her near-perfect life this morning was work! Melody shook her head, acutely aware *that* feeling was back again. A feather was tickling the part of her brain responsible for calling out to nature. She was not a woman who felt "desire" as Veronica so glibly put it. Work was her natural high and love, but there was no denying the wakefulness of her body. Melody inhaled deeply, swung her long legs over the side of the bed and raised herself to a sitting position. She wasn't about to have a girlie fantasy.

Walking across the room, she lit a cigarette: a little indulgence she allowed now and then. Aside from a dull ache in her head, life was great. She was in tip-top shape. Just great! Chronic Fatigue beaten. After the merger, if she ever got the courage, she'd take a dream vacation. If it weren't for the upcoming emergency Trinity meetings, her life would be perfect. Those goddam meetings drove her crazy!

Melody arrived at her office early. It was as though she'd been gone a year rather than two weeks. The hellos and resounding greetings were heartwarming.

"Good morning, Angel," Melody chirped, hanging her coat in the spacious closet of her office suite.

"Oh, Ms. Adams, I'm glad to see you're well. You look great. How do you feel?"

"Alive. Rejuvenated. You're wearing a new outfit today, Angel."

"Yes. I bought it on Saturday." Maybe her boss hadn't recovered after all. She never made small talk.

"Have you spoken with the guys from Microtech? Let's see," she stenciled through her PDA, "when should they come in."

"I took the liberty of scheduling them for Wednesday since your calendar was not back-to-back, you have a four-hour break." Angel smiled with smug satisfaction at her efficiency.

"Since when do you make such a decision without my input?" The old Melody was back.

"I just thought…."

"Don't you know better than to think for me?"

"I'm very sorr…."

"Stop explaining. What's done is done. Get Microtech on the phone. Tell them I'll fly to San Francisco to meet with them on Wednesday. Cancel the rest of Wednesday and Thursday. It's the least I could do. Check the flights and let me know what's available. United only."

"Right away, Ms. Adams."

"It's a good idea to do a site visit. Don't you think?" Miss. Hyde's persona was back.

"It's a very good idea," Angel said cautiously.

"Yep. Since we're a couple of months behind on this project, we might as well kill two birds with one stone. "Now," Melody continued, "how did the big boys take my absence?"

"Go into your office and see," Angel said wearily, not knowing if it were Jekyll or Hyde who would answer.

"Wow!" Melody said with delight. The credenza, side tables, coffee table, lunch table, and massive oak desk were covered with every floral arrangement.

"That's all I did yesterday. Sign for flowers. Everyone is excited about your return," Angel informed. "Coffee, Ms. Adams?"

"Tea. Green tea." She'd heard it was good for menopause. "I had no idea so many people worked here."

"If we don't have green tea, would you prefer herbal or regular? Those beautiful yellow roses are from the gentlemen at Microtech."

"Herbal. Good. They know how to schmooze."

Melody looked over each bouquet and smiled. Comtech had been wonderful to her. Recognizing her talent, the founder, Edward Heidleman, had schooled her personally. Not only did they enjoy a special relationship as her sponsor, but he'd pushed her hard until she'd landed on the leadership track. When all her psychological scabs had been fully buried under the pressure of her torpedoed rise to power, she had become as much a part of Comtech as its founding fathers. Edward had been the first to say it was good she'd get some rest before the chaos of a merger.

Pushing aside a fragrant vase, Melody rested her valise on the credenza. For a second, she stopped to inhale the exquisite scent of flowers in hues that lit up the cockles of her heart. Melody, choked up, wasn't used to feeling sentimental, so she quickly distracted herself. What the dickens was going on with her? She was way too cynical and angry to have such emotions. *If only a man had sent her those flowers,* the irrepressible thought floated into her head.

"Melody Adams, you need to quit," she said aloud. "A man did send you these flowers. Many men, in fact. Just not your man." She picked up her schedule and left her office without her tea.

When Melody walked into the boardroom, everyone was already there.

"So, you're human after all?" Edward said, rocking back in his maroon leather chair. The massive glass and brass table were laden with breakfast food.

"It was just a test," Melody quipped. "I needed reassurance of my value. Thanks for the flowers."

"Anything to make sure you know we adore you," Edward smiled, getting up to kiss her cheek.

The review meeting was everything she had hoped for. The merger was well executed down to the finest detail. The only thing left to do was present the offer to Microtech and get their signature on the dotted line.

"I've arranged, or rather, am arranging to fly out to San Francisco to present the offer to Microtech."

"Isn't it better to have them on our territory?"

"Hardly. But I'm good at what I do anywhere." Melody was confident this sweetheart of a deal was a shoo-in they wouldn't pass up. If they did, they were more foolish than she'd have thought. "Plus, I want to kill two birds with one stone."

"She's back." Edward smiled.

By seven p.m., Tuesday, Melody was on her way to O'Hare, San Francisco bound. She liked San Francisco. Too bad she didn't have a schedule that allowed a few days to enjoy the city. A driver, holding her name on a placard in the baggage claim area, took her overnight bag when she identified herself.

"There's a stocked bar, Ma'am, the paper and some snacks in the cupboard. We have about a thirty to forty-minute drive, depending on traffic. Is there anything else I can do for you, Ms. Adams?"

"No. Thank you." Melody pulled open the larder. She looked regretfully at the packet of M&Ms, shrugged, and proceeded to open them. Munching away, she pulled out her brief.

Microtech was a top-of-the-line company. She could see they were doing well even beyond the financial statement. Happy employees were hard to come by. She loved excellence. Forty minutes later, the driver pulled up to the Fairmont hotel. She was glad for the time advantage. A uniformed attendant glided over to open the door, and Melody alighted. All check-in arrangements were pre-done, so she headed to her suite. Nodding her approval of the accommodations, she was impressed Microtech had picked up the tab for the trip. Yup. Top of the line, all the way.

The spacious bathroom boasted a deep sitting tub outfitted with magazines, chilled glasses, expensive wine, and candles on the custom ledge. *For lovers,* she thought regretfully. "Well, my dear sweet girl," she filled the tub with delightful fragrances, provided compliments of the hotel, "no love in the world is as rewarding as the love of self." As soon as the tub was ready, Melody poured herself a glass of wine. "Muuum," she said, looking at the label. This is how wine should taste. She'd remember to take the label for Veronica. Sliding down into the deep tub, she closed her eyes and emptied her mind of everything.

Later in the evening, Melody ordered herbal tea from room service, plumped the pillows, and switched on the TV. She clicked through channels. "Your destiny is only a phone call away," some guru was advertising their services. Opening her briefcase, Melody searched for Microtech's annual report to review the financials. Like everything else in her life, she just needed the fact; all the fluff could go by the wayside. Had she left it in the car? Along with her other mid-life maladies, she was losing her sense of detail.

The door rapped, and Melody let the room service attendant in, then climbed into bed after she left. Stretching her long body, she inhaled deeply and felt herself fading fast. Before she could drink her tea, she was asleep.

"Housekeeping," the knock at the door woke Melody with a start.

She'd obviously forgotten the do not disturb sign. "Oh, no." Melody leaped out of bed. It was ten-thirty. The meeting with Microtech was at noon. "Come back later," Melody growled at the second knock on her door. With the sudden flurry of activities, nausea overcame her. Feeling dizzy and faint, a band of ache tightening around her head, Melody sat on the bathroom stool, took some deep breaths, and waited until she began feeling normal again. Something still wasn't right with her. When she got back to Chicago, she'd have the complete check-up she'd been putting off. Enough was enough! Melody hastily got ready and phoned the driver.

A young Asian woman was waiting for Melody in the stunning glass-enclosed atrium of Microtech. "Ms. Adams. I'm Beverly Wong, District Manager for the Midwest. Welcome to Microtech. I hope your flight was comfortable."

"Yes, thank you."

Melody looked around the lobby. Impressive. "This is a very nice building."

"We're proud." Beverly moved efficiently down the hall. Melody followed the woman through the lobby and up the escalator. Beverly and Melody's heels reverberated against the deep green marbled floor. She'd never seen a green marble floor! How Melody wished her head would stop pounding. "I get into Chicago every three months or so. It's not a hot area for us, but it's up and coming."

"A good marketing plan will solidify that," Melody said confidently, glad now to be walking on plush carpet. Halfway down the corridor, the women stopped before solid mahogany double doors. The words "Executive Dining Room" were embossed in pewter.

"We're here." Beverly pushed open the door.

"Very nice," Melody said.

"Enjoy your visit." Beverly smiled, greeted the other staffers, and left the room.

The dining room, though understated, was magnificent. The inlaid wooden table seemed to have been carved from one piece of wood and could comfortably seat twenty people. Formally set, white linen, crystal, china and silver service, swan-shaped napkins flanked each of the seven place settings. A chef, pleated hat, and all, was on standby, ready to prepare food to order. Melody, duly impressed, wondered about the owner of Microtech. This sort of style was only privy to those born into the meritocracy. He was probably the son of some dynastic family where success was a matter of throwing family money at an idea—a Michael Dell spin-off sort. She tried to recall the company's history but drew a blank about its founder. Had she not been late this morning, she'd have boned up on the company beyond its financials. What she did know, and what was important, was that a mere sixteen-year-old company had sales of nearly one billion dollars. This, by anyone standard, was an impressive company.

"Ms. Adams," a young, preppy, attractive white man came toward her. "We are so glad you could make it out. It's a pleasure to meet you finally. I hope you are fully recovered?"

"One hundred percent."

"Glad to hear it. I'm Justin Bladen. VP of Sales and Marketing. I was one of the people out in Chicago. Our legal counsel, COO and CEO will join us shortly. I'm afraid they got delayed in an earlier meeting, but Charles' assistant just called to say they were on their way. Why don't we sit over here?" he pointed to a burgundy leather sofa. "Tea, coffee, wine, or something stronger?"

Melody was a bit unnerved by Microtech's savoir-faire. She hadn't quite prepared herself for this level of sophistication. It's a good thing she was confident in her knowledge and experience to pull off this merger. Once talking business, the self-assured Melody Adams would emerge and take control. Plus, she remembered her company was the buyer here, not Comtech, albeit style-challenged, was ten times Microtech's size. They were barely seated before the double door opened, and four virile, clean-cut men and a woman walked into the room. One Indian, one White, one Asian, and one Black, all in their early forties, she was guessing. Diversity at its best. No wonder they were rocking the world.

"Ms. Adams. I'm so pleased to meet you. I'm Charles Bell." The well-dressed man outstretched his hand.

Holy Mary, Mother of God, Melody, who wasn't even Catholic, almost dropped her purse. She felt as though she was having a religious experience. The man before her was a looker; fine, fine, mo' fine, "bazoom," and "phat," as Veronica's twelve-year-old would say. Charles Bell had Tiger Woods's eyes, Ming Lee Ho's smile, looked like the Badshah of Bollywood, Shar Rukh Khan, only African American, and to top it off, he had Jeffrey Holder's voice, for Pete's sake. How could anyone resist Jeffery Holder's voice?

For a minute, Melody thought she would faint. Had her overdue date with the inevitable love finally come? What an unnerving experience! Mr. Bell," Melody imagined, with disgust, the silly grin on her face as she flashed him what she'd hoped was a gorgeous smile. Stepping back from the hypnotic moment, annoyed but recovered, Melody chided her stupidity. This was so unlike her. But to be real, she had to give herself some slack.

Even Lot's wife would have stirred at the six-foot-five inches stallion of a man in front of her. Her brother had been exactly that height. His short cut gray speckled hair was brushed to brilliance, and she was now more convinced than ever he was an ex-IBMer, disarming Melody further.

So far, the merger had reached the negotiation stage with Attorneys and CFO, and Melody wondered why, as she assumed he was the lead counsel, she hadn't at least made his phone acquaintance. Then the name Charles Bell exploded in her head as her recall buttons activated. Why did she know the name? He couldn't be! Charles Bell was the owner of Microtech!

"Mr. Bell. The pleasure is all mine." A smile spread across her lips. "I'm so sorry about canceling our last meeting," Melody said, recovering her calm.

"What's to be sorry about? Sickness doesn't announce itself in time for proper planning now, does it?"

"I suppose not," Melody said.

"We're sorry you were ill but pleased that because of it, we were able to get you out here, and I get the pleasure of attending the meeting." It was Charles Bell's turn to flash a gleaming smile. He introduced the other players on the team and then announced, "Let's eat and get right down to business."

"Guest first," The VP of marketing announced.

"Salmon Caesar," Melody said confidently.

"Coming right up."

Melody discreetly kept her eyes on Charles Bell throughout lunch, especially his left hand, second finger. No arc from a wedding ring was evident. A man like him had to be married, she mused. Then from absolutely nowhere came the most jarring thought. *She had met her Michael Chen, the financier she admired most.*

Lunch concluded; Charles Bell wasted no time in getting down to business. Pushing back in his chair, he rose, strolled over to the credenza, and picked up the reports Melody had set out. "We can move to the conference room, but I rather like being at this table," he said, handing a copy of the bound document to the meeting participants. "Any objection?" The staff shook their heads and glanced, un-hurriedly, through the report. As she quietly observed the men, Melody was acutely aware of the team's synergy. It was as though they were able to communicate without verbal exchange. A nod here and a sigh there simultaneously conferred the essence of thought. There was, from what she had seen, a total sense of belonging and respect. Each, no doubt, to be included in this prestigious circle had proven themselves exemplary. It was obvious why Microtech was successful.

"I'm impressed with the look of this package," Charles's voice startled Melody.

"It's a terrific offer." Melody was pleased.

"It is Ms. Adams," Charles Bell stared, his eyes fixed on hers, "with one exception. I want a clause that every employee at Microtech remains employed for at least one year after the sale. Senior and executive management, except for myself, must have a three-year severance or employment, whichever pleases your company."

"You've got to be kidding! That's impossible! Lunacy!" Melody said, snapping back to the reality of the deal. Her business instinct has swiftly annihilated any fleeting notions of romantic love. "Mr. Bell, that is non-negotiable."

"Everything is negotiable, Ms. Adams. Didn't they teach you that at Stanford or Northwestern?"

So, he'd checked her qualifications to conduct this deal. The man was meticulous. "You are driving too hard of a bargain, Mr. Bell. I will never get management to agree to this. I don't care how much cajoling I do. I, for one, think it's suicidal. Comtech must be free to do what's in the company's best interest." She ignored his comment about her education.

"And companies are made up of employees. People with lives and families." Charles's voice was calming. Effortless and genuine. "The employees at Microtech are among the best. I want each of them to have the chance to go out and find another opportunity equal to or better than what they have here. If they are not needed at Comtech, they'll have no problem finding work elsewhere, but this is a safety net for them should my assumptions be wrong. If this can't be accomplished, Ms. Adams," his gaze blazed through her, "I will not sell." He meant it. She could see that from his eyes. What the hell did he think, Comtech was the Salvation Army?

"From where I sit and what I know of Comtech, it will never happen. But I'll see what I can do." Melody rose, throwing her shoulders backward, indicating the negotiations had ended. "Mr. Bell. I caution you to think of a compromise. This is a sweetheart deal, and you know it. Don't lose it because of …well, never mind. I can see you have made up your mind. As soon as I have an answer, I'll be in touch."

"Thank you, Ms. Adams. I'm confident in your ability to deliver the deal as discussed. It's just a single change. Please allow me to walk you back to your car."

"Your car." Melody corrected.

"Maybe. But not for long if my hunches are right." Another dazzling smile. The man was seamless. Almost Zen. She wanted to shake him into reality as much as she wanted to enter his temple of enchantment. She wanted to stay in his presence forever as much as she wanted to escape. How could she walk away without saying a word? How could she say a word? It was impossible. Intimacy meant sharing, and Melody had nothing to share with anyone. Then her mind dealt a lethal blow. It kept saying—*marry him now, for as God is your witness, you have just seen what you need. Yes, girlfriend, you've found your man with the slow hand.* The feeling left her weak, and Melody struggled to remain on her feet. The indomitability of love had struck. For God's sake, she was coming undone.

"Thank you again." Melody mustered enough strength to move toward the car, and as soon as the door opened, she quickly slid inside.

"Are you free for dinner tonight?"

She wanted to scream *the whole goddamn night* but instead said, "I'm afraid not, Mr. Bell. I have a flight out in a short while."

"Why hurry back? San Francisco is beautiful."

"To get you an answer."

"I'm in no hurry. Eight o'clock? I'll pick you up. I'll have someone change your flight to tomorrow morning. Oh, by the way, what's your cell number?" It wasn't even a request. It was an order. Melody's usual urge to rumble at being commanded was rendered mute. At thirty-seven, it seemed her elevator was no longer going all the way to the top. She gave him the number. In the elevator, Melody felt her forehead. She had no temperature, but she felt like she was in the middle of a cauldron. Her cell phone pinged with a message. "I'm thinking about your strategy for Comtech. This very minute, it came to me." She clicked the attachment. The Dinner Place! I'll tell you there. Melody busted into an uproar of laughter.

"Can't wait," she tapped out.

CHAPTER SEVENTEEN

APRIL CURLED HER body into a ball on the floor. Her will firm, she passed a trembling hand across her mascara-streaked eyes to wipe away the last residue of tears. Enough! No more crying. No more tears.

"No more," she said loudly, struggling to her feet. Unimaginable pain gripped her as she stumbled to the kitchen, grabbed an open bottle of wine from the counter and walked somberly into the great room. Staring aimlessly into the dark fireplace, she felt the fray of madness descending. She needed to call her mother. She grabbed a crystal figurine from the mantel, smashing it into the unlit fireplace. "Get a life," she shouted. What she needed was some light. A fire to illuminate the dark, dank corners of her life, to expose what's buried far too deep for far too long.

The fireplace was central to the room. On hands and knees, April reached up and flipped the flue to open. Pushing hard on the ignite button, she watched as a golden hue roared to life, spewing jagged bolts of light into the air. It was a poor imitation of a good old fireplace where wood scents and sparkles sizzled and crackled. Like everything else, the damn fireplace was an imitation! What would it be like to step into the flames and disappear? April bet it wouldn't be half as bad as the madness that now consumed her. Swigging a generous mouthful of wine her thoughts ricocheted. What had she to lose? A nagging mother and an abusive husband? "Wouldn't it be lovely?" April swayed, gazing as the flame leaped boldly inside its boundaries. Instead of smashing the wine bottle into the fake flames, April got up, wrapped herself in the Afghan and stretched out on the sofa. She took a final swig and put the half-empty wine bottle on the coffee table. Closing her eyes, she thought of sleep. Sleep was the beginning of regeneration, of newness, of hope. Would anyone believe it if she just slept away permanently? Would they report her death as natural causes or suicide?

"But they were such a nice, loving couple. We never suspected anything at all! Depressed? Unstable? No way. They were always happy and friendly." The neighbors would chirp to the news anchors as they carried her out on a stretcher. What was wrong with death, anyway? She liked Manna, didn't she? What if she didn't go to heaven? No one she knew had a near hell experience, so she wouldn't know what to expect, except for the silly jokes people told about hell.

"But I thought hell was filled with dancing girls and guys. That's what I saw, wasn't it?"

"Yes, my dear child, but that was just a demo." The Devil would grin, exposing jagged teeth as smoke puffed out of his ear.

How much of this fiasco was her fault? April wondered. Since returning from Jamaica, she'd purposely avoided serious conversations like job promotion and babies. It hadn't been hard, as Sam's travel schedule had suddenly picked up. What difference would any discussion make now? Everything was over. Done. Kaput. What the hell was the use of trying to hold on to her so-called perfect life, anyway? Now marred and no longer perfect, she was free to do as she pleased. To the world, April and

Sam appeared to be the perfect couple. Perfect careers, perfect home, idyllic vacations, and a once perfect sex life. Since their return from Jamaica, Sam had not as much as reached for her hand. April's eyes focused on the glittering flame. Why was it all going wrong?

Outside the expansive glass windows, glowing lanterns twinkled. How beautiful the landscape had been this past summer when life was in bloom; the floral medley; the smell of peat moss, and freshly mowed lawns. Now, like in her life, the season had changed, and it was cold. Like feisty trees hold on to the last summer leaves before accepting the defeat of winter, she too had tried, the best she could, to hold on to a dying marriage. There was indeed a time for every season under heaven. Soon life would bloom again for the flora, but maybe never again for her.

April's mind drifted to a dark place. To go there, she had to take another swig of wine, maybe two. Why would Sam mess up all this for some unknown like a baby? What if the baby was crazy? Not normal? Not all he expected? What then? What did he know about babies? Little babies. Babies with chubby toes and furrowed legs. She had wanted her baby. She had hoped and prayed. If Sam knew she hadn't been honest with him about babies, he'd have left her for good long ago. Why hadn't she trusted him with her secret? Why…why?" She guzzled another mouthful of wine. Why was he in such a hurry anyway? They had time. For Christ sakes, you'd think it was his biological clock ticking away!

As she mellowed under the wine, burrowing deeper into the sofa, April listened to the dance of the crackling flame. *Babies. Babies who looked just like Sam. Just as good-looking and just as….Babies who looked like her, deceptively small ;babies who looked like them both…tall, long-legged, long-necked, burnt-sugar brown with long lashes. "Sam," she murmured as her lids drooped heavily. "Oh, Sam, where did you go?"*

What right have you to complain if you do nothing to change the plight of Black folks? Here you have an opportunity. An opportunity to control the media and, therefore, the minds. An opportunity to see your story on the silver screen the way it should be told, not how Hollywood tells it. Write your check tonight and rewrite history.

The man at the podium had an edge. A sharp, jagged edge. It attracted April like a bolt of lightning. She couldn't take her eyes off him. They were transfixed, glued to his deep-set eyes. He wore a Kangol turned backward, a black cashmere sweater, sleeves shoved up to his elbow, and black Cords. He was the guest speaker in a room full of two thousand-dollar suits, yet he was entirely at ease in his attire. The occasion was an investment meeting of Black wealth to underwrite a movie from a new director. Sam Summers was the entertainment attorney making a name for himself as a brother with a purpose. Women swarmed him. April turned away.

April had never dated an American man. Her mother's overly colonial educated Caribbean social group was her playground. Sam Summers was not in her milieu. At the bar, nursing a martini, she was mulling over Sam's powerful effect on her when someone whispered in her ears, "Earth Angel, Earth Angel, will you be mine."

If that wasn't the cheesiest line! The voice belonged to the man who had detonated her heart.

"Yes, I will."

That night emotions erupted like a volcano shooting its contents miles into the air, burying doubt under hot, molten lava mounds. The ground fertile, April Summers had found love.

Gabriella Dixon had been shocked, stupefied, and dumbfounded her daughter would marry a Black American, any American for that matter. She warned of the dangers of mixing cultures;

quoted the Bible, "yoke with your own kind," and pleaded with April's father to talk sense into his daughter's head. But none of it had worked. With Sam, April experienced a stronger synergy than any hold Gabriella had over her. They'd married eight months after meeting. The bliss of their passion had taken eight years before love's glow dulled under the pressures of reality. Now their passion had dimmed to a humm.

What was the use of trying hard if everything always deteriorates into nothingness? As of tonight, April was no longer going to do what other people wanted her to do. Whether beholden to her mother or to have babies so Sam could love her again, she was going to damn well do as she pleased. *Screw them all.*

So, what if she blotted out life's dreadfulness with work and a few drinks now and then? Tonight, Sam was the beneficiary of her drinking. She could pretend his behavior, which had shot way over the line, was simply a borderline human emotion from anger. Unsteadily, April made her way to the Bluetooth and turned it on. She pressed Spotify on her iPhone, and Eminem's fabulous song *Love the Way You Lie* came on. By the time the playlist reached her *African playlist*, April was twirling around the room in uncontrolled spins. She knocked over a framed picture of her and Sam but did not bother to pick it up. Tonight, music and wine were her comforts. Had she not majored in economics and business, she would have been a dancer or maybe a pianist, as was her mother's wish. Who knows, had she tried harder to please her mother, she might have gone the way of *Shine*; David Helfgott's descent into total madness, trying to play Rachmaninov. April gyrated, her body changing gears to the dance of her motherland…Africa.

Sam Summers burned some tires. Smoke. Pungent-smelling rubber. At the end of the street, he gunned the engine and imagined the skid marks on Gabriella Dixon's forehead. He blamed her for everything that was wrong with April. But even that didn't calm him. His anger was not at April or Gabriella. He had to face up to his shortcomings. How had he allowed himself to lose control? Sam eased onto the ramp that merged into I94 to the loop. God, how he regretted his diabolical behavior! He pulled the car into the valet parking line. This was a bad idea from day one. Even though Sophie Watkins was a dangerous woman, a temptress, she was no antidote to his glaring problem tonight. She was not the answer. Far more than eye candy, his wife had an enviable mind, a wicked sense of humor and a personality that intrigued. He'd loved her from the moment he had set eyes on her, and nothing had changed. She was his "Earth Angel." Sam reversed and turned the car in the direction of home.

A waft of heat met him. He followed it to the great room. On the hand-woven carpet was a circular, red stain, and an empty bottle of wine. April, prone on the couch, her hand flopping over the sofa, was sleeping soundly, her breath drawn in angry rasps against the night. Sam sat on the floor beside her and buried his head into her abdomen. "I'm so sorry," he lifted her carefully, carrying her to bed. In this vulnerable, helpless state, April was fragile and so very beautiful. Who would ever believe that by day she was a helluva corporate czarina? Sam undressed his wife, still awed by the smooth, soft almond skin. Her size thirty-six breasts heaved up and down with each breath. He had hurt this beautiful creature. As he brought her into him to remove the only remaining article of clothing she wore, her bra, the fresh lemon scent of her hair wafted across his face. Gingerly he placed April into bed, pulling the covers over her. He lit the bedroom fireplace so her naked body wouldn't feel the cold and tiptoed out of the room. He loved his wife so very much, and now he had betrayed her in more ways than she knew.

Sam's brows furrowed, and his thoughts went to his mother. His family life had been one of constant rage and broken hopes. He dialed the phone.

"Hello." The old but still sweet voice said.

"Hey, Ma," Sam said softly.

"Son. Is something wrong?"

"No, Ma. I just felt like hearing your voice."

It could be said, without a doubt, Fanny Mae Summers was a ball of burning fire. She made no bones about promising to kick anybody's ass who interfered with her sanity, which included her husband but never her children. But Fanny had also suffered in silence. Sam knew that. He could still hear the nighttime howls followed by the morning welts on his mother's body. One day Fannie Mae had changed. She'd decided not to take it anymore. It was the day his father had come home drunk and without his check. The fool had left it down at the speakeasy in a few bottles of whiskey. After some serious railing and cussing, barking, and berating, and when Fannie Mae realized the money to feed her children was gone, she'd reached onto the stove, grabbed a frying pan, and pelted her husband on the head with it. He never came home again. My God! Sam suddenly acknowledged. He'd become his father.

CHAPTER EIGHTEEN

AT THE AIRPORT, Tony and Veronica went their separate ways. Arizona already felt light-years away, their illicit morning tryst a fast-fading dream. As much as she tried, Veronica couldn't hold onto the memory. Feelings of loss, remorse and dread overwhelmed her.

At 3:35 p.m., Veronica, deep in deliberation, swung her maroon Mercedes truck into the driveway of her Hyde Park mansion. A loud metal bending noise crunched under her wheels, and she quickly reversed into the street. Sticking out on the side of the driveway was her son's dirt bike, the rim now all bent to dickens. Worse, there was a dent on the bottom of her truck. Welcome to reality and bird-brain children, she said aloud, storming into the house to give her absent-minded son holy hell. Suddenly Veronica stopped dead in her tracks. Her toothless six-year-old daughter, dressed to kill in a brand-new sweater, was racing down the stairs. Her daughter's face and brand-new sweater were covered in makeup. Instead of annoyance Veronica felt a warm gush of love for the child who dived into her legs.

'Hi, Mommy," the toothless caper grinned. "I'm pretty today."

"That you are, Missy, but why are you so dressed up?"

"Because I wanted to sing for you. Do you want to hear me sing, Mommie?"

"Of course, pudding face. Shall I sit down?"

"Okay," her daughter said, rushing first to turn on her iPhone and then went to stand in front of the fireplace. Veronica sat straight up and readied herself for Jenny's debut performance. The young diva clasped her hands before her, and within moments, a beautiful and lilting little voice filled the living room. "I believe I can fly. I believe I can touch the sky. I believe I can soar."

Tears welled in Veronica's eyes. When did her daughter learn to sing like that? She had missed so much of the children's growing up. Why would she dream of disrupting their lives? She hated this guilt. She hated this affair. She hated her life. "That was wonderful, darling. You are such a star," Veronica bit back tears, hoisting the child and kissing her warmly. "And girlfriend, you have a set of pipes on you! Jenny, who taught you that song?"

"Daddy. We sang it after school today. He told me never to forget that I could touch the sky. Can I mommie?"

"Without a doubt, my kitten. Without a doubt." In times of joy, this was a happy home. The children were secure and full of mirth. Laughter abounded because Randolph, even though precise, was a very funny man. Veronica often joked that if he never made it as a writer, he could always do stand up at Second City. No longer was the house a palace of happiness. Veronica sensed how hard the children, who suspected all was not well, were trying to pull her back into the family. "Jenny, you are a wonderful singer and thank you for sharing your song with me. I'm going to arrange singing lessons for you. Now, where's your brother?" She lowered Jenny to the floor, ruffling her bangs. Veronica wished she and Randolph could go back to the way things were. He was such a good father. The weight of her infidelity gripped her soul.

"Watching TV with Daddy."

Veronica and Jenny climbed the steps to the entertainment room on the third floor of the magnificent house. A dream house Veronica never imagined possible, even with lofty dreams. There was more talking than television watching as she entered the room.

"Gerald," Veronica's voice was stern. "How many times do I have to tell you to put your bike into the garage when you're finished riding it?"

"I did… ."

"Aaa Aaa. Don't try it. That bike is sitting in the driveway crushed to death."

"You didn't. Dang, mom." Gerald jumped to his feet. "Are you blind?"

"And don't you ask me to buy another one," she shouted after him as he stomped down the stairs, followed closely by his sister and Toby, the pain-in-the-ass fur ball of a cat. Her twelve-year-old son was growing into a take-it-for-granted kid. It was time for a life lesson. No way was she going to be responsible for turning him into a useless noose around her neck, into an ambitionless, rich, spoilt, selfish kid. No way. Veronica looked with regret at her husband, whose eyes had not left the television since she'd walked in. She wanted to be nice. She wanted to thank him for being such a great dad. She wanted to say she was sorry about where they were, but instead, she lashed out at him.

"Randolph, it's 4:15 p.m. Monday. You know the children have piano lessons in thirty minutes."

"We're not going today."

"What do you mean not going today?"

"Things are going to change around here. It seems you have forgotten who you are in this house. I have changed the children's lessons to Saturdays so you can take them. You need some time to bond with your family."

"What the hell? Are you nuts? Why didn't you say a word to me about this?"

"I didn't think I had to. They're my children as well."

"I don't believe you. I can't…."

"Look, you don't want to start anything tonight. I'm not in the mood."

"I hope you're in the mood for a divorce." Veronica bellowed.

"Don't bother. I've already contacted a lawyer."

"You've what? Christ almighty Randolph, have you gone mad?"

"Haven't you? Look. If you want any questions answered about the divorce, talk to my lawyer." Randolph turned up the volume on the television.

"And who's paying for the lawyer, pray tell?"

"All the years I've spent supporting your success. I'm sure that's worth something in court"

"You make me sick. Randolph, why couldn't you have talked to me about this?"

"I would have if you were ever home. When are you ever in this house when anyone is awake?"

"I am now," Veronica said cocking akimbo.

"Why? No more patients, students, laboratory rats, conventions?"

Veronica snorted. "If I had a gainfully employed husband, maybe I wouldn't have to work so hard."

"Don't blame your ambition on me. I'm doing exactly what we said we would do. Didn't we plan this? You're the one who gave up on me. How could you, Veronica? How could you? How could you give up on our dreams?"

"Dreams? Dreams? Randolph, we had dreams. We had vision. What have you done about them in the past three years?" Veronica's voice trembled with emotions.

"Don't make me seem cheap like a common gigolo. What do you want me to do, Veronica? You said you need time to re-evaluate. You want me to beg you to stay? Beg you to spend time with your neglected family? That'll never happen!"

"Why don't you find something to occupy your time so you can get off my case?"

"I suppose to you it seems like I do nothing. Why don't you look at your children? They, thank God, are having a childhood. Anyway, I'm not going to have this conversation one more minute. I have just one thing left to say." Randolph grabbed Veronica by the wrist. "Hear me and hear me well. I will not, under any circumstance, be treated like a parasite who brought no value to your life. Think carefully about the next step you take."

"You're always good with words, aren't you?" She wrestled out of his hold. "But isn't it time to take your head out of the sky and walk your talk?"

"If you were so distressed about my writing going nowhere, why didn't you say something?" Randolph stood up; his fist clenched at his side.

"Say what? I'm ashamed to introduce you as a househusband. What exactly do you want me to say?"

"I find the person you've become most despicable. Where's the humble woman I used to know and love?" Randolph's voice was sad. "As I said before," the sadness turned to anger, "from this day forward if you want to speak to me, speak through my lawyer. If you have something to say about our children, put it in writing."

Veronica felt dismissed. Her husband had a way of making her feel small. Back in the projects, he'd been unconquerable, unflappable, and had an extraordinary sense of fair fight when facing adversity, which persisted to this day. Above all, he'd never lost his dignity no matter how angry he became. Randolph's eyes burned through his glasses, lasering her with anger.

"Why don't you take your dead ass outta my house? Let me see if you're still superior when you can't live off me. I swear I married a fool."

"Veronica, I'm warning you …."

"*Pa-leaze.*" Veronica glared at him. "Are you threatening me? I don't want to hear this shit either, but man, you got some nerve serving me divorce papers. I'm gonna talk till I'm blue in the face. What're you gonna do about that?"

Randolph's knuckles were bloodless, gripping the back of the chair.

Veronica's emotions teetered on the edge, but nothing could stop her. She was livid. Enraged. Fuming. How dare he threaten her? "You want to know what I'm doing." She spat. "I'm trying to get a life. Some time for myself. Christ, all I do is work to support this family. Tell me, where do I fit into all this happiness you keep talking about? This togetherness? This family? Is getting a life so damn bad?"

"You can choose happiness if you want. You're the one running away from us."

Tears glistened in Veronica's eyes, and her voice broke. "Randolph, to tell you the truth, the thought of leaving you and the children to feel alive again is very, very tempting. But I haven't left yet, have I? Why would you file for a divorce?" Her face creased with hurt. "If anyone is to be blamed for our failing relationship, it's you. My career is about to skyrocket, and my marriage is falling apart because you want to be a friggin' writer." She turned on her heels, grabbed Gerald's books and marched down the stairs.

"Mom," Gerald was on his way back up the stairs. "You ruined my bike."

"Me? How did I ruin your bike?" Veronica snapped. "You're the one who left it in the driveway. How many times have I told you to pick up after yourself? Here," she thrust the pile of books into his hands. "This is your homework and go get ready for bed."

"But Mom."

"Don't 'but Mom' me nothing. I said, go to your bed."

"I'm not gonna. I'm gonna ask Dad if he can fix my bike." Gerald stormed past her. He never bothered to take the books.

Veronica wasn't downstairs twenty minutes before her beeper went off. It was the hospital. Hopping into the truck, she backed out of the driveway. Rage rose in her like bile. Filing for a divorce had never entered the realm of her reality. Veronica wiped a hand across her eyes. No matter how long you live with a person, you never really know them.

Traffic was light. Veronica drove up the parking garage ramp as though she was Evil Knievel. Pulling into her parking space, she saw Tony getting out of his car.

"We've gotta stop meeting like this." He smiled at her. "C-section. How about you?"

"Ectopic." She wasn't in a friendly mood.

"What's with the grim face?"

"Nothing. I have to go. I'll talk to you later."

"Can I walk with you, at least?"

"Sure." She said. She shouldn't take her problems out on Tony.

"Wanna talk about it?"

"No."

"C'mon, Veronica. What's wrong?"

"Tony. Didn't I just ask you to leave it alone? If you want me to walk with you, then back off, okay?"

"Fine. Fine. Just you go on and treat me like a stepchild."

"I didn't mean to snap but going home makes me crazy. Tony, everything is wrong. Randolph filed for a divorce. I have a feeling he suspects something. Not you and I in particular, but he suspects something. We can't see each other anymore."

"How could he?"

"When you've been married for eighteen years, listen to your partner's breath next to you every night, believe me, you know."

"That's crazy. Veronica," He grabbed her arm, spinning her to face him, "I won't be without you."

"Tony. Don't make me crazy."

"After surgery, let's have coffee and talk this through, okay?" He pulled her into him. "Every problem has a solution."

"Okay." Veronica looked around nervously. "I'll page you."

When she arrived on the OB floor, the nurses informed her the patient was in quite a state. "Could you please have a word with her," the nurse begged, "before we wheel her into OR." Typically, Veronica never saw patients until they were prepared and on the operating table. An ectopic pregnancy was a no-brainer. Thirty minutes tops. On the way to the patient's room, she glanced briefly at the chart the nurse handed her. "A first-time mother." The nurse said. "Been trying for four years."

"Mrs. Milton, I'm doctor Whittaker. I'm on call for your doctor. I'll be doing your surgery. I wanted to stop in to see how you're doing."

The woman's face was contorted with grief, tears streaming down her cheeks. "Please, doctor, do something. I want this baby. I need this baby," she wailed. The woman's eyes, through the tears, were wild and assailed with fear and the bloodless hands gripping Veronica's coat.

"Mrs. Milton." Veronica pried the woman's hand off her coat, holding them between hers. "I can hardly imagine your pain, but we have to go to the operating room now. I wish I could give you better news." Veronica was empathetic. "Believe me, if it were in my powers to do, I would do everything to save your baby, but I can't, and it's *your* life that is most crucial right now. You can have more babies," Veronica said softly but with urgency, "I promise." She touched the woman's tear-streaked face. "I'm so sorry, but we must go to OR now."

Mr. Milton was sitting catatonically beside his wife, holding her hand tightly. Veronica touched his left shoulder reassuringly. Randolph had held her hand through both of their children's deliveries. Gently. Kindly and supportively. He had never left her. Turning away, she quickly went to the OR.

As the Betadine brush swept up and down her arm, Veronica thought of Randolph. She was lucky to have a man as great as him in her life. If she could take back the horrible words, she'd spoken to her husband. If she… ."Gown." The OR nurse held the green scrubs. As she pushed her hands into sterile gloves, Veronica thought of her family. Family, the last bastion of a civilized world, was dying, and she was guilty of contributing to its demise.

With the surgery completed, Veronica took the left bank of elevators to the doctor's lounge. Emotionally and physically exhausted, she slumped diagonally across the God-awful twin bed provided for over-worked staff. As her body made contact with the bed, her lids fluttered closed, and a vision of her children floated above her tiredness. She had failed them miserably. Did she know how lucky she was to have a man like Randolph? Many Black women were screaming to have a man in their lives, much less a good decent man. Randolph was why her children were carefree and happy. It certainly wasn't because of her erratic schedule. Her beeper went off. She didn't want to answer it, but she did.

"Hey. Where are you?"

"In the doctor's lounge."

"Shall I come up?"

"No, Tony, I have to go home."

"Veronica. What use is it going home to fight? Let's talk about this. Devise a game plan."

The thought struck Veronica as odd. How do you devise a game plan with a secret love? "I'll be down."

Seeing Tony in the parking lot smiling warmly at her, she was struck for the millionth time by his incredible magical charm, charisma, and his deep hold over her. "I'm going home, Tony." She said solemnly.

"Are you trying to make me crazy? Isn't having my heart enough? Just a little coffee. That's all."

"Drumroll, please." Veronica pulled the brim of his Chicago Bulls cap over his eyes. "I can't stay long, is that understood."

"Clearly."

"Where to?"

"How about my place?"

"Ah, hell." Veronica's beeper vibrated. It was her answering service. "I gotta take this. Go on; I'll follow you shortly."

"Call me on my cell if you've got to go to surgery again."

"Will do."

CHAPTER NINETEEN

APRIL SUMMERS AWOKE slowly to a throbbing headache. She was no longer on the sofa in the great room but in bed alone and in her birth suit. Sam, it seemed, had already left. That was wise, for if she had to face him this morning, she would bury a dagger of words, if not one of steel, into his heart. April opened the bedside drawer, swallowed three aspirins, and washed them down with a glass of tomato juice, no doubt, Sam had left. Surprisingly, instead of lingering on the fight, her thoughts were on losing her safe harbor. Sam understood her as no one did. Now all that was gone. He gave her no choice now or reason to save their marriage. She pulled on a robe and headed to the kitchen.

"Good morning." Sam was at the table, nursing a cup of coffee.

"What's good about it?" She said, avoiding his eyes.

"Not much." He eyed her sheepishly. "How are you feeling?"

"How would you feel if you were used as a punching bag and a sex slave?" April pulled a cup from the dishwasher. She ran a shaking hand through her hair.

"April, I'm so very, very sorry. I don't know what came over me. Can you ever forgive me?"

"Forgive you? Can you forgive yourself?"

"It's going to be hard." His eyes were glued to the brown liquid in his cup.

"I don't want to talk about it this morning." April held up her hand in a breaking gesture.

"April," Sam pleaded, "it was a mistake. I went crazy. I swear." He looked up and could still see a faint red blotch on her cheek.

"A mistake? It was barbaric and cowardly." April slammed the mug on the table. Sitting opposite Sam, reaching for the carafe suddenly seemed too much, and she wept. Sam put his mug down, took the coffee carafe from April's shaking hands and poured coffee.

"Here," he lifted her head, handing her the cup of black coffee. He watched her closely as she raised the cup to her lips.

"I'm truly sorry. I'll make it up to you. You'll see." He touched her shoulder encouragingly. Never would he consciously hurt his "Earth Angel."

"That's what every batterer says to his victim." April hurled back at him.

Rising, Sam put the morning paper in his briefcase. April sat rigidly in front of him. She glanced sideways at him. There was dullness and a shame in his eyes she couldn't bear to see. He deserved it, she thought.

Sam snapped his attaché shut. "I'm no batterer," Sam said, slipping on his goulashes. "You know that. Have I ever touched you in all our years together? I'm no batterer."

"My face can't believe that right now." April sipped more coffee. The aspirins were not doing a damn thing for her headache.

"I've been feeling vile lately. Everything is wrong. You won't talk to me. You won't discuss a family. All you want is your job. I just lost it. I swear it will never happen again. April," Sam was serious. "If we're going to make it, I'd like you to consider quitting your job."

"Quitting? S&G? You can't be serious. Sam, it's not just a job. It's my career. I could be the next CFO. Do you understand that? You knew I was a career woman when you married me."

"Our marriage needs this."

"We have no marriage anymore."

"What do you mean?"

"How can I stay with you? We don't want the same things anymore. I can't be what you want me to be. Sam, answer me one question. Could some of our problems be because you feel competitive about us?"

Prickles. Anger. Familiar dander. It was time to go. He couldn't go there, not after yesterday. "I was only trying to… never mind." His tone was resigned.

April looked up sharply.

"I have to go."

After Sam left, April sat at the kitchen table, trying to get her act together. Her success threatened Sam! If that was the root of all this, she didn't know how to deal with it. She needed help, but it was not from Eve or a divorce lawyer. It was from The Trinity.

"Hi." She said simply when Veronica's nurse answered the phone. "Is Dr. Whittaker in office today?"

"I'm afraid not. She's in surgery. Are you a patient?"

"No. I'm a friend."

"Would you like me to page her?"

"No. I'll reach her later. Thanks a lot."

"Don't mention it. Have a good day."

CHAPTER TWENTY

IT TOOK MELODY four minutes after returning to her hotel room to ring Veronica's. Her cell didn't pick up, so she tried her work number.

"Dr. Whittaker's office."

"Is she there? This is Melody Adams."

"No. ma'am."

"Do you know where she is?"

"She's headed to the operating room," The operator said with a "do-I-look-like-her-keeper" tone.

"How do you get a hold of her in an emergency?"

"We page her." Nonplused.

"Then page her, damn it." Oh boy. Now she had a permanent new vocabulary to match her new mid-life crisis personality.

"And where can she reach you?" The ill-mannered woman barked.

"At the Four Seasons Hotel in San Francisco. Tell her it's an emergency. The number is triple five-9876, room 845. And thank you"

By the time the phone rang, Melody felt like an eternity had passed.

"Hello, Vee?"

"What's up?"

"What took you so long to call me back?"

"What are you talking about? It's been five minutes. What the matter with you, anyway, and Melody, what are you doing in San Francisco? Are you all right?"

"Yep. Never better."

"So, what's the emergency?"

"Veronica, promise not to laugh."

"I promise, but could you get to the point. I'm dying of curiosity over here, not to talk about the surgery I have to do like now."

"I'm in love."

"What? What the hell? You called me in an emergency to tell me you are in love?"

"C'mon, Vee. Do you know me to be this crazy?"

"I've always suspected your tight ass had a wild streak."

"But I've never been crazy, right?"

"Awh right, awh right. You're in love. So, pray, tell, with whom are you in love? The iceman cometh?" Veronica laughed.

"With Charles Bell."

"Who? Melody, would you volunteer a little more detail so we could get to the point here."

"Okay. Okay. I'm here on a business trip."

"Okay Sherlock."

Ignoring the interruption, Melody continued. "Remember the meeting I had to cancel a month ago. Well, I flew out here to meet the folks. The owner of Microtech is the most gorgeous Black man I have ever seen in my life."

"Hold on. Just hold on a minute. You mean to tell me you met this man a few hours ago, and you're in love?" The snigger turned into uncontrollable laughter. "Girl, when you have a breakdown, you go all out."

"That's it. I'm not telling you another word."

"Okay. Okay. Okay. I'm serious. So, at what juncture did you decide it was love?"

"At first sight."

Veronica cackled so hard, Melody herself started laughing. "Jesus wept. I have never heard some shit like this. Girl, I had no idea you were a romantic. Not your prissy tight, behind."

"Tight? Do I deserve that?"

"Melody, you're so tight you squeak, so if this man is the oil-man, go for it, love, or no love. Seriously though, was this being in love feeling after you hacked up the man's body, or before? You did take him into the cosmos, didn't you?"

"Veronica! Don't be ridiculous. I'm no two-bit hussy."

"Yeh. Well, you know what they say. Woman in the board-room and the other in the bedroom. Especially when the man has Bell as his name. *Ring my bell, bell. Ring my bell.* "Veronica sang.

"My, you're corny. Why did I call you? I have no idea why I'm confiding in, for that matter, even speaking to you. You're crass, downright disgusting and— ."

"And so should you be. Are you seeing him again before you leave?"

"Yep. Tonight, for dinner. I'm petrified."

"Oooh, wee. I'm scared of you. Sharpen your hatchet, and girl, don't do anything I wouldn't do." The laughter again. "And that's nothing. 'Course, you might want to get a broomstick first to get rid of cobwebs. I know. I'm a prize-winning female doctor."

"You got that right," Melody echoed one of Veronica's favorite sayings. "Let me get off this phone, so I can go sweep."

"Yeah, the anesthesiologist is blowing up my phone."

Veronica was beginning to love this new Melody. "I'll call you later after my surgery." She was in fits of laughter.

"All right, Vee. Goodnight, and thanks for listening."

"Okay, baby. Anytime." There was a sadness now.

"Veronica. Is everything okay?"

"Yeah, girl. Everything is fine. See you when you get home. You have to tell me everything, okay? And make sure he's not married. A girl like you could be a wife's nightmare."

"I've already established that. I looked for skid marks on his fingers. Didn't see a hint."

"Wooooo. Okay, okay, okay. Now you're talkin' like a real sistah. I was so worried about you, girl. But all I have to say now is, go on with your bad self."

"Talk to you later." Melody hung up the phone. Her cell pinged a message.

"Hope you got back safely. Looking forward to tonight. CB"

Melody sat for five minutes trying to think of a clever response. "Back. Yes…I'll see you later." He really loved his cell phone.

CHAPTER TWENTY-ONE

RANDOLPH WHITTAKER switched off the television and sat in the darkness. He reached for his pipe, stuffed it with tobacco, hooked it over the right side of his lip, lit it and drew hard on the tip. He was hurt and angry. A common gigolo was how his wife thought of him? How dare she? It's not as if they hadn't agreed on their plan eighteen years before. He would work while Veronica got her practice established, and then he'd take time off to write the great American novel, which, still in his mind, was a noble plan.

How else would they have raised their two beautiful, well-adjusted children? Didn't she understand the horrors children face out in a world, day by day sinking into anarchy? So, what if it had taken him longer than he'd expected to get published? One had to be brave when they embarked on the profession of writing. Unlike the convincing arguments of business, his diatribe, rants, and raves of conglomerate publishing's evils were lost on his agent, herself incapable of discerning good literature. Publishing houses weren't exactly waiting for what a Black man had to say unless it was a tell-it-all confession on how the jail system rehabilitated him. He wanted to holler all right but not at the system, at his once beautiful, kind, and decent wife.

Disgusted, Randolph went to check on his kids. On the way, he passed the hall mirror and stood looking at his reflection. He was an average man in looks, style and chic. He was a professorial type, prone to tweed and flannel rather than some dashing hunk outfitted in designer garb. He was a good and faithful husband, which should count for a lot.

"Gerald," he pushed his head through the door, "you're supposed to have lights out by now," he scolded. But Randolph could never be angry with his children for long. If only grown-ups were as accepting and non-judgmental as children, the world would be a better place.

"I'm reading, Dad."

"Finish tomorrow."

"Dad. Could you ask Mom to get me another bike, please? Everyone will be able to ride to the park but me."

"Gerald. You should've put your bike away."

"I know, Dad," Gerald said glumly.

"I'll look at it tomorrow. I bet I can fix it."

"You can, Dad. I know you can. Thanks, Dad."

"Anytime, sport."

"Are you sure you don't want to read with me?"

"Yeah, I do. I want you to get some sleep so you can ace that test tomorrow. What are you reading anyway?"

"Oh, it's this book Joseph gave me. It's called *Basketball's All-Time Greats*. I want to be just like Mike when I grow up."

"Yeah?"

"Yeah. Who'd you be, Dad?"

"Cassius Clay."

"Who's that?"

"Muhammed Ali."

"Who?"

"Pa-leaaaze. You don't know who Muhammed Ali is, son?"

"No. Who is he?"

"The greatest boxer who ever lived. Boxing has never been the same since. I'll tell you what, if you promise to turn out the lights, I'll take you to see a movie about him. It's called *When We Were Kings*. It's an old movie but it's playing at the artsy downtown."

"That's cool"

Randolph kissed his son, switched off the light and went down the hall to check on his little princess. Jenny was fast asleep with her Elmo doll tucked in beside her. Closing the door gently, Randolph went to his study. The last thing in the world he wanted was for his children to be fatherless. Single parenthood was not just a Black thing. It was one of America's worst social nightmares. In a few years, Gerald would need a man who could understand the perils of teenagerhood. Still, he had to go. What else should a man do when his wife calls him useless? Randolph didn't want a divorce, but he would not be insulted.

Veronica had been the love of his life and the reservoir from which he drew strength. They'd been high school sweethearts. And together, they had lived the promise after escaping the empty life the street promised. When kids in the neighborhood were sneaking away to smoke cigarettes, tote alcohol, drag on weed or inhale crack, he and Veronica sat in the park, planning how they'd make it out of the ghetto. Often when they played Scrabble, they'd spell out words that portended their future and their dreams. SUCCESS. CAREER. ZENITH. He'd always believed he'd be married to Veronica until his mortal life had slipped away. Was this life she was handing him any better than the hollow life in the streets?

Randolph sighed. She was winning. Doing exactly what she said she would. This time it was not a game. It was real life. The two-million-dollar three-story house in Hyde Park, the cars in the driveway, and the kids' expensive private school were ample reminder Veronica had reached her dream. Though he was in the dream, it was not his. Suddenly, the starkness of his professional failure hit Randolph hard. Did he just buy into Veronica's dream and ride her coattail to success? Was her success his success? He didn't see himself as a failure. He wanted more than anything in the world to write. It was his superpower, but he couldn't catch a break! Had Veronica even noticed his disappointment? Most people would have given up on their dream by now. Had she noticed he hadn't? Randolph couldn't deny his growing disappointment at the rejection letters or that he'd considered giving up. Could he blame her for wanting to leave? After all, he did owe her a dream.

Jaw set in determination, Randolph went into his study, pushed the power button on his Apple computer and watched as the half-eaten Apple logo floated onto the screen. Something, maybe uncertainty or fear, was blocking him from putting the final touches on his masterpiece. Tonight was the night he would finish his opus, and he'd get it published if it cost him his last breath.

Veronica stared at the disconnected phone. Love was a joy and a pain. For the first time in years, Melody sounded happy. *Take it while you can*, Veronica thought, *'cause love isn't promised forever*. Veronica reached for the ringing cell phone clipped onto her waist.

"Veronica?"

"Hey, Ma."

"Weren't you supposed to be here today?"

"Oh hell, Ma, I'm sorry. I just got out of surgery."

"I thought you were at a convention."

"I got back earlier today." This was the third time she had promised to visit and didn't show up. Hell, where was she to get the time? And now Tony was like a drug, blurring everything else in her life.

"So, how's it going, Ma?"

"I'm surviving.'" The loud noise in the background almost drowned out her voice.

"What's all the racket?"

"I'm running the blender. I'm making myself some sweet potato pie. I promised to take two to church tomorrow night."

"Save me some."

"You suppos' to been here last week, and the week before that and the week before that, to take this niece of yours to the beauty parlor. When you plan on comin'."

"Ma, you know how it is with my schedule. Can't plan anything." Veronica said. Veronica usually tried to help out as much as possible since her stone-cold loser of a sister had dumped her daughter on their mother and ran off with some two-bit hustler. The woman never even bothered to call.

"Well, I can no mo' comb this chile head. You'd better come soon."

"I swear, Ma."

"So, how's my grand babies?"

"They're fine. Ma, you should hear Jenny sing. She's got some pipes on her."

"She got that from me. You should bring them on over to church. She ain't too young to start singin' with the choir. And what about that big head boy, Gerald?"

"He's doing fine, too."

"Good. Now Ronny, when is you coming over here for real?"

"I'll come after work tomorrow."

"What's wrong with right now?"

"I've gotta go see my lawyer," she lied.

"What you seein' one of them, thieves for at this time a night? It's eight o'clock."

"Randolph and I are getting divorced."

"Lawd, have Mercy! What did you say? Why in heaven's name would you do some foolishness like that? They ain't no better man out there than Randolph. What he done? Keepin' some woman on the side? I can understand that. You ain't never home."

"Ma! Why does it have to be my fault?"

"'Cause you don't know what it's like to be a good wife. You put everything else before your family. Randolph wouldn't hurt a fly, and he's put up with your foolishness for eighteen years. Why you wanna go get no divorce?"

"Actually, *Mother,* he is the one who asked for a divorce. I suppose he's tired of having me supporting him." Veronica said bitterly.

"Shut up with your stupid self. He works harder than you! He's raising two wonderful chillen'. Like I raised you. Don't think it was you alone, girl, who delivered you from the Southside. Not only that, the man's gifted. He gonna be somebody someday, mark my word. That book business ain't like delivering babies and getting paid by the insurance company. He's up against a lot to write them books and get them published. You ain't been bothering him, have you?"

"I swear I don't know why you called. Randolph might as well be your child rather than me."

"Now you know there ain't no truth to that. I *loves* you both equally, but baby girl, you is making a mistake."

"Fine, Ma."

"Veronica, you knows, I tell you like it is."

"Yeah, Ma. I can always count on you. I'll see you tomorrow." There was heavy sarcasm in her voice.

Veronica adored her mother, but the woman was too frank. Tongue dipped in arsenic and wagging all the time, unfortunately, spoke words of wisdom. She didn't want to hear any wisdom today though she was acutely aware her practical side and cut-to-the-chase attitude came from her mother. Right now, Veronica wished she'd been more like her father. A math whiz. As his name aptly suggested, Able Johnson was a stable and steady man who always made good choices. A laborer all his life, even in the face of survival, he had never given up on his dream to become an accountant. Finally, when he retired from the Wrigley plant, Able went back to school. "That man is one idiot," her mother had said when he announced his decision, but it was she, in the first row at his graduation, who had grinned like a Cheshire cat when her husband walked across the stage to get his diploma. "I always said that man was gonna be somebody," she'd piped.

"Yeah, Ma. We know," the children had echoed. Veronica only hoped she'd inherited her father's ability to stick something out to the end.

CHAPTER TWENTY-TWO

AT EIGHT O'CLOCK, not a minute before or after, Melody's room phone rang. "A Mr. Bell is in the lobby," the front desk informed her. Melody took one last look at herself, grabbed her purse, and headed for the door. She was nervous but knew she looked fabulous. She darn well hoped so after spending the entire afternoon shopping for the little black dress tastefully hugging her sleek body. Melody spun around one last time. *It's okay, I think, not too tight and not too loose. Enough cleavage to show off my enticing bosom and maybe get a rise out of Charles Bell. Go on. Go on.* With only a few hours to make a good impression, it was an all or nothing attempt to woo Charles, for what only God could tell. But as they say, love rules. Melody, convinced that these strange behaviors were all due to a mid-life crisis, vowed to study the malady on her return to Chicago.

"Mr. Bell," Melody's golden smile accompanied by a demure voice brushed the air as daintily as her outstretched hand.

"Mr. Bell? You're not going to call me that all evening, are you? As long as you can deliver what we asked for, our business will be concluded. So, please, call me Charles." He took her by the hand and spun her around. "You look breathtaking."

Bold and riveting, the above-the-knee black dress tailored to her body revealed enough to pique the imagination but not too much to incite uncontrollable passion.

"Thank you." Melody genuinely blushed. This femme allure stuff was giving her a right headache. Will one night of passionate lovemaking put her midlife crisis nonsense to rest? She damn well hopes so because this damsel shit was a right pain in the ass. She'd read somewhere if you are thirsty, drink and be done with it, but this was too much work.

Charles stared flatteringly at Melody as a deep sigh sagged his shoulders. The woman took his breath away. Exquisite beyond words. Statuesque, her large, languid, expressive, but sad black eyes, met his stare briefly before fluttering to the ground. As she took her place by his side, she was erect, sensual, and proud. His heart drummed a rhythm of desire, and he was acutely aware that at his side was where Melody Adams belonged.

"Charles, you look rather dashing yourself." She smoldered him with a down-turned glance before casting a crimson puckered smile at him. He held the door, and together they walked outside. Her black hair brushed away from her face, danced and gleamed under the streetlight. Charles swore she was the most enchanting woman he'd ever met. Instinctively he reached for her hand, which curled and interlaced with his as he led the way to a black Mini convertible. Melody was not too surprised at his choice. Everything was different about Mr. Bell.

The evening had cooled to a comfortable sixty-five, a slight mist casting its spell of enchantment. There was something magical about the dusk, more than the beauty of the weather, and suddenly Melody knew her life was about to change. Charles Bell represented the thawing of a very long, lonely, and cold winter.

"I can put the roof up, but it's such a nice night. Do you mind? I know ladies don't like their do's ruffled."

"Oh, no. I'd love to have the top down," Melody downright lied. Demurely, she untied the scarf hooked to her bag and tied it over her hair. "This is what one would call a perfect evening for a convertible ride."

"I'm going to miss this weather, all right. I wasn't much for the windy city. Chicago is for Eskimos." Charles faked a shiver.

"Almost killed me when I first got there. But you'll soon adjust," Melody consoled.

"Where did you come from?"

"This side of the world. Charles," Melody's voice cautioned, not alarmingly but firm, "you're about to go through a red light."

"Fasten your seat belt," he instructed as he screeched to a halt. "Sorry. I'm in a dream here. I'd better pay attention to the road instead of you. You're doing strange things to me, Miss Adams."

"Why, Mr. Bell? Do you hear chimes?" *Oh my God, where did that come from?*

"You bet. But you can ring my bell anytime."

Melody flushed. Now he sounded like Veronica. She felt like the lead character in a movie.

"I chose a Creole restaurant in the Gas Lamp district. Closest thing I could find to crawfish on the Bayou. Is that okay with you?"

"I love Creole food," Melody said. Another lie. She hated Creole food. *He must be from Louisiana. No accent, though.*

"You know something, Miss Adams. I think we're hitting it off. Don't you?"

I hope so, Melody wanted to say. *I sincerely hope so.* Instead, she said. "It's my turn to ask. Are you going to call me Miss Adams all evening?"

The restaurant was a short drive. Charles pulled the car to the valet stand and was by her door in a flash, opening it! As she got out, he moved to her left and held her by the elbow as they climbed the short flight of stairs to the restaurant. Their table was on the balcony, overlooking the pier. Even a picture couldn't do the scene justice. Was this man for real? Romantic, thoughtful, handsome, and successful? It just didn't add up. If he turned out to be a jerk, this was the perfect place to knock him into the water. Somehow, she knew that wouldn't be necessary.

"So," he said when they were seated, "How long have you been with Comtech?"

"Twenty-two years."

"No, kidding! You don't look that old at all. That's wonderful." She smiled engagingly. "And you?"

"Sixteen years. I started the company then. It seems like only yesterday, but it also seems like a lifetime."

"I knew that, didn't I? In the real world, it was only yesterday, but for technology companies, it does spell a lifetime. Why are you ready to get out of such a profitable situation?"

"I don't want to, but I have no choice. Or maybe I'm looking for an excuse. But mine is, both my parents are getting on in age and need my help. I'm an only child, and it's time to give back. I've gotten a lot from this life I wouldn't have without them."

Melody was so impressed she almost choked on her saliva. "You mean you're selling to go look after your parents?" She said incredulously. "Why not just take a leave of absence or hire some home care help?"

"There are people to help out, but I wouldn't dream of putting them in a nursing home or anything like that. I believe there is nothing like a child's love when parents become older. My parents are the best of the best. And if I can't take a little time out to help them, I'm not much of the man they raised."

"Charles, this is unbelievably good of you." Melody felt sorrow about the state of her own family. "Why not just move for a while and have a virtual office?"

"I thought about that. I've been lucky so far, and there is no point in being greedy. Thanks to you, I dare say I won't be a pauper after this deal. After my parents are stable, I can start something else. If I did it once, I can do it again."

"Charles, that's impressive. I'm awed."

"Oh, you're modest. I'm sure you would do the same for your parents if necessary. There aren't too many of you around, Melody, so they must have raised you exceptionally well."

"Yes. I suppose," Melody said softly, her guilt threatening to spill out. Quickly, she shrugged off the moment. There was no time for remorse. She had done what was necessary to survive.

"My parents' case is special," Charles continued, "My father has terminal cancer, and my mother is getting senile. You see, I wasn't born until my mom was forty and my dad forty-two."

Melody had pegged him, early to mid-forties. That means his parents were getting on in age.

"But there has to be a way." Melody pressed.

"There is always a way, Melody. When I started the company, it was never to sell. I wanted to keep it until I had someone to pass it on. Start a generational thing, you know. But Microtech took all the time I had, and I have sacrificed a lot for its success."

"Such as?" Melody asked. She saw before her only a life of outstanding accomplishments.

"A wife and children. That's a big enough price, isn't it?"

"That depends." Melody was ecstatic to learn for sure he wasn't married. She could take care of the marriage part, but hell, he wanted children, and she was already forty-two! Then she calmed down, remembering his mother had been forty when she gave birth to him. She'd better propose tonight! "Marriage is quite a rocky road."

"So, I've heard."

"It's hard for me to imagine women letting you slip through their fingers. But Charles, it's not too late to have either of your wishes. You're young, handsome, and, might I add, quite a wealthy man. A catch, as they say."

"Really?" He profiled. "How handsome?"

"Quite." Melody slapped him playfully. "Let me take a picture and show you." "Romance is one of the things I'll be paying closer attention to. I suppose if it had happened before, I wouldn't have been opposed to it, but most of the women in my life were career oriented. If you mentioned children to them, they got spastic. I want to be with a mature, focused, maternal woman who knows how to love."

Melody was beside herself. Any minute now, if this guy said he loved the Sunday crossword puzzle, she'd propose. "Love? What's love? Does anyone understand love these days?"

"Love is a feeling that shows itself in everyday life. Love understands imperfection."

"Imperfection?"

"Of course. Why would the perfect need love? They already love only themselves. No room for anyone else."

Melody twisted her napkin. Over and out. It was too good to be true. She hated imperfection. Melody snapped back to reality. The woman with studied grace and daily caution was back. They were the exact opposite of each other. Cordially, she said, "Where are your parents, Charles?"

"Chicago. That's where I was born."

That's it. Christ almighty, it was a sign if she ever saw one. But why now? Hadn't she given everything to a life of deceit? Hadn't her pact been enough? Why was she being punished again after so many years of sacrifice? How could she tell this wonderful man before her that she'd worked like a dog to reshape every imperfection of being having been born on the wrong side of the tracks? That the thought of imperfection spiraled her into a dark abyss?

"Why the silence?" Charles looked curiously at Melody. She had gone to another place.

"I was just thinking that you had to be kidding?"

"Nope. That's kind of why I took a second look at Comtech. A geographic allegiance, so to speak. What about you?"

Panic. "As I said, I'm from these parts. Los Angeles. I went to undergrad at Stanford and then grad school at Northwestern. That's how I ended up in Chicago, and I just sort of stayed when I was done."

"Yes, I know about your schooling, remember. I bet you miss being around your family. It was hard for me to leave, but Silicon Valley was where I had to make my move. I figured if I could make it big before my parents got too old, I could spend their later years with them."

Melody couldn't do the family bit. How would she tell him about the Demon of Darkness called the ghetto, where empty lives could only find release from the discarded liquor bottles or at the end of a crack tube? How could she tell him her brother's and sister's lives were buried under the crack and heroin addiction debris? Or that in the face of such hopelessness, alcoholism had plagued her father. Too much at stake here. She was not ready to tell him anything about her estranged, dysfunctional family, so she steered the conversation in a different direction. "So, where did you go to school?"

"MIT. Both undergrad and grad. I loved Boston."

"And how did you get into business?"

"My dad always wanted to own a business. He used to tinker in the garage with all kinds of things. By the time he retired, he had some thirty patents for his inventions. He was an engineer at IBM. Back then, Black folks were shoeshine boys, so you can imagine how bright he had to have been to get into MIT. He worked all his life at IBM and saved all his money so I could live his dream. I wasn't a bad tinkerer myself. When I graduated, I went to work for Intel and then AT&T. Armed with all the knowledge I needed in a practical world, I took my show on the road. And as they say, the rest is history. My only regret is I couldn't sell to a Black firm, but there aren't any big enough to afford us."

"Any ideas what you'll do after this?"

"I had a mind to bring my father's inventions out of the chest. He had some pretty good stuff."

The waiter, who had been hovering, looked impatiently in their direction. They couldn't believe conversation came so easily and that they'd hit it off so well.

"I think we should order," Charles whispered, leaning his head toward the waiter.

They ended up talking all night. Not only at the restaurant but at the jazz club and then on the way home.

"I don't seem to want to leave. May I come up? Don't worry; I only want to see how Microtech treats our guests."

Melody was powerless to stop her feeling of admiration. She felt at peace with Charles Bell. Being with him was how she had imagined life with a man. Effortless. Obediently she handed him the key. The worst part of this whole and absolutely ridiculous situation was she did not mind him being in charge. Inside her, a little voice kept reassuring that acquiescing her power to Charles would not be so bad. He wouldn't abuse the vulnerability of her love.

"I don't have anything to offer you." Melody couldn't think. She was speaking about herself.

"Of course, you do. That refrigerator is stacked with over-priced champagne and vodka. You name it. Go check around and I'll provide the ambiance." He switched on the radio.

Melody kicked off her shoes and padded to the refrigerator. It was packed with more than alcohol. It had delectable goodies, an insult to her toned body. Nevertheless, she emptied the bottle of Macadamia nuts into a bowl and set them on the coffee table. Pouring two glasses of champagne, she handed one to Charles. On the radio, Marvin Gaye was crooning *Let's Get It On*. Charles rested his glass and took her by the hand.

"Shall we dance?"

Moving into his arms with ease, Melody felt a belonging. Charles pulled her close, his narrow hips pressing against hers, she resting her cheek in the cradle of his neck. He curled his arms around her waist pulling her even closer as Marvin Gaye's smooth and sexy voice crooned, Get it One

They danced around the room and waited until the next song came on and danced some more. Melody felt it. Her life was morphing right in front of her, and as the song changed, to Etta James *At last*, She knew serendipity had played its ace card.

When Charles finally had to leave, it took every ounce of Melody's willpower and restraint not to throw herself at his feet and beg him to stay. Oh God, she thought in desperation, *such were the follies of higher love.*

CHAPTER TWENTY-THREE

THE EMERGENCY meeting of the Trinity would live up to the reputation of the number three. Far too emotionally vulnerable to be with a couple of soul-searching women, Melody had tried every excuse to cancel, but neither of the other women would let her off the hook. She wasn't up to this nonsense gathering, especially now. What she needed was quiet time to quell this lunacy that had overtaken her mind. Ah well, best to get the day started. Melody bundled up against the cold morning.

It was the middle of March, the dead of winter. A walk along the shore where everything was frozen into stillness was sure to put life into perspective and, in the process, return her heart to its rightful place. Melody slipped into a fur-lined, full-length coat and matching hat. Sinking her sock-clad feet into fur booths, she stuffed a thick scarf and gloves into her left pocket and left the apartment.

Under the white, heavy cold sky, Melody felt alone. She needed someone, other than her caged heart, to talk to—someone who would tell her how foolish she'd been, but she wasn't ready for the frankness of the Trinity. Something in her had changed from the moment the plane landed in Chicago. Deep regret met her at the door, and she was keenly aware the fairytale romance and the happily ever-after fantasy, now wreaking havoc in her head, had to end. She decided Charles Bell was a dangerous man. The thought of anyone getting close enough to get a whiff of her dysfunctional life petrified her. Rendezvousing with Charles had been a mistake. *But Everyone makes mistakes,* she consoled, pulling the coat closer around her body.

Pensively, she sat on a bench, looking out over the frozen water. In another month, the edges of the lake would begin to soften. Spring was hiding somewhere just beyond, ready to take its rightful place a few weeks from now. Melody heaved loudly, allowing her usually erect shoulders to slump. *The key to mistakes is simply to correct them, and that was what had to be done. But how would she handle the thoughts of Charles ambushing her without warning?*

"You scoundrel." She said softly into the wind. You unscrupulous knave. *What else could you want from me? Haven't I paid a handsome price in exchange for my life? If you must continue to extract your pound of flesh, why not choose a different punishment for me? One that I can understand,* Melody wanted to take back the IOU she'd made with the devil for her life of material success. "Can I," she whispered?

The cruel answer was the replay of her incredible night with Charles. Remembering felt like tumbling into a bottomless, dark abyss, yet powerless to stop the free fall. Light snow began to blow against her cheek. Never in this life had she expected to find a Charles Bell. Excruciating pain jabbed at her heart. Was she silly enough to think the devil might have forgotten its bargain? The likelihood of such a love would mean payment would now be due in full. The free-fall into mania—the other side of romantic love was nothing she wanted to experience. Melody, with utmost regret, knew rejecting Charles was not an option; it was survival. *You damnable man. You're wonderful and the man of my dreams, but I can't have you. You see, I already belong to someone else. I have traded love for all I now have…, please, understand.* She buried her face in her hands. How could her heart have betrayed her head so completely? Failed her one moment of weakness.

Determined their togetherness had ended that very night, Melody turned in the direction of home. As realization informed, her only romance in ten years was over before it had started. Steeling herself as she'd done so many times in her life, Melody left the park, the remnants of useless emotions buried. It was the only way to soldier on. In San Francisco, she had felt like a young girl bathing in the warmth of first love, breathing in vital elements to revive a life too long dead. For a split second, wrapped in Charles's arms, life was no longer in monochrome but in the most radiant technicolor. Wakening up in the comfort of his arm had been life-giving. *You'll have to forget,* Melody advised her psyche.

Too many emotions, in too short a time, were giving her vertigo. Melody pulled the collar of her coat up against her ears and hurriedly made her way home.

The phone in her pocket vibrated.

"Are you bundled up?"

"Excuse me." She said aloud.

And as if he heard her, his next text was: "I know you're out trying to clear your head and figure out what happened. Since I'm not there to warm you up, just make sure you're bundled up when you go outside. Don't think too much about us because it's not something you can control. It just is."

Melody did not answer the text, instead, dropped the phone into her pocket.

Exquisite flowers, a Hallmark card, and a return ticket to San Francisco for a weekend greeted her on her arrival at the office. Tugging relentlessly at her resolve was hope—the belief that anything is possible and that if you believe it enough, it might come true. Hope the last emotion of a dying person.

"Angel," Melody buzzed her secretary, "Please send a thank you note to Microtech for the flowers."

"Will do, Miss Adams. Anyone in particular?"

"No. Just the staff. Also, re-confirm lunch reservations at Morels for noon. Three people?" As much as Melody wished she could share her feelings, the thought of the confounded meeting gave her hives and the fear that they, too, would find out she was an imposter was more than she could handle. Melody passed a hand across her blurry eyes. She was falling apart. The trilling phone saved her some brain cells.

"Hey, hey, hey lady. What time is lunch? The Trinity needs some Eucharist."

"Noon. I'll call back if there's a change of plans, but as of now, it's at Morels."

"Better not change any plans. We need to meet. I know I definitely need to," Veronica confessed.

"Since when? I've been trying to find you a lot lately. Where have you been?"

"Girl, I have to tell you later. I'm looking forward to seeing you at noon."

"Can you come a little early? I'd like a word before April gets there." Maybe she could unburden a little on Veronica but definitely not with April there.

"Melody, stop it! We're friends. April is one of us, Melody. What will it be, Miss Pain-in-the-Ass, friendship, or competition as always? You know competition is a testosterone thing, don't you? Let's not do that to each other."

"It's not that; it's just that...."

"Melody! Friends are friends."

"See you at noon."

"That's a girl."

Veronica was at the restaurant when Melody arrived. She looked sad and withdrawn until the moment she said, "Hey, girlfriend."

"Hey, Vee."

"I hope you're glowing on the inside too, 'cause you look great to me today." Veronica smiled mischievously.

"Lower your voice." Melody looked nervously around the room.

"Girl paleeeze. Don't make me hit you today. How can you be in a bad mood after falling in love at first sight?"

Melody sat down. Vee's deep, gravelly, Eartha Kitt-type voice was floating over the restaurant. "Veronica, your voice travels."

"So. The problem is you care too much about what other people think. I am talking in my normal voice. It's the one God gave me."

"But could you lower it a bit?"

"No. I am not going to be whispering all through lunch."

"Okay but try."

"The only people who might hear me is the table over there. Do you know them?"

"No. But...."

"All right then."

"Why do you look so tired, anyway?"

"Didn't sleep much."

"I thought you might be overworked, but I knew you were fine as soon as you opened your mouth."

"The face of a clown, my dear. I loved the circus when I was a kid. Learned how to hide everything under a mask."

"Is something wrong? Really?"

"There's always something wrong. That's life, right?"

"Why are you so dressed up today?"

Veronica, who had the most enviable chestnut complexion, smooth as a baby's bottom, looked dapper in an aqua tropic-dotted silk dress as dainty as a gossamer's wing and most inappropriate for the inclement weather. More surprising was, her hair had been styled, and beneath the tiredness, her flawless skin glowed with makeup! Until a couple of months ago, as long as Melody had known Veronica, the woman had never worn makeup, nail polish, high heels, or her hair out of a ponytail. Something crazy was going on with her. Once Melody had asked what she did to her face to have such a flawless complexion and got the answer, "go to sleep." Veronica was a wisecracker that way. Five feet-seven inches, Veronica was graceful with a generous helping of hips and a tight rump she called her calling card. "Men love them," she often joked. Which "men" was anyone's guess since Veronica had been married to her childhood sweetheart for eighteen years.

"Hi there." April sidled up to the table, feigning joy. "Don't you look fab?" She eyed Veronica's new look.

"Didn't think I could clean up, huh? Well, I'm tired of you and Melody always looking like some prize models and me looking frumpy, so I'm changing my attitude and my look. What do you think of that?"

"You'll be the next Tyra Banks." April pulled out a chair.

"Hell no! That girl looks like a rail. *I* will be the next *new* thing everybody wants to look like." Veronica's unusual smoky voice carried long distances, and Melody could see nearby patrons smiling. "We were just about to order drinks. What will you have?" Veronica waved the waitress over.

"Martini. Maybe two." April said.

"Two Martinis? I'm scared of you." Veronica placed their orders.

"Rough week. So, did I interrupt something? You two looked deep in conversation." April's spirit was flat.

Everyone seemed out of sorts.

"Naw. It's a long shot, but I was just trying to find out if dumb butt here *shuttuped* this guy she met in San Francisco, but she is more concerned about the timbre of my voice." Veronica said.

"What guy?" April looked from one woman to the next.

"Wound tight here called me from San Fran and said, 'as God is her witness….'"

"Veronica, shush."

"How can you tell a grown woman to shush? You are rude and out of order."

"Do you want the entire restaurant to hear my business?"

"What business? You have no business if you didn't *shtupped* the guy. Stop changing the subject and answer the question?"

"I'm not trying to change any subject."

"Girls. Girls. You sound like barnyard hens." April informed.

"Tell that to Miss-Goody-two-shoe. Lighten up sometimes." Veronica rebutted.

"All this because I don't want to answer your nosy question?" Melody huffed.

"Why are you so secretive anyway?"

"This is pretty pathetic." April sipped her Martini.

"I was only asking a simple question, especially when this woman called in the middle of my surgery to tell me she was in love."

"Veronica, it's not what you asked; it's how you asked. Let me try. Melody, Veronica wants to know if you made beautiful musak with the nice gentleman out west." April grinned.

A deep tint dimpled Melody's face. "I'm …."

"You're going to answer that?" Veronica interrupted. "I don't believe this."

"I was going to say if you'd let me finish that I'm not answering any questions about the man out west."

"That's 'cause he probably wouldn't go near your polar behind." Veronica snapped.

"Lower your voice, would you?"

"Why? Who here knows you personally?" Veronica got louder, annoyance speckling her voice.

"Okay, you two. Cut it out. This is supposed to be a spirit-lifting session. We are supposed to be helping each other remember, not ripping each other apart. These meetings are our safe harbor from the cruel world."

Melody never knew Veronica to get brusque.

"You're touchy today. Is something wrong? Did you and Randolph have another fight?" Melody asked.

"Let's not start with Randolph." Veronica hardly got that out before she said. "You wouldn't believe what that sonofabitch did. He filed for a divorce. Do you know what he wants? He wants the house, alimony, custody of the children and child support. Now tell me if you've ever heard some shit like that. I swear, the gigolo is smokin' rocks. Serves me right. That's what I get for marrying a bum."

"Oh my God, Veronica, why didn't you tell me on the phone?"

"I wanted to. Believe me, but you sounded so happy. I swear I don't know why life has to be so complicated. Why can't we all live our lives without having to answer to others."

"Because life doesn't happen in a vacuum. Everything we do affects everything else in the world, and that's a right pain-in-the-butt if I've ever felt one." April sighed. "Why is he filing for a divorce?"

"How the hell should I know?"

April took a swig of Martini and eyed Veronica. "I'm going to file for a divorce," she pulled up her sleeve to show a bruise on her arm. She needed honesty today. The Trinity was all she had.

"What happened to you?" Melody asked.

"Sam. We had a nasty fight last night. He hit me and tried to force himself on me."

"Hit you?" Melody was agog.

"Hit and tried to rape you?" Veronica echoed.

"Can you rape your wife?" April asked.

"Oh, Jesus?" Veronica said. "His ass can go to jail for some shit like that. Are you going to press charges?"

"No. I couldn't do that. I don't know what came over him. He's never done anything like this before. I think my career threatens him."

"Oh, Lord. So now what?" Veronica asked.

Melody cast a look of disbelief at the young woman on her left. The poor girl had no idea what the real world was like. How did she think the ghetto got so overcrowded? Heck, in the ghetto, people fought nightly and then screwed their brains out to forget the pain. Next thing, there were twelve angry children from two angry parents to terrorize the neighborhood—the burden of the elite. So, book smart and clever, yet so unwise.

"I don't know. I honestly don't know." April sighed.

Veronica put a consoling arm around April's shoulder. "How can we help?"

"Help." Melody chortled. "Which of us here is better off than the other?" Melody said sarcastically. "In case you haven't noticed, we're all up shit's creek without a paddle. You don't know why your husband is asking for a divorce. I can't stop having hot flashes and minute-by-minute personality changes, and April here can't figure out if she's been raped!"

"Are you blaming me for feeling stifled in a suffocating marriage? For trying to get some breathing room?" Veronica felt slighted.

"Not blaming, per se, but you're the one disrupting your happy home. You're the one asking for change. I was simply pointing out a reason for Randolph's decision."

"Who asked you to point out anything, Melody Adams? What makes you think I need your damn permission to live my life? How can a person like you even feel at liberty to give advice? Do you have a life? How would you know what it feels like to be trapped? Like a caged animal. What would you know about that Melody ice cube? You won't even allow yourself to feel. At least I'm taking chances and experiencing life. You're so damn self-absorbed, so disconnected from your own life, you have no life at all. You should be glad to have hot flashes. Something needs to melt your staid behind. I have no problem if self-preservation and low risk are how you want to spend your life, but don't you judge me. Do you hear me!" Veronica's defenses got the better of her.

Melody visibly shrunk from Veronica's attack, folding her arms to protect herself in the line of fire. She was lost to such emotions. She had to disengage. Emotions like determination and deception were in her memory bank, but emotional confessions were not in her realm of learned behavior.

The outburst detonated all conversation. Veronica gulped her gin and tonic; April examined her fingernails repeatedly, chugging Martini; and Melody, jiggled the ice in her glass of Bailey's on the rocks. Somehow in the heat of the moment, the women knew their emotional venting and honesty had created a new bond.

"Randolph wants a divorce because I'm having an affair," Veronica said quietly, "and I can't seem to stop. Beats me how I even got there. I'm becoming someone I despise, and I can do nothing about it." Veronica had a faraway look in her eyes. "From the time I was eight, I mapped every journey of my life. Planned it to a tee. Now, here I am, recklessly throwing it all away, and you know what, I don't care. Can you believe I called my husband a gigolo?" The tremor in Veronica's voice was unusual. "Randolph doesn't have a control gene in his body. He is the fantasy-perfect husband." She continued, "sometimes, we women kid ourselves that we want sensitive, caring men. We don't. What we want are strong, controlling, ambitious and successful men. The equality bit we spout is just a notion. I'm a prime example. I'm ashamed my husband has nothing important to show for his life other than being a struggling writer, which amounts to a househusband. At social functions, when they ask him what he does, I cringe. He's a great guy, the best father and husband, but it's not enough for me anymore? My success demands more. If I have the ideal life that so many envy, then tell me why I'm having an affair with a man ten years my junior?"

"Veronica, why?" Melody said, a plea clearly in her voice.

"That's what I just asked," Veronica said solemnly.

"But you have to have an idea." Melody insisted.

"With Tony, I can share my accomplishments without feeling guilty about leaving him behind. We're intellectually and professionally matched. I don't feel pity for him. All I feel is the excitement, the rush, the desire my life needs. I've never felt the excitement or the possibilities of love as I do with Tony. I feel alive."

"What are you doing?" Melody snapped. "Veronica! Where is your common sense? Be very careful about the choices you're making. They can start a spiral that will leave you at the bottom of the heap. Veronica! You have two children and a husband. Believe me, sometimes what's too good is never good for us."

Melody felt unexpectedly choked up. For a second, Veronica thought she was going to cry. Melody's eyes had widened, and tears clung to her lids—but just as suddenly as they appeared, they disappeared, replaced by her usual composure. Melody moved her head to one side, trying to clear away blurry vision and the funny feeling in her head. All this damn girl talk was for the birds. She's such an idiot to keep coming to these meetings. To be frank, she would rather not be a part of the "Holy Trinity." Too much togetherness for her. She didn't need a Trinity. She had integrated her pain a long time ago, and apart from dealing with her mid-life crisis, she wasn't about to exhale. How on earth could April, who she so aspired to be, have problems? How could Veronica, whose marriage she secretly envied, be so naïve? In all honesty, Melody was beginning to feel a real kinship and renewed respect for April, who, even in a state of emotional frailty, was braver than she could ever be. To bare her most vulnerable soul, in Melody's eyes, made her a giant. It takes a brave person indeed to expose their innermost fears.

April looked at Veronica. Melody slumped in her chair. Deep within her soul, Melody was trembling. These kinds of emotions would test her mettle. Melody shifted uncomfortably in her chair. Until this damn group, she never dealt with shit like this. She had nothing to share. Why would she even contemplate trusting these women with her emotions? She wouldn't trust a soul in this life. Where the heck did it get people? She trusted her Mama, and where did that get her? Melody looked at her vibrating phone. "I see you have fallen for me completely, no answer?" Melody hit the delete button.

That day they transcended competition and career and entered the realm of friendship.

"Do you want to stop?" April said softly to Veronica.

"I don't know. I feel so much lust for Tony, but I love my family more than anything. I'm sorry," Veronica said, smiling weakly. "Maybe I should have saved this for Eve."

"I'm sorry too," April said. "I didn't mean to start this mess."

Melody, unable to deal with Veronica's confession, turned to April, "What do you think you might do about your situation?" Melody's concern was genuine.

"I thought of filing for a divorce. Last night, I was sure of it. Today, I'm not so sure anymore. It's sick to think a woman like me wouldn't walk from a situation like this, but I love Sam. I'm trying to be level-headed, but who knows what he'll do in the future now he has opened that door. Sam came from an abusive home."

"Acorns don't fall too far from the tree." Melody cautioned. "Physical violence is out of our league. Maybe you and Sam should both see a therapist."

"What would you do in a situation like this, Melody?" April asked.

"I'd leave him before God got the news," Melody scoffed. "Men! They say they want independent, strong, and striving women, but when you start climbing the ladder, they find a way to pull the rug out from under you. If you agree with their power-striping ploy, in the name of love, they knock you up and keep you in the kitchen barefoot and pregnant; then you can have their undying love. If not, you'd better watch out. Men are so insecure."

"It's okay. Don't work yourself into a tizzy." Veronica patted Melody's hand before turning to April. "So, do you believe Melody is right about the power struggle?"

"Maybe unconsciously. Sam is quite successful. My success shouldn't threaten him, but who knows."

"You can rationalize all you want, but men will always try to dominate women with anything they perceive they can hold over their heads. It's in their nature. And to make it worse, they have the nerve to make you feel it's your problem. I swear every woman's problem is a man." Melody shook her head in disgust.

"I now know why I don't have one. I couldn't take the burden of relationships. Plus, if I have to bring home the bacon and have it scoffed off by a greedy pig who tries to tell me how to live my life, I will most likely commit murder."

"So, what are you gonna do about the guy whose name is stamped on your forehead?" Veronica deadpanned.

"I'm gonna keep coming to these sistah meetings so I can be reminded why I should keep away from him." Melody laughed.

Veronica was glad to get the conversation on lighter grounds. "Before you bury the man for good, can we ask if you *shuttuped* this miraculous guy?"

"No! You may not. But I'll tell you one thing. I was very attracted to Charles. I'm not kidding. My name was indeed stamped on his forehead and his on mine, but I'm no fool. He is too good to be true." That's as much as Melody could share.

"Uh-huh. Well, you know what they say." April spun one of Melody's tired expressions. "When something is too good to be true, it usually is."

"So, Charles was too good to be true, huh?" Veronica pushed the envelope. "Well, it's better you didn't *shtupped* the guy. Now you'll never know if he was all you wanted or not."

"What? Where are you going with this?" Melody's brows knitted in confusion.

"What if the man only had a one inch?"

"A one inch?" April interrupted understanding the drill. "Nah. How about making it a tickler."

Even Melody had to laugh at the ridiculous turn the conversation had taken. "Do you people ever think of anything other than the reproductive anatomy?"

"I'm a doctor. A coochie doctor at that. What else do you want me to think about?" Veronica wiped tears from her eyes with the table napkin.

"How about Randolph over there?" Melody's smile disappeared.

"Where?" Veronica's head spun around like Linda Blair's in *The Exorcist.*

"Veronica. Do you have to be so obvious? Wait a moment; he's looking in this direction. He's four tables to the left with a blond woman."

Veronica twisted, not just her head this time, but her entire body, to face the direction in which Melody was looking. She was livid, and a funny feeling crept over her. It was the green-eyed monster, jealousy. Jealousy! "Well, I never. I'll be a rat's ass. Damn, that no good louse. I swear. He was probably having an affair before me. He was using my absence as an excuse to ask me for a divorce. I'm going right over there to kick his ass." Veronica balled up her napkin and laid it on the table.

"Please, Veronica. Don't do that. This could be very innocent."

"Like the Virgin Mary."

Just then, Randolph looked up and saw Veronica. Her look ricocheted across the room at full laser speed into his. He whispered something to his companion, eased out of his chair, and strolled over to their table.

"This man's got to be crazy. He'd better not be paying for this meal on my credit card." Veronica said chewing the lettuce so hard puree was forming at the side of her mouth.

"Veronica. Melody, and Madam," he addressed April. "I wouldn't have expected to see you power-women in a place like this."

Veronica was trying hard to control herself. "I would say I'm the one who's surprised to see you here. The blond is paying, I hope?" she said vengefully.

"What does it matter? You'll be paying one way or the other," he spewed acid. "She's my divorce lawyer."

Veronica slumped back in her chair, Melody concentrated very hard on her coffee, and April kept folding and refolding her napkin on her lap. She couldn't bear to see grown folks embarrass themselves. "I have to go powder my nose," Melody tried to excuse herself after a moment of uncomfortable silence.

"No, that's all right. I'm leaving." Randolph turned on his heels.

"Bastard. The man is over the top. I just can't believe him. I'll fix his ass tonight"I'm glad you didn't make a scene." Melody was relieved.

"I swear, I can't understand this. Eighteen years and he's ready to throw in the towel just like that. We're too old to have to deal with all this shit."

"How come all of a sudden, I'm old. I thought you called me a babe in the woods?" April said.

"Problems age one quickly."

CHAPTER TWENTY-FOUR

APRIL WORKED LATE into the evening, as she had done almost every night since the blowout fight with Sam. Though she had forgiven him in her heart, he needed to feel the chill. Maybe she'd thaw out when Spring arrived. Sam had moved into the guestroom, which made avoiding him easy. By the time she usually made it home, Sam would already be asleep, and she'd bolt out the door in the morning before he woke up. She would have the conversation they needed to, but in her time and on her grounds.

After a restless night, Melody found herself again in the park by the lake, watching the sun kiss the night sky before heading to the office. According to the weather report. It was going to be a windy but sunny day in Chicago. Even though she'd been in bed by nine, Melody was exhausted. She sipped the black coffee she'd taken with her as the conversations at lunch the day before played back in her mind. It'd disturbed her a great deal. She'd been completely surprised by April's confession, but she was outdone by Veronica's. The unfortunate thing was it scared her silly, and now no matter what she felt for Charles, she was sure it would never work. Served her right to have lost her composure and control! She should've left San Francisco as scheduled. Given her track record for control, how could she have imagined her evening with Charles would have ended in a hotel bed! Never in her wildest dreams had she envisioned herself so enamored to sleep with a man on a first date. And since meeting Charles, she had come to know discontent all too well.

"Good morning, Ms. Adams." Angel smiled warmly.

"Angel. What is it?" She looked at the quizzical look on her assistant's face.

"Enchanted Gardens just delivered something for you. A basket of delectables." And what a basket it is. It's from Microtech again. A Mr. Bell in particular."

"How nice. Put it in the lunchroom."

Unfortunately, the old take charge Melody had a hard time surfacing all morning. She was flat, depressed and wanted to be alone. She didn't want a life of more problems, and from what she gathered from the other members of the Trinity, men came with problems.

Melody glanced at her watch. How could it be twelve-fifteen already? Feeling the need to cocoon herself from the world, she considered canceling her hair appointment. Duty or self-imposed neurosis, however, compelled her to gather her belongings and make her exit. Chantel would probably cheer her up anyway.

"Angel," Melody said on her way out, "Would you send another thank you note to Microtech?"

"To Mr. Bell?"

"No. Just to the executive staff. Also, call April Summers and let her know the next Microtech meeting is scheduled for three o'clock p.m. next Wednesday."

"Yes, Ms. Adams."

"I hope you liked the basket. Melody, you can't avoid me. Don't be a wuss."

The text made her dander go way up. Melody's fingers flew across the iPhone. "You are so full of yourself! What makes you think you can just text me when you feel like it. We're not that kind of friends."

"We aren't. Well, let's change that."

OH, JESUSSSSS! Melody threw the phone in her bag.

Instead of returning from her hair appointment, Melody found herself driving toward Eve's office. A heavy burden weighed her down. Trinity or not, there were things only Eve could hear. Damn the confounded Trinity. It was their fault she was having these disturbing memories. With all the emotional sharing and the touchy-feely nonsense in the group, Melody was dredging up more and more unsettling feelings. And now there was Charles Bell. What on earth was wrong with her!

"Come in, Melody." Eve eyed the woman. They had been working together for some time, but Eve never felt she was getting anywhere with Melody.

Melody sat in a single chair rather than on the sofa. She needed to be contained. Mercilessly she was wringing her hand.

"You seem agitated today. Has something unusual happened?"

"Oh, everything is going to pots. I can't keep it together anymore," Melody blurted. Tears clung to her lashes, and a single drop settled under her eye, stubbornly refusing to slide down her flushed cheek.

"Why don't you tell me about it?" Eve soothed.

"It's a long story."

"Comtech can afford to pay me. Come on, Melody. Let's do this."

"Why do you bother with people's issues? They can't be pretty pictures."

"Not all pictures have to be pretty."

"It's even uglier when you start life behind the eight ball." Melody began hesitantly. "I have seen the worst pictures one could ever see. I have seen the streets claim six of my siblings. I've seen the neighborhood girls going to church on Sundays and to the delivery room nine months later. I have seen deep into the eyes of hopelessness."

"Yes." Eve prompted at Melody's hesitation.

"There's a lot you don't know about me. Things are sometimes not what they seem. We all have secrets. We all have to find a way to cope with the life we were given. Some of us embrace or succumb to the tragic life of the streets, and others run away. I chose to run away as far as I could."

"Go on," Eve prompted.

"This is the whole story. I was born in South Central L.A. Walking to school in my neighborhood was an obstacle course to survival. There was so much to distract you. Brothers would show up on the street corners to drink and smoke weed as though it was a nine to five job. Others promised a way out if you'd just deliver this one package to the man in the suburbs. Coming back home every day from the white school with brand new textbooks and fancy gyms was like walking through the gates of the underworld. I was always as determined as I am today, and I wanted more. I saw how those children in the 'burbs lived. I saw the hope in my eyes was simply entitlement in theirs. The only way out was to use the talent inside my head. I remember once when I had a nasty fever, and Mama kept vigil over me, holding a cold compress to my head. I resolved not to surrender to the fever and tried to get up. I kept saying, 'I'm feeling better now, Mama. I need to get up and do my homework.'

'Stay in bed, child,' Mama had implored. 'What makes you think you have to be so perfect all the time?' It's true I was always prissy and strong headed. I was always neat as a pin, too. Not a strand of hair was ever out of place on my head. Mama used to brush my hair every night. One hundred strokes, and then she would tie it tightly with a scarf. The next morning you couldn't tell I had slept on it. And my clothes were always neat and pressed. I was the last of eight siblings. The last hope Mama had. Until I was five, I did everything little girls did except get dirty. Watts was home, and nothing about it had seemed abnormal to me back then."

"When I got older, South-Central L.A. was no picnic. Living in Watts was a hellish nightmare. In reality, a nightmare cripples, destroys, or otherwise disenfranchises any Black kid. Talent and hope were washed away at the end of the empty bottles lining the street. By the time I was ten, my mother's protectiveness had saved me from the streets. When I came to Chicago, I took on a new identity and left Watts far behind. I was glad to leave Watts. The day I left, I vowed never to return. My decision created quite a chasm between my beloved mother and me. The identity I have lived every day since is a fictional life." Melody rocked back in her chair, wiping the corners of her eyes. Her vision was blurred as montages flickered through her mind. Melody remembered the very day she had made up her mind to alter her destiny. Voice little and frightened, she continued. "One day, while playing hop-scotch on the sidewalk, a brand-spankin' new Cadillac pulled up."

'Where is that thiamin' brother of yours?' the gruff man inquired.

"I don't have no thiefin' brother," I'd sassed.

'Don't play with me, girl. Where's Eric.'

"He ain't here. Do you want to speak with my Ma?" Her voice had quivered, and she became frightened, but Eve did not interrupt.

'Nah, we ain't looking for your mammy. We looking for your thiefin' brother.'

"The men were angry and big. But everyone in Watts was angry. As soon as the car left, I ran inside the house and headed for the kitchen, where my mother was always cooking something good.

"Mama." I'd tugged at her skirt. Mama turned around and looked down at me. It was always a loving look, even when the words from her mouth were harsh."

"'How many times do I have to tell you to take off them shoes when you come into my house? You deaf or dumb, chile? Which one?'"

"I hastily ran back to the door and deposited my shoes on the green mat. 'Mama, there were some mean men outside looking for Eric. They said he's a thiefin' brother. Why are they looking for Eric, Ma?'"

"A worried look crossed Mama's face, and she at once stopped chopping onions, wiped her hands on her apron, and hastened over to the window. Mama's apron was like a uniform. She never took it off unless it was on Sunday when she was all dressed up for church, so I knew something was wrong when she took it off.

'Lawd, have mercy.' Mama shook her head. 'Melody, go to your room and do your homework. I'll call you when dinner is ready.'

"I'm done with my work, Mama."

'Do some more.'

"I've read half the dictionary, again," I said indignantly.

'Chile, if you don't belt up and do as you're told, I'm gonna whup your ass.'

"I slept on a cot in my parents' room. That night I was pretending to be asleep.

'That boy don't have long to live. I'm tellin' you. What is you goin' to do 'bout it, Hubert? He won't stay home. He runs them streets every day and every night. Them streets gonna kill him. You hear me? I hear he's selling drugs. God help us, Hubert. I used to be so proud of that boy. So bright. As bright as Melody. Now, this. If he'd done just stick with them books, he could've left out of this rat hole a long time ago.'

"As I listened to Mama weeping, I made up my mind to be everything a mother wished for in her child. To do everything to get my parents out of that bad place that sucks the life out of people. From that night on, I followed my mother like a shadow, and when I wasn't hanging on to my mother's skirt, I was studying my books until my eyes hurt.

Less than a month after the men drove by our home, my brother was shot down in the streets before our house like a common dog. His life extinguished as though he never existed. My heart died watching Mama, who day, by day lost, her hopes and dreams. And as the streets continued to claim six of my siblings in one way or the other, I was more determined than ever to be Mama's hope. I was determined to make her proud. By tenth grade, I was a straight-A student. Mama's eyes brightened with each "A" she read on my report card. There in her eyes was a glimmer of hope. It was tough to have hope in my neighborhood where guns were the norm, teenage girls bore babies, school kids pulled knives on each other for sneakers, and luck was on the other side of the state. But I won.

'I'm so proud of you, baby. You gotta continue to do well in school, my Melody; that's the only way outta here. If not, you'll be like your brothers and sistahs. Please, baby, don't let your Mama down.' Tears had welled in my Mama's eyes.

"I scored 1490 on the SAT and had a perfect grade point average."

'You gonna be somebody,' Mama had said proudly at my high school graduation, and I believed her. I was accepted into

Stanford, Berkeley, UCLA, Princeton, and Yale on scholarship. Mama cried like a baby.

'Now listen here,' Mama wiped her eyes with her frilly Sunday handkerchief. She was wearing her Sunday best to take me to school. 'Don't you come back here pregnant or married after one year? Go all the way to the top and show them, folks, back here getting outta here can be done. Remember baby, as a smart Black woman, you gonna carry a big burden for your entire race.'

"In college, I lost or found my way, depending on how you look at it. That's when I began getting obtuse about the story of my life. Although I never really said so and did nothing to dispel misunderstandings by senior year, everyone thought my lineage was deeply entrenched in the Black bourgeoisie— mother in the Links and father in Boule, the private clubs for elite Blacks. Even I was beginning to believe it. I no longer believed that unless it was a miracle from the hands of God, my circumstances pre-ordained me to a death sentence. I realized then it was education that controlled my destiny and that with education, I could win. By then, you see, I'd figured out the miracle I'd craved didn't come from above. It came from my Ivy League education. I, and not God, was responsible for the outcome of my life. I became a card-carrying member of the 'pull yourself up by the bootstraps' philosophy. Education liberates, I preached. I blamed apathy and poverty on ignorance and when thirteen and fourteen-year-old girls in the neighborhood were getting pregnant, still heeding the words of the pastor every Sunday, I was preaching my sermon. To those who had called me an assimilated cog-negro, cognitive negro, responsible for betraying the motherland, Africa, all I had to say to them was 'show me *your* money.'

"Mama disagreed vehemently. The last time I saw Mama, her body had spoken in a language I'd never seen before. Her words were tainted with anger; her voice was grave but calm and rung of an unspeakable betrayal. 'Careful of the walls you build, chile. They'll shut you in as much as they shut us out. This falseness, this pretense, this person you've become is gonna mess up your mind. Make you an enemy to your people. Do you think nobody here wants to live in this rat hole, Melody? Do you think Black people came to America and said, Jesus, let me go sit in this ghetto and rot? Wake up from all that white brainwashing, girl. This world don't see you. Education or no education. Don't you ever come back into my house 'less you can give thanks from whence you came. It's the ghetto that brung you, girl, and it'll be the place that sets you free. You'd better not forget it.'

Melody swung her arms before her in a crisscrossed pattern, hugging her body tightly and exhaling loudly to revive waning energy. "I felt so betrayed. I'd done what I did for Mama. After that, I did what I had to do to survive," she said calmly.

"Yes. We must all find the best way we know how to deal with such traumas. Melody, many people do worse. Why are you ashamed you chose success?" Eve said softly.

Melody hadn't seen it that way. Not that way at all.

Eve was glad for the breakthrough. Now she could help Melody.

At the office again, Melody did not work for the rest of the afternoon. She just couldn't concentrate. She fiddled with memos Angel had given a week before as well as new notes. Charles Bell had been calling incessantly, leaving every conceivable number, including three cell phone numbers, where he could be reached, and his texts were constant.

Reading the messages repeatedly, Melody picked up the phone ten times, only to put it back in the cradle. She felt relieved, having confided in Eve something she'd locked away for so long. Ever so slightly, a burden had rolled further down her shoulder. Sometimes sharing is hearing, someone once said to her. If she kept working with Eve, maybe she could go home one day. All in good time.

Looking over the messages, again and again, Melody desperately wanted to call Charles. She couldn't without good reason, such as an answer about the merger. She couldn't afford to give him the wrong impression. Tried as she did, memory blazed vividly and with a daring hard to ignore.

It had been a wonderful evening. A spectacular night. An extraordinary night. From the moment Charles walked into the executive dining room, she knew he had altered her life. Why had she not been more cautious? Charles was a testament to men's ability to derail lives, for all she'd done since was sit around all day wondering what it would be like to have him in her life forever.

The profundity of it all was the fleeting familiarity she'd met Charles before. According to Veronica, who had been on a metaphysical trip for all of a month, past-life theory was the explanation. Apparently, they were born as each other's separated half and had been waiting many lifetimes to rediscover and reconnect with each other. Maybe he'd been her twin soul, soul mate, her yin to his yang, because in her, he had created a void she could not explain. Melody could not be moved no matter how often love had reared its prophetic head.

Melody closed her eyes, recalling every single detail of their incredible night together. His perfect lips nuzzling the back of her neck, his dark, crinkling eyes smiling at her, his soft fingers blazing against the small of her back, his strong, muscular legs pressing hard against hers as they danced in total unison. His heart had beaten rhythmically, matching her every throb, and finally, when her resolve had vanished, Charles had cupped her face in his hands, and she had felt every inch of him and had allowed him to take from her everything she had to give. Every detail was crystal clear. She had allowed herself to be drawn into the magic, and now she couldn't forget.

No matter how her mind had fought to stay in control, it had lost the battle to the simple touch of his hands on her bare skin. Lying to Veronica and April was the only way not to admit Charles Bell now owned her, lock, stock, and barrel, but as corny and clichéd as it might be, that's how it was. Melody jumped up from her chair. "Not me, Melody Adams. No one owns me!" Yet her feelings for Charles Bell frightened her; confused her sense of order and control. "Damn the confounded man," Melody said, dropping the phone back in its cradle for the eleventh time.

CHAPTER TWENTY-FIVE

APRIL HAD BEEN mulling over the lunch conversations for days. She wasn't crazy—no one gets a pass on problems. She would do something about hers, starting with her mother, who was a thorn in her side. As soon as she heard Sam's car pull out of the driveway, April quickly got out of bed and peered through the window to ensure he was gone. Hurriedly dressing, she jumped on her speed bike and rode the two miles to her mother's house. By the time she rang the doorbell, her determination to confront Gabriella had wavered.

"April, what are you doing here this early in the morning? Aren't you supposed to be at work?"

"Normally, but Mummy, I have some important matters to discuss with you."

"Well, come in and have coffee. Do you want breakfast?"

"No. I'm fine." April followed her mother to the kitchen. With renewed interest, she looked over the well-appointed, unassuming style of the home, very much like her own. Even her style was a copy of her mother's, and which spoke to the woman's deep influence over her. April accepted the cup of coffee. She needed more than coffee to confront her mother.

"Why do you look so agitated?"

"Mother," April said, tension sliding down her neck. She placed the coffee cup in the saucer on the kitchen table. "I want to talk about me before I lose everything I value."

"I don't understand a single thing you're saying. Who are you losing?"

"I'm talking about you, me, and Sam." April's voice quivered a decibel louder.

"Why are you shouting?"

"Because on this subject, you are deaf. I need you to be open with me right now, Mom, because I think my marriage is falling apart. I have to face a few things about myself to move forward."

"What do you want me to say about your marriage? As far as I'm concerned, it's good riddance to bad rubbish." Gabriella calmly added cream to her coffee.

"Damn it, Mother." April slapped the table. "You are so insensitive."

"I have been this way all my life." Gabriella was curt. "What is it you'd like me to do?"

"I want you to tell me about the hospital and the baby, Mom. Tell me why we never talk about it. Sam wants to have a baby. What reason should I give him why I can't?"

"Is this some kind of joke? Did you and Sam have *another* spat? Is this why you're hysterical?"

"We had a spat, all right. So much of a spat he hit me."

"He didn't!"

"Yes, he did, but Mother, it's not your business. And it's not why I'm here." April said sharply. She shouldn't have blurted that out.

Her mother hurled past her answer as though she hadn't spoken. "When did all this happen?"

"Mummy!" April riled. "Get over it! Husbands and wives have problems they need to work out themselves. I'm sure you know about that. What I want to talk about is family secrets, mother. That's part of the reason why Sam and I are fighting. Because of family secrets."

"Personally, I think his going is a blessing in disguise." Gabriella again ignored April.

"Jesus Christ, Mother. How can you be in such denial? I don't know who is worse, you or Aunt Josephine. Why did I even bother coming here? I'm such a fool," April shrieked.

"April, I told you …."

"Don't start the nonsense again about Sam is not good enough for me. He is Mom. And I love him. It's partly your fault why he's leaving."

"Me? What do you mean me?"

"He thinks you're stuck up, and he thinks you have too much influence over my life. And he thinks I'm just plain crazy. He isn't far off, is he, mother? Not on the crazy part."

"What has gotten into you, April? What is this man doing to your head? What Sam is saying is poppycock. I'm not the one married to him, so what would my being stuck-up have to do with him?"

"Mother, face it. You are not a pleasant person when you don't want to be. And you've never been pleasant to Sam. Why do we sweep everything under the carpet and pretend nothing matters? Pretend our way is the only right way? Why can't we ever talk about anything unpleasant? Like my being in the hospital and the baby?" Like the fact that I'm a Black woman in America, Mother. That makes a difference. This is not Jamaica!" April was not letting her mother off the hook.

"April," Gabriella was visibly agitated. "You didn't tell him about the hospital or the baby, did you?"

"I didn't, Mother but know I wanted to. Sam has a right to know. He has a right."

"That would be very silly. Very silly indeed. Dear, I know you're upset, but this kind of behavior should make you see I was right about Sam. He's not good for you. How could a man beat his wife and then leave, desert her? I told you…."

"What? What, what do you swear?" April began stuttering, getting more hysterical as the moments passed.

"Listen, dear. Take control of yourself. We can talk about the hospital in good time. Why don't you go on home now and get ready for work? Come by this evening, and we'll talk this through."

"Mother, I'm not a kid. I am thirty-two years old. Why do you have to tell me to get ready for work? I'm not leaving until we talk. And if you don't talk to me, I am cutting all ties with you forever! Do you hear me!"

"All right, All right. Let me get dressed and come with you. We don't want to get your Dad involved in this now, do we?" Gabriella went to the stairwell and looked up. He knows nothing about any of this."

John, April's father, wasn't due downstairs for twenty minutes. For the forty years they'd been married, every morning, he locked himself in the soundproof room and blasted classical music for thirty minutes before starting his day. It was an idiosyncrasy she had got used to.

"Coming over is probably not a good idea. Sam already says he goes limp with the three of us in the bed. My work, me, and you. I don't think he could take four."

"He said what?" Gabriella's face went bloodless. "I can't believe he subjects you to such vile language. By God, the man is downright crass. I told you not to marry that—that guttersnipe. Why couldn't you have found a nice Jamaican guy like Noel Brumfield?"

"Mummy," April shouted. "Shut up. Just shut the heck up. You drive me crazy." April threw the coffee cup into the sink, watching it splinter.

Gabriella was speechless. For the first time in her life, she was silent. The time had finally arrived when she would have to deal with April's 'hospitalization.'

"Let me repeat Mummy. If you don't come clean, I am walking out of your life forever. There will be no competition between you and Sam. He will win hands down." April glared at her mother and bolted from the house, slamming the door so hard it bounced back open.

She was frightened. She rode with a vengeance hoping to ward off the closed-in feeling descending on her. April didn't remember much about anything these days. Spinning out of control, she felt the need to imbibe more and more. Sam's constant demands, her mother's high society delusions, and her stress at S&G all intersecting were pushing her over the edge. April felt herself losing control. She was definitely not an alcoholic as Sam like to intimate, but she did turn to her liquor now and then when she needed to forget her troubles. Her anger bubbled up threatening to choke her. When April got back to the house, tears blurred her vision. The door opened before she could turn the handle, and she damn near ran head-on into—

"Get outta my way." She snapped.

An arm enveloped her.

"Sam! What are you doing here?" She looked helplessly at him.

"I came back. I wanted to be here with you today. How about if we spent the day together? Maybe take a little trip."

"I'd love to, Sam, but I have to get into the office. I have a three o'clock meeting to prepare for. Look, I know we need to talk, and there's something I have to say to you, something I should have said a long time ago. I promise we'll talk, but I can't find the strength today to stand up to my mother and have to fight you too."

"Please, April. Stay here today."

"No, Sam. I can't. I have a lot to deal with right now," she slid past him and up the stairs.

"Like what?" Sam followed her.

"Look, I just told mother to shut the heck up. That's a lot to deal with right there, okay."

"You did what?" Sam rubbed his head with disbelief. April never confronted her mother.

"Yes. You heard me right. Just as I said it and not in such nice language either. I've had enough of people running my life and, in the process, running me raggedy. Sam, I have to go to the office. Truly I appreciate your being here, but there are some things I have to work out on my own. I'll come home early tonight, and we'll talk."

The doorbell rang. "Don't answer it," April warned. "It's probably Mother. Minutes later, April could hear her cell phone ringing. She didn't answer it. Then Sam's phone rang.

Downstairs after she thought her mother had left, April searched frantically for her keys. "Is tonight good?"

"Tonight," Sam handed her the keys right in front of her eyes.

"I really do have to run," she brushed past him. "I'll call you later. Could you look to make sure Mother is gone?"

April pulled out of the driveway, only to park her car a few blocks away. She sat behind the wheel for the longest time, trying to find courage. She was jittery. She didn't have to be so mean to her mother. It was unnecessary. Who, after all, was there for her? Misstep or no misstep. It was her mother who'd helped put her problem into perspective, and it was her mother's explanation of what happened that kept her going. Until April saw *Life is Beautiful,* she never quite understood her mother had consciously altered her reality like the father in the movie had altered his son's. Finally, April started the car and made her way to the office. She'd get it together just as soon as this CFO stuff was over. That had to be the reason she was feeling so nuts—that and the "deep thinking" effect that the Trinity meetings seem to have on her.

It took Melody almost four weeks after returning from San Francisco to put the final report together. So much was going on at Comtech that needed her immediate attention, and the merger deadline was more than three months away, so she kept putting it off. To be frank, she wanted to put as much distance between herself and Charles Bell as possible. She glanced at her watch. Three p.m. It was time to give her report to the executive team. Melody dabbed her face with powder and made her way to the boardroom. She would call Charles Bell when there was news, which might be a moot point since Evan wasn't going to like this deal one bit. However, she'd promised Charles her best pitch, and she would keep her word. The deal was still a good deal for Comtech, and it was her job to secure the buy. Moreover, she wanted Charles to have the opportunity to be with his parents.

"Well. It's Miss M&A."

"Funny?" Melody smiled, knowing Evan was needling her about the length of time it took to get the report done. "I'd hoped to have had this in before, but… ."

"You're full of buts these days. Not like you at all." Evan outstretched his hand. He seemed relaxed. Who wouldn't be? He was retiring at fifty-five!

"I figured since no news is good news, bad news could wait a bit," Melody said.

"I smell trouble on the deal."

"Not exactly."

"Great. What did you think of Microtech?"

"The company is top quality. The building is beyond classy. A nice asset to pick up."

"So, what's up with the package you presented in San Fran?" Evan knew Melody too well. She was hedging.

"It was a nice package." Melody saw her opening. "But the operant word here is, was. Charles Bell, the President, and CEO of Microtech, is requesting some changes to our proposal. He likes almost everything about the deal, and believe it or not, he didn't even haggle over price. I expected that would be the only hitch, but it's something more…how shall I put it Sentimental."

"Like what? Move the building to Chicago by truck?" Evan chuckled.

"That would probably be easier," Melody cautioned, handing out the revised proposal.

Evan's face sobered. "Do we need a scotch?"

"Double." Melody grimaced.

Just then, April was ushered into the room. She swept in with an air that was radiant, upbeat, effective, and springy. It was after all Spring. Gone was the sad, forlorn girl of weeks ago. The confounded woman was such a class act. Melody smiled warmly, feeling a kinship with April, who stared down life's challenges with grace and style like herself.

"Gentlemen." April smiled broadly. "I apologize for being a little tardy."

"Come in, Miss Summers. Have a seat." Evan pointed her to a spot on the sofa. "Melody was just about to go over what sounds like a ridiculous meeting with Microtech. Maybe you'll want to join us in a double scotch as she suggested."

"No thanks to the drink, Evan. I've been working with Melody on the revised numbers. I'm glad I'm the backer and not the buyer," her eyes flashed to Melody. "But by all means, dull the pain, for there is some pain involved. I had the honor of hashing out the new deal personally."

Pretentious lush, Melody thought grudgingly, stifling a grim. How can anyone hide so well behind a mask? Mask. What the hell was she talking about? Her own life was mummified behind many layers of masks.

"Continue." Evan turned his attention back to Melody, handing her a glass of sparkling water.

"Charles Bell wants us to retain *all* the company's executive management for at least three years after the merger unless they decide to leave. The rest of Microtech's staff must be retained for at least one year. If our answer is no, the deal is off." There was no easy way to present this pill.

"Impossible! No way in hell! No wonder he didn't haggle over price." Evan boomed. "Who is this man? Does he understand the cost of labor and load? We don't need that kind of noose around our neck. Absolutely and categorically not! We don't need…. Ah, hell, cancel the deal." Evan said.

"Let's not be so hasty," The VP of Human Resources piped up, "How many employees are we talking about here?"

"Three hundred and fifty."

"And he wants full salary and benefits?" He whistled. "Holy kakaroo!"

"Bull." The SVP of Finance slapped the desk.

"It may not be as bad as it sounds," Melody hastily jumped in to defend the deal. "First of all, more than half of those people won't want to relocate to Chicago. If they don't, then it's goodnight, Irene. This man kept a lean and mean Exec team. They number only fifteen, including him. I'm sure most of those people, with their track record, will be snapped up by the competition, especially if they think they know trade secrets. And we can always sell the building. It will be worth a lot."

"Actually," the VP of Sales and Marketing interjected. "We may want to keep Microtech just where it is for the next three years anyway. It's got a stronghold in Silicon Valley, and its sales activity can certainly support its staff. That will give us time to start a proactive marketing campaign in Chicago and build market share here. If we move them immediately, just the sheer geographic move, we will lose some market share. Let's give this some real thought before making a hasty decision."

"Yes. That's true. I met with the District Manager for the Midwest while I was there. As a geographical region for Microtech, Chicago is tepid. From a financial point of view, what April proposes could be a winning idea. April, why don't you go over some of the ideas and the numbers you came up with?" Melody tapped a button on the conference table, revealing the hi-tech flip chart.

"Let me preface that at first, I thought the entire idea was preposterous. But under closer scrutiny, it might just work in Comtech's favor. I can assure you I have seen worse deals come out smelling like roses. Okay." April got up and began writing on the flip chart. "Here is scenario one." She continued until she had outlined four possibilities if Comtech wanted to move forward. "Let me reiterate, none of these," she pointed to the chart, "is ideal, but there is no ideal state in life. We can effectively manage the risk in all these scenarios, and I assure you if you choose to move forward, the bank will finance any of these options."

"Leave me the information, April. The group will meet in the morning to finalize a counteroffer. If we can offer fewer dollars upfront, it will reduce our debt to service substantially. "Evan said.

Melody felt a sense of pride in April.

"Don't let dollars stand in the way. The ROI is strong." April cautioned.

"Very well. Taken under advisement. Does anyone have questions?" Evan looked around the room. No one moved.

"Great. Gentleman and Melody," April emphasized, showing Corporate America hadn't come far. There was always only one woman at the top rung of management in every corporation. "If that's all, I'll be on my way." Another dazzling smile.

"April," Melody's smile was extreme, "thanks for your help. Your strategies were very helpful and well thought out."

"As they say so commonly, that's why they pay me the big bucks." With that, she exited the room reminding Melody of a swan gliding on water. Melody watched as the woman floated away, envy and sadness rising in her. Even, after all, she'd been through she was a class act.

"Well, this will be your first baby as CEO." Evan refreshed his drink.

"Right. I figured." Melody continued, turning her attention back to the group, "I believe only thirty percent of the staff might accept the offer. Who would want to move from San Francisco to Chicago, anyway? Look over these numbers. See their impact on your department. Come back with any suggestions, improvements, concerns." Melody said, reaching for the folder on the desk. It took only a moment to realize, though she was trying, her hand was not moving. What the hell? There was numbness in her entire right arm. Alarmed but in control, Melody reached for the folder with her left hand. "Until tomorrow then," she left the room significantly more composed than she felt.

Inside the bathroom, Melody panicked. Suddenly her arm started to tingle, and then her fingers and then it was as if nothing had happened.

Back in her office, pouring a glass of water with shaking hands, Melody sat behind her desk, frightened and unable to think clearly. What was going on with her? Maybe she should call Veronica. She looked around the room, eyes wide with terror. What? What could be wrong? Her body was giving off signals. What had changed in her life? Her logical mind searched for an answer. That damn Chinese food she'd ordered in for lunch! That had to be it. She was probably having an allergic reaction to the MSG, or worse, food poisoning. Indeed, she was beginning to feel queasy.

Melody buzzed Angel. "Would you arrange a car for me? I forgot about an unscheduled appointment. I'll be ready in ten minutes." She couldn't possibly drive herself in this condition.

"Right away, Miss Adams. Do I need to prepare anything else?"

"No. That will be all."

Maybe she should ask Veronica for a referral. The thought of communicating her physical challenges of the last few months to Veronica flashed through her mind again, but she decided this was something best kept under wraps until she knew what was going on. No point in being an alarmist.

Dr. Henry's office was crowded when Melody arrived. She signed in and sat among the sea of faces, some gaunt and obviously in pain. She watched a little boy who was holding his mother's hand tightly. His head was bald except for a few fuzzy hairs, and Melody suspected he was probably dying of cancer. A cranial scar from front to back indicated he'd already had brain surgery, yet he was chatting eagerly with his mother, smiling at her from time to time. He was the only person in the room who smiled. Melody looked around the room from one hopeless face to the next. Suddenly she got up, grabbed her purse, and left the office. Whatever was happening to her was not that serious. She'd wait a bit longer to see if she got better. Yet a nagging feeling that she was unwell dwelled in the back of her mind. Whatever was happening to her was not just midlife crisis.

CHAPTER TWENTY-SIX

VERONICA STROLLED around the eclectic two-story condo. Nothing like she expected. It felt more like the home of an artist than a doctor. Keeping her promise not to see him had not worked out and she needed a jolt of admiration after Randolph's stupidity. Still, she intended to close the barely read chapter.

"This condo is fabulous. I'd never have guessed you had this kind of creativity in you."

"It's in the genes. My mother is an artist. I actually wanted to be a filmmaker when I was younger and even toyed with the idea of being a musician. I played bass in a band called the Scalpels in med school."

"How fitting." Veronica laughed. And then?"

"Then I thought, okay, maybe I'll write music for films. And then my mother won."

"Mothers have a way of doing that." Tony's phone rang. He excused himself and went to the kitchen. She could hear him saying. "Yes. Next weekend. It'll keep. You bet. Yep. I love you too."

"My sister," he said, coming back into the room. "She wants me to help her move into her new apartment next weekend. Her first time living on her own, and she's driving us all crazy."

"How old is she?

"Twenty-one. The accident, baby. Ten years younger. She's just graduated college and is moving to the Big Apple. She is the real artist in the family. She'll be understudying a curator there. Artsy stuff, huh?"

Veronica gulped. He's only thirty-one! Reason enough to sober up. "Darn," Veronica swore at the sound of her beeper but was glad for a reason to make an excuse.

"Don't answer it."

"Are you mad? We're doctors."

"And humans," he added.

Looking at the message, Veronica said, "Tony, I have to go. My daughter." She grabbed her purse and sprinted out the door.

Randolph and Gerald were in the corridor when she arrived at the emergency room, where her daughter had been taken.

"What happened? Where's Jenny?"

"You'd know if you were ever home." Gerald snapped.

"Stop," his father cautioned. "Jenny's all right. She fell off the see-saw on the playground. I think her arm is broken. They're setting it now."

Five nights before, she had promised to talk. It was minutes to midnight, and she was still not home. Sam refused to go to bed. Whatever conversation April was avoiding would be had tonight! But why would she be afraid to talk with him? Didn't she trust him? Frankly, he wasn't sure who needed to have a conversation more, or be trusted more, him or her. If their relationship was going to make it, there were conversations that needed to be had.

It was well after midnight when keys jingled in the door. Sitting in the library, he heard footsteps and the clinking of a glass from the kitchen.

"Isn't it too late for that?"

April jumped in fright. "Damn it, Sam. I wish you wouldn't creep up on me like that," she fumbled with the faucet. "I'm only getting some water, and even if I wasn't, I don't want you to think you can start telling me what I can and cannot do, okay?"

"You're right, April. You can do exactly what you want, when and how you want. Why the hell would one compromise in a relationship."

"I compromised. I compromised a lot."

"Yeah. How come you don't bother to call anymore when you're going to be late?"

"I lost track of time."

"It's been over a week now since you've been losing track of time. Is it you don't want to have the conversation you know we should have? You promised."

"I know. I'm not ready. I'll talk when I get good and ready, so please don't push me," April snapped. She was mad as hell. She was supposed to be home, but she had worked late. Her five days of sloughing off were spent working on Melody's deal. What in God's name did he want from her?

"The least you could have done was call. You are the one who said tonight five nights ago."

"I'll have the conversation when I'm good and ready. I'm thirty-two goddamn years old, and I'm not going to continue feeling like I always have to explain my life? To mother. To S&G and now to you. Why don't you people leave me the hell alone?"

Sam felt the hairs on the back of his neck rise. "Talking with your husband. Now, what was I thinking?" He said sarcastically.

"I'm not sure, Sam. What are you? Who are you? We've become ugly together, and I'm not sure. Sam, it's been a long day. I'm not trying *not* to have this conversation, but I need some time to think about all this. The past month has been difficult. You've avoided me as much as I've avoided you, so don't put all the blame on me. We'll talk about this but not until I've finished with the deal at S&G. I can't take on any more stress right now. I just can't. So, let's talk about something else. Something that will keep us going until we can find the time to really talk. Speaking of which, are we having our Memorial Day party as usual? If we are, I need to start planning."

Sam shook his head. He couldn't believe April. How could anyone hide so far away? How could she be so insouciant about their problems? "So, after your little chat with Mummy, it's business as usual, huh? I see she has reminded you how to sweep the ugly stuff under the carpet. Sure darling, why not? Memorial party it is." Sam went out the back door to the old carriage house. In there, he would find solace.

Frank Easton categorically did not want to go to the last dinner party of the clandestine eleven, now twelve. He was hard-pressed to think of himself as a man who'd betrayed his values and tainted his soul for greed. Usually held at Kusak's house, the function had been moved to Fallwell's since April Summers's discovery. The disbandment of the S&G betrayers was synonymous with the Last Supper. Like him, everyone there tonight would be haunted or potentially haunted by the skeletons in each other's closets and who would be most likely to squeal under pressure if this damn scheme blew up in their faces. Eleven men and Martin! How the hell could Kusak have been so careless?

"What's the address?" Frank grunted at his wife.

"It's the house on the left. At least according to this address." Lindsey Easton said.

Falwell had just moved into a new ultra-luxurious abode— a multimillion-dollar home he was able to afford from the dirty money made from their conspiracy. Frank Easton swung the silver Mercedes up a winding driveway. A quarter mile up, he came to a gatehouse. The attendant checked a list, looking from Frank's face to a paper before opening the electric gates. At least Falwell had the good sense to guard himself behind a wall. After leaving the gatehouse and driving between perfectly manicured evergreens for what seemed too long a time, the house finally came into view. Eleven cars lined the circular driveway, and he recognized them all but one. That had to be Kusak's. He was told to rent a car. The eleven traitors and a blackmailer, Frank thought somberly, regretting being dragged into this so-called foolproof scheme. Lawyers, money managers, accountants—Chicago's barons could have their lives destroyed with a slip of the tongue. They couldn't even do one damn thing right. If they had wanted to play God, they should've had twelve disciples to begin with—Disciples! They were more like Lucifers. He, for sure, had committed more than one deadly sin. Of course, everything worked out in the end because they now had twelve. Twelve, Martin Spiro, the slob, was the last disciple. Why did he feel there was going to be hell to pay from their tangled web?

Inside, the men greeted each other, asp eyes darting from face to face for a clue of who the Judas might turn out to be. At their monthly dinners, the most interesting news was whose wife was the newest. It was fascinating to see slug eyes crawl up and down the bodies of the latest beauties who were there only as decoys and entertainment. Tonight's dinner was a formal event with each bejeweled wife trying to outdo the other, their catty barbs flying around like daggers. Dinner was a somber event and much shorter than usual. Leaving the women to a game of bridge, the men retired to the soundproof library. It was time to conduct business. And this meant making an exit strategy that left no trail past Kusak. Kusak had to be the sacrificial lamb, which seemed to cause him little concern. Frank knew he couldn't stall his final meeting with April Summers much longer. Calling for her return urgently after New Year's for a meeting was simple craftiness, but now it was time to move things along, or they would start looking suspicious to more than Martin.

The more Frank thought, the angrier he got. Finally, he bellowed, lighting a cigar to calm his nerves. "Kusak, you're a dumb cluck! How the hell did the woman get so close?"

"Ahaa. I really screwed up this time, Frank. Let my guard down because I didn't think she had it in her. Underestimated Ivy League education as affirmative action. I'm sorry but rest assured I don't think she suspects anything beyond me. It'll all die down, but you absolutely cannot give her the job right now. She's far too smart, and unfortunately, she's not corruptible like Martin here. We'll have to put Martin in to clean up this mess and fast. I'll work behind the scenes to ensure that happens." He gave Martin a spiteful look. "Any more April Summers investigations before then would be risky and, let me remind you, gentlemen, if I go all the down, we're all going down. I'll take the heat, but I won't be cooked!"

"This is your damn fault," Jeffery Osborne, COO, was mopping sweat from his brows.

"We already established that old boy, so let's not fink out, okay." Kusak's confidence irked everyone but himself. "Every problem has a solution. If we do as I say, no one will get hurt by this. As I said, I'm willing to take the fall. It'll be minimal. My father has every judge and lawyer in the city in his debt. I can weather this. I promise."

"You're still a dumb cluck. Martin," Frank could not keep the disdain from his face, "if necessary, you'll help us with a smear campaign, won't you? Prove to us you've been worth all the money we've paid you." Frank didn't care a hoot about Martin's feelings. He was now in and, as such, exposed to the brutal honesty of mobsters. Do or die.

"What smear campaign?" Kusak eyed him curiously.

"Well, Martin has been quite busy with S&G's business and April Summers. He had a friend who was a classmate of Summers who thought she had some problems in her junior year at Harvard. Spent a semester out. Nothing reflects on her transcript, but I'm sure we can find out what if we dig hard enough."

"Whew." Osborne whistled.

"Hell no," Kusak cautioned. "We won't touch that with a long pole. Let's not try to bring undue attention to this situation. The blame game would kill us, and it should stop with me."

"But she's going to squeal racism if she gets blown off. She is, in fact, legitimately the right person for this job. How are you going to deal with that?" Martin spoke for the first time. It seemed no one even cared he was there.

"Oh, for Christ sakes, did the president bang Monica Lewinsky or not? Did he remain the President?" Kusak slammed his fist down hard on the table.

"Barely," someone answered.

"He was still the President, okay. That's what power expects. Exception from the law." Kusak bellowed. "She is going to get the position but just not now! Do as I say, leave this to me, go on with the screening process, and stall until I tell you. I'm sure no one here would like the outcome of this fiasco if the truth came out."

"I sure hope you know what you're doing this time. 'Cause, my friend, you're a dead man if you fuck up again. No questions asked. Just like that. Badabing, Badaboom. Dead. Tomorrow I'll make an appearance at April's Memorial Day party. I'll see what I can find out casually. I suppose it's politically correct to show up, and I can't find a way to say no." Frank said, emptying his glass and pouring himself another gin and tonic.

"It's politically correct, and you damn well better show up! She wants you to see she is more than you could ever imagine." Kusak downed the brandy in his glass in one swig. His eyebrows twitched with fear.

CHAPTER TWENTY-SEVEN

APRIL WAS GLAD she hadn't canceled the Memorial Day affair after all. It was the perfect place to keep up pretenses and allay any real-life intrusion. Something she was excellent at doing. Thank goodness she had a fickle, externally driven mother with impeccable taste to rely on and who considered her hysterical behavior a mere personality flaw. She still wasn't speaking to her mother, but this was business, and she couldn't do without her input.

Sam had no idea when April and her mother had resolved their differences. Certainly, it had been more successfully resolved than she had with him. He blamed her mother now more than ever for the problems in their marriage. April had decided there was little point in trying to change or defend her choices until she was certain what her actions should be. Until a solution was crystal clear, she would lay low while the cold air blew over. The changes necessary to make all this right were not just hers and her mother; Sam had a big role to play. She looked ruefully over at Sam, chattering away and playing his role perfectly. Seemed he was having a good enough time despite the charade. Her heart stirred at how handsome he looked in his short-sleeved cotton shirt and khaki pants, play-acting on her behalf. "No point," she murmured, turning away from the repentant emotions swelling in her. Throwing her shoulders back in resolve, April's face took on a sanguine look. She jabbed her hands into her pocket, put on her plastic face and advanced into the crowd. *Do what you do best, Summers, for all this world is your stage.* Tears stung her eyes. *C'mon, girl,* she admonished, *get it together. Move your hiney.* April moved toward the milling crowd with a gleeful smile fixed on her face.

It had been five a.m. when April first eased her body out of bed. Stuffing her feet into terry cloth slippers, she'd padded to the Italian-style kitchen, adorned top to bottom with preserved fruits and decorative olive oils. Filling the kettle, she had sat down to have a cup of tea before starting her day. Neurosis got the better of her though she had little to do to make the day perfect. Second-guessing her mother's incredible attention to detail was like asking God if he had made the earth in six days. April sat idly twirling the teacup in the saucer. Suddenly, with great passion, she felt a deep urge to have a baby. A baby she had thought resolutely would give her and Sam a lasting bond. As soon as the thought gelled, April knew the true but clandestine reason for her decision was to tie a noose around Sam. She needed him. She couldn't face her life without him. A baby would give them someone to focus on other than themselves. Maybe a grandchild would be good for her parents, too. Draining the teacup, April looked for a clue in the leaves' pattern at the bottom of her cup. The only thing it said was go check on the china; check to make sure the curtains were changed; check to see the valet stand was in order and go back to bed. Instead of going back to the master bedroom, April made her way to the guestroom, where Sam had been sleeping since their unresolved fight.

Sam stirred as April lifted the sheets and slid in beside him.

"Sam," April shook her husband lightly. His body heat warmed her. "Do you think we could talk a little while?"

"You pick 5:30 a.m. to have a conversation we should have had weeks ago?"

"You're right; go back to sleep." She swung her feet back out of bed.

"Stay." Sam pulled her back into the bed. April turned to look at her husband. In the morning dawn, he was incredibly soft. No anger. No persecution. No fears.

"Why are you in here?"

"I'm tired of fighting. I was hoping we could talk, finally."

Sam sighed loudly. "Look, April, I'm sorry about everything. I made a mistake, and I promise it'll never happen again. I promise you on my life."

"I know that Sam. Really I do. Sam, there is something I'd like to tell you."

Sam felt his wife's body tremble beside him. "Go on, April," he sensed her hesitation. "You can trust me."

"There are things I should have told you a long time ago. Things that may explain some of my avoidance behavior."

Sam pulled his wife to him. "No matter what happens between us, April, you'll always be my "Earth Angel.""

April looked sharply at Sam. What did he mean, no matter whatever happens? What she wanted most was for Sam to hold her, her to receive him and give him the child he so badly wanted; instead, she'd climbed out of bed.

"Where are you going?" Sam was surprised.

"Sam, I'm sorry." April rushed toward the bedroom door. "I'm just not ready."

"Don't do this, April." Sam pleaded as he heard the door shut softly. He switched on the light watching steam rise from his ears.

His schedule on overdrive, Memorial Day, arrived faster than Sam wished. Unprepared, his psyche wasn't ready for the necessary stage acting, but he would dust off his acting skills for April.

Sam watched his wife work the room. Despite his despair over the state of his marriage, he had to acknowledge April, and her battle-ax of a mother were wonderful hostesses. She was glancing at him from time to time. He missed her, her laughter, her quick mind; her biting sense of humor; even their cultural disagreement. They used to be so good together. Where had all that love gone?

"This has to be a mistake." Frank pulled into the circular driveway, centered by a Greek marble fountain spouting water into a lily pond. He marched up to the massive double doors and rang the bell. The chime was a very soft rendition of some classical music t he'd be damned if he knew. A uniformed attendant greeted him offering to park his car.

"I believe I'm in the wrong place," Frank said, holding onto his keys. "I'm looking for the home of April Summers."

"You've found it, Sir."

Frank, truly surprised, beckoned to his wife. The door was opened by April herself.

"Frank. How lovely to see you. I hope you didn't have much trouble finding the place. Do, do come in." April smiled at the woman standing beside Frank, whom he seemed reluctant to introduce. She was a Marla Maples look-alike, just as young as when she'd met the Donald.

"I'm Lindsey Easton." The woman smiled back. She was at least thirty years younger than Frank and, if April's observation was correct, out of her league. A trophy wife, no doubt.

"Delighted."

As they walked into the vast marble and gold-flecked hallway, Frank Easton was impressed. When the hell did Black folks get this affluent? But it wasn't just the affluence; it was the style, class, and worldly chic.

Gabriella Dixon breezed into the foyer. "Dear, you are needed in the kitchen," she said to April, smiling politely at the people in her company.

"Mother, may I introduce Frank Easton, my boss and CEO of S&G, and his wife, Lindsey."

"Charmed." Gabriella turned to her daughter. "Go on, dear, and I'll take care of your guests." Gabriella turned her attention to Frank and Lindsey, leading them toward the garden. "You are April's boss. I don't understand much about investment banking. All I know is it is an obsession with money. A little vulgar for my taste. If I could have convinced April, I'd have preferred her to be in a more fulfilling profession. A classical musician or something more intellectually challenging and meaningful such as research." Gabriella sighed loudly, "Too bad we don't have much control over our children these days. Such a pity."

Frank Easton was in shock. Did this silly woman know to whom she was speaking? How could she address him as though he were some common laborer? He was damn near the richest man in Chicago! Somehow, he didn't think it mattered to her.

"Investment banking can be quite an intellectual pursuit," he stammered. "What else do you consider a better occupation?" He was not amused but awed by this gracious Black woman who spoke with an autocratic and highborn charm and an accent as heavy as the queen of England's.

"Medicine. Literature. Law. Money is quite an unnatural equalizer to intellect. Money puts people where they don't belong."

Frank knew how true that was for him. He was one of those kids who knew the burning ambition and desired never to see poverty again. He would have compromised his soul and did to be where he is today.

"John. John, darling," they had reached the bar, "may I introduce Mr. Frank Easton and his—Gabriella looked the woman up and down with disregard; blond, teased hair and, no matter how expensive, clothes, not worn right— wife, Lindsey. He's April's boss." Gabriella was glad to leave the wannabes to her husband's charm. "Do take care of them, will you, darling?"

"How do you do?" John Dixon's smile was welcoming. "May I offer you both a drink? I'm not supposed to be here, but I do such a good job, April lets me."

"What would you rather be doing?"

"I don't do much nowadays. A dabble here and there in brain research. I'm mostly retired now. I teach a few classes in Neuroscience at Northwestern School of Medicine now and then. Gabriella shares the load. She teaches when I don't much feel like it, so as you see, I'm really quite the slacker."

Frank wondered if he was in a time warp. This had to be a dream, or he had been catapulted to 2049. He had been warned about the rising minority workforce of the millennium. The browning of America. Humm, he thought, April Summers represents change. Wonder how Kusak thought he was going to control this!

Lindsey, too busy gawking at the magnificence of the unusual house, its unique landscape and the party buzzing under two large tents pitched on either end of a Japanese bridge, had not listened to a word that had been exchanged. She absolutely loved the house. Maybe Frank would find her one just like it!

"Come in, ladies," the pleasant butler who opened the door urged when Veronica and Melody hesitated, entering the house. "The party is going on outside. Just follow me" It was Melody who kicked Veronica into action. It took quite an individualist to have a home like this. It reeked of a unique and confident personal style. She had never seen anything like this. Never imagined it. For different reasons, Melody and Veronica had overspent to make sure their homes were magnificent, but the house they stood in was incredible. Melody felt herself shrinking. One could never emulate this; it was the taste of aristocracy. Set back from the road, the mansion nestled itself behind shady trees. Melody walked with her head spun in all directions. She wanted to drink in every detail of the luxurious home. From the frescoed walls to the twinkling hand-blown Italian chandeliers, from the stone hearth at the center of the magnificent Tuscan great room dotted with breathtaking hand-painted Italian furnishings to the carved bannisters. The home was beyond compare with intricate wainscoting archways leading to grander and grander rooms, and the spectacular leaded glass windows to the perfectly manicured lawn. The house wore its surroundings with the ease and confidence of its owner. A marvelous mahogany Steinway, visible on their way to the garden, dominated the music room. On top, sheets of music were casually strewn. In Melody's house, there would be no such casualness. The music would've been neatly stacked in the piano stool. Melody Adams was riveted and ill at ease. For a brief moment, Melody hated April and resented her birthright.

It was Veronica's turn to nudge Melody into action. The butler was waiting patiently as the women meandered. "Girl, can you believe this shit!" Veronica chimed. "Next week, I'm having a decorator come in to gussy up my place."

"This isn't decorator territory," Melody answered. "This is inherited taste."

"Melody. Veronica." April said, gliding toward them. She wore a shimmering purple and chartreuse Capri pants topped with a snugly cut, purple, sleeveless linen blouse. She looked exquisite. Regal.

"I'm so glad you guys made it. Come, I want to introduce you around," she pulled them by the hand over to a well-stocked bar. "Father. This is Veronica Whittaker. She's the doctor you talk about incessantly."

"Dr. Whittaker, it is my distinct pleasure." John Dixon was from behind the bar in a flash. "Your research is outstanding and of the highest caliber. I dare say I haven't turned out anything quite as good in forty years."

"Mr. Summers, Aren't you kind. Thank you," Veronica beamed. "But do call me Veronica."

"I will if you call me John, John Dixon," He winked and outstretched his hand.

"Gosh, I'm so stupid." She'd called April's father by April's married name.

"I would hardly say so. April, unfortunately, gave away our name when she married and became a Summers."

"And this is Melody, Daddy."

"*Enchante,*" John said in a perfect French accent. "Now, how about a drink for you lovely ladies?"

"Baileys or Martini," Veronica said.

"Cranberry juice, please," Melody said.

"I'll have a scotch and soda, dad," April said. "In a few minutes, I'll take you to meet the other guests. I think you'll enjoy the people."

"Is that who I think it is?" Melody was staring at the gorgeous woman coming toward them.

"Oh. Sophie." If you think she is a Hollywood actress, yes." April said. "Sophie, Sophie," April called, waving a slender hand around. A darker, taller version of Vanessa Williams glided towards them.

"I can't believe you know her." Melody dug her elbow into Veronica's side.

"Know her! She's, my cousin."

"Your cousin? How come you never said?" Melody asked incredulously.

April shrugged. "I suppose because it never came up."

"Hello, darling." Sophie's smoky voice was competition to Veronica's.

"You look fantastic, as usual, Sophie. This is Melody, and this is Veronica. You know the Trinity I tell you about. They are the other members. With them, you don't need a shrink."

"I can always ask for my money back and join your group. I certainly could stand keeping more of my *moolah*. Delighted." Sophie smothered the women with a glittering smile but did not give her hand to shake.

"Delighted, too," Veronica said casually while catatonically Melody stood by her side.

"Where is Sam, darling," Sophie asked April. "We're so overdue for a visit. Ah," she said before April could answer, "I see Aunt Gabriella. Ladies, excuse me." Sophie trotted off.

"She is gorgeous," Veronica said.

"Oh, shut up." Melody jabbed her in the side.

"So now you can talk." Veronica cut her eyes and made off down the path behind Sophie.

Black and White, Chicago's power elite, were engaged in lively chatter in April Summers' magnificently landscaped backyard. When Melody and Veronica finally met Sam Summers, they were quite taken with him. Sam exuded a sense of power which matched his wife's, and to their surprise, April's incredibly conversant husband seemed the complete opposite of their vision of a wife beater. To Veronica he had the look of the very man she so often hoped for at her side. *How the grass always looks greener over the septic tank.*

"Melody," April propelled her through the crowd, "please let me introduce you to Frank Easton, President and CEO of S&G. Frank, Melody is CEO elect of Comtech, one of our largest clients." Frank Easton knew her by name, as it was bantered around all over Chicago's papers—as a testament to Black female *savoir-faire.* "And this is Dr. Whittaker. She's the foremost infertility doctor. Has just been nominated for a top commendation in medicine."

Frank Easton bowed. He didn't offer his hand, as they were covered with barbecue sauce. "Ladies. Very nice to meet you."

"April, Sweetheart, Smudgekins." Two lanky, anorexic white women, flashing perfect orthodontically altered teeth, came down the path. "It's been far too long. We haven't seen you since last summer in Greece or was it Spain? Oh, I can't quite remember. Age is catching up with me," the taller of the two said. They air-kissed both April's cheeks before turning their attention to Frank Easton. The women were from old, old, and extra old money. Melody could tell by the casualness with which they wore their Cartier. Their wealth was evident down to the mute color of the polish on their toenails.

"Frank Easton," the taller of the two women said without much interest. "I've been reading about you."

"All good, I hope."

"That depends, doesn't it? I suppose I shall think so if you contribute to our charity for underprivileged children."

April ducked out of the conversation, leaving Melody and Veronica in rich and richest hands. Veronica and Melody later found out the women were millionaire friends of April's from

Brown and Harvard. They were heiresses, scions of corporate bastion, women who did not need to figure out how to blast through the glass ceiling of corporate America. In the cases of Sandy and Juliet, their names, their contribution to the world was to head influential charities that pacified the guilt of being uber rich and carefree while others struggled to find food. As April moved up the path to greet other guests, the women stayed back under the tent. Shortly, Veronica and Melody made their escape too.

"Alan, Alan Bladen." April was beaming with delight. "I didn't expect to see you. I just keep sending invitations to be cordial."

"That's the problem with expectations. They lock a person into patterns they'd rather not be in. I brought a friend. I hope you don't mind. I suppose I should've called."

"And spoil my surprise?"

"This is Charles. Charles Bell."

"Welcome." April smiled, escorting the men to get drinks.

Gabriella was at the bar talking to her husband and complaining about the ineptness of the catering service. "I see you're still as diplomatic as ever," Alan Bladen hugged the woman from behind.

She spun to face him. "Alan, you scoundrel." A light beamed on Gabriella's face. "Why have you been away so long?" As usual, he was debonair and charming and, without question, the man April should have married.

Sam, noticing the camaraderie, moved away from the mingling crowd.

"There you are, Sam, darling." Three kisses. "I've been trying to get away from these tiring people to find you for over ten minutes now. How are you, darling?"

"Sophie," Sam was surprised. "How could you come here?" His voice was a whisper.

"What do you mean, darling? April invited me, of course. I hope you're glad to see me. I've really missed you."

"Let's not get carried away."

"Why are you being insufferable?"

"Look, what happened in Jamaica was situational."

"And the time after?"

"Situational."

"So is this. Meet me inside when you can get away."

"Not here."

"Then I'm at the Drake."

"Sophie…."

"Darling, I hate a bore. Come on, Sweetie, April has no clue about us."

"There's no us," Sam said angrily.

"Isn't that what makes it so hot?" She purred. "Get away, darling. I need you tonight."

Melody Adams was sitting under a tree near the bar, back to the queuing lunch crowd. She was wondering how anyone with April's life could be in distress. Again, she felt like an imposter.

"Mother, isn't it swell to see Alan." April was saying.

"My dear, it's delightful. And who is his handsome friend?"

"Mr. Charles Bell," April said softly but not softly enough that Melody had not overheard the conversation.

Melody's body stiffened. She dared not look up. Charles Bell. It had to be someone else! But when the man spoke, there was no mistaking Charles Bell had arrived at April Summers party! She had no idea. She watched from the corner of her eyes as he bowed courteously to Gabriella Dixon, laughing with verve at some comment she had made and listening with great interest to her story of Alan and April. She missed nothing. She wanted, however, for the world to open up and give her an escape. She couldn't face Charles today. Melody jumped quickly to her feet to find an escape route, but just as she rose, April, who was heading toward her, Charles Bell in tow, said, "Melody, I hope you're having a good time?"

Melody glanced at the striking man looming at April's side. He was more handsome than she remembered.

"May I introduce my friend Alan, and Mr. Charles Bell. We've only just met ourselves, but Charles is in your line of business. I thought you two should meet."

"Ms. Adams, it's good to see you again." Charles's eyes laughed at Melody.

"You two have met before?" April looked curiously from one to the other.

"Yes, Mr. Bell *is* the CEO of Microtech," Melody said calmly. "It's good to see you again too, Charles." She allowed him to clasp her hand.

"This *is the* Charles Bell? Well, well," April said with renewed interest, "it's my pleasure to meet the man with the golden heart. I'm the investment banker on the deal. You drive quite a bargain, Mister."

"Only because I'm in good, capable and understanding hands." Charles never took his eyes off Melody. "And may I say, Mrs. Summers, you have a most beautiful home."

"Thank you."

Melody shifted her weight from one leg to the other, looking around frantically for Veronica. *She had to get out of here!* Veronica was a few feet away, chattering with some guests. Veronica, who happened to look in Melody's direction, saw the look of panic on her face. Excusing herself, she quickly made her way over to where Melody stood.

"Are you all right?" Veronica spoke to Melody, never taking her gaze off the man staring Melody into the ground.

"I'm fine. Thank you. Veronica. Meet Charles. Charles Bell."

"Charles Bell. Oooohmygod. It's you! You are the infamous Charles Bell I've heard so much about you?" Veronica gushed, ignoring Melody's murderous stare.

"I sincerely hope so," Charles's eyebrows arched as his lips crinkled into a smile. "What sorts of things have you heard? Good, I hope.""

Melody looking positively faint, said, "I'm going to get a drink. Would anyone else like one?"

"Let's all go. Lunch is served, and mother will be petrified if we are off schedule." April chuckled softly, moving in the direction of the lunch tent. Melody was positively mortified. Charles fell in step beside April as they walked toward the tent.

"You no good, knucklehead," Melody whispered to Veronica as they lagged. "Of all the stupid high school comments to make. Couldn't you think of anything more suitable to say? Sometimes, I think you must have gone to a Podunk school instead of Northwestern."

"Chile, you need to take a chill pill. Why don't you admit what's got your hormones raging? That man is gorgeous! I could've said all you ever do is chatter about him. Maybe I'll tell him over lunch. Ask him if his ears burn all the time."

"And I'll break your neck. Anyway, I haven't talked to you about Charles since San Francisco, so I have no idea what you're basing your facts on."

"Really? You make it seem so casual, but next time, notice we never really have a conversation without chatting about Charles Bell."

"Let's just get out of here?"

"And miss lunch? Are you crazy? Girl, I'm having the best time, and I'm not leaving. If you want to go, ask Charles Bell to drive you home." Veronica jested.

"Don't be crass."

"Girl, you've got to stop being such a stick-in-the-mud. Go on over there and smile at that incredible hunk of a man. Melody, the man, is phat! You've got to be crazy if you don't want to get to know this guy." Veronica shook her head.

The timber voice pierced through Melody's annoyance. At the voice, air seeped out of her lungs in a wheeze, and sweat as it usually did in times of stress, gathered on her upper lips. "Hello again," Charles said, sitting next to Melody. Under the table, she was wringing her hands, but her tone remained monotone and unaffected.

"Are you having a good time?" He set his plate on the table. It was loaded.

"A great time," Melody fibbed. She hated every minute she was in April's house. Every turn of her head reminded her this kind of ease with wealth did not come from the contrived packaging she represented. To think she had never 'left' America. Sure, she'd visited hotel rooms in other parts of the world, but she had never left America. Renting houses in Spain, Italy, France, or whatever for holidays hadn't ever occurred to her. Such thinking was not in her reality.

Seeing Charles beeline for the table, Veronica made her way to a different table. She'd have to suffer Melody's angst, but she didn't care.

"You didn't return any of my calls." Charles leaned over to whisper in her ear.

"I have no new information about the deal yet. I was waiting."Melody sipped her Mint Julep in a generous gulp.

"Melody, you know that's not why I was calling. I was calling about us."

"Us? What about us, Charles?" A veiled surprise. "What made you imagine an 'us'? Because we had *a* lovely evening together doesn't make us an us."

"Melody. Dear. Do stop babbling."

"Excuse me?"

"You heard me. Stop babbling. Spare me the banality and defenses. I know you are scared of what happened between us. Just say so and stop babbling. Because I want you, I will make you want me more."

"Excuse me! You are a very, very insufferable man."

"Sure, I am, but tell me, would a woman like you give the time of day to anyone less insufferable, less intense? A man like me is a threat to you, but at least I'm a challenge. And challenges turn you on, right?"

"And you are irritating. I really can't believe you are sayi…." Charles cut her off again.

"Honesty is the best policy."

"Platitudes?"

"Sort of. You are desperately trying to avoid me because you find me irresistible. The truth is you wanted to see me."

"Sure, I was planning on seeing you. The next time we meet on the merger deal. Before that, I wasn't planning to look you up."

"And now I'm in town, will you go out with me tomorrow?"

"I'm already committed." Melody stammered out the words. Never had she met anyone so—so—so.

"Uh-huh. With what?"

"With what, what?"

"What are you busy doing?"

"I'm going to a ballgame with a friend."

"That sounds like fun. What time? I'd love to go. Can you bring a date?"

"What makes you think I'm not going with a date?"

"Are you?"

Their private conversation was interrupted as other people began joining their table. Melody was relieved beyond words.

"April," Melody said at about a quarter to seven. The party was breaking up by then. "Have you seen Veronica?" It had been a delightful evening for everyone except Melody.

April looked pleadingly at Charles.

"I'm taking you home," said Charles, who was standing close to Melody.

"That's not necessary. I have a ride." She slung her purse over her shoulder, walking off to find Veronica.

"No, you don't. I told Veronica she could go ahead."

"You did what?" Melody spun around; her eyes were flashing a lethal red. She looked at April.

"It wasn't my idea," April said, hardly perturbed.

"Well? Are you going with me or what?"

"It seems I don't have a choice." Melody spluttered and hissed before following Charles silently to his car.

CHAPTER TWENTY-EIGHT

"WHAT DID YOU think of Frank Easton?" April asked Sam as they sat in the kitchen, having a nightcap.

"I didn't think of Frank Easton?" Sam said, still aware of their war and accepting that April thinks she can just pretend things don't exist and they just go away; the one flaw in his wife that drove him insane.

"Not one thought?" April pressed.

"He looks like all the other crooked white men I've seen."

"Okay," April got up. "Never mind."

"What I did think about was how your mother fawned over Alan Bladen." Sam, too, rose from the table.

"That she did. But she's always loved Alan."

"I know. She told me he was who you should've married."

"Did mother say that today?" April asked, her anger flaring at her meddling mother.

"How about five times."

"You have to ignore mother," April said.

"I've been doing that pretty much for eight years." Sam climbed the stairs. Tonight, he was not allowing anything to get on his last nerves. All he could think about was Sophie's offer. The woman haunted him. After her cameo at the party, she had called him six times on his cell, each call more promising than the other. The only thing he wanted to think of right now was the quickest way to get to Sophie.

April went to the great room and flicked on the television. An hour ago, there were seventy-five people in her home, and now there was none. As usual, the party was a huge success, but without Sam to do the post-mortem, she felt very alone. Usually, after their Memorial Day party, they would take a bottle of wine to bed, dissect all the guests, get nice and tipsy, and then celebrate their success with wanton lovemaking. Tonight, the severity of their ongoing feud, which meant April had to sleep alone, was daunting.

Forensic Evidence was on television—a story of how a lawyer murdered his wife because she wouldn't give him a divorce to be with his younger mistress. Afterward, when he thought of the freedom the money would give him and his home wrecker, he committed insurance fraud, and that was what undid his cleverly planned crime. Greed.

"I have to make a quick run," Sam said, coming into the Tuscan room. He was now natty in eveningwear.

"I hope not to the corner store," April said sarcastically, eyeing his attire.

"What difference is it to you?" Sam had almost barked but caught himself before his anger got the better of him.

April pushed the volume button up. "Don't flatter yourself." She shouted as Sam slammed the front door shut. She did very much care where he was going. Maybe tonight, she would have crawled into his bed and have makeup sex. She cared her plans for reconciliation were now null and void. Where could he be going? For a moment, April had an urge to get in her car and follow him, but to be honest she had too little energy left for that sort of thing.

April's mind strayed to Frank Easton. He seemed very much at home at her party. She hoped he had been impressed with her gathering, confirming in his mind she had the social skills to be the CFO of S&G.

A hand came swiftly around the door, caught his tie, and yanked him into the room. "Purrrr. Oh, Purer." The voice caressed his ear. "I have been waiting for you, darling."

"Can't you even offer me a drink?" Sam was breathless.

"I'm darling. Can't you feel how much water is in my well?" The hand pushed him to his knees.

CHAPTER TWENTY-NINE

EXCEPT FOR THE soft music on the radio, Charles and Melody drove back to the city in silence. The night was still. Balmy. Melody felt unbelievably sanguine, and though she wanted to be mad, hostile, and insufferable, she was very happy. They drove unhurriedly.

Charles was the one who broke the silence. 'Why don't you trust your instincts? This could be love."

"Now, who's being banal? What's love got to do with anything?"

"Are you saying you don't believe in love?"

"Only as much as Tina Turner. 'Second-hand emotion.' "

"I couldn't tell that in San Francisco."

"A moment of weakness."

"What's wrong with weakness?"

Melody was not in the mood for banter. She wanted to sit quietly in the car beside Charles and dream the impossible dream of love. "Listen, Charles," Melody said urgently, "you don't want to get mixed up with me. I'm as confused as I am confusing. You said you'd wasted a lot of time on foolish women. It's important to spend what time you have looking for the love of your life in all the right places."

"I believe…."

"Don't interrupt me," Melody ordered before continuing. "Just because you want us to be, doesn't mean it's so. I'm not available for love. I've a hard enough life living with myself. Why in heaven's name would I want to take on someone else's problems? Not only that, I'm damaged goods. Psychologically inferior. My life has been a real challenge, one you shouldn't have to bother about."

"Really? So, life has been a challenge, huh? Tell me, who do you know who doesn't have a 'poor little old me' story? Lover left, mother left, father emotionally unavailable, spouse abusive, and even those experiencing pain from self-inflicted reality or delusions cry at the injustices of their narcissism. As for my hard life! I had to live up to my parents' expectations of excellence. Mind you, it was good for me, but I struggled with it as a young man. Who doesn't have to get over some hump or the other in life? All one has to do is stand as far back from the hill as necessary to gain enough speed to jump the obstacle. We have to, for no one can do it for us. The truth is, there are safe places to go to practice until you are ready to jump. Safe havens where injuries and wounds can heal before the attempt is made. If you're wounded, Melody, I can be your safe haven. Let's bury our pain in each other's hearts."

Melody felt the wind change. She sat for a moment, speechless. "I've always been my own safe haven," Melody said, her words soft. She had walked alone all these years; where did he get off lecturing her on hills and mountains to climb? Who did he think he was?

"An open offer." Charles stared lovingly but didn't press the subject. He already knew the outcome of this love. "So," he chirped, "will you tell me where you live? Turn right. Left. Keep straight?"

"Oh," Melody said triumphantly, as though this oversight made her obedience to Charles's demands more tolerable. "Lake Shore Towers. Do you know where it is?"

"Who doesn't?"

In their game of cat and mouse was contentment needing no words. When the car pulled up to the entrance of Lake Shore Towers, Charles said, "I want to come in."

"I'm sorry, Charles, you can't."

"I won't take no for an answer."

"I'm afraid you're going to have to." Melody retrieved her purse from the car's side pocket.

"Stop it," he grabbed her by the arm as she was about to open the door. "I'm who you have been looking for, and you know it. I certainly know you're who I've been looking for, so why do we have to play this game? I won't go back to San Francisco until I find out if there is an us, please." He let his grip slacken on her arm and instead took her hand into his. Melody allowed her hand to rest there.

"Why are you doing this to me?" She squeezed her lids tightly over her eyeballs, hoping to re-center her emotions. Resisting what she knew was right in her soul was near impossible with Charles so close to her. As a stab of desire mixed with excruciating pain pierced her body, and she shuddered, she could feel Charles' fingers closing tightly around hers.

"Because I think I love you. I want to lose my heart to you?"

Melody saw her entire world in Charles's eyes at that very moment "Love. Friendship. Happiness. "Charles, some people live with dreams forgotten. I am one of those people. You can't love me."

"How close will you let me get so I can make you believe in me?"

Melody leaned heavily on the headrest. She bit her lips and squeezed her already shut eyes tighter. Clearly, she saw the cliff she was about to walk headlong over, but there was no way to stop. "Stay only a little while," she said. It was a plea.

Upstairs, Melody poured a snifter of brandy from a decanter into two glasses. In her glass, she poured a double shot. She needed more than brandy to handle this situation she'd gotten herself into.

"I will not talk about us," she said, sitting next to Charles on the sofa.

"Who cares to talk?" Charles up turned her face and, while staring unflinchingly into her eyes, touched his lips to hers.

You stupid child. What do you expect? That I would give you back your soul? You stupid, stupid child. Showing badly decaying teeth, the old woman laughed hauntingly, and she suddenly pushed Melody over the cliff.

Melody sat bolt upright, the places under her armpit soaked. Her breathing was labored, and her heart racing. Her naked skin, which glistened with perspiration, felt cold and clammy. It was still dark outside except for a blade of light piercing the room from the overhung lamp. Melody, holding her body still, tried to calm her edgy nerves from the frightful dream when Charles stirred beside her. Fright squeezed her heart, and just as she was about to faint away, she suddenly remembered she was not alone. Melody stared down at him in utter disbelief. In twenty years, there had never been a man in her bed! Holy Mary, mother of God! What in hell had she done—again?

Stirring had not awakened him. Melody slid quietly out of bed, made her way to the bathroom, and opened her dresser's bottom drawer to pull out a pack of cigarettes. She turned on the fan and sprayed air freshener before igniting the lighter. Inhaling deeply, she sat on the side of the tub and cried. She had to be crazy to have started something she knew would be impossible to finish, but by God, she loved Charles Bell so very, very much.

Charles stirred when she climbed back into bed. Resting her head in the crook of his arm, she felt safe. Could he indeed be her safe harbor? Her knight in shining armor, who would slay the demons of her psyche? Her one true love? The wonderful man, resting peacefully at her side, exceeded her expectations in every way, and she felt ready to fight the devil for her lost soul. She would barter anything.

It was ten a.m. when Melody finally got up to open the curtains covering floor-to-ceiling glass walls. Through the walls of the magnificent bedroom, the Chicago skyline glowed majestically. She stood with her arms folded across her flat naked belly, staring out the window.

"That's how beautiful your life could be with me," Charles said, encircling her waist from behind.

"You know something," Melody stared ahead. "That's what scares me."

"Why would that scare you?" He turned her to face him.

"It just does."

They were both unclothed, yet Melody felt no need to cover her body, and Charles was so at ease with his own she thought nothing of his nakedness. She felt as though she was home sitting in her most comfortable Lazy-boy-chair.

"You'll tell me what ails one day soon enough." He said confidently.

"When did you get into town?" Melody nodded, changing the subject abruptly.

"Not long before I came to the party. One, maybe two, hours before. I touched down precisely at noon."

"Humm. Sounds like a good flight."

"Always is when I'm the pilot."

"You're a pilot?" Melody was trying hard not to be impressed, yet her eyes could no longer avoid Charles's nakedness. His body was rippled with muscles, and he was moving in the direction of excitement.

"Does that bother you? Flying?"

"No. I just can't imagine flying my own plane."

"It's a lot of fun. I'll teach you one of these days. It's easier than driving a car and a lot safer, too."

"We'll see about that," Melody retrieved her robe. "Now tell me. Mr. Bell, are you famished?"

"Humm." He fingered his chin. "What do you think? Great sex always makes one famished."

Melody was purple with embarrassment. She threw him a terrycloth robe and hastily headed to the kitchen. He followed.

"Do you want coffee?"

"That would be great. What else?"

"Carrot sticks and Melba toast?"

"Why doesn't that surprise me?"

"How about we have lunch in New York?"

"Huh?"

"We'll fly up. I'll take you to this amazing place with zero calories," he grinned.

Melody decided to try this thing called love.

Melody and Charles became inseparable. No one would ever have believed love could transform a person as much as it did Melody Adams. The woman glowed, the woman purred, and the woman became even more hauntingly beautiful. The only thing that didn't change about Melody Adams was her sense of style and charm. If April was a tastemaker in the divine Trinity, Melody was the perfection of that taste.

CHAPTER THIRTY

"**O**KAY. IF THIS isn't the best steak you've ever eaten," Tony pushed a fork into Veronica's mouth, "I'll eat my hat."

"Mmmm, this is yummy." Veronica said.

Guilt ridden, she had again tried using absence to cure her addiction to Tony and had succeeded for all of four weeks. After April's party, however, she'd yearned to be with him and here, not twenty-four hours later, found herself back in his arms. Tonight, she was finally going to tell him it was over.

"You know, you're the only woman I've ever cooked for."

"Tell me another lie."

No matter how tasty the morsels, she needed to go home to her family. Her children, especially Gerald, had started acting out. Veronica suspected Gerald knew something different from normal was going on at home, especially since she and Randolph no longer spoke to each other, though he didn't know what, In the past, the children would have to pull their parents away from each other to get to school on time.

"I don't lie. You are not just being kind, are you?" Tony said, coaxing another compliment out of her.

"This is good. Really good and tender. What did you put on it?"

"It's a secret."

"Like us," Veronica said, placing the fork on the plate. "Tony, I came… ."

"Don't go there tonight. Why can't you just let it go and enjoy life?"

"That's what I've been trying to do for four months. Trying to let it go. I hate all this creeping around and I hate hiding behind a wall of deceit."

"I hate it too." Tony flipped a steak on the grill.

"Then if we both hate it, why are you and I having an affair?"

"I'm not having an affair, Veronica. I'm single."

Veronica got up and paced. "You know what I mean," she retorted. "I came here tonight to break this off for good. It's so damn hard to think of no more you in my life, but I must."

"Why?" Tony grabbed her shoulders. "I can't and don't want to be apart from you. You make me feel so alive. So successful. So understood." Tony's eyes blazed.

"That's what is so frightening to me. I'm in agony over losing those comforting feelings, but I'm a married woman, Tony. Last night, I lay in bed, staring at the ceiling, re-evaluating my life. Sure, I don't like some things I see, but I have children who depend on me for their routine, values, and morals. What do I tell them about choice and consequences? Last night, I realized how much I love my husband even though I no longer lust after him the way I do after you. I have loved him for eighteen years, and I just can't walk away. What we have is pleasant. It's dependable and true. On the other hand, you make me feel young, beautiful, wonderful, and happy, but I have responsibilities my choices created long ago."

"Responsibilities shouldn't take the place of happiness."

"You're wrong, Tony. Sometimes responsibility is happiness. Joy even. Everything we do affects something or someone else. We don't live in a vacuum. How many people have to get hurt so you and I can be happy? I have a six-year-old. What about her happiness? I have the responsibility not to cause my children pain because of my choice with you."

"Veronica. Stop this right now. Do you think I fell in love with you because I wanted to? Love has its own agenda. Its own cost. Its own rewards. I had no control over my feeling for you."

"Neither did I, Tony. Neither did I," Veronica said, standing to face the man making her happy beyond words. She loved Tony in a sensual way. In a way, which revitalized her soul, but she loved Randolph in a knowing way. They'd shared all the joys and pains of life. "Yet we can all control our feelings if we want to. We can feel them and yet not act on them. We, who experiment on lower animals and proudly separate ourselves from them because of our ability to choose, should know how much control we have because of our ability to reason. We, Tony, are humans. The superior species."

"Why are we having this conversation today?" Tony was becoming gruff. He threw the spit into the sink, gathered the entire dinner, and dumped it into the garbage can. "You sure know how to mess up a perfect moment," he banged the cabinet door.

"I'm trying to save my marriage," Veronica said, her shoulders heaving. "Don't you think I want to continue to feel what you give me, but I can't sacrifice my entire family for such a selfish reason? I chose the life I have a long time ago and like my oath in medicine, I must live up to my marriage commitment."

"Till death do us part. Then get out of here now!" Tony said, striding angrily toward the door. "And don't let the door hit you where the good Lord…."

"Tony," Veronica stopped him before he yanked open the door. Veronica wanted to stay with Tony for the rest of her life, and she knew it would take every ounce of her willpower to walk out the door. "I need you tonight," she said softly, lowering herself to the chair. "I really need you."

Tony yanked her out of the chair. "Do you think you can play with my emotions anyway you feel? This is not a goddamn movie set," he shook her by the shoulder. I can't make love to you and let you walk out on me. "You either want to be with me, or you don't. I need to know. I have to know. There are things I need to do if you stay."

A knock on the door stopped them both from giving in to each other. Their attraction was intense and demanding and was not the kind of bad habit one could go cold turkey on.

"Who could that be?" Tony said, bad-tempered, crossing the room to open the door. Damn these door-to-door Christians. He pulled open the door.

"Surprise." The chic, stunning woman at the door threw her arms around Tony. He went ashen.

"Tia?" His voice was low.

The woman was staring past him, looking directly at Veronica with a glint of anger in her eyes.

"Hello," she pushed past Tony into the room. "I'm Tia. Tony's fiancée."

Veronica was speechless. It took her a full minute to recover. "I'm Dr. Whittaker."

"Oh!" The woman's attitude changed. "Tony speaks so highly of you. I didn't mean to barge in, but Tony has been working so hard he hasn't come home to look at our new house in months. I thought I'd surprise him and bring pictures. Were you working?"

"We were just about finished." Veronica gathered her belongings. Thank God it was her idea to end this crazy relationship, but the pain of betrayal stabbed her like a hot knife through cold butter, goring her insides to shreds. What did she expect? She was nine years his senior. The woman before her could not be more than twenty-five. Veronica mustered her courage, numbness spreading over her like she'd been anesthetized. As her cheeks thawed and finally pulled into a smile, she said, "Tia, it's a pleasure to meet you. I hope we get to see more of each other soon," she said, fleeing the apartment.

CHAPTER THIRTY-ONE

FOUR WEEKS AFTER Memorial Day, at 6:30 a.m., singing and feeling great, April clipped down the stairs. Today was the big day. She'd waited for six months and finally, it was time to climb the last hill to her career dream. If Frank Easton had had reservations about her social skills, they'd surely been vanquished on Memorial Day. It could only have been better if her mother hadn't been quite as unfurling, but Gabriella was Gabriella.

"Morning." She glanced over the paper Sam was reading. After she got the confounded job, she would deal with her decaying personal life once and for all. Get everything in kilter. "Today is the big day. Wish me luck." April said to Sam. Since Memorial Day, they had warmed up a bit toward each other but not enough. Sam had seemed calmer somehow and almost a little regretful. Yes, indeed. After today, she would make peace with herself and her husband in one way or the other.

"Good luck." He kept reading.

"What's your day like today?" She wanted to invite him to lunch if she got the job.

"Same ole, same ole. Trying to beg for more money for this star and for wannabes. Tomorrow I'm going to LA."

"But you'll be home tonight, won't you?" April's stomach lurched. If she did get the job, though he'd probably be pissed, there was no one in the world she wanted to share it with but Sam,.

"Yeah. I'll be home."

"Tonight, Sam. As God is my witness tonight," April promised, her voice laden with urgency. I'll make it right with us."

At seven thirty a.m., Frank Easton walked into the pre-meeting with S&G's department heads, which now included Martin Spiro and the other traitors. He'd wanted them assembled an hour before April came into the room. The captains and keepers of the gates of Babylon watched closely as Frank ambled over to his seat. "We have concluded our investigation into the activities of our past CFO. Each of you will be briefed on the responses, PR spin, and any material effect Kusak's shenanigans had on your particular department. All the missing funds have been replaced, and I assure you this unfortunate event has been contained." The betrayers looked anywhere but at Frank, who was very convincing. "I'm glad to report it's business as usual, with one exception. We need to announce our new CFO today. That's why we are here this morning." He avoided looking at Martin and, for that matter, at all the traitors in the room. Those not in the know were attentive and anticipating. Frank paused. The silence was palpable. "Well," he continued, "we've asked Martin Spiro to join us because he is the one who has worked closest with April Summers. I think his input will be valuable to all of you and will support the choice we must make. Martin, go ahead." Frank shuddered at the thought of the charade taking place. Everyone in the room except fifteen people were in the know.

Martin smiled at the unsuspecting department heads and the members of the traitor group. He concentrated on those he did not know. "This is an awful spot to be in," Martin began; his voice was cold and steady. Frank watched him carefully. The man was a schlock. Vapid and swarthy. What was he even doing in a company like S&G? Ah, he remembered. Favors returned for favors done. And now a blackmailer. He should kill Kusak, and he still might.

Martin felt a right Uriah Heap, and though this was all play-acting, he needed to make it look as though he were a chosen CFO rather than a front. "April Summers is top drawer," Martin continued. "There is no doubt about that. She has all the credentials and the skills to make her an outstanding CFO here at S&G. I couldn't sit here and say otherwise, but," he cleared his throat, "we have more than April Summers to consider. We have our clients both internally and externally. If you look over the poll we have taken, I'm afraid if we make April Summers CFO, our clients might not quite like our choice."

"Ah, they'll get used to it. It's the trend in Corporate America." Martell Gilmore, EVP of HR, gruffed. He hated what was happening to the American industry. "It seems promoting Blacks to top positions is a growing trend. The research says it is not about Black; it is about economic survival—an economic necessity. The landscape of America is changing, and money is shifting in its power base. This is the reality of our world we have to deal with over the next many decades. It would be a strategic decision to push the envelope on this. To be a leader."

"I second what Martin has said," Herman Stauss, VP of Sales & Marketing, offered. "It is true and maybe even an imperative in mass markets such as the car industry, clothing establishments, utility companies and others with heavy consumer clientele. These companies must reflect the population at large. But we are an exclusive investment institution. Our clients represent the top five percent of American earnings. I assure you those clients are not Black. They don't want their future in the hands of mass hysteria over the makeup of workforce 2049 or whenever. What would we have to gain? We might have a lot to lose. Perceptions don't change that fast among rich, white men."

"That should not be a consideration. Miss Summers earned the right to be considered for this position because of her excellence, not her color." Raymond Pruss, VP of Information Systems, one of the outsiders, said laconically. He was young and of a different generation and a newbie who played rap music and bopped around the halls all day. "What reason would we give Ms. Summers why she would not be offered the position?"

"That's the concern we have here, and we need consensus. We have to be very careful about discrimination. We can be sued, and that's why we've come up with what we think is a brilliant solution," Frank said regrettably. He'd have fought tooth and nail for April Summers as his CFO in another time or place. She was brilliant, but unfortunately, was not bribable. "I think you'll like our solution." He said, knowing he had sealed his and April Summers's fate so many years before when he consented to become a part of the embezzlement scheme now commonplace at top corporations. Frank sat erectly in his chair. It was time for him to retire. Blot out his name from the annals of S&G and retire. Hell, what would a man of his age do in prison?

"I wish reality were different," Martin looked pained. "But it isn't. I have worked with April for eight years. I know she can do this job with her eyes closed but that's not the only question here, though, is it?"

Frank suddenly understood the snake in Martin. His evil was totally underestimated. Like father like son. "We need to be on the same page once she walks through that door."

April was seated at her desk, glowing. Everything will work out just fine. And if not, giving some thought to Sam's plan 'B' was not at all that unpleasant. In fact, it warmed her insides—a little Summers. The idea was beginning to gel. Scanning the *Investor's Business Daily,* her eyes registered nothing. Her nerves were on edge, and she read the same line ten times. April had been waiting patiently, well not so patiently, for the call from upstairs. Once her position as CFO was confirmed, she would take a well-deserved vacation. She'd take her husband back to Jamaica. And they would make a little Summers.

The phone on April's desk jingled. For whatever psychological issues it salved, she made it ring longer than usual. It was one of those moaning jingles she'd meant to change since the new phone system got installed, but the task never made it to the top of her to-do list.

"Hello," April said excitedly.

"Hey. It's Veronica."

April was disappointed. "Hey, friend." She said flatly. "How are you?"

"Is this a bad time for you?"

"No. I was just expecting another call. Did you have a good time at the party?"

"The best. Haven't seen a hide or hare of Melody since then, either." Veronica said.

"Well, now. I guess the mark on her forehead is getting bigger and bigger. I think it's time for a Trinity meeting."

"Lord is it ever. I left Tony. Randolph and I are going to give our marriage a chance."

"Is this what you really want?"

"It's what I want," Veronica said, unsure of how she would face each day without Tony.

"Let's plan to get together soon. I'll really need my Trinity after going before the honchos today begging for my job."

Begging. Ah, don't think so. Good luck, old girl. What time is your date with the men in grey?"

"Actually, I thought you were them."

"Knock them dead. Hold up the rights of women all over the world. Especially the BBBs."

"Right." April chuckled.

"Anyway, I called for a different matter," Veronica said.

"What?"

"Do you know what you get for being the 'hostess with the mostest'?"

"Let me see. Two prepaid tickets and the key to a beach cottage in St. Barts."

"That was behind door number one. Sorry. But you, my dear, get an invitation to this wonderful shindig."

"That sounds great."

"Not when you hear that it's gonna cost $1,000 dollars per ticket. But it's for a good cause—a benefit for infertility research. I'm a committee member and have to sell ten tickets. With you and Sam, Melody, Charles, Randolph, and I, I'd only have four more to gooo." Veronica sang.

"I hope you know the can of worms you're opening. I sit on six committees that have yearly benefits. When is it?"

"Next Saturday."

"So soon. I'm sure I have nothing to wear."

"Neither do the rest of us. We're shopping bright and early Saturday morning. Come and meet us."

"Okay. Where?"

"How about in front of Prada on East Oak."

"Which door? North, south…"

"Ah, shit. I wouldn't know north from south if they gave me a compass. Let's change the venue. How about in front of Chanel? Michigan Ave. Ten o'clock sharp. Only one door there. The other Miss Thing will probably want to go in there anyway. I swear the girl spends a fortune on 'occasion' dresses. Half the clothes in her closet still have tags on them. Me. $300 tops, and I'd better be able to wear it again."

"Count me in."

April's assistant poked her head around the door. "Ms. Summers, Mr. Easton's assistant, just called. It's time."

"Dead woman walking," April said and hurriedly hung up the phone.

"Thanks." April rose from behind the mammoth glass desk, stuffed the envelope with her resignation letter into her briefcase should things not go as expected, and went over to the mirrored wall in her office to examine her appearance. She peered at her reflection. Confidence and assurance looked back. "Well, Chickadee," she said to the image, *this is it. Today will change your life in more ways than one. I hope you're doing the right thing,* a little voice squealed in her head. Her stomach lurched. Here she was, April looked around the room, standing at a door that could open wide, yet to her back was one that would surely close if she didn't get the job. Every ending is a beginning, she repeated as she walked through the door.

At thirty-two, standing at the crossroads of her life, April Summers felt frightened. At Harvard, she'd been the only Black in her social group. Well-appointed, sexy, educated, and glamorous among a sea of white intellectuals, April had proven herself smarter than most, many whose only presence there was due to nepotism rather than intellect. Despite her brilliance, or maybe because of it, she'd not been spared the reality of her heritage. Contrary to her mother's belief, April understood America's original sin's deep roots could overshadow her impeccable record and outstanding achievements at S&G as it had at Harvard. In a few minutes, her professional life would culminate either by being selected as the best-qualified candidate to be the

CFO at S&G or by facing a decision hinging solely on society's prejudices. Deep feelings of doubt began to surface, but April choked them back with a vengeance. *Too late now, baby. There is no turning back. Get your silly ass out of there and do what you do best. Win.*

"I don't know how long this is going to take, Danielle, but I'll be back," April said to her assistant, every ounce of courage back where it belonged. Her feelings of uncertainty had taken flight, replaced by her fighting spirit.

"Miss Summers. It's going to be a piece of cake. Congratulations ahead of time."

"What confidence!" She playfully punched Danielle's arm. "Thanks."

As April strode down the corridor to the elevators, her mind trailed to Melody Adams. She had maneuvered her way into running one of the biggest deals in town. That Melody would be the first female to make a fortune 500 company CEO in Chicago made her a little jealous. She felt awful about her thoughts, but she was being honest. She didn't envy that it would be Melody, and not her, who would be the female unicorn, remembered. If she had to fight this hard for CFO, what would she have had to do, and how many more years would it take to land the CEO position at S&G. *I can do this.* April erected her shoulders. *Seize the day, for there's no day but today.*

April turned right off the elevator and walked hastily towards the conference room. She had been in that room a thousand times, and if she didn't get the CFO position, this would be her last. On the spot, she would resign. April turned the door handle calmly and entered with utter confidence. "Gentlemen," April said solemnly. "Good morning""Mrs. Summers. Come in." The men rose.

Around the table were a couple dozen C-level white men and Martin. Not a single woman. The air was heavy. *Martin!* The thought registered as her eyes made four with blubber. *What the hell was Martin Spiro doing here? Surely, this was not a good sign.* She extended her hand to the President and CEO, nodded to the other department heads, and sat solemnly in the only empty chair.

"Mrs. Summers," Frank Easton began. "After that wonderful party, I feel I can call you April. I had a wonderful time."

"Frank," April extended the familiarity. "It was a pleasure to have you."

"Who made that fantastic barbecue sauce?"

"The caterer." April deadpanned.

"Make sure you leave me their name."

"Definitely."

"April," Frank stared at her, "I've had an opportunity to review your records since you've been here with us at S&G. It's impressive. Very impressive, indeed."

Good so far. "I thought so," April said. She was not about to kowtow.

"As impressive as your record is …"

Aha, here comes the double talk. April straightened her spine. *Nah. He was not going to do that old, tired ass 'build them up before you tear them down' number.*

"…being a superstar at one level does not ensure success at another. Managing a department and being responsible for multiple functions and people is different from managing the entire company's portfolio. Peter Principle, you know. We have some concerns about this, so we brought you in to ask a few more questions."

Peter Principle, my ass. Why don't you say we're not sure a Black woman can fit in at the top? "I'm well aware of the Peter

Principle concept, but I truly don't believe it applies in this case, Mr. Easton. However, I will answer any questions that will *further* put you at ease about my qualifications for the job. But might I remind you I have been running the finance group for the past five years—the people, process, portfolio, and the lion's share of S&G's business. Though I didn't have the title, I have been the CFO of S&G for the past five years."

"Yes, Mrs. Summers, we've garnered that."

Martin Spiro cleared his throat and took a sip of water. "I can say, between April and I, we did have much managing to do in Kusak's absence."

Frank, too polite to address Martin, looked straight ahead.

April almost murdered him with her stare.

"Well, err…that's basically what we found. We have a proposition. I'd like to run it by you to see what you think."

April felt the thermostat of anger and hormones turn way up. She sat still. *The ugly, short, hooked-nose, prehistoric creature.*

"We would like a transition period. We want you to consider being a co-interim CFO in the next six months. Based on your past performance here, I know it may be an insult to you, but you will agree it is in our best interest. If you can live with that, we'd like to offer you the opportunity to work closely with Martin in the CFO position. We are prepared to re-evaluate in the next six months." It was the best Frank could do.

Martin. The dunce? What an insult! April allowed her shoulders to relax, giving no clue to the somersault inside her stomach. They were offering her the CFO position with conditions. Conditions they called a transition with the dunce Martin as her spy and watchdog! Well, that did it. As far as she was concerned, America had failed again. April looked around the room calmly. "Gentlemen. I've worked hard for this company. For eight years, I dreamed only of this day. I have prided myself on being educated, fair, and, above all, I believed in S&G. I was convinced education would be the great equalizer of opportunity and that ability, rather than the color would create a new reality. I see now that I have been living a dream—an illusion. I appreciate your consideration, but you have indeed insulted me. Martin Spiro is a dunce. How dare you put me in the same category as him?"

Martin went beet red.

Frank choked on his water.

"Gentlemen, you lack self-respect; I'm going to choose to believe, for your sakes, you made a bad decision because you still believe that S&G must have a white male CFO. A business imperative, so to speak. I thank you for your offer, but unfortunately, I must decline." She reached into her briefcase, "You can accept my resignation."

"April." Frank Easton was on his feet. "It was not that way at all."

"Really, Frank. What way was it? Are you saying you didn't sit here and discuss how my image would affect your wealthy patrons? Didn't you consider my color at all? In hindsight," she continued, "I believe you made the right decision. I just want to remind you there is a basic law of science and nature. Gates, Mr. Easton, keep out as well as keep in. Time will prove, a company like S&G, if such was the thought pattern that led you to this decision, is on its way to extinction. I look forward to that day. But as of now, Sirs, this horse is out of the stable, and I intend to gallop to the finish line or to my death." April searched their faces in front of her. There was fright. She knew they were petrified of a lawsuit, but she wouldn't waste her time. Frank was squirming, Martin was distressed, and the others were mortified. April spun on her heels, walking briskly out of the room.

In her office, she didn't stop to answer the eager question hanging on anyone's lips. She simply cleared out her office and walked out of S&G without looking back.

Frank Easton went dejectedly to his office. As soon as the fire quelled, he would resign.

When he looked up Martin was behind him. "You can't leave it like this. If you do you are dead either way. April Summers is not one to lie down and die."

"And so, what do you suggest?"

CHAPTER THIRTY-TWO

RANDOLPH WAS IN his study when Veronica arrived home. She stood momentarily at the door, watching him. Totally engrossed, his fingers moved at lightning speed across the keyboard; his jaw was set with a determination she hadn't seen since they were children. Veronica tiptoed up the stairs, going directly to their bedroom—now hers alone. She'd made an utter fool of herself, and as suddenly as it started, not because of her but because of Tia, she jettisoned her feeling for Tony. He'd lied. He was her junior by nine years, and he had lied. How could she have cheated on Randolph with such a man? For eighteen years, he'd been her everything. What on earth had come over her? For the past couple of months, they had been civil and unspoken covenants had been made but the ice had not thawed.

In the walk-in closet changing her clothes, Veronica felt a nostalgic jolt as her eyes landed on a pair of Randolph's old black flip-flops. He'd had them for as long as they'd been married. She slipped a foot into the well-worn grooves. Like the imprints of a dental cast, her foot, with ease and comfort, molded to the grooves known to her as the symmetry of their life. How could she have been so insane to think of leaving this man? She knew every crevice of his heart. His very soul, and though not perfect, it was enough. The velocity of her love for Randolph hit her like a bolt of lightning. Thank God the woman had walked in. She could have made a terrible mistake.

With determination, Veronica hastened down the stairs. She stood in the study archway, watching as her husband intensely stuck key after key on his computer.

"Eighteen years," Veronica said, unsure which of the bitter emotions running through her head caused the spill from her soul—Tony's betrayal, her betrayal, or anger at Randolph for giving up on their marriage so easily. "Why didn't you fight for me?" Her voice trembled with uncertain emotions. "Why did you file for a divorce without even a fight?"

"What did you want me to do?" Randolph didn't flinch. "Come to claim you with a stick?"

"You could've fought. Fought for me. Make me feel I was worth fighting for after eighteen years."

Randolph stopped typing and swung his swivel chair to face her. "Veronica, you are a brilliant, successful, and grown woman. I can't force you to love me, but that doesn't change how I feel about you. I have always loved you, and I suspect that I always will, even if we divorce. But I don't fight. Don't you remember even that much about me?"

"Break your rules for me, damn it," Veronica said. "I know I have behaved badly, but sometimes Randolph; I don't think you deserve me…you should have fought." Her voice faltered.

"Behave? For heaven's sakes, I have never known you to behave. You always had a filthy mouth, an erratic streak, an obsession with success and a deep survival instinct that helped you beat the odds. That's one reason I married you because you knew how to fight when I didn't. Have you ever known me to fight a dirty war, Veronica?"

"I'm your wife!" Veronica was indignant.

"Are you? I'm not the one who's changed, Vee. That was you."

"I haven't changed. I fell prey to the one thing I said I wouldn't. Unbridled ambition."

"No argument here. But ambition is good. It's the byproducts of ambition that cause problems. Ambition is God's test of the poor. He grants wishes, and what does he get back? Hubris."

Veronica stood still. How could she have forgotten Randolph had always been head and shoulders above most? Sticking to his values, no matter what?

"I'm sorry we've come to this, Vee. When the treadmill started running too fast, we needed time to adjust, but we didn't make time."

"And now we've run our way into a new world."

"Not me. I see no difference between our world now and when we were kids. We're still on the same path. You just got to the finish line first. But you no longer love or believe in me. What should a man with dignity do but go without another word?"

"Oh, God, Randolph," Veronica covered the space between them. "I made one mistake. I'm not perfect. Don't you think I tried? Why? Why didn't you fight for me?" Veronica wept openly.

Randolph turned back to his computer. He was overcome with emotions and too much pain.

"Please look at me. Look at me, Randolph, and remember. I don't want a divorce. I need you to forgive me. Give me another chance. Let me love you again. Please."

"Why should I?"

"Do you remember the day in the park just before we went off to college?" she asked.

"Yeah. Like it was yesterday. We were so young. So invincible, he got up and paced the room.

"You'd written your bestseller then. You told me the entire story, remember? It was a great story, Randolph. I want to be here for the end of the story. Whatever happened to it?"

"I've finished it." He paused. "Just last night. To tell the truth, I'm scared. Scared to send it out and have it rejected. I wouldn't be able to write again."

"Oh, Randolph. They won't reject it. It's a marvelous story."

"That's easy for you to say. When you take an exam for med school, you either pass or fail. It's different for me. I always feel like a failure if my work is rejected."

"That's ridiculous." Veronica sniffled. "A rejection letter is entirely subjective. If mysteries aren't selling this year, not even a well-known author can get a lucrative contract, much less a first-time author."

"Maybe. But the story of the struggle gets tiring. It did for you, didn't it, Veronica? Isn't that why you wanted to break up our home?"

Veronica was very still. She could not utter a word. She was no better than the cold, heartless editors slowly taking away her husband's dreams. What she felt for Tony was no fluke. It was a mistake, but no fluke. She cared about him more than she wanted to admit. But could she live on the fumes of impetuous love? Randolph was safe, dependable, kind, and a wonderful father, and he loved her. Maybe he no longer ignited the same passion in her as Tony did, but she loved him. She always had. She would never tell him about Tony. Never.

"I'm going to bed." Randolph headed toward the door.

"Randolph," Veronica called after him. She had to do something. She had to. As Veronica watched her husband cross the room, she saw him with new eyes. He was still the most handsome man she knew, and there was no question she wanted to go home where she belonged.

"I want you to come with me to the awards dinner. I have so much to thank you for because I couldn't have done anything without the freedom you allowed me to have. I need you by my side," she'd tried anything to keep him.

"As what? A clown, a jester, a pauper, or a spurned husband? I don't think so. After all, I wouldn't want to embarrass you."

"Randolph, please. Come with me."

"As what do you want me to come as, Vee. Answer me?"

"As my husband, what if I said I'd like you to come with me always in this life in every sense of the word?" Veronica had to go for the bold.

Randolph stopped in front of her. The look in his eyes was one she'd known for eighteen years. He still loved her. Veronica knew her decision to be with Randolph was the only decision she would've made. *Good-bye Tony*. She moved slowly toward Randolph, unable to deny the loss slowly sweeping over her. Tony had been more than an intrigue or a fling. The lust, the need and the inferno of their desire had been as real as the man standing before her. In another space and time, she would've been able to love Tony as much as she did Randolph, but as much as Tony had reacquainted her with the pleasures of a paradise long gone, she'd gone there and beyond with her man who had taken her to nirvana. Randolph watched her closely. Ever flicker in her eyes—every muscle in her face.

"Is this how you solve problems?"

"It's one way," Veronica whispered.

"How badly do you want me, Veronica? For the rest of your life or just for tonight?" Randolph blazed a steely gaze into his wife's eyes. They were glistening with watery pain.

"I want you," her husky voice whispered in his ear. "For all time. Oh, God, Randolph," she pleaded, wet streaking her face. "Forgive me for hurting you. I can't live without you. Please, take me back to where I belong."

"Who do you belong to?" Randolph caught her by the hips.

"You."

"Where?"

"By your side."

"For how long?"

"Forever."

"So, your fire still burns for me, huh? Show me, Veronica, where your fire burns for me." Randolph pulled her to him. "Show me where it will burn for all times."

Veronica pulled back, took his hand, and placed it over her throbbing heart. "Here," she said softly, "always here just for you until life puts it out."

Randolph wept. His tears mingled with his wife's, and together they wept in each other's arms. "I've missed you so, so much," he buried his face into her hair. "So very much."

CHAPTER THIRTY-THREE

THE SILENCE IN APRIL'S head was deafening. She waited and waited for the madness to descend, but all she heard was the ticking of the clock in Eve's office. How long had she been sitting there? What the hell did it matter? "Tell Eve I'll be back." April smiled weakly at the redhead, moving trance-like toward the elevator. She should go home. It was time to tell Sam she'd finally got religion.

No one could fault her for wanting a drink today. April stopped by Michael's, the neighborhood's bar, for a drink and to wait until it was time for Sam to get home. She downed drink after drink at the bar; dead, arid, devoid of any hope of recapturing her idealism for a just world. Gone was the hope of ever transcending the vileness of oppression. In the haze of the alcohol-induced stupor, she found momentary peace.

"I should call you a cab," the bartender offered. The woman had been sitting in the bar since three o'clock. He looked at his watch; it was eight p.m.

"I'll be fine. I haven't had much to drink, have I?"

"You put away quite a bit there, ma'am."

"Get me a coffee to go, will you, Mike? I'll wait this out in my car. Don't worry. I'm fine, and I promise not to drink and drive. Scouts honor."

April stumbled when she tried to get up.

"I'll call Mr. Summers." Michael appeared from nowhere. Obviously, the inveterate bartender had told Michael of her condition. Michael's was at one time Sam's and April's favorite watering hole. That was until they no longer had fun together.

"Michael," April slurred. "Don't make a fuss. I've left here in worse condition than this and made it home. Plus, I told bozo I'd wait it out in the car. All I asked for was some damn coffee, not the martini Gestapo!"

"I'm coming to check on you in half an hour," Michael said, handing her the Styrofoam cup of coffee. "Don't move until then."

Michael's was not far from her home, and April felt sober enough to drive, so she did not heed his advice. She started the car and pulled out of the parking spot, tapping the car's bumper directly behind her. About a mile down the road, April found focusing on the road near impossible. The relentless pounding in her head blinded her vision. When the world seemed to be spinning very fast on its axis, April, too drained emotionally, physically, and from drinking too much, was forced to reconsider her decision. She pulled her car to the side of the road and locked the doors. She was one foolish woman, she thought as her head drooped to the steering wheel. Sam would be furious she'd behaved ridiculously over some stupid job. Today she was one stressed-out girl, and stressed-out girls were allowed a drink or two.

April turned on her hazard lights and turned on the stereo. She felt twice as old as her thirty-two years, maybe even older. Well, old girl, what are you going to do now? You are unemployed, your husband will probably leave you after this fiasco, and you're so drunk and numb, none of it matters. April pushed the phone button on the steering wheel that said home.

Sam was sitting under a lamp reading. His eyes scanned the same passage over and over. All day, he'd waited on a call from April. He wasn't happy about a job promotion, but she could have at least called! When he hadn't heard from her, he decided she must have wanted to surprise him, so he'd left the office early to be home when April got there. His own surprise, a romantic dinner, now a crisp. It was nine o'clock, and she hadn't bothered to call. Sure, he was feeling guilty about Sophie, and he was still ashamed of his volatile behavior, which had prompted him to be kinder about this job business than he would've been, but it was still pretty maddening his wife was so self-involved . He wasn't going to take it anymore. Sam jumped to answer the ringing phone knocking over the lamp.

"Sam, it's April." He didn't mistake the slur in her voice. "I'm afraid I'd better not drive home. Could you come and get me?"

"Where are you?" Sam howled.

"I was at Michael's. I just pulled onto the highway, but I'm afraid I'm in no shape to drive."

"At least you used good sense for once," Sam barked. He was livid. "Keep your lights on and lock the door. It'll take me a few minutes to get there. Don't leave the car," he ordered. Is that understood?"

"Yup." April hiccupped, gagging as a sudden wave of nausea rose into her throat. What was she to do now? The rising bile made her decision easy. Urgently, she yanked at the door tumbling outside just in time to throw up on the grass. How the hell did she come to this? "April's eyes filled with tears. Drunk by the side of the road?

She was relieved when the shadow moved toward her. "Sam," she whispered, grateful to him for rescuing her. Resolved, April decided never again would she be so stupid.

"Don't move," a sinister voice from the shadow ordered, pressing something cold to the back of her head.

"It's okay, Sam. I feel better." April moved sluggishly as though in a slow-motion dream—maybe even a nightmare. She turned slowly, and instead of Sam; she came face-to-face with two menacing-looking men. She stared at them blankly, not registering much of what was happening. She smiled weakly. "Thank you for helping, but I'm waiting…"

"Shut up bitch, and don't move," one man said as the other rummaged through the car.

"Not much in here, but this is a nice ride. Let's just give the bitch what every bitch deserves and then take the car."

"Yeah. I've never banged a high-class bitch before." The man with the gun was smiling, running his tongue over his lips.

"Maybe we should go, let's just scare her."

"Com'on man. Just a bit of fun."

April, even in her stupor, realized she was in danger. A panic rose in her, and she tried to run for her car. One man grabbed her by the hair and dragged her behind the car, out of view of passersby. They couldn't possibly hurt her here on the road. But there were no streetlights, and April knew no one in Chicago would stop at night for a car parked on the side of the road. One man bound her hand with a rope that appeared from nowhere. The other guy was trying to rip off her blouse.

As Sam approached where he thought April should be, there was what appeared to be a commotion. Police cars and an ambulance with flashing lights and sirens surrounded a vehicle. He inched closer. It was April's car!

Sam slammed on the brakes and sprinted to the scene.

"Step back. Get back. This is police business," a blue coat ordered.

"It's my wife. You don't understand. That's my wife's car." Sam pushed forward.

"Step back," the cop ordered again before he understood.

"What happened?" Sam was near hysterical.

"A passerby called when he heard screams. The screams, it seems, scared off the men."

"Please, may I go to her?"

April was prone on a stretcher. Just before the EMS attendant covered her, Sam could see her blouse had been ripped. .

"April," Sam jumped into the ambulance earning him a cautious look from an attendant.

"The husband," the police indicated.

April's face was bruised, and she seemed dazed. Sam reached for her hand. "I'm here, honey. It's going to be all right."

"I'm so sorry, Sam," she wailed, "So sorry."

"Don't speak now. It's going to be okay. Did they—they—" He turned to the ambulance attendant.

A shrug of the shoulder did little to allay Sam's worst fear. They couldn't have. There was no time. He'd been there in ten minutes.

"Can I go home now, Sam?" April was clutching his shirt, her knuckles bloodless.

"No, sweetie. We're taking you to the hospital."

"Please don't, Sam. I've made such a fool of myself. I don't want to embarrass you anymore. Please take me home and promise you won't call mother." He could tell she was already trying to block out the trauma.

"April," Sam said firmly, "We have to go to the hospital."

"Okay." April searched her husband's face for some clue of what he was feeling. Disgust, pity, hatred? What did it matter? She was a failure, regardless.

"I didn't get the job, Sam," April explained. "I just needed a little drink." She wilted.

"Don't worry about that now."

"I can't believe —"

"Shush. It's okay. It's S&G's loss, not yours."

Though thoroughly disgusted with his wife, Sam Summers closed his arms protectively around her.

At the hospital, April was examined. Her blood-curdling screams had scared off the assailants.

"Mrs. Summers." The attending physician said. "We would like to keep you for a day until Dr. Bringham sees you."

"Who is Dr. Bringham?" April asked.

"He's chief of Psychiatry."

"Why do I need to see him?"

The doctor affirmed, though he believed she was not in physical danger, he feared she would experience post-traumatic syndrome.

"I'm fine." April insisted.

"You may feel fine now, but…."

"I'm fine." April was taciturn.

April insisted on being sent home. She was downright belligerent about it. Sam tried to talk her into staying for an evaluation, but she would have none of it. No way, not in this life, would she see another crazy" doctor.

"Sam. I'm going home, and don't try to stop me."

"April," his voice was no-nonsense, "this is ridiculous. What are you doing? You have to deal with this. The doctors are concerned about post-traumatic syndrome."

"Tell the doctors to bugger off." April turned her head away, very angry at Sam for trying to control her.

"April, I'll go through this with you every step of the way, but you have to promise to get help now. You have to get help now."

"Get me out of here. That's all the help I need."

Sam got Dr. Bringham to prescribe some sedatives just in case and to give him a referral for an outpatient psychiatrist in their neighborhood. In the car, April was silent all the way home. It was one-thirty a.m. Friday morning, when they arrived home, April went upstairs and into the shower. She turned the water to as hot as she could bear it, lathered her rag, and scrubbed her skin until it was raw. No matter how much she washed and scrubbed, she could still feel the filthy hands creeping up her skirt. She could smell the man's putrid breath as he lunged forward. He smelled of alcohol, or was that her? Suddenly, she was scared. A new wave of anger swelled within April, and her body shook uncontrollably.

April scrubbed harder as sobs rose in her throat and escalated into wails of anger. The wails brought Sam running into the bathroom. April was fighting off an invisible assailant in between, scrubbing her body raw. Sam threw open the shower door and, fully dressed, got in. He turned off the scalding water and held April until she was somewhat calmed.

Just as the doctor had predicted. Drying her off, Sam pushed her arms through a cotton robe and put her in bed. He gave her a tranquilizer. April didn't fight as Sam held the tablet to her lips. She rolled it over her tongue and took a sip of water. How would he ever forgive her? Would she ever be the same? Then in her head she heard the words *just scare her*. Who were they? April squeezed her eyes shut. Sam stroked her head until she showed signs of drowsiness and when she'd nodded off, he pulled the covers over her and left the room.

The next morning Sam entered the room. He placed a glass of water and a cup of coffee on the bedside table. April was groggy, but awake. He made no move to cuddle her, nor could he look her into the eyes that begged for forgiveness. He dialed the phone number of their housekeeper. "Nancy, I need you to come over this morning. April's car broke down and I have to go and get it. The tow truck won't take it unless someone is there."

"There's no need for all that," April sat up against the pillows. "I'll be fine."

"Nancy will be downstairs. Just ring the service bell if you need her." Sam slipped his cell in his pocket.

"Go on then." She looked at the clock. It was now 10:30 a.m..

CHAPTER THIRTY-FOUR

MID-JUNE, Saturday morning and it was blistering. As always, Michigan Avenue was a zoo.

"You can tell all the people in this group who were potty trained early," Veronica said as Melody sidled up to the door exactly on time. Both dressed in walking shorts. Melody wore a striped couture short set, while Veronica sported cut-off jeans and a T-shirt.

"Global warming and anal retention. I live for it." Melody laughed. "If you'd asked me, I'd have put money on it that April would be the first to arrive."

"Why would you even say that? April has always just been on time for Trinity meetings. I'll go across the street and get us lattes, and you wait here for her." Veronica said.

"I'll have a double mocha caramel macchiato."

"Huh, I see Charles introduced you to something new." Veronica smiled.

"A whole lot a new." Melody blushed. "Remind me to tell you about what he did last night."

After forty minutes of waiting with no sign of April, Veronica flipped open her Samsung and dialed April's number.

"Hello." The woman on the line said.

"This is Veronica Whittaker. Can you tell me what time April left for the city? We've been waiting for forty or so minutes."

"Mrs. Summers didn't leave today. She had a pretty bad accident on Friday. I'm afraid the doctors have sedated her, and I don't think you should expect her."

"What kind of accident?" Veronica looked worriedly at Melody.

"I'm sorry, what I told you is all I know. Mr. Summers will be back in an hour. Maybe you can call back then. I'll tell him you called."

"How is she?"

"She'll be fine."

"And you're sure you have no idea what happened?"

"No, ma'am, but Mr. Summers will be back in an hour." The woman repeated the previous information as though she'd rehearsed it.

"What's wrong?" Melody, who could only hear Veronica's side of the conversation, asked.

"April had an 'accident,' Veronica put the word accident in finger quote marks, and the housekeeper isn't giving up any info. Said to call back when Sam returned. It's bad. I can tell."

"That man is abusing her again? We need to go over there."

"That could be possible, but knowing April and her hysterical self, I bet she didn't get the job and is moping. Or maybe she did have a legitimate accident."

"I'd feel better if we checked on her." Melody insisted.

"Since when did you like her so much?"

"I don't know, but I do like her a lot. So, let's go."

"What about our shopping?" Veronica said.

"We have enough in our closet to wear."

Melody and Veronica hastily made their way to the parking lot.

"I've come to like April, but I still can't imagine what real problems she could have. Her life seems so perfect."

"Oh please, we of all people know life's a bitch, and then you die. Girl, it's not about things; it's what's on the inside. Pain is pain, and when it's up close and personal, it feels like the end of the world, no matter how much money you have. I think wealthy folks have more problems in life."

"Life sure is a humdinger?" Melody said as she got into the car.

"Isn't that the truth? And sometimes, it doesn't matter. You want what you don't have, and when you get it, you use it to destroy your life."

"The golden ghetto." Melody went silent.

"I'll tell you one thing." Veronica sped down the spiral parking ramp. "When I was struggling to rise out of the ashes, I was so much happier. All I thought about was the struggle. Now I'm a hotshot look at what the nonsense almost cost me. I replaced struggle and hope with shame and vanity. Ain't that a bitch?"

Everything Veronica said stood for her life. "Veronica, do you always drive this crazy?" Melody held on to the armrest for dear life.

"We are in a hurry, aren't we?"

Veronica drove around the circular driveway and stopped in front of the door. A woman opened it to their knock.

"Hi. I'm Veronica Whittaker, and this is Melody Adams. We're the ones who called."

"I'm afraid I can't let you in. Mrs. Summers cannot be disturbed."

"Who said that?" Veronica demanded.

"Mr. Summers. And I suppose the doctors."

"Are you sure you can't tell us what happened?"

"No more than I told you on the phone. She had an accident. Mr. Summers has gone to get the car towed. I'm sorry, ladies, I wish I could help."

"Couldn't we just come in? I'm a doctor." Veronica reached for her ID.

A crash upstairs sent the woman flying up the stairs two at a time, but not before slamming the door shut on them.

Veronica and Melody were now seriously concerned. "What's with all the secrecy? Something is fishy here," Veronica said, looking at her watch. She was pressed for time as she had to help out before the gala.

"People have a right to their privacy I suppose," Melody said, following Veronica down the steps.

"Family matter or not, if we don't hear from April or Sam by tomorrow, I assure you it'll be a different story."

April was drowsy. She'd moved her head slowly at the sound of the doorbell and, trying to raise herself, knocked over the lamp. Whatever she was taking, the feel-good medication was fading and darkness descending. Darkness is absolute. In the darkness, one never has to see or feel. In its mercy, it allows those prone to self-combustion to exist in their world of denial. Unfortunately, April was lucid enough for a beacon of light to enter her darkness.

"Mrs. Summers," The housekeeper came running into the room. "Are you alright?" The source of the disturbing crash was the crystal lamp, now splintered on the floor.

"Sorry, I was trying to get up and missed the mark."

"What's going on?" Sam who'd just arrived home came into the room.

"The lamp fell over," April said.

"Two of Mrs. Summers' friends came by just now. Did you see them when you came in? I asked them to come back when you were here."

"No. I didn't see anyone. Thanks Nancy. I'll take it from here. She'll be fine."

"What exactly happened?"

"A carjacking."

Nancy covered her mouth. "You're kidding, right?"

Sam shook his head and walked Nancy to the door.

When Sam returned to the room, April was weeping. "Go away." Her hand balled into a fist, and she seemed ready to strike.

Sam held her flailing hands. "Who do you want to go away?"

April stared blankly at Sam. "Life is nothing but a great big lie. What are you to do when even your mother lies to you?"

"How did she lie?" Sam was very confused.

"She said I was equal to every other human being and that through adversity, the human spirit would triumph and if I worked hard, I could have anything I wanted. She lied to me Sam. She just plain lied."

"She didn't, April. You will triumph."

"No, I won't. I'll never be good enough. Black folks will never triumph."

"You're wrong. But we don't need to talk about this now."

"Yes, we do. I am telling you, Sam, nothing changes."

"Here. Take this," he held the little white pill to her lips.

"I don't want any more drugs. It's time we talked."

"Sweetheart. That can wait."

"No, it can't." April raised herself to a sitting position. Sam, I need to talk."

"Okay," Sam nodded.

"When I was a kid, my circle of friends wasn't what you'd call diverse. They were mostly white and Asian. The Asians and I were always the honor students. It was the same when I went to Harvard. I was only seventeen, and I felt free. I wanted to feel grown-up. Harvard is not as progressive as you'd think. I suppose because slave money built it, it felt invincible in its discrimination. In my junior year I dated this guy Liam. We were good together and came from similar backgrounds. I got pregnant, and he asked me to marry him. I was so happy. So, so happy. We had it all planned. We both had trust funds, and he would continue on in school while I had the baby, and then I would go back to school when he graduated.

My mother went ballistic, as did his parents. They would have none of it. We were overwhelmed. We didn't know what to do. Where to turn. Mother was so furious I'd messed up her perfectly orchestrated life for me 'you cannot, and I repeat, you cannot have this child.' She took me to have an abortion. I was devastated.

Back at school, I skipped classes and spiraled into a very dark place. I felt hopeless and suicidal. I slit my wrist," she proffered her left wrist with the barely visible scar as proof. "The suicidal bit put my mother in a tizzy. She thought I had the "family" disease. My uncle, you see, has been in and out of mental institutions since age eighteen. No one talks about it, but I know his illness was one reason mom went into neurology. I didn't want to kill myself really, but I just couldn't reconcile having killed an unborn child. I wanted to share the pain. That's why Sam, I don't deserve to be a mother."

Sam sat in utter disbelief. He'd been married to April for eight years and had never heard this story. Though he wanted to understand, all he felt was abject betrayal. Finally, however, he understood her fear of motherhood.

"Sam," her eyes beseeched. "Please understand. Please don't judge me. I know I should have told you before," she grabbed his arm, tears streaming down her face, but I was ashamed. I was so scared and afraid."

"Take this." Sam slid the pill between her lips.

CHAPTER THIRTY-FIVE

VERONICA PEEKED into the crowd from backstage to see hardly a seat empty. She looked in the mirror, renewed her cranberry lipstick and took a deep breath. Overall, except for her momentary indiscretion with Tony, life had been worth living. Funny how she rarely thought of him these days. After the Tia incident, she asked that he leave the research project, and she'd finally stopped going on rounds where he would be present.

"Dr. Whittaker, it's almost time for you to make your speech." A volunteer pushed her head around the door.

"How long before I go on?" Veronica nervously cracked her knuckles.

"Right after this. Five minutes or so. Can I get you some water?"

"I'm okay." Veronica clasped her hand behind her back.

"I'll be back to get you in a jiffy." The woman disappeared around the door.

The door creaked open again. "Congratulations." Tony's voice abruptly stopped her from doing the stress-release arm exercise. "You look sensational."

"What are you doing back here?" Veronica was astonished.

"I'll just take a second, but I couldn't let you get up there tonight without an explanation about Tia."

"Tony, this is not about you, and it's certainly no time to throw me off balance." Though he was standing close to her, and her heart was beating irregularly, Veronica remained in control. "Anyway, what exactly is there to explain? You're engaged. I'm married. Our relationship had to end. Please let's be the grown-ups and move on."

"I just can't go on without you. Veronica, let me see you again."

"Tony, go home to Tia."

"There is no Tia."

"Dr. Whittaker," the attendant called.

"My answer to any question you could ask me, with or without Tia, Tony is no. I have got to go." Veronica said as her name was being called.

Veronica approached the podium with a glittering smile for the audience. "No discovery is made by one person. It is only from building on ideas, theories, and through thousands of observations that breakthroughs are possible. Many patients have sacrificed their time and shared their pain with us to allow physicians like me and Dr. Tony Reifenburg to come to our conclusions. Dr. Reifenburg is, in fact, a significant contributor to this research, and I would like to acknowledge him by asking him to join me in accepting this award."

Tony Reifenburg struggled to hold back the emotions he was feeling. Overwhelmed with feelings of both joy and pain, he rose, buttoned his jacket, and joined Veronica on stage. He really loved her.

Randolph examined his program. Patrons cheered nonstop.

The way Tony looked at Veronica when he got on stage meant he could have been his rival. He had a hunch, but he didn't want to know. Melody, too, was observing the couple on the stage. She now clearly understood Veronica's attraction. Tony Reifenburg was indeed fine. As she watched them, she understood the passion that had fueled their love and, for the first time, released her anger at Veronica.

"You were sensational," Melody said when Veronica joined her friends from the podium.

"Congratulations. That was some honor." Charles Bell clasped her hand warmly.

"Thanks."

"You done good, baby. Real good." Veronica's mother's lips quivered with pride as she handed her daughter a beautifully wrapped present.

"You got that right, Ma. That's because you raised me right. Thanks, Mom." Veronica kissed her mother's wrinkled cheek. It was Veronica's time to tear up. "Thank you, all of you. You are all so very special to me," she turned to her husband, reaching for his hand. "But a special thanks to my husband who has loved me more than I ever deserved."

Tony had left after the presentation, but without question, he had renewed respect for Veronica Whittaker. He understood why she had to leave him.

Onstage, some crooner was crooning. There was an all-star lineup of musical artists. From rap to love songs. The old and the new. Who says they are so different? Melody almost jumped out of her skin when Boys II Men came on. She adored the song they were performing, humming along with delight. "You'll make the greatest mistake of your life don't do it, babybee. Ohh, Ohh, Ohh, Oh, awoo."

"Okay, enough of this sentimental stuff. Let's go celebrate." Randolph said.

"I can't. I have to go backstage now to help out." Veronica's smoky voice was even huskier than usual.

Veronica's mom shook her head. "That woman has a voice on her. Whoopi has nothing on my baby."

"Only those wacky dreads." Melody laughed.

CHAPTER THIRTY-SIX

THREE WEEKS HAD passed, and no one had heard a peep out of April Summers. Veronica and Melody were worried sick. On one of their early morning power walks down Lake Shore, Veronica announced. "I'm going over there, and I will kick down the door if no one lets me in." She swung her arms with exaggeration.

"I can't believe her husband won't let us see her. Talk about *Boxing, Helena!*" Melody said, shaking her head in disbelief.

"Whatever it is, three weeks is a lot of time to stay cooped up even in an ultraluxe house!" Veronica said. "I'm going over there first thing this morning."

"I'm coming with you."

Veronica, NASCAR racer extraordinaire, beeped her horn repeatedly at what she termed the damn fool drivers of Chicago as she sped down streets with twenty-five-speed limit signs at forty-five miles an hour. They made it to April in record time.

"Maybe we should mind our own business," Melody said, seeming to have a change of heart.

"We are minding our business. April is our business. Remember. Holy Trinity."

"We are that."

The women banged on the door and waited.

The housekeeper opened the door a fraction.

"We're here to see Mrs. Summers."

"Mrs. Summers is resting."

"If you don't let us in, we're calling the police." Veronica put her foot in the slightly cracked door.

"On what grounds?" The housekeeper asked indignantly. "Mrs. Summers is resting." She repeated.

"Then we'll see for ourselves and be on our way."

"Wait here," the housekeeper said, letting them into the foyer and disappearing upstairs.

"Follow me," she said moments later from the top of the stairs.

The room was in darkness. Heavy drapes blocked out every bit of light. "April," Veronica felt for a light switch.

"Don't turn on the light, please," April's voice reached them.

"Then I'll just draw the curtains a bit."

"Don't do that either," April said wearily.

"What the hell is going on?" Veronica demanded.

A sliver of morning sun strained through the drawn curtains. Melody couldn't stop herself from taking in the elegance of April's bedroom. Done in mint and beige, the room was neither masculine nor feminine.

April dragged herself to a sitting position. "I'm so sorry I couldn't make it the Awards event, but you didn't have to come all the way out here to see me. How was it."

"Veronica was amazing!"

"Congrats. So, deserving."

"We called, and we visited and then called some more. What is going on? Why hasn't Sam called us back?"

April patted the bed, and the women sat down.

"I asked him not to. I asked him to give me some time. I'm okay. Really, I'm. Just taking some time to sort myself out. Even my mother thinks we're on vacation in Italy. What time is it anyway?"

"Ten o'clock."

"What's going on?" Veronica insisted. "I had to threaten to call the police to get in here this morning."

"That's drastic."

"Okay, April. Enough. Cut to the chase," Veronica demanded.

Melody sat transfixed. So, this is what happens when high born people get disappointed. Hell, April would never have survived South Central L.A.

April fidgeted uncomfortably. "They didn't give me the job. Well, they gave me the job, but they didn't, so I resigned."

"Yeah, so what does that have to do with your being in bed for three weeks?"

"After leaving S&G, I went to Michaels and got so drunk. I couldn't drive home, so I had to park on the street. I called Sam to come and get me." Her eyes rolled back as though she was reliving the nightmare. "Sam told me to stay put, but I never listen to anyone as usual. I felt like I was going to spew my guts up, so I went out to throw up outside. Was I supposed to just throw up in my car?" she said as though such a thought was not a possible choice. "Two men carjacked me. I was almost raped, and it was all my fault." She hurried past the point. "All because I didn't do what I was supposed to."

"Come again? Where?" Veronica was agog.

Even Melody couldn't stop the fury of bubbling emotions welling inside her. "How could almost being raped be your fault, April?"

"If I hadn't…."

"Yeah, if we all hadn't bothered to live. Girl, this is a doozy." Veronica shook her head. "But we'll get through this. I want you in my office tomorrow morning. You got that? If you don't show up, I'll come and get you myself. You can't stay behind these curtains. We have to get you past this. I'll take you to see Eve, myself. She's good. Really good."

"I can attest to that." Melody piped.

"You do understand, don't you? I'm sorry to have worried you. It was rather selfish not to call, but I've been emotionally borderline since the incident. I've been taking some pills and just can't seem to get moving."

Veronica picked up the bottle of pills and read the label. "Understood. But you can't take pills forever." She walked into the bathroom and dumped the contents of the vial. "April, you have to see a professional. Post-traumatic syndrome is real, but you don't have to be doped up to deal with it. These friggin' pills are addictive. You don't want that problem."

"I'll try." April's voice was small.

Melody, who had never heard April's voice small, was relieved when Veronica's beeper went off. How she identified with the rage April must be feeling. For a different reason but rage no doubt.

"Damn it. This isn't even my patient."

"Dr. Lam's answering service, Dr. Whittaker. I understand you're on call for him?"

April took comfort in the girls. They were here to help, and they didn't judge her. She supposed that's what friends are for, but it was still a new experience. Indeed, she believed in the Holy Trinity.

"Gotta go girl. But we'll be back. I only have six deliveries to do for Dr. Lam. I swear that man is crazy. With six deliveries due, how can his ass go cruising?"

"Cruising?" April said.

"Yeah, as in "tiny bubbles" island cruising. Someone else takes over at six, and I feel sorry for them. They're going to see a lot of meows tonight."

"Meows?" Melody looked quizzically at Veronica.

"Better than the P-word."

April laughed for the first time in three weeks. "I'm so angry."

"As you should." But, Melody, fully acquainted with pain, added, "every day that passes, this will get better."

It'd probably never be all right again, but April was glad to have her friends around.

On the way back to the city, Melody was very quiet.

"Hey. She's gonna be okay." Veronica patted Melody's hand.

"Life is such fuckin' insanity."

Veronica took her eyes off the road to look at Melody. Never! Never had she heard the woman use an expletive. This must have affected her badly. "Let's plan a getaway for all of us. How about we take our asses on a tiny bubble cruise too… ."

"Cruise." Melody was aghast. "Hell no. April is used to renting villas all over the world."

"Okay! Okay. How about a villa in España. Belgium, France, Prague, Italia, South Korea, Japan, Kenya, Tanzania. Which?"

"Beats me, but it'll do us all some good wherever we go." Melody's voice became more concerned. "How are you, really, Veronica?"

"I'm doing okay," Veronica said softly.

"Vee." Melody pressed. "How are you?"

"Honestly, I'm doing great, but I have my days. Whatever choice I made, there would be pain. I don't think my feelings for Tony were fake, but I wasn't willing to sacrifice my children and husband."

Melody was silent. God, the burdens of expectations and perceptions. "Are you sure of your decision to give up on love and happiness?" Melody finally asked.

"Love and happiness!" Veronica said. "I've always had love and happiness. I lost sight of that for a moment. I really love my husband, and I'm going to do everything to make it up to him. He has no idea I had an affair, and I'd like to keep it that way."

"Isn't that starting over with a lie?"

"No, Melody, what one cannot see in their mind's eye does not exist. He doesn't need a reason to doubt me. I can live with this lie. Anyway, whatzup with you and Mr. Chime?"

"I've turned into a blabbering fool."

"Yeah. Love rules, doesn't it?"

"Don't you see the mark?" For the first time, in Veronica's opinion, Melody's tone was reconciling.

"Looks like the mark of Charles Bell to me."

Melody chuckled. "It is."

The following Saturday morning, Veronica and Melody arrived at April's house in a limousine. They had planned a surprise spa day where they would discuss their trip to wherever.

"Hey, girlfriend. I brought the chauffeur. So, our day of relaxation starts now."

"This is some get up."

"Yeah. We know." Veronica said.

How are you holding up, chickadee?"

"Fine. eighty-five percent. I've been seeing Eve."

"After our planned day, you'll be at ninety-five percent. And after our villa in España, Tanzania, Japan or wherever, you'll be at one hundred percent. Wait and see."

"So, where's this spa we're going to?" April asked.

"Right here." The driver pulled up to Melody's building.

"Really. I didn't know they had a spa in this building." April said, pushing the elevator button.

"Let's hurry to my place and get changed. In ten minutes, three wonderful Swedish masseuses will arrive. After which, we'll have three competent women to do our facials, manicures, and pedicures." Melody opened the door to her ultra chic apartment. "Then we hit the sauna. I have one in there," she pointed to a room off the bathroom. "And then, let's not forget the hairdos."

"Three hairdressers?" April asked.

"Yep. After we have pampered ourselves silly, the caterers will serve an early dinner. And then, my dears, we'll plan our getaway. I have rented videos for every taste, or we can do whatever we want."

"Ummm. I can't wait. Lead the way." April said.

"Madam." Melody pointed to the changing room—the bathroom.

Come, April, let's change into something more comfortable."

"Melody, make sure yours is a straight jacket." Veronica said bringing up the rear.

"Veronica, is this what you came here to do? To harass me?"

"No." Veronica grabbed Melody and gave her one helluva hug. "This is how I show my exciiitttement."

"Why don't you just get your big behind in here and shut up." Melody yanked her friend into the bedroom.

"This is going to be one helluva day. I can tell." Veronica said.

The women returned to their spa base decked in terrycloth robes and slippers, with logos of the various hotels from Melody's travels. "Let's prepare ourselves for a good and productive day of self-care." Melody plopped down on the couch. The women followed suit.

The day was superb.

"I'm not ready to go home yet," April announced.

"Me neither. Let's get some jams going to set the mood for the evening. I'm only hoping Melody has the motherland in her veins. You know how it is, April. People like you in America with their high yella complexion sometimes get confused about their identity."

"How many times do I have to tell you I was born here, stupid?"

"Melody, did you hear that? Girlfriend is back to her caustic, sassy self. Now let's see," Veronica riffled through the neatly stacked CDs, "if there is any saving grace to your Stanford behind missy. I feel like some Luther."

"Some who?" Melody teased, examining her newly polished nails.

"Lord, I am the only authentic sistah in da house. Melody, who the hell are these?" Veronica screamed, as though the world was about to end, holding up CDs by Police, Meatloaf and Rod Stewart.

"I looove Rod Stewart," April piped up excitedly.

Melody grabbed the CDs Veronica was waving around and handed her Wyclef's *Carnival.* "Here."

"Who the hell is Wyclef?" Veronica looked at the back cover. Haitian? "What on earth? Voodoo music?"

"He's from the Fugees. Expand your narrow horizon." April had fun siding with Melody.

"Hey, hey. Now you're talking. I love the Fugees. *Killing me Softly With His Song.* A certified jam. Put on that bad boy and turn the musak loud. Before you do that, though, gimme one of those carrot sticks in your refrigerator. I'm famished. And dinner is not served for another hour." Melody couldn't believe she had that much fun in one day.

"I just remembered something," April said as the music came to an end. "One of the men who attacked me said something like, they just said 'scare her.' I am sure I heard that."

"You are kidding. Do you think…."

"I don't want to."

That night Melody drove excitedly over to Charles's. With the deal almost wrapped up, Charles was spending more time in Chicago. Tonight, she would tell him how much she loved him, and that love wasn't bad, after all.

The beautiful, newly renovated brick house next door to the very house he grew up in was extremely tasteful. He'd paid a premium to get the previous owners out so he could be close to his parents. Like Charles, the house was understated and impeccable. Sparsely furnished but with rare pieces, it made one want to roam. This guy was some kind of special. Most people would have put their parents in a nursing home. Momentarily Melody wondered how her parents were doing. From time to time, she'd contacted her father by sending checks to a bank account in his name so her parents didn't have to worry about money in their old age. To Melody's disappointment, they never moved from the run-down, drug-infested, gang-ridden neighborhood. When she'd pleaded with her father to use the money, he'd said. "I'd much rather have my Bella than a new house. How do you expect me to tell her how I got the money to afford a snazzy house in Brentwood Park? She'd probably throw me out if she knew I speak to you." *Not now,* she admonished herself, throwing her arms around Charles, and hugging him tightly.

"My. What a nice greeting."

"For a nice man." She kissed him with abandon.

"How is April?"

"Doing great. I think she's gonna be okay."

"Wonderful," he pulled her to him.

"Hey. Watch the do. It cost a pretty penny."

"Really?" Charles raked his hand through her hair.

"Charles!"

"I read it in a Kama Sutra book. The hair is very sensual. So, what do you think of the place?" It was his first night there.

"It's beautiful." She'd learned a lot about Charles. And day by day, she loved him more. She followed him into the room he'd set up as his painting studio. Charles's presence filled the room. The beauty of his work struck her. Melody couldn't believe a man like Charles was a painter.

"There is nothing more relaxing or fulfilling than this," he waved around the room.

"Such an odd hobby for a corporate tycoon."

"Why would you say that?"

"I don't know exactly. I just think of painters as tormented souls. I would have made a great painter."

"I think you'd make a better model. Go on, pose for me."

"Me? Pose. How?"

"Nude."

Very early the next morning, Melody woke with a smile on her face, promptly wiped away by the throbbing in her head. The headaches were more frequent now and she could tell by them if it was going to be a bad day. *Aspirins. If she took them right away, it'd help.* Looking lovingly at Charles, she groggily got out of bed. How she loved him, she thought, padding to the bathroom to find any form of painkiller. There were no drugs in Charles's bathroom. She reached up to pull down the paisley robe hanging behind the door before making her way to the kitchen. He had to have something somewhere.

Suddenly Melody grabbed her head. A blinding pain was shooting through her right eye and into her neck. Her vision blurred. She saw flashes of light, and the room began to waver, tipping from one side to the next. The headache was excruciating, and Melody groaned just before she felt her body convulse, hitting the floor with a thud.

Charles, hearing the racket flew out of bed and went in the direction of the noise.

Melody was convulsing, thrashing around on the kitchen floor. He grabbed a spoon and put it in her mouth, called an ambulance and cradled her until they arrived.

CHAPTER THIRTY-SEVEN

VERONICA ARRIVED at the hospital in record time and met Charles in the emergency room. April was minutes behind her.

"Thanks for coming," he got up to greet them.

"Oh my God, Charles, I'm so glad you were there. What on earth happened?" Veronica's training as a take-charge doctor was evident.

"She collapsed, just like that. She was in a lot of pain. I could tell, but I couldn't get her to talk. Not a word?"

"Not a single word."

"Is she pregnant?"

"I hope so." Charles was relieved, thinking about the apparent reason she might have fainted, but why would she convulse?

"I'll go in and find out what I can. May I get you coffee? Anything?"

"No, thanks. I'm fine."

April, who hated hospitals more than anything, was ashen. "Pull yourself together and take care of Charles while I go inside," Veronica said

Just as Veronica was about to leave, Dr. Kurtzwell entered.

"Percy. Hi," she said with relief.

"Hi, Veronica. What are you doing here?"

"That's my best friend in there. This is Charles Bell. And April Summers."

"Family?"

"No."

"Is there a family member we may contact?"

"No. I'm afraid Melody's parents are deceased. She is an only child." Veronica was concerned. She didn't like the tone of this. "Mr. Bell is Melody's companion. Her significant other. So, what do you think, Percy?"

He hesitated.

"It's all right," Veronica reassured, "I know."

"Great. Let's talk over here," he led her away from Charles and April. "We did an MRI. There is a lesion in the frontal lobe. It's causing a lot of pressure, and it's quite big. I'm surprised she hadn't complained before. We'll do further tests, but if I were to take a guess, I'd say it's a glioblastoma."

"Oh, my God." Veronica slumped to the chair. "Oh, Percy, no. I thought she was pregnant."

"We'll check for that."

Veronica had no idea how to break the news to Charles. Should she? Yes, of course, she had to. "Charles," she began making sure to take hold of April's hand."

Charles had no idea what exactly had just transpired. Whatever the medical terms meant, it sounded grave. What he was sure about was, he wasn't about to be a daddy.

April was shaking all over. Having grown up with neuroscientists, she knew exactly what was going on.

Melody, regaining consciousness, raised her head off the pillow to see a woman in a white uniform fusing with an IV disappearing into her arm. She was in a hospital room, and she didn't even remember how she got there. What on earth had happened? One minute she was basking in one of the best moments of her life, and the next, she was spiraling into darkness. Though she felt completely normal, she'd been aware her body was betraying her for some time. If this was a midlife crisis, it was cruel and uncalled for punishment. The door opened, and three men and a woman entered.

"Miss Adams. I'm Dr. Kurtzwell." The others she assumed were residents. "How are you feeling now?"

"Quite normal. Though I know something is wrong."

"We have the results of the MRI" Melody didn't quite know how, or if she did remember, being pushed through a tunnel. Yet in her head, she could hear a voice say, "Don't move. Please. It's very important." She had been as still as a mouse, but it wasn't because her body was responding to her mind's command. She could not move on her own—the sensation evoked in her a feeling of being slid alive into a coffin. The worse part of the entire ordeal was the droning noise that threatened to deafen her, yet no words could come from her lips. Melody was a realist. She had learned to cope with pain and disappointment. She knew how to dissociate from pain, failure, and fate. Whatever it was….

"Three of your friends are outside. Would you like them to come in? A Charles Bell, April Summers, and Dr. Whittaker."

"Yes. I'd like that."

One of the residents left the room and soon returned with the gang. Their faces were solemn but supportive. Charles moved quickly to Melody's side, sliding his hand easily into hers. She didn't resist. What if she was really sick? Should he be there? She was grateful he was.

"The pictures show a large tumor in your brain. It is pressing on your frontal lobe and causing you to have these spells. I'm sure this is not the first of the episodes, is it Ms. Adams?"

Melody didn't speak. She looked furtively at the faces in the room. Was this a dream? They couldn't have said what she thought they said. A tumor? Cancer? Impossible! She could handle anything but this. She had overcome....

"Are you sure," was all she could say.

"Yes, Ms. Adams, but I suspect you've had some episodes before," the doctor repeated, "this is not the first time, is it?"

"No, it's the third or fourth in the past few months, but none has made me collapse." She answered the question calmly.

"Did you seek any treatment before?"

"No."

"Well, the tumor looks like a very common but serious tumor. We need to begin treatment immediately as the prognosis, if left untreated, could incapacitate you in five months or less."

Veronica hated that shit. Doctors are always going on as though they were some kind of God, predicting times of death and shit. She had fought against that all her years as a doctor, but very few physicians were sensitive to the fact that time frames on death could subliminally control outcomes. The argument against it was people's right to know. Valuable time, perhaps to put their business in order. Such nonsense.

Melody felt numb. Fatally wounded right through the heart. Maybe, just maybe, her saving grace was she was ruled by the head and not the heart. But hadn't they said the cancer was in her brain? Melody's fingers tightened around Charles. Winded, she was unable to speak or cry. She felt Charles pressing back reassuringly on her hand, but her only thought was, she had let her mother down after all. Melody looked from one face to another, searching for a hint of reassurance, a glimmer of hope. There was none. She stared past the faces out the window and into the brilliance of the sunlight. She was caught in a storm, yet the sun was pouring in. Cancer. She had cancer.

"Ms. Adams, are you all right?"

Melody did not answer. She shifted her gaze and stared ahead at the blank white wall. Tears spilled over Veronica's cheeks, and Charles slumped into the chair next to the bed.

"Give her some Valium in the IV." Dr. Kurtzwell ordered.

"No," Melody said softly. "I don't need it. Dr. Kurtzwell, I understand the gravity of what you have said. I'm not in shock. And I understand the urgency with which you must act, but I need a few weeks. What are the chances of controlling the blackouts with some form of medication? Diet?"

"Melody," Veronica interjected. "Please."

"I know. I know. I just need a short time."

"Well, we could try a few drugs that will reduce brain activity and erratic impulses but not impair your ability to function. You won't be able to drive. However, we strongly recommend we begin treatment immediately. If you want a second opinion, we encourage that, but I urge you to hurry. This is a nasty disease."

"Thank you, Dr. Kurtzwell."

Charles refused to leave Melody. She insisted. What she needed was solitude and an action plan. If she was going to die in five months, she had only one thing to do. She had to go home. Had to hold her mother's hand and ask her forgiveness. Her other "business" was relatively simple. Suddenly, it dawned on Melody she had to be crazy. They had told her she had cancer; as in malignant; as in dead, and she was calmly planning her exit. This was not normal, but neither was her life. Disappointments and struggle had prepared her for anything. This extraordinary ability to defuse a potentially volatile situation was where she excelled. Hadn't she been the living dead all along anyway? No matter the reason, she was in control again.

Veronica didn't know she could feel this much grief. How could such bad things happen so suddenly? *Why God? Why do you create and destroy? Why do you punish the innocent and let the guilty go on living?*

"Because death is a new chance for happiness. Life is the real punishment when you screw it up." Veronica spun around to see whose voice answered. There was no one. Did the voice come from her subconscious? She turned to the other side of the room, fear mounting in her heart. Someone had spoken. She heard it. All she saw was Randolph coming down the stairs.

"Hey, Sweetie. I didn't even hear you come in. Was just on my way to the kitchen for a cup of coffee. Want one?"

"Yeah. That would be great. Randolph," Veronica looked curiously at her husband. "Is that the first time you spoke, just now?"

"No. I started talking at eight months, 'Dada.' My Mom said."

"Oh, stop. I meant tonight. Oh, never mind, I don't know what I mean."

"Why? Are you hearing voices?"

"I thought maybe I was. But it's been such an awful day anything is possible. Melody has a brain tumor."

"What? What did you say? My God. How did that happen?"

"Who knows Randolph? Who knows what goes on inside our bodies at any given moment? Who knows?" But a hum behind her was increasing. She looked around furtively, but there was nothing. Out of nervousness, Veronica picked up the mail and riffled through it. She paused at *Time Magazine,* wondering why the face on the cover looked so familiar. It was the face of a man shrouded in a three-dimensional light, but she had no idea who. It was too spooky. Strange voices and familiar pictures. The title of the *Time Magazine* article was "Heroes of Medicine." Veronica flipped through the pages that talked about these miracle workers and began reading. Suddenly a name jumped out at her, and she began reading closer. Dr. Cox, a world-renowned brain surgeon? Her body trembled. Then it shuddered, and then she was covered in goose pimples. She had graduated with this guy! They were friends in Medical School. Was this a sign? He was the world's foremost brain surgeon who'd pioneered a new technique to remove brain tumors that were a sure death sentence only ten years before. Unbelievable. With his new technique, hope became a reality, and he'd been prolonging lives for years, the article said.

Veronica raised her face to the heavens. To the God, she'd just heard. She was sure of it, for neither the voice nor the answer came from inside her. *The answer will come when you need it*, she affirmed, looking at her watch. It was five p. m.—Chicago time. Cox was at Cedar Sinai in California. She would call. It was clear this was a sign.

April wept all the way home.

Comtech was in an uproar when they heard of Melody's request for a leave of absence. No one other than her had been groomed to take on her job, so Eric's retirement plans were in jeopardy.

"I'm going to be fine, Eric." She kept the unpredictability of her future a secret. There was no need for the truth just yet. Not only that, she wouldn't give into excessive sympathy. The most important thing was done. The Microtech deal had been signed on the Microtech's side. "I know you can handle this. I have some pressing personal business to take care of, but I'll be back as soon as possible. As for the deal, I get the papers in order later this week."

"Don't worry. The deal is practically done. I will countersign the papers immediately." Eric reassured.

"Fantastic."

"And Melody, take as much time as you need."

The deal, as said verbatim by Charles Bell, was concluded. Melody was given an indefinite leave of absence with pay. Looking around her office as she packed her personal belongings, Melody was devastated. That was when the news hit her hard. She wasn't going on a leave of absence. She was never coming back. Her eyes scanned the familiar sights; her awards, diplomas, the letter nominating her CEO elect of Comtech. Tears welled. She wondered who would take her position at Comtech, the only home she had known in well nearly twenty years. Walking around the room, touching the artifacts she'd collected, Melody suddenly stopped and slumped in her high back leather chair. She would never see this office again. She ran her hand over the Regency desk she had handpicked. It would outlast her. She pulled open her top drawer and removed the last picture of her mother she'd ever taken. She stared at the proud woman. Tears that clung to her lashes fell unabashedly onto the glass frame. It was only then she fell to her knees and soaked the plush carpet with salty tears.

What would she do now? How would she fill her days between chemo and radiation? Was she going to let them mutilate her, or would she accept her pending death with dignity? Melody got up and walked around the office for the last time. She had been reared at Comtech. Found her strength and purpose and was rewarded for a professional life well lived there. A cold technology company run by people with the warmest hearts. Abruptly, she turned and walked out the door. At the front entrance, she balanced her little box, touched her fingers to the gold insignia and walked to the parking space that usually said VP of Finance. It now read CEO. Inside her car, she felt as cold as the letters on the door. It was 5.00 a.m.

Charles grew extremely respectful of Melody. He had never quite seen anyone with such dignity. He wished she would cry with him. Throw a vase, thump her fist, or chastise life for being unkind, but she never did. He was committed to being there for her, but his agony was deep. For the first time, he'd found a woman with whom he wanted to spend the rest of his life, and now this.

"Charles," Melody reached for his hand as they sat on the couch in her apartment. "I'm so glad I found you. Maybe we won't have a lifetime together, but we have now. I don't know how long before my body gives out, but I want you to know you've come to mean everything to me in these short months."

"We're going to beat this. I know this in my heart. Not only will we have a lifetime together. We'll have grandchildren. Stay positive and focus on getting well."

"I will."

"Let's get out of here for a minute before we take the next step. What do you think?"

Melody laughed half-heartedly. "Where are we going?"

"Anywhere you want."

She started to cry. "I've always wanted to take you to Bora Bora."

"So, I'll take you there. I'll let you fly."

"I don't want to die before I have to." She laughed.

"I'll let Veronica know we'll be gone for a week."

Of course, Veronica protested but in her heart she wished them the best. Charles and Melody flew to Bora Bora. She had never had so much fun being his co-pilot. The eighteen-hour flight had gone by faster than she had ever imagined, as the pilot took over from Melody and Charles an hour into flight and they retired to their sleeping cabin. If Melody didn't understand the power of money, she did now. Charles had paid attention to every detail of their accommodations from the thatched cottage nestled among coconut palms, citrus and breadfruit trees, and a grey stones' barrier dam protecting overflow from the surrounding aquamarine lagoon outside their bedroom window. Their exquisite over-the-water bungalow showed a clear vista of the extinct volcano rising to two peaks on Mount Pahia. A tiny hideaway only six feet long and two miles in diameter, they did not explore the French Polynesian island but opted to stay close to home, relaxing, swimming in the lagoon and eating the healthy meals their cook prepared. Only once did they venture into the town of Viatape on a Sunday when all the stall vendors selling their wares added to the beauty of the small island. Charles bought Melody a strand of black pearl necklace, and hands interlocked they entered one of the churches on the main corridor. There, holding each other they prayed. And they prayed.

For two weeks, Charles did everything for Melody; he washed her hair, did her pedicure and as they walked along the shore, hands intertwined, pull her close into his heart. He couldn't believe she was dying. She seemed so vibrant. He silently kept praying to God to have mercy. For a miracle. To let him have her forever. But if he had to take her, he begged for a peaceful transition. Melody too knew how precious the moments were and thank God she was well enough to enjoy this time with the man she so desperately loved. She did not feel the slightest symptoms of her illness. Maybe they had made a mistake.

"Charles," Melody said as she nestled in his arms on their last night of vacation. . "I'm so sorry; so sorry."

"For what," he pressed her closer.

"For being the first to leave. I didn't want to run away again, but it seems I'm going to."

"Look, let's take it one step at a time. Mind over matter is important right about now. Miracles do happen, you know."

On their return, like a project, Melody delved into preparing for her ordeal. First, she had to know everything about her disease. To fight it, she had to understand what she was dealing with. In front of the bathroom mirror, she stared at herself. She looked perfectly normal. "Damn you. Damn you. Damn you," she picked up a bottle of Dolce Vita and threw it against the mirror. The burst of smell nauseated her, and she stumbled out of the bathroom.

The doorbell rang. Melody pushed the medical book into the top drawer of her desk, wiped her eyes and darted back to the bathroom to quickly wash her face. She should never have given her access, as now the doorman no longer called when it was April or Veronica. She deliberated answering the door, but Veronica kept banging and calling her name.

"Quit with the racket, would you? I'm not going to kill myself, okay. So please feel free not to come by every second." Melody yanked the door open. Veronica and April were standing there.

"We're going to LA. Where is your luggage? I booked us on a nine-p.m. flight." Veronica ignored the angry outburst. It was quite understandable.

"Excuse me." Melody looked up. What did Veronica know of her connections to LA?

"Look, she threw the *Time Magazine* on the coffee table. I went to school with him. I already called, and he gave us an appointment for Monday." It's Sunday. "How was Bora Bora?"

"It was great but….

"Melody, I couldn't believe it when I got home from the hospital the night you fainted, I saw this article. It was a sign from God. We have to go."

"Yuup. I have nothing else to do. I quit, remember?" April's arms spread in a statement of disbelief.

Melody didn't argue. She walked to her bedroom, followed by her guardians, and got her suitcase. It was wise to act swiftly before the pernicious illness claimed her reality. "Let me call Charles. Call him from the plane. What the hell were you doing? Trying to drown yourself in perfume?" Veronica choked on the excessive fumes in the air.

"Wouldn't you say it would be a better alternative?"

April was driving. She veered the car in a direction Melody could not fathom.

"Wrong terminal for United," Melody noted."

"We're taking Charles' plane."

"Hell no!"

"That's why we didn't tell you," Veronica admonished.

Charles was standing by the plane ready to fly them out to LA. "Hey, Lady." He kissed her.

"Hey," Melody responded.

"I thought you'd like this better."

"Charles. We just returned. You have to be exhausted?"

"A little. That's why my pilot is here. He'll fly us out?"

"Is your pilot as good as you?"

"The best."

"Why isn't he working for United?"

"Because, he's better paid." Charles chuckled and put his arm around his love. "Plus, I'll be right there beside him as co-pilot. It won't take long, and you can sit with the pilot and me in the cockpit. I'll teach you to fly. I plan to stay with you that's why he's flying us. He'll bring the plane back."

"You can't take any leave now," Melody insisted."

"Why not?"

"Now the deal is done, you've got to get back to San Francisco to prepare your staff."

"That can wait."

"Charles, this is what I want. Life goes on, you know. Trust me. I'll be back to you in a flash. Don't worry; I'm one helluva fighter. If you knew me, you'd understand."

"Believe me, I do," Charles said, "But I'm coming."

"Listen to me," she turned to face him. "You can't. I will be fine. Fine. And I'll be back before you know it. If you want to help me, do as I ask."

"Okay, Melody. But call me. The moment the plane lands. Better yet, call me from the plane every hour."

"Why not." Melody smiled reassuringly, walking up the steps of the plane. "Charles," she turned and looked back at him.

"Yes? What is it, darling?" He came toward her.

"I tried so very hard not to love you."

"I'm glad you failed."

"So am I."

CHAPTER THIRTY-EIGHT

THE ENTIRE WORLD seemed to be fawning over Courtney Cox. His status as a life-giver led to deferential and lauding treatment. If his name was mentioned, people bowed in awe. The image he presented when Melody met him was entirely different. A tall, handsome, unassuming Black man, he seemed embarrassed by the accolades bestowed on him, insisting he was no life-giver but merely a life preserver. Yet, from within him came a wonderful glow. The same calm that had surrounded his picture on the front cover of *Time Magazine*. Of all the doctors in the special feature, he was the only Black man in the group, and he was chosen for the front cover. The brown eyes that held Melody immobilized were kind and wise. Wise beyond his years. With Dr. Courtney Cox, Melody felt calm. No matter how hard the days ahead might become as her physical body debilitated and chemotherapy drained her energy, she would feel her soul safe with him. He smiled at her but didn't speak. He simply sized her up before turning to his classmate.

"Veronica. How on earth are you? I've tried to contact you repeatedly when I've been in Chicago but never connected. Either you don't get messages, or you don't return phone calls?"

"You know how it is. Time. The time difference between LA and Chicago makes it worse. Several of us are in Chicago, and we don't even see each other often."

"So, how are the dynamic graduates of the class of nineteen ninety?" They embraced.

"Those I'm in touch with are doing about as well as the rest of the nation. Married, divorced, children, none, gay, straight. You know?"

"You're still funny. What's your story?"

"Married, two children, boy and girl, almost divorced until I wised up—the usual. But I'm so proud of you, Courtney. And thank you so much for seeing us so readily."

Melody and April felt as if they were voyeurs. Something was happening they didn't understand.

"Miss Adams," Dr. Cox finally turned to Melody, reaching for her hand. "It's wonderful to meet you. Veronica filled me in on your diagnosis, and I can tell you we have work to do. You'll be in good hands, and I'll do my best, but I cannot give you false hopes. Your condition is very serious, and maybe the best I can do is guide you to accept the inevitable."

"I understand. Thank you." Melody whispered, loving his forthrightness.

"Please follow me."

Melody reached for her friend's hands, dragging them along.

The next several hours were spent in consultation. Courtney spoke about her diagnosis, the course of treatment, being careful not to seem overly optimistic, and about her faith. He'd seen the reports of the MRI, and he was optimistic with the location of the tumor. He reassured her a new technique he had perfected, if successful, could possibly remove most of the cancerous cells. He was concerned about the size of the tumor, which he told her had been growing for a long time and that there could be metastases in other parts of the body yet undiscovered. However, he would do his best to move quickly and successfully. They said their goodbyes, and he promised to see them in the morning.

"Okay, girl." Veronica stroked her friend's arm. "This shit is a doozy, but Courtney is it if we have a chance. Let's go get some dinner. I know this great restaurant. Are you up to it after all that?"

"Let me get your sweater," April insisted.

"April! Stop it! If you start treating me like an invalid, guess where your siddity behind is going? What am I going to do with a sweater in eighty-degree weather?"

"Wear it. Okay. No sweater. How about a hat?"

"Veronica! Get this woman away from me."

"Sure. I'd be delighted. April, bring your dead ass over here without a hat or a sweater and let's go eat."

Melody, though reticent, laughed. There had been too little laughter and too little fun in her life for too many years. She would make sure she laughed a lot throughout her entire ordeal. "If I only have five months to live, I will live it to the fullest. April, may I have my sweater and hat, please? Shall we go?"

"If it's true that only the good die young, girl, you have very little to worry about. Don't believe that nonsense about five months. No one can predict the end of life, and Melody," Veronica felt compelled to put things in perspective, mind rules body.'"

The women, Chicago's Holy Trinity, joined hands and walked the short distance to the restaurant. The Crystal Palace was not very large, but it was exquisite. And every bit of the six-course meal was scrumptious.

"Let's order the best bottle of sherry in the house." April sat back, satisfied.

"I won't do alcohol," Melody said. "No brain stimulant until I understand what's going on?"

"How about cherry pie?" Veronica pointed to the dessert tray, passing their table.

"That I can do." Melody touched her friend's hand. "You're the best friend anyone could ever have; you know that? Please don't feel you have to pretend to be cheery or protect me from reality. I know how serious my illness is, but I'm not going to spend the rest of what's left of my life weeping."

"Agreed," Veronica said sadly, "but…."

"Hey, all I need is for you to keep on being Veronica, caustic, funny and real. That's the person who brought joy to my life. You guys have brought me most of the happiness I've had in my life, trying Trinity meetings, the rotten jokes, the great massages, the wonderful laughter, and the most giving and healing friendship. I need to say how much I love you both and how much I need your strength now. Don't go changing trying to please me."

"Who's changing? I'm too set in my ways to change. April, she must be speaking to you, girl."

"I'm all about change," April said. "I'm more ready than ever before to learn about anything I can to be real. And I do have something to say. I'm so grateful to you both. Thanks."

"I echo that," Melody said. "Veronica, if you only know how much I appreciate your always being there when I've had no one. I cherish our friendship so much. More than I've ever expressed. I don't want another minute to go by without telling you I love you."

"April, she smiled broadly at her friend. "I have to be honest. I didn't like you for a long time. Even after Veronica forced us together, I thought you were stuck up and spoiled. It didn't take long to realize my anger and jealousy of you were misplaced. It had nothing to do with you. It was all about me. Today I love you like my very own sister."

"April. You'd better check how much love that is. Melody has no sister." Veronica said.

"I had four sisters and three brothers, and my parents aren't dead," Melody said. "It's time for me to tell you both the truth," she continued, "I believe the time has come to bare my soul." She repeated the story she'd told Eve.

April was bawling. She wasn't crying she was bawling, paroxysms of pain shaking her body. She pulled a packet of Kleenex out of her bag, blowing her nose loudly, trying hard to control her emotions. Halting between tears, she said. "Life is a chore, so damn deceptive."

"I'm so sorry. I didn't mean to deceive anyone. It was the only way I knew how to cope."

"I'm not talking about you. Hell, I'm a real coward. I skirt around issues, never addressing them. My whole life, I've wanted to tell my mother off. To tell Sam, my career came before him and child, family. But you know what's real. I was scared to have a family, and I was scared to lose my mother. Why didn't I have the balls, to be honest? The reality is, neither would have left. Sam has been my rock, and so has my mother. Believe me, perception may be far greater than reality, but it doesn't have to be true!"

"Life is nothing more than the tyranny of the weak over the strong. A society, a situation, a family member who has hopes for you in all the wrong ways." Veronica added. What will you do now? Are you having any regrets about your decisions, Melody?"

"Not a lot but I'd love to see my mom. To make peace with her. To tell her thank you. Were it not for her faith in me, I could have gone the ways of my brothers and sisters."

"And?"

"I'd wish to let her know I turned out okay."

The women sat quietly. Each spiraling into their own pain. Facing it, examining it, accepting it.

"If I don't make it," Melody said to her friends. "Please keep Charles in your lives and please find him someone who will help him heal from losing me."

"Love sure is a healing journey. But I don't think that would happen any time soon. That man loves you to pieces."

"It may be too late for me," tears welled in Melody's eyes, "but I thank God for Charles. God!" she banged the table, "I was just beginning to feel good about him, but how can I continue? I need to let him go."

"What do you mean? You've already felt his love. The question is, as he fully felt yours? Don't you dare cut him off now, Melody," Veronica admonished. "Don't you dare."

"How can I be so selfish? Why should I force him to watch me die? He should move on now and get on with life. He told me he'd waited to find the right woman for his entire life. He wanted to get married and have children. He, too, wanted someone to ask the answers to the Sunday crossword puzzle. Why should he see me die and have a setback for years?"

"Because he is a great man, and he can handle it. A man above men, and he loves you. Plus, your stupid ass cannot die."

"Love doesn't grieve, Melody. It rejoices." April added. "Above all, Charles is your friend. Like us."

"When you part from your friend," Melody recited a verse from her favorite writer, Kahlil Gibran, "do not weep for, in the dew of little things, the heart finds its morning and is refreshed."

The women reached across the table and linked hands. They sat for a while, just being.

"Everyone probably thinks we're gay." Veronica suddenly laughed.

"You think? Well, let's give them something to ogle," Melody reached over and pecked her friend's cheeks. "Lesbian ménage-a-trois." As usual, they did what they did best. Double up in laughter.

Veronica flew back to Chicago the following morning, and April stayed on for another week. When she left Los Angeles, she had never felt such clarity about her life. She was sure of her path for the first time in her life.

CHAPTER THIRTY-NINE

"WHEN DID YOU get into town?" Sam asked.

"Last night, darling. Where is April?"

"In your neck of the woods. Her friend, Melody, you met her at the Memorial Day picnic, has cancer."

"How awful. Is it serious?"

"Yeah, I guess so."

"So, you've been alone for how long?"

"A week. She'll be back any day."

"Do you want to have dinner?"

"Sophie. I don't think that's a good idea."

"Sam. Why deny the inevitable? Darling, I don't want to marry you, but we have fun together."

"That's over now. April and I are doing a lot better. I was carried away with my grief."

"Ah, grief. Why are we such slaves to explanations? Why can't we just do what is so natural?"

"Don't you feel any guilt about cheating on your cousin?"

"I'm not cheating, darling. I'm not married. And even if I were, I'd honor the physical as much as the spiritual. Monogamy is artificial. It's not in our DNA."

"Maybe not for you, but for me, it is. I don't think dinner is a good idea. Come over when April gets home."

"And you think that's enough protection. Sam, we're great together."

"Sex together is what's great. Not you and me. I'm not a plaything Sophie. We have sex the few times you come to town. In how many other towns do you have sex with other people's husbands?"

"Darling. Hollywood has no boundaries. It's the norm."

"No. I won't see you. Final."

"Don't count on it, darling." Sophie dropped the phone.

Melody insisted on seeing April off to the airport. Exhausted when she made it back to her room she flopped onto the bed noting the lights on the phone blinking. She didn't pick up the messages. By five the next morning, the phone was ringing nonstop.

"Hello."

"Melody, it's Charles."

"You're an early bird." She looked at the clock on the bedside table.

"I've been calling all evening. Where were you?" He was angry.

"Out with April. She left last night."

"Well, I FedExed you a cell phone."

"You did what?"

"FedExed you a cell phone. I need to be able to reach you anytime, or I'll go mad. If not, I'll be right out to stay until you come home."

"Courtney says I can't have a cell phone."

"You don't have to answer it. It'll just let you know I'm trying to reach you and you can call back. Keep it in the closet and turn the volume up high. Okay. Got it? I'll expect a call within five minutes, from a landline or wherever. If you can't call because of tests, have the nurse call. I miss you so much, Melody."

How unbelievable was this man? Most men would have bolted after the first night of sex, much less at the news of their lover's grave and debilitating illness. "I miss you too."

"I'll be out on Saturday, but until then, what do you have to tell me?"

"We'll. I'm having this fantasy."

"Oh, boy. I like the sound of that."

"Not that kind of fantasy, Charles," Melody scolded.

"Oh." Disappointing. "What kind?"

"Well, it's not a fantasy. It's a recurring dream. Maybe even a nightmare. I dream that we are about to get married. I'm so happy. Radiant. I see you down the aisle. Beaming. I can't wait to get down the aisle to you. The music starts, and I begin the slow walk. With each step I take, my dress constricts further until, by the time I get to you, it has suffocated me. I fall at your feet, never to get up again."

"Sweetheart. Given the situation, it's normal. Your fear is understandable. I promise though you'll reach me, and I will smile into your eyes, and our hearts will take flight as we say the words 'I do.' "

"Charles." Melody choked. "Was that a proposal?"

"Most definitely."

First thing in the morning, Melody went to see Dr. Cox. She was happy. Charles had proposed. Suddenly she was scared. Scared she wouldn't live to be his wife.

"What's that look on your face for?"

"I was just wondering how long before I might be able to go home?"

"Home? I'm afraid this will be your home for a few months." He stopped writing for the first time since she entered the room. "I was just going over a list of residences near the hospital.

Something more functional than what you have right now. The nutritionists have to be able to cook for you every day. We are putting you on a Macrobiotic diet. I'm hoping you could take a couple of days to check them out. Make sure it's somewhere you'll enjoy staying. Most of them are within walking distance of the hospital and offer hotel-type services, laundry, etcetera." He circled a few places, handing her the list. She had expected him to delve into needles and x-rays, more MRI and chemotherapy, but he seemed more interested in her being settled. Within two days, Melody was settled into a new corporate apartment. On the first day of official treatment, Dr. Cox walked into her new home rather than she into his office.

"Nice place."

"Thanks to you."

"Are you ready?"

"As I'm ever going to be."

Dr. Cox pulled the blinds and instructed Melody to sit on the couch. He pulled a chair in front of her. For a moment, he said nothing.

"Now, Melody." He looked gravely at her. "What is it that has caused you to have this illness?"

"I'm sorry?" Melody looked sharply at the man in front of her. He was leaning forward now, looking deeply into her eyes.

"Diseases are not just of the body. They are of the mind and spirit as well. You must cleanse your heart, soul, body, and spirit of any unfinished business before we begin. If your recovery is going to happen, it has to be done with a free heart. Think, Melody. Where does your spirit need work? I need your help to give you back your life if possible."

Melody couldn't believe her ears or her eyes. Tears were streaming unabashedly down her cheeks. Where did the sudden deep emotion come from? Until recently, she had hardly shed a tear since she was nineteen. All the energy and affirmations behind her career successes, seeing her name in the *Tribune,* or her face on the television delivering a speech, had been motivated by anger, not tears. She was a powerful businesswoman but maybe her work was over. Experiencing success must have been her call to destiny, and now that it had been fulfilled, she was being called home. Before that, however, she needed to go home. Home to South Central LA. Melody looked up at Dr. Cox through a blur. Now she understood why he'd earned the love and respect of his staff and his patients.

"I need to go home," she whispered, "I need to go home." Melody never thought it would have been this easy to say.

"We just talked about that."

"Not that home."

"What is home, Melody? Where?" Courtney prompted.

"Right here."

"In L.A.?"

"Yes. South Central Los Angeles."

"Okay, Melody. We're going home."

They sat for an hour as Melody shared the story of her life. The denial of her heritage, the pain of her arrogance. The spontaneous eruption of her deep pain, so quickly and effortlessly rising to the surface, was evidence she had not buried her pain as far as she'd thought.

CHAPTER FORTY

EVERY NIGHT, Sam longed for his wife, deeply aching. He longed to smell the lemon shampoo in her hair and the scent of her perfume on the bedsheets—though he was still smarting for many reasons. One, had she not left the island, Sophie, who called him nonstop today was a dangerous stalker. Of course, he empathized with April wanting to be with her friend Melody, but what about him? Didn't she know he was hurting too? Everything it seemed came before him, and his life was at a boiling point.

Sam left his office in a huff. He only realized the depth of his anger when he slammed on his brakes, bringing the car to a stop in the parking lot of Michael's. He'd have a couple of drinks and then head home.

"Absolut. On the rocks." He sat at the bar.

"Twelve-fifty or a tab."

"Tab," Sam grunted.

"Yes, sir."

"Hey, buddy." Michael came through the door. "Hey, what's with the sad face? How's your wife? Is everything okay?"

"She's doing fine, Michael. Thanks."

"So, what's with the long face?"

"Life, just life, man," Sam said, nursing his Vodka.

"I thought you'd be here," the deep, smoky voice caressed his ear. "I know you don't want to see me, but I thought I'd at least be a friend. Why didn't you answer my calls?"

"It was a busy day."

"Why don't you tell me what's going on? Why are you drinking away your sorrows when you have me?"

"Sophie. I've gotta get home." He put his credit card on the counter. How did you find me here. Are you stalking me? I can't…."

"Sam, stop being a nutjob. I stopped by your house and when you weren't there I thought I might find you here. It's your favorite spot. Let me comfort you tonight. The after-effects will be better than Vodka."

"You went to my house. How dare you?"

"Ah, lighten up, will you. Even if April was there, she's my cousin!"

"That's the point. How can you live like this? How can you betray your own cousin? Don't you want more from a relationship?"

"You, tell me. Do they work? Come on, Sam, let's get out of here. Let me take you home."

"I'll go home, all right, but not with you." Sam paid his tab.

"I'll leave with you." Sophie acquiesced.

Outside, the rain had just begun to spray a light drizzle. Sam, the consummate gentleman, pulled off his coat and put it around Sophie's shoulders, who, in a halter top, needed it more than he did. Sophie took the moment to mold her body against his. "You're lonely, aren't you, darling?" she whispered against his lips. "What harm can there be in my comforting you? After Jamaica and the party, I didn't bug you now, did I? We live in the moment, Sam, and at this moment, you need me." She moved her body against his.

Sophie was an exciting and unconventional woman. Never had he been so sexually charged with any woman, not even his wife. "I am lonely but…."

"But what, darling?"

"I'm so very lonely." Sam felt a rising desire.

"My place or yours?" Sophie breathed softly against his lips. "Where's your car," she was practically stripping him in the parking lot.

"Not here, Sophie. Let's go to your hotel. I'll follow you."

"No, darling. My driver will bring you back to your car. Was it not for the chauffeur, she would have pulled over on the side of the road, traffic violation, or no traffic violation.

Back at the Drake, Sophie ran bathwater and lit scented candles in little holders all around the bathroom. "Let's get out of these wet clothes." She urged a reluctant Sam.

"I'm fine."

"Okay, I know what you need."

"You do?" Sam said.

"A drink." She was annoyed he was playing hard to get, and when he was burning with desire. To punish him, she intended to make him wait. To make him beg. "Sit down," She used her foot to push him back onto the sofa. "I'll get you a drink. "If memory serves me right, you drink Glenfiddich?"

What he wanted, Sam thought, was to explore the delicious curves of his wife's body, not Sophie's. Drink be damned. He watched Sophie move with catlike precision to the bar. It was all April's fault this was happening. She was the one who'd left him in Jamaica with Sophie. Didn't she know her cousin was a sexual predator? On the white sands of the beach, Sophie had seduced him in the dead of night. For four days, every available waking moment was spent at her rented house, between the sheets. He had expected it to stop when he left, but now Sophie was showing up in Chicago far more often than he wanted, and even to their Labor Day party.

Sam jumped as the cold, amber liquid hit his skin. Sophie was pouring it from the bottle.

"Let me get that," she purred.

What a paradox life was? Melody's illness had devastated April, but it also gave her a new perspective on a life not promised. All my life she'd had nagging doubt about herself. Doubts her mother could comprehend. She suffered racism her mother would never understand. The slights. The oppression. The micro aggressions that had her fighting a war against herself. Who am I? Where do I belong? Growing up with Caribbean people who think differently, and discounted race in America's as their stupidity, was all her mother understood.

Beginning today, she was going to set some things straight. First her mother and then Sam. Once and for all. But more than ever she was ready now to leave behind little footprints she and Sam created. Maybe they would have two, maybe three children.

At five fifty-four a.m., the red eye touched down at O'Hare. Sam will be very surprised by the new April Summers and the future mother of his child. She had never felt better or happier. April hurriedly pulled her roller luggage to the waiting Uber. She wanted to surprise Sam and was impatient for the cabbie to reach her house. At six forty-five, April made her way quietly up the stairs. She tiptoed into their bedroom, but the bed was empty. She ran to the garage. Sam's car was not there. Just her luck, he had an early appointment.

That evening, April sent the housekeeper home early, called her mother, with whom she had not spoken since Memorial Day to let her know she would be over the next day to finish their chat. Then she got all dolled up to wait for Sam. After the evening she had planned for them, there'd be little doubt about the path their lives would take. April waited. Since LA April had stopped taking the pill, and though she couldn't conceive right away, she hoped they would conceive soon.

When Sam had not arrived home at ten o'clock, April finally broke down and called his private line. No answer. Maybe he was on an overnight trip, but he'd have mentioned it. April paced and paced. Finally, it dawned on her to listen to the answering machine. Maybe there would be a clue to his whereabouts. There were messages. One from Charles and one from Sophie saying she was in town, but there was no message from Sam. She dialed his cell again—still no answer. April's heart began thumping in her chest. What if her assailants had come back for revenge? They had, after all, taken her purse. Frantically April dialed the housekeeper.

"No. I didn't see him this morning when I got there."

Which wasn't unusual as Sam often had early appointments. But something was fishy.

That night he never made it home.

At eight a.m. sharp, the following morning she called the office. No answer. She called every half-hour until Sam's secretary finally answered.

"Mr. Summers wasn't in the office yesterday. I thought I'd forgotten to write down an appointment, but maybe I didn't. He was toying with the idea of visiting you if you hadn't come home by the weekend, but I didn't make a flight for him. I'm sure he'll be here momentarily, and I'll have him call."

Finally, April decided to call Sophie. Maybe she'd know something. Why didn't she think of that before? She'd left a message saying she was filming in town for a few weeks and was at the Drake. Sam, who was handling her contract, could be with her going over the deal! Still, Sam should have informed his office. April felt a little calmer and dialed Sophie's number. The phone was busy. Quickly showering and dressing, she left the house. April backed the car out of the driveway and turned on the radio to find out how traffic was moving as she headed in the direction of the Drake hotel.

"And if today is your birthday, you share it with celebrity Sophie Watkins, the rising new star who happens to be in Chicago filming her new movie, *Daring Love*. She turns thirty today."

How could she forget it was Sophie's birthday? April found a floral shop near the hotel and picked up a dozen red roses.

"I'd like to get Sophie Watkin's room number, please."

"Let me dial for you," the attendant offered repeatedly.

"No. It's a surprise." She held up the roses.

No matter how hard she tried, the receptionist would not give her the room number. "But I want to surprise her," April insisted. "She's my cousin, and it's her birthday. Wait a minute." April dug in her bag and pulled out a picture of her and Sophie. One she'd meant to mail since the picnic. "Here, we are together. I'm really her cousin. How would I know she was here if she hadn't called?"

"Ma'am."

"Mrs. Summers."

"Mrs. Summers. I could get fired for this," The receptionist explained.

"Fine. Go ahead and call up. I'll just spoil my birthday surprise."

"Okay, Mrs. Summers. But if anyone asks, I didn't tell you."

"I'm going to guess she's in the penthouse. Just nod if I'm correct. Then you really wouldn't have told me, right?"

The receptionist nodded, and April handed him a folded bill.

The last time Sophie was in town, she'd stayed in the penthouse. The sign on the door said, do not disturb. April was about to knock when she noticed the door was not all the way locked, so she twisted the knob, and it yielded. It'd be a real surprise. There'd been a party. She could tell from the half-eaten room-service food, liquor bottles, and clothes strewn around. This was a bad idea, April thought, turning to leave. She would call from downstairs. She placed the roses on the table. She was about to leave when familiar laughter stopped her dead in her tracks. She'd have sworn—no, she was crazy. April moved through the living room toward the bedroom door, but something else stopped her…the blue and white tie she'd bought Sam. The door was shut. April advanced slowly. This was insane. It was nine in the morning, and she was an interloper. How many women could have bought that tie? April pressed her ear against the door.

"I've got to go, but I'd better call my office. They will be sending out the search squad if I don't show up again today."

"Don't go, Sam. Let the world go on without you for another day. So, what if they missed you. It's about time someone did, right?"

"Let me make this call."

"What the hell," April threw open the door and let out a curdling scream calling Sam's name over and over. "Sam," she wailed, "how could you."

"April! What are you doing here?" Sam was mortified.

The look in April's eyes lasered Sophie! Her trusted cousin and once best friend. She looked from one to the other in total bewilderment. "How could you both? How could you.?" She turned to leave.

"April, wait," Sam was in his boxers and pulled the sheet to cover his nakedness. "I can explain." He shot to her side, unaware the bedspread had not yielded to his tug and he was damn near stark naked in front of his wife in another woman's bedroom.

"Cover yourself up." April slapped Sam hard, pinning him with a gaze of utter disbelief and anger. "Oh my God, Sam, how could you?" She backed away. "Sophie!" She looked at her cousin.

"It's not what you think, April. Come on, get a grip. Let us explain."

"Get a grip? Get grip? Are you goddamn crazy? Do you think I'm a fool? Don't you dare? What are you going to tell me? That you and my husband are both almost naked, and it's not what I think?"

Sophie got out of bed and casually pulled on a silk robe. "I'm sorry, April. You know I wouldn't do anything to hurt you. It's nothing, really, nothing!"

"Why, Sam." April ignored Sophie. "Why. Answer me. Why?"

"Listen to me," Sophie pleaded.

"Get the hell out of my face, you harlot. You evil witch!" April slapped Sophie even harder than she'd slapped Sam. Sophie staggered backward, bringing a hand to her face. "My face." She fled to the bathroom to examine the damage. "Jesus Christ," she exclaimed. She was to begin shooting in the morning. "Really, April, you're over-reacting. "God!" She looked closely at the fingerprints across her face. "What's the big deal?"

"Shut up, dammit." April went into the bathroom and hurled a crystal vase that whizzed past Sophie's head.

That was it. Violence. No way. Sophie pushed April out of the bathroom and quickly locked the door, leaving Sam to somehow get out of this pickle. This was such nonsense. She had no intention of leaving the bathroom until the tornado had subsided.

"April," Sam advanced cautiously. This was a mistake. It means nothing to me. I know, but I was so lonely. Can't you understand?" Sam pleaded with his wife. "I love you, April. You and no one else."

"And this's how you show it?" A shoe whizzed past his ear.

"This was a mistake. A big mistake. The other night I was at Michael's. Sophie dropped by. We were drinking, and I was asking her for advice about us. She was the closest I could get to you. I'm sorry." Sam reached out for understanding.

"Don't touch me!" April slapped his hand away. "I should never have married you. I should have listened to my mother. You're nothing. Do you hear me? Nothing."

Sam was enraged. "I don't give a damn about your mother. I'm sorry about this. I have no excuse. But don't you dare bring your mother up in my presence. She's part of our problem. After today...."

"There is no after today. I want you out of my life for good. Do you hear me? Out."

"April. Stop this! Shut up for just a moment and listen to me. I don't give a hoot about Sophie...."

"Sam. You are a narcissistic, selfish, indulgent ass. I will not shut up. I will not shut up. And as for Sophie, she might as well be dead, right along with you. Do you hear that? You are coward of a man. "And, you Sophie, the husband thief, are DEADER THAN DEAD." April shouted through the bathroom door. Throwing anything close at hand at the door.

"Stop this, please."

"Or what? You'll hit me. Go on, Sam hit me. Hit me because *you* betrayed me. 'Cause, *you're* cheating on me with my cousin, for quitting my job. Hit me because I'm pissed *you* have betrayed our love. Go on, spin this if you can. Make it my fault. I don't know where you get off telling me to stop this."

"April, Sophie, and I didn't mean to hurt you. You've got to believe me."

"Sam don't patronize me. I'm already humiliated, downright mad. I've been an ostrich all these years. Shouldn't I be mad that

I'm standing in a hotel room, where my husband, who's was in my cousin's bed, is telling me, a fucking four-point-O student, that he can explain?"

"April. Sophie and…."

"Sophie is vile, and evil, and morally corrupt."

"Why are you saying such things," Sophie shouted through the bathroom. "Don't listen to her, Sam. April, you've always been stupid. Crazy as a bedbug. If you keep this up, you'll lose a good thing."

"Good thing, huh. He may be good enough for you, Sophie, but not for me. You both belong in the toilet. Go on, Sam, join your lover in the toilet." The look on April's face was one of pure hatred. "Get out of my life for good. No one is going to take me for a fool ever again. By the time I get home tonight, I want you out."

Sam was frozen. April was joking, he thought.

"April," Sam spun her to face him. She looked him up and down with utter scorn.

"Get out of my life, or I'll kill you." April dropped her voice to a whisper.

CHAPTER FORTY-ONE

TONY WAITED UNTIL Veronica's office hours were over before stopping by. He hadn't seen her for three months and thought things might have cooled down by now.

Veronica refused to open the door.

"Veronica. Please. I just want to thank you for your kind words at the awards dinner."

"You're welcome. Tony," she opened the door. The man still made her quiver. "They weren't just kind words," Veronica said, "They were true words."

"May I come in for a minute?"

"No. That's not a good idea," she said.

"I accepted a position back on the East Coast."

"That's a good decision. Maybe you can come to your senses with Tia."

"No. That's really over. Just for the record, I was never engaged to Tia. She always did that when she felt I was interested in another woman. Honestly, we did date, but that was before I met you and the house business; it's her house, not ours. I know what love is now, and Tia deserves better than a man who loves another woman."

"Tony don't…"

"Don't what? Don't tell you how much I love you? Don't worry. I won't bother you anymore. I'm leaving because I can't stay here any longer. Each day I don't see you is like torture, and I die a little inside. I didn't mean to cause you any pain, but I really do love you, Veronica. If there is any hope for us…."

"None. Tony, the decisions I made eighteen years ago are still valid today. I don't feel the same rush in my heart when my husband holds me at night as when you hold me. I don't feel the madness of serotonin, but I feel very good, Tony, for many more reasons than you could understand. I'm home where I belong."

"Let me be with you, Veronica. We can build memories too. Please, give me the chance to love you. Let me make you happy. I know what we did was wrong, but I also know our love for each other is real. It's destiny. I can't live without you, Veronica."

For a moment there was silence. This was a weird conversation to be having with a door between them. Luckily, no one would be around at this time.

Finally, Veronica said, "Tony. Believe me. Time and distance will heal the wound in your heart. What you feel for me now, I have felt for my husband, and in time, we would get to the same point—mature love. Besides, would you be able to trust me?" Veronica stared at her toes, unable to look Tony in the eyes. "Tony, even if "love" was what we felt, and we know better, that's only a fraction of the commitment it takes to make relationships work. What happens when I turn eighty-eight, and you are sixty-nine? Our time has passed. I want to send you into the world knowing that obligation, loyalty, commitment, and duty are what romantic love settles into when the dust all clears. That's the kind of love that moves mountains. That's what I have with Randolph. Make the right choice, Tony. Go on back East and know I was just a catalyst to the love you'll find. Your soul mate is yet to come."

"I will never love again."

"Nonsense. If it makes you feel better, know I have a great deal of respect for you and I thank you for saving my marriage. Know that and take that with you wherever you go and use it however long you need it."

"You are one helluva woman Veronica. It'll be hard to find the woman to replace you, but as they say, it's better to have loved and lost than not at all."

April's face was swollen from crying. It didn't matter whether Sam meant to hurt her or not. He had. Sophie's phone call, pleading and offering long explanations in defense of Sam, did nothing to ease her pain. "I don't know why I did it, April. Bloody hell, April. I wanted something you had. Better me than someone looking to break up your happy home. Come on. You know me."

"I thought I did, Sophie. I really thought I did." She had mumbled at the ranting messages.

Maybe she was being naïve again. Men cheated on their wives all the time for no reason at all. But there was no reconciliation possible for them. April looked over the divorce papers. She was unsure this was the right thing to do, but it was the only thing she knew how to do. She played a role in this debacle. She's never been easy to live with. She wasn't a pliable woman. In fact, she was known to be impetuous, uncompromising, and unapologetic, but she'd never been unfaithful. How could she ever forgive Sam? Trust him again? Trust anyone, for that matter? Her cousin, whom she'd befriended and protected as a child. How could she? Sam had been whimsical. To hell with Sam. She didn't deserve infidelity, and she wasn't going to take it. April shuffled the papers on her desk once more before folding the notarized letter into quarters and pushing it deep into her pocket. Walking down the driveway, she felt a profound loss. April flipped her cell phone and called Veronica.

"Hey."

"Hey, girl."

"God, you sound awful. What's the matter?"

"Nothing I can't handle. Whatsup?"

"I'm going away for a little while. To the mountains. Hiking. Just wanted to give you the number to reach me. Tell Melody I needed some time, but I'll be out to see her as soon as I get back."

"I won't ask if you don't want to talk."

"When I get back. I'm checking out for a couple of weeks. I have a few things I gotta work out. I'll tell you everything when I get back."

"Are you sure?"

"I'm sure."

April decided to do one of her most favorite things in one of her most favorite places on earth. Colorado Rocky Mountains… Aspen in particular. Winter, Spring, Summer, or Fall, she loved Aspen. As much as she wanted to see the spectacular view Aspen Trail afforded, she decided to opt for a less populated trail. She needed time to herself. *Lost Man* trail which just about summed up her life, with its rugged terrain and steady incline afforded a lake view of the Alpine tundra. As she climbed the mountain, April's found herself thinking of Frank Easton. Why would a man as smart as he was choose Martin as a co-CEO. It just didn't make sense. She couldn't believe in two months so much could have changed about her life.

That evening as April dressed for dinner in town her grooming was interrupted by her trilling phone. She ignored it. She had no intention of talking to Sam or anyone else and she was sure it was Sam who had called every day so far. The phone stopped and then started again. She finally picked it up after this continued four times to see Martin Spiro number on the screen.

"Why on earth are you calling me, Martin? You finally get that you can never do the job you were offered. It's been only two months."

"April," Martin's voice sounded grave. "Where are you?"

"On vacation and it seems you have a habit of always interrupting them."

"I must see you."

"That will never happen."

"Listen to me. Nothing is as it seems. Not even you hijacking."

"It's a conspiracy."

"What are you talking about?"

"The entire Kusak thing. It's a front. You won't believe this. I can't talk on the phone. When can you meet me?"

April went silent.

"Are you there. Everything has been orchestrated. I am telling you…I can fax you something."

"Martin, I have to go." April hung up the phone and sat on the bed.

After thinking it over, April called Martin and had him fax over evidence of the conspiracy. April poured over the reams of paper in her rented cottage library, contemplating charging the louse for using so much of her paper. Sitting at the table, she read over and over again the stack of papers she'd gotten from Martin. It was unbelievable. Kusak had only carried on with a scheme started when his father had been CEO of the bank. All the rank and file were involved. April would never have made it to CFO no matter what she'd done. What was Martin's motive for giving her this information, and what the hell would she do it? Why didn't he use it himself? Was this an attempt at recruiting her to get on board with his clandestine plan? Frank had semi-retired, and Martin had assumed the permanent position of CFO, so why would he do this? Were they attempting to offer her the CEO position if she cooperated with their clandestine plan? Were they looking for a fall guy?" She wasn't going to be used for their convenience and cowardice.

April read on. "And that accident was no accident. We wanted to scare you in case you thought of filing a racism claim. We had to stall you for a few months while they cleaned all traces of wrongdoing."

April dropped the pile of papers on the floor. She didn't give a flying hoot about S&G. Let white folks fight white folks' battle. She ought to send the stack of papers to the Federal offices but she was shaking and before she knew it she was crumpled up in tears.

CHAPTER FORTY-TWO

I T WAS THE END of August. Eight months had passed since the women had first met in Eve's office. So much had happened in that time. She'd lost her job and was facing a divorce. Veronica had an affair and Melody's illness has thrown them all into a tizzy. April stared at the phone in her hand. She had only one person to call.

The urgent call that came in over her answering service for Veronica had her in a panic. She removed her surgical hat and gloves and went to the wall phone of the OR. She was forever alarmed when she got an urgent call, praying it had nothing to do with Melody.

"Veronica." She picked up the receiver.

"Veronica," the tears were coming, and the sobs garbled every word April said.

"April! What's going on."

"I'm too pissed to talk."

"Is it Melody?"

"No. It's…."

"It's what? April?"

"It's everything."

"Okay. I know. I'm in OR right now but as soon as I get out I will call you. Stay put."

"Okay," the meek voice said.

Shacked up in a hotel for two weeks now, too ashamed to go home, Sam ordered room service and sat in front of the TV with a glass of wine. April wouldn't return his calls. Sam stuck his fork mercilessly into the salmon steak. He'd said medium rare, damn it, and the Salmon was dry as a bone. What the hell was he doing living in a hotel room? Sophie had insisted the director move the shoot, so she had abandoned him too. Not that he would have looked for solace in her arms ever again. Pressing the volume dial on the TV changer until it was too loud did little to drown out the noises next door— four hundred dollars a night for a confounded room with paper-thin walls. The last thing he needed tonight was to hear knocking headboards. Bet they were people having an affair.

It wasn't right, but Sophie was the only woman he'd ever strayed with and it would, he was sure, cost him his marriage. If only April knew how heroic he'd been all these eight years, especially in his line of business where women found him, as they said, "irresistible." He bet April was filing for a divorce and avoiding him until she could serve him papers. All over again, Sam was mad as hell. He had to convince April to take him back. There was no one for him but her in this life. He supposed he could try waiting her out, hoping she'd come to her senses, but something told him he would be waiting until the cows came home, as she often said. He had to make the first move. Had to get her to understand. Beg on his knees. Sam switched off the light and pushed back into the chair. Plots swarmed in his head. Half an hour later, he picked up his keys and left the hotel.

April was nowhere to be found. The house was dark, the doors locked, and his keys no longer worked in the front or back door. Sonofabitch. She'd changed the locks. Sam tried his garage door opener. At least that still worked but the lock to the garage door did not. Sonofabitch, he banged on the door.

CHAPTER FORTY-THREE

INSTEAD OF GOING back to Chicago Charles and Melody had flown to Los Angels and she'd checked into Cedar Sanai for what was to be the fight of her life. Melody had never fought physically. She'd left that to her brothers and sister. Her fight had always been the mental struggle to rise above her destiny. But life had punched her squarely in the face, punctuating her rise to power with little hesitation. She hunched over the emesis basin, green fluid flowing from her mouth. It had been six weeks now since she'd started chemotherapy and radiation. It took every ounce of her will to live, to hold on. Her beautiful black hair was coming out in clumps, and her complexion, pasty. She'd already lost fifteen pounds. Melody lay back on the treatment bed. Courtney thought it best she stayed in the hospital while in treatment. She hated the hospital. She hated seeing all the people, most of whom never came back after a few weeks. When she'd inquired about them, she'd gotten that look. They had died. Why should she fight? Who was there to live for? Why would she saddle Charles with an invalid? This was her journey. Her burden. She had told Charles as much. She'd hurt him, she knew, but what else was there to do?

"Let me help you, Miss Adams," said the nurse cleaning her up with a wet towel.

"Thanks," Melody smiled weakly. "How much longer will I have to go through this?"

"Another four weeks or so. It's the only option." The nurse looked sadly at the young woman on the bed. "You know, Melody, I'd like to leave you a book," she pulled out a little white book from her pocket. *Conversations with God*, the title said. Jody had the most beautiful, calming voice. Soft like a whisper in the wind.

"How many of these do you hand out?" Melody looked at the title.

"Many."

"Oh my." Melody fought back a tear. "This is the second time I've heard of this book."

"The next book you read, the next song you hear, the next thought you have. There is always a message." Jody smiled as she straightened the pillows.

"Thanks. I'll read it."

Melody looked at the little book but did not open it. All the ethereal stuff exasperated her. And if God was so great, why was he taking away her life? Why had he taken away her family? Any day now, she was expecting Monica and Della from *Touched by an Angel* to tell her what her life lesson was and to remind her how much God loved her and to have faith. So why should she have a conversation with God!

"Ms. Adams," Courtney came into the room, and the nurse exited.

"Yes?" Melody hoped for good news. Some miracle so they could stop this god-awful treatment.

"I want to listen to your vitals, and I have to order a few more tests. How are you feeling?"

"I suppose as well as could be expected under the circumstances."

"Uh-huh," he put the stethoscope in his ear. "I had no idea you were interested in this kind of literature." Courtney was listening to her lungs when he noticed the book on the night table. "I have this wonderful book called *Many Lives Many Masters*. You should read it.

"How does a hard-core scientist like you believe in this stuff?"

"Because I see miracles every day. Melody," he stopped examining her. "Every time I try to save someone's life, I realize there is a force greater than me. I work on the brain, but I did not create it. Someone or something did. The brain is so marvelous, so complex, and so life-giving. I'm but a servant to the universe. Life-giving?"

"It's my brain that is taking my life." Melody said softly.

The next day a copy of the book arrived. Many times, Melody reached for it, and many times she halted. Just as she was about to pick up the book again, the phone rang.

"Hey, girl. How's it going?"

"Hey, Veronica, how are you?"

"Hanging in there. What about you, Mel? You sound weak. It's pretty awful, eh?"

"Yes. I'm tired all the time, but I'm holding up. Courtney says only four or so weeks to go. How is Charles?"

"Sad. Confused. Annoyed you're trying to dump him."

"Veronica, I can't involve him in this. It's not his load."

"How do you know? What if he was contracted for this part of your life? He wouldn't have met you if it weren't his journey."

"What do you mean?"

"Look. Every one of us is here for a reason. Maybe we are here to learn a lesson or to pay back a debt. I don't know, but maybe Charles is your guardian angel."

"Oh, Christ! Not you too. What's with all this stuff everyone is spouting?"

"Who else?"

"The nurse. Courtney. Is this a sort of rehearsed oncology story for people destined to die? Is it supposed to make the after-life better?" Melody was acerbic.

"Yup. You're feeling sorry for yourself again. Tell me, missy, how is that going to help? A positive mind is what you need."

"Courtney has been encouraging me to make peace with my parents. He says it's a part of my treatment. I've tried writing my mother a letter, but I just can't."

"Maybe you should let Charles drive over and bring her to see you this weekend?"

"Look, damn it. I don't want Charles to come this weekend. Nor you or April. I don't want to die with an audience." Anger rose like bile. Uncharacteristic. Melody never got angry. She was too logical. Android precision. It took a brain tumor to remind her she was human. "I want to do this my way—alone."

"Have you entertained the thought you might not die or that if you keep up these temper tantrums, it will not be angels taking you away? Anyway, no worries, only the good die young."

"Yes, I should take comfort in that," Melody managed a weak smile.

Veronica's voice became more serious. "Melody, Charles loves you. He's the man you've been looking for all of your life. And girl, I can assure you, you can't get rid of him."

"I'm sorry," Melody sighed. "You're right. I'm feeling sorry for myself. I know you mean well but Charles doesn't need all this Vee. He just doesn't. Look, I'm forgetting things. Yesterday

I accidentally peed on myself. I need my dignity. Please understand. I don't want Charles to see me like this. Don't pressure me, Veronica. I need to do this my way. Ask him not to come."

It was going on the sixth week of therapy. Melody felt like a rag doll. Today, however, was one of her better days. Courtney said the radiation should have shrunk the tumor in another week enough to operate. After her radiation and chemo treatment were done, Courtney would let her go to Chicago to recuperate until he was ready to do the surgery. She would be glad to be in her home, among her things. She wanted the familiar. No matter how sterile her home might be, it was hers.

Melody checked herself in the mirror. Her hair was now completely gone. Her beautiful, black mane shed to completion. She'd almost died of shock when the first clump came out. Going bald has been frightening, but like everything else, one gets used to change when there is no alternative. She was toying with the idea of doing the Princess Caroline thing—fashionable turbans—yet chose to stay just the way she was. Another good thing about the day was the arrival of a package from Microtech. In it was a sign that said CEO.

The midday sun was pouring through the window. Funny, she had never paid much attention to the characteristics of light. How it casts shadows, faded the curtains and chairs in its path, and sped up decay while also giving life. There was something extraordinary about today's sunlight. The blade of light cut through the glass effortlessly. It changed with each breeze as though it carried a message. Melody felt compelled to pick up the books by her bedside. There were a few magazines, some work-related stuff, a couple of novels and the new book Courtney had brought her, *Many Lives Many Masters*.

Melody's mind lingered on Courtney. He was different from any man she had ever met. After spending these weeks with him, she found herself curious. How does such a brilliant man remain so humble? He never spoke of himself but rather about her. How was her night? How was the letter to her mother coming? How was her, Charles? She had no idea if he was married. Had children. Where he was from, and yet, she'd shared every aspect of her life with him. She'd felt no shame, no triumphs, just an absolute peace with him. Looking into his empathetic black eyes, she could tell he was born to do this work. His kismet had been fulfilled. Courtney was a man who believed himself an instrument of a higher power.

Melody picked up the book and, without turning to the cover flaps, began reading. So totally absorbed was she; she hadn't heard him come in.

"It's wonderful, isn't it?"

Melody jumped, looked up from the book, and swore a new kind of light had entered the room.

"Marvelous," she accepted the tissue he handed her. "What's this for?"

"You're crying."

"Oh!" Melody touched her cheeks. You're right. Thanks. Can you stay awhile, or do you have to run off?"

"It depends."

"On what?"

"You."

"Me?"

"My surgery was canceled this afternoon, and I thought maybe you'd like to go have lunch."

"Courtney, not that cafeteria! The food will probably kill me before the tumor."

"That's quite possible. I have to go and see a few post-op patients. I'll be back in half an hour. Is that long enough?"

"Yup."

She'd lost quite a bit of weight by now, but she still looked reasonably healthy except for her hair. Her complexion had evened out, and she hadn't had any more fainting episodes. If she weren't just so tired, she'd have been hard-pressed to believe her own body was betraying her.

Melody chose a butter yellow belted jacket and an A-line skirt. Yellow was her favorite color. Her home was decorated in yellow and blue. The sun was yellow, and the light that would come to take her away would be yellow. Melody was startled by the thought. Had she accepted death as a way out? Had she stopped fighting? Maybe she had because she no longer felt like being brave. She felt like crying and crying and crying. And that was what she did. After composing herself, she applied a light touch of make-up and skillfully wrapped her head with a silk scarf. On top of the scarf, she donned an English Nanny hat. Surveying herself in the full-length mirror, she was pleased. There was no Essie to ask, and she missed that. She would call her housekeeper when she returned.

April placed a call to Veronica when she landed in Chicago. Then they called Melody to tell her they were both coming out for the weekend. The problems to be solved required the Trinity.

The phone trilled. "Yo, yo, Ma." It was Veronica again.

"Whatsup, this time, hips." Melody said.

"Whatsup?" She could hear April who was on a three-way call. "You sound great. How are you feeling?"

"Tired but okay. I'm on my way to lunch with Courtney."

"Oh my. Do you see how lucky you are to know me?" Veronica said.

"I've always known that." Melody was earnest.

"We're just calling to say we'll be out this weekend."

"Veronica, April, don't."

"Melody, why don't you ever mind your own business."

"I look forward to seeing you."

"And Charles is coming too."

"Ready?" Courtney was at the door.

"Yes. I'll be right there. Veronica, not Charles, please. I've gotta go. Courtney's here."

"Give him my love and eternal gratitude, will you."

"Will do."

"The restaurant is only a couple of blocks away. Do you think you can make it? I'm positive. That was Veronica again. She calls every minute on the minute. She says hi."

"Good, tell her the same when you talk to her again in the next minute," he chuckled. "It's a beautiful day. The sunshine will do you good. Yes. I think we'll walk. We'll go slowly."

And indeed, the sunshine was rejuvenating.

"You know I've meant to ask." Melody put on her sunglasses. "How can you take such personal care of each of your patients?"

"I don't. I take excellent care of my patients, but you're different."

"Why?"

"When I was in med school, I had a crush on Veronica, but I was too shy to tell her. I was, he chuckled, "a brainiac. Brainiacs are usually shy people. One day just before the Christmas break, I finally got the courage to tell her how I felt. I thought she was going to die laughing, but she didn't. It never amounted to anything because she was with Randolph, but I was grateful she didn't laugh at me. It made me confident. So, any friend of Veronica's is a friend of mine because she never laughed at me."

Melody felt a twinge of sadness. He was a loner.

"And you never married?"

"Yes. I did. I got married, right after my residency, to this wonderful woman. She's a brainiac too. He chuckled. "We have two beautiful brainiac children."

"So, how does your wife deal with your being gone so much?"

"Ah. My wife understands we can only serve one master. My destiny is my work, and she understands that. She's busy with her life, and when we're together, our world is complete."

Melody felt jarred. Somewhere along the line, she had transferred her feeling of love and need entirely to Courtney.

Veronica, April, and Charles didn't come out because Melody had again squelched the idea. Four weeks went by slowly. But it had gone by. The chemo and radiation were over. A nutritionist came daily to Melody's new apartment to teach her how to cook macrobiotic foods. Once she mastered her nutrition, medication, and vitamin routine, she could go back to Chicago. She couldn't drive, but Courtney encouraged her to go back to work. He wanted her to resume as normal a life as possible until the surgery. That night, Melody sat at the corner table and pulled out a writing tablet. She started six letters, only to crumple them into the wastebasket. What could she say? What could have been said was sealed a long time ago? Instead, Melody sat with her foot on top of a towel. She was going home soon. Around her were bottles and bottles of nail paraphernalia. She picked up the one called putrid green, a reminder that she'd made it through a horrible experience. She couldn't believe she'd been doing this beauty nonsense for so long that, even now, she felt compelled to maintain her beauty routine. She wanted to look special for Charles. "How could you be so damn superficial?" Melody balled up the entire towel filled with nail polish bottles and threw it at the wall. It shattered, leaving a collage on the wall. She didn't hear the door open.

"Nice" Courtney stood in the doorway. "I had no idea you wanted to be a painter."

"I'll pay for the repainting. I'm sorry."

"Feeling sorry for yourself today, huh?"

"Wouldn't you, damn it? Wouldn't you?" Suppressed anger erupted from deep within her.

"Yes. I'm sure I would." He gathered her flailing arms. "But don't let the anger get the better of you. How're you doing with the soul healing?" he said softly.

"I've tried to write."

"And?"

Melody sniffled. She didn't want to die. She just didn't want to die.

"Melody," Courtney held her close, "It's going to be rough. The surgery. We have to start treatment as soon as you're strong enough. I will tell you this; I'll feel much better about doing the surgery if you make peace with your mother."

"It's so hard. When you've been lying all your life, the truth is hard to find. I can't make peace with Mama just to tell her I'm dying."

"Think, Melody. If you died tomorrow, what is the one thing you'd have wished you could do?"

"Tell my Mom how much I loved her. How strong and courageous I thought she was. How her dreams gave me my life and how much I thank her for the opportunity to know another world."

"Then, you will have to do it. Find the words."

Melody licked her lips. They were dry. Chapped even through her lip gloss.

"I will," she murmured. "I'll find my way home. You know Courtney," she looked up at him, her eyes filled with tears, "I'm scared." She welcomed his comforting arm around her shoulder. "It's okay to know you'll die at some time, but it is downright frightening when every time you close your eyes, look in the mirror and hear your voice, death is beckoning you into its embrace."

"I wish I could take away your fear. I wish I could tell you it was all going to be okay. But I can't. I want to operate under the best conditions possible, and in all my years of believing in miracles, they often happen when people are at peace inside. For you, and for me, Melody, find the words."

When April pulled into the garage. Sam's car was inside. Her body stiffened. She pushed her key into the door and it didn't work. She went to the front door and tried to open it. It was fine. Maybe she'd forgotten to change the garage door lock but she was sure she had.

"How did you get in here? I had the locks changed." She walked past Sam who was sitting at the dining table.

"I had the garage lock changed."

"Well change it back. You no longer belong here."

"April," Sam said softly.

He was standing behind her now. April swung around, her face coming within inches of his. She gasped at how drawn he looked. His eyes were dull, and his complexion gray.

"Why are you here?"

"I've been coming here every day for five days. Where have you been?"

"That's none of your business? Didn't you get my letter?"

"Yes. That's why I'm here. I have to talk to you, April. You're making a big mistake."

"I'm making a big mistake! Don't you mean you made a big mistake?"

"I did. I admit, but it was… ."

"Sam, I'd like to listen to you beg, but that's impossible right now. When we meet, bring your lawyer. I assure you I do want you to beg, but a word of caution, it won't help. I'm going to take everything you own."

Sam caught her by the wrist. "I will do no such thing. You will listen to me tonight or else… ."

"You don't learn, do you, boy." April was livid. "What are you going to do? Try to force yourself on me again? Lucky for you, I left that part out of the divorce deposition, but I can add it if you'd like. I did tell you, didn't I, about this professor of mine at Harvard. He spent ten years in jail for alleged rape. What if I have proof of a rape? How much time will you spend in jail, buddy?"

"April, listen." Sam stepped back.

"No, Sam. You listen. I've been my mother's alter-ego. I've been your disappointing wife, who you were forced to betray. I've been S&G's jester, and now I just want to be my own best friend. Is that so hard to understand? Leave me alone. I'm not as mad as before about your affair. I don't have the energy left to stay mad. Actually, you've liberated me."

"Sophie is the only person with whom I've ever been unfaithful. Listen to me. I just needed to be close to someone. I know I was wrong but please; I was, I was lonely."

April looked away sharply. She couldn't bear to see Sam this way. The pain in his eyes. The drooping shoulders. The broken spirit. Why was she being so hard on him? She wasn't the easiest person to live with. She knew that. Having taken the pill throughout their entire marriage, she, too, had deceived him. And though her perfected art of avoidance had refused to hear his cry on so many occasions, he hadn't left her for not want-ing the child he so badly wanted for the past five years. Their lives had been rocked by a gargantuan boulder. He'd betrayed his "Earth Angel," so what could be left of their love? If she took him back, they would face an enormous uphill battle. Could they fight it out to the bitter end? She wasn't sure.

"I'm sorry, Sam. We just can't go back. We don't fit anymore."

"Please. Please, April, reconsider."

"Sam," April stopped him. "In time, maybe I'll be able to for-give you, and we can be friends, but right now, I just can't. You want me to take you back, have your child, trust you again, but I don't know if I can ever do that. I'll have to do a lot of work on myself before giving you an answer."

"I'm prepared to wait."

"Then wait." April got back in her car and sped away.

CHAPTER FORTY-FOUR

"**T**HERE IS NO SUCH word in the English language," Randolph was adamant.

"Who says? Get the dictionary," Veronica rebutted.

"Veronica! Accept defeat. There is no such word," Randolph insisted.

"Are you challenging me? You know you'll lose your turn?" Veronica's head did an Egyptian dance.

"All right. All right. While I find the Scrabble dictionary, you replenish the drinks." Randolph shook his head. "There's no point arguing with this woman without proof."

"I'll make the drinks," Charles offered. "And just in case Veronica changes up the board, April, you stay here."

"The gall. Are you calling me a cheat? You, people, know nothin' about Black folks' language."

The scrabble party was in honor of Melody's arrival the following t day. They were scheming how to arrange for Charles to pick her up, especially since she forbade it. The girl wanted to take a taxi home. April, who had been quiet all evening, poured more peanuts into the bowl.

"I feel so badly for him. Melody should be more reasonable." April said when Charles had left the room.

"Do I hear the pot calling the kettle black?" Veronica inquired.

"Veronica, that's not fair. He cheated with my cousin, for God's sake!"

"The actress at that?" Sarcasm was obvious in Veronica's voice.

"Yes. The very one. What I can't fathom is what she could want from Sam. Sophie's M.O. is to sleep with powerbrokers from whom she needs results, but Sam? What can he do for her?" April shook her head, still in disbelief.

"Maybe she's just evil. But how can you forgive me so easily and not Sam?"

"That's different."

"No, it isn't."

"Randolph doesn't know."

"I wouldn't count on that. My husband is real smart. Because I didn't tell him doesn't mean he doesn't know. April, I have to defend Sam just a little. Believe me, it's so easy to stray when things are all messed up in your head. I never thought I'd cheat on Randolph. Yes I became obsessed with Tony, but my affair with him had nothing to do with Tony per se but with my need to escape reality. Sam's probably feeling ashamed of hitting you, frustrated you refuse to have his child and not being able to protect you against an assault."

"But cheating with my cousin? A stranger would be easier to take."

"Yeah. That's hard."

"By the way, what did you decide to do with the information Martin gave you? You should discuss it with Sam. He can help you."

"Let's not talk about that anymore. It'll only upset me. I did what should be done. I sent it anonymously to the law!"

"You did?"

"Yes, all except the part that they planned the assault on me. I couldn't bear the thought of having to go through a legal investigation and have the whole nightmare brought up all over again. I know what else I forgot to tell you. I meant to when we met for lunch, but so much was going on. I was ready to really try to have a baby. I'd stopped taking the pill."

"Don't tell me. You mean you were on the pill when Sam thought you were trying to conceive?" Veronica didn't flinch, but her eyes glazed over. "How can you call betrayal when you are also a betrayer?" She finally asked.

"It's not the same."

"It absolutely is, and worse."

"It'll be great to have Melody home tomorrow?" April said, changing the subject.

"Yeah, it will. She'll want a few days by herself. After that, we'll break down the door."

"So, how are we going to get Charles to pick her up?"

"Beats me."

In the kitchen, Charles made a pitcher of rum and coke. He added crushed ice and felt very much at home. He wanted to give Melody a home like this. He wanted to build tree houses for their children. He wanted to shake the hell out of her for refusing to see him for weeks. For not wanting him to pick her up. His anger erupted unannounced. How could she be so cold? So afraid to let him into her life? Did she think he was so superficial he would walk out on her? Charles leaned against the refrigerator for support.

"Hey, man," Randolph, who had come down the back staircase, said. "It's going to be okay. C'mon, man, let's go back inside. She'll be home tomorrow."

"Yeah. Tomorrow." Charles said though it did not resonate through his being.

"You alright, man?"

Charles nodded. He was now composed, just like a big boy.

"I've got the dictionary," Randolph announced, pushing the door open.

"And I got the liquor." Charles followed him.

"We're armed and dangerous." Randolph put the dictionary and a wad of papers in front of April and casually laid an envelope in front of Veronica. It said Random House. Veronica picked up the envelope to hand back to her husband, then stopped. She looked at Randolph. "Is this what I think?" She covered her mouth.

"Look and see. Read it, Veronica. Read it to me."

With trembling hands and quivering lips, Veronica opened the neatly folder letter. The paper was expensive linen with an insignia watermark.

"Dear Mr. Whittaker." She began. "We are excited about your submission. *Never On A Sunday*. The story is poignant, suspenseful, and totally engrossing. Though we have some suggestions for the rewrite, we would like to make an offer on the work. We can have an editor assigned to you immediately, and we would be happy to fly your agent out to get the contract signed."

"Oh, my God. Randolph. You did it." Veronica rose to squeeze her husband tightly.

"We did it, Veronica."

For a moment, the room was silent. Only the coughing wheeze of the heat through the vent broke the silence. An understanding passed between Randolph and his wife. Instinctively Charles hugged April. And she, in turn, hugged him back.

"Congratulations," Charles slapped Randolph's back.

"I wonder how much of an advance they're willing to offer?" Veronica, now recovered, was all business.

"I don't care. I'm just glad someone accepted my work."

"My ass. They're going to pay a pretty penny for the last fifteen years you've been submitting excellent work. I'm gonna quit my job to become your manager."

"Talk that talk, girl." Randolph kissed the top of his wife's head.

"Yeah. You think this is only talk. Then wait, my lovely, and watch me walk that walk."

"Amen," Charles said.

"And now Veronica since I have been ordained a wordsmith, April, you may check, but I assure you, your word is not in the dictionary. Please take up your tiles and lose a turn." Her husband said lovingly.

The foursome broke out in ear-splitting laughter. Predictably, the game was prematurely concluded.

"All that's left is a toast, then," Charles poured rum and coke for all.

April dropped a couple of ice cubes in a glass and raised it in a toast. "To the next titan of the publishing industry."

"Here, here." Everyone raised their glasses.

"I've got a toast," Veronica said. "To seeing Melody tomorrow."

"Here. Here. Cheers."

"I'll definitely drink to that." Charles raised his glass. Celebration was in the air.

"Let me warn you all now. She's as feisty as ever. I offered to fly out and pick her up. You know what she said to me?" Charles was shaking his head in disbelief. She said, "I can only deal with the fear of death in one form at this moment. But thanks anyway. Then she said she'd take a cab home. Just wait and see. One day, I will teach her to really fly if it's the last thing I do."

"I didn't know you'd spoken to her," Veronica said. "Maybe we should just let her take a taxi home. She'll call us in a couple of days. Let's be patient."

Veronica, true to form, was all choked up. She didn't want to spoil the evening for everyone, so she dashed for the bathroom as she felt her tear ducts filling. Under her arm was the bound manuscript her husband had presented to her.

She read the Dedication

"There is no greater love than the love of understanding, patience, and faith. One should never give up on a dream, for it will always come through. I dedicate this work to my wife, who deep down believed in me even in the face of doubt and frustration."

"Oh, God." Veronica wiped her eyes. "I could have given up on the greatest love in my life." How could she have even thought it? Veronica was crying hard. She was crying for Melody, April, Charles, Tony, Randolph and, most definitely, for herself.

The phone in the bathroom rang softly, and Veronica grabbed it on the first ring.

Hours earlier in California

Courtney hooked the film in the reader to take a final look at the scan before signing Melody's release papers. It was late, and he wanted to be in her apartment bright and early with the good news. She was very excited about going home, and he was happy for her. "Dear God!" He was shaking uncontrollably. "Dear God," he repeated, slumping back on the desk. Melody's tumor had grown considerably since the last test that had shown it shrinking. Almost doubled in mass in less than two weeks. He had never seen anything like it. Fear rose so great that he had to seek refuge in the chair behind the desk. Despite the chemotherapy and radiation, which had shown promising signs, despite the last battery of tests and x-rays which showed the same results, the tumor has growing aggressively in the past week. Courtney did not understand how this could have happened and how it had not affected Melody's physical or neurological condition. Debilitated or not, if there was any hope, he had to operate immediately. Wearily, he put his head on the desk. Courtney Cox was distraught. If there were a time he would have wished to be God, it was now. He had treated thousands of patients. He knew how to behave when the prognosis was bad. Today, however, he felt defeated and, for the first time, wished he were in another profession altogether. He had to go to her immediately. How would he break the news? Before Courtney made his way to Melody's flat, he dialed Veronica's office.

"Dr. Whittaker's answering service."

"This is Dr. Cox."

"Is this an emergency? Dr. Austin is on OB call tonight."

"This *is Dr*. Cox from Cedar Sinai in California. And yes, it's an emergency. I'll wait on the phone while you try Dr. Whittaker and then patch me through."

The operator suspected from the authority of his voice, it was better to act than to question the caller. "Yes, Sir. Just a moment."

Chicago.

"Dr. Whittaker. I have a Dr. Courtney Cox on the line."

"Put him right through, Rita. Hey Courtney?"

"I'm glad I caught you."

"We're having a pre-welcome home celebration party. I was going to call later. What time is Melody getting in, do you know?"

"I'm afraid she's not."

"What do you mean? What's wrong?" There was obvious fright in Veronica's voice.

"I just looked at Melody's new scan, and the prognosis is really bad." He sounded shaken.

"What do you mean bad. I thought the….How bad?" Veronica's voice was shrill.

"Bad enough I think you should come immediately. I have to take the chance and operate right away within twenty-four hours. I haven't told her yet. But I'm on my way there now. I'll stay with her tonight, but I would like it if you would come out. I can't fathom how this could happen. I have never seen it. Her tumor has grown."

"I'll be on the next plane," Veronica said calmly. "I'll be there."

"Veronica, do you know where to find her mother? She wants to go home."

"I'll find her, Courtney. I'll find her."

The world had stopped. Veronica was transfixed. Without warning, a deep wail welled in her, broke free and filled the house. Charles was the first to reach her as she came out of the bathroom; her body doubled over as if she were in excruciating pain.

"Veronica. What's the matter?"

"That was Courtney." She wailed.

"I'll get the plane ready." Charles had gone ashen.

CHAPTER FORTY-FIVE

THE NIGHT HAD been rough for Melody. She had been sick to her stomach, throwing up repeatedly. At midnight she broke out into a cold sweat and was shaking all over. Panicked, she'd tried to get out of bed but felt too weak. She was desperate to call Courtney, but her arms were too heavy to dial the phone. Frightened and alone, she curled into a fetal position and prayed she would feel better soon. "Please, God," she begged. "Don't let me die alone."

Tossing and turning, Melody suddenly threw up. The projectile vomit soaked the bedspread and the walls. She tried again and again to move, but she was too weak even to lift a finger. "Oh, God." She cried, but the sound was only in her head. "Please, I beg of you, don't let me die alone. I need to say goodbye to my mother." Lying still, with a vomit-soaked bedspread over her, she resolved her end had come. She was trembling and afraid.

Courtney strolled up to the door of the apartment. He wasn't looking forward to telling her the news. Squaring his shoulders, he knocked on the door. There was no answer. He looked at his watch and knocked louder. Suddenly he panicked, rushed back down the hall, and ordered the doorman to have security open the door.

The air was heavy with the stench of vomit. He rushed toward the still body. "Melody! Melody." There was no movement. He began shaking her.

"Call 911 and tell them to get an ambulance over here, stat," he shouted to the security guard. "Now!"

Melody felt strangely calm. Too much radiation was making her feel really terrible. Was she having radiation? She was certain she could hear Courtney's soothing voice, but she couldn't see him.

"Dial 555-2598," Courtney ordered the guard. "Put it on speakerphone."

"This is Dr. Cox," Courtney shouted to the O.R. nurse. "I'm on my way to the hospital with an unconscious patient. I want to take her directly to O.R. I suspect she has fluid on her brain. Have everything ready, do you hear me? Everything. And have an ICU bed ready. Life support on standby and quite a bit of Morphine. I'll be right there, and I don't want to wait."

Coutrney dialed another number.

Brenda Cox listened to her husband. He was prattling. He never panicked, but tonight he was somewhat hysterical. Courtney was an awesome, compassionate doctor, but he was always in control. It was a first.

"Courtney. What is it?" Brenda Cox tried to snap through the incoherence.

"It's Melody. That patient I was telling you about."

"Yes."

"She's unconscious. I'm in her apartment, about to take her to O.R. I won't be home tonight."

"Courtney," Brenda spoke softly. "I trust you know what you're doing."

"I thought I did, Brenda. I pray, I do."

"Just remember, darling." Her voice was soft and understanding. "Don't try to play God."

"Are we ready to go?" Charles asked the pilot.

"Yes, Sir. Ready when you are ready."

"Thanks, Dwight, you're a good man."

Charles sat beside Veronica, buckling his seat belt. Neither of them spoke, but they could tell by the redness around the rim of each other's eyes neither of them had stopped crying since the call. Charles was a take-charge person if Veronica ever saw one. It had been less than two hours since the call from Courtney. From the plane she texted April to let her know what had transpired.

"You look awful," Veronica said. "How are you?" She covered his hand with hers.

"Not good. But I'll try to get some rest now, and I'll shave before we get to the hospital. I want to look presentable for Melody"

"Have this," Veronica handed him eye blinders.

Charles was silent the entire flight, and Veronica allowed him his solitude.

"It's worse than I thought." Courtney held Veronica's elbow and led her down to the cafeteria. He was exhausted. He wasn't sure the decision to operate was a good one. He had lost his objectivity.

"Did you go to surgery already? It…"

"We didn't do much. The surgery confirmed the worst. There was no way to get the tumor out. Even worse, it has metastasized. I've just gotten all the reports back. She won't make it."

"Can we take her home? Melody would want that."

"Did you find out where her parents are?"

"I mean home to Chicago. But I will find her parents. I promise you I will."

"She is a mystery to me. She is quite the gal. You can go in an see her in the morning. After a couple days you can take her home. We didn't do much so there should be no problem flying."

"Thanks for everything. I know you did more than you had to."

"I'm so sorry, Veronica. I'm so very sorry."

"Go home and get some rest. Charles and I will take it from here. I don't know how I'm going to break this news to him. He was so hopeful. How long do you think?"

"Not long. Not long at all. I'm going to the doctor's lounge. Here's the number. If anything changes, call me right away."

Veronica went to find Charles. She was not looking forward to the conversation. "Let's have a cup of coffee," Veronica said to Charles.

"Straight up. Just tell me straight up."

"The news is not good. Courtney says we can take her home in a few days. She may seem normal to you for a minute but the cancer has metastasized and it's only a matter of time."

"What's that mean?"

"Not long, Courtney said. Not long. Five to six months."

"Can we see her?"

"She is not awake. She'll sleep through the night. We'll see her in the morning."

The following morning Charles stood in the doorway of Melody's room. She was awake and didn't seem as bad as he had expected. "You didn't call me today,

Why are you here? Why are you here?" Melody squeezed back tears.

"I couldn't wait any longer. I heard you were up to all kinds of shenanigans?"

"I was doing so well. I don't know what happened. Oh Charles…." There was no holding back the tears.

Charles was next to her in a minute. He held her until the tears stop flowing, caressing her hair, and resting his head against hers. "Has Doctor Cox spoken with you?"

"Yes. I am aware. I just want to go home. Please I don't want to die here. I just want to see my mother once more."

"You will. Dr, Cox says we can take you home in a couple of days. Tell me how to find your mother."

The black SUV pulled up to a dilapidated frame house. No way could this be the right place. Veronica knocked on the door.

"Yes." An elderly woman peered suspiciously through a chained door. Nobody came to visit her and certainly not in a car like that!

"We're looking for a Mrs. Adams. The mother of Melody Adams."

The shock on the woman's face was severe, and then her eyes took on a look so sad Veronica was encouraged. "I don't know any Melody Adams. You have the wrong place." She began closing the door.

"Deloris," a handsome, old man came to the door. He looked just like Melody.

"Come in." He pulled open the door. The house was worn, but neat as a pin.

"I'm a friend of Melody" Veronica began, "I'm Veronica Whittaker, Dr. Whittaker."

"Is something wrong with our baby?" To her surprise, it was the mother who spoke.

"I'm afraid so, Ms. Adams. I'm afraid so."

"I'd love to bring you back with me to Chicago to see Melody. Can you be ready to go in a couple of days? I will be back later with your flight details. We will be at the airport to pick you up."

The flight home was uneventful. Melody slept all the way. Charles stared at her and found it hard to believe she was dying. Charles moved into Melody's apartment. He wanted her to be in familiar surrounds, Today her parents would arrive and he hoped it wouldn't be too much for her. She was resting when the doorbell rang.

Veronica ushered Mr. and Mrs. Adams in. Deloris looked around the place in awe. "Is this Melody's home?"

Veronica nodded.

"She's still so perfect. She was my perfect child. Can we see her now?"

"She is sleeping, but you can just sit with her until she wakes up. I'm Charles Bell, Melody's partner." Charles took Deloris hand in his. "Come this way."

"You are her husband?" Deloris asked.

"Yes. In my mind I am."

Melody's father helped his unsteady wife to a chair by their daughter's bed, Deloris sat, staring at her Veronica. She wanted to hold her hand but instead prayed to God to have mercy. *Why would God take so many of her children, even those who did good?*

"It's my fault." Deloris Adams wilted into the chair, voice but a whisper. "I'm to blame. She only wanted to help. All Melody wanted was to make things better for our people. I wanted to protect her. I wanted her to stay away from the neighborhood. The streets are hard and I was afraid she'd come to harm. I'm glad she built this kind of life. I'd rather lose her to success than to the streets." Deloris Adams hung her head in sorrow. "I watched for her every day. Every move she made, and I'm so proud of my baby. I have a scrapbook this big of all her accomplishments."

"Mother. Is that you, mother?" No one noticed that Melody had awakened.

"Oh, my chile. Who else could it be? Now, don't you worry 'bout a thing you hear. Your Mama is here."

"Mama. Is it really you?"

"Yes, chile. It's me and your daddy."

Paroxysm of sobs left Melody's body shaking.

"Coffee?" Veronica mouthed to Charles and they left the room. Melody needed this time with her family. "I'm sorry, Mama. I'm sorry" 'Sorry 'bout what. I'm so proud of you. Look at this wonderful home you made. Look at all this "Can you forgive me? Can you?"

Deloris rose from her chair and enveloped her daughter. "Forgive you for what? Do you think I had no idea about you? I followed your every move…every single one…didn't I Lawrence? Deloris opened her purse and pulled out an album of pictures including one in the *Chicago Tribune* for her nomination as one of Chicago's most influential women.

"Is it true Daddy?"

"You see, don't you. Every day she scours the internet for news about you. Yes, she even learned them computers so she could follow you on those social things."

Melody looked at the pictures. Then she looked at her mother and father,. "Mama, I think you're proud of me."

"Not just proud of you? You're the best thing that ever happened to me in my life. I've always been proud of you, Melody. I watched you soar. I watched you fly, and not for a day have I regretted the path you chose. I know it didn't seem like it, but I never wanted you back in Watts. I did what I had to do as you did what you had to do. I would do it again and again. I have never been prouder in my whole life."

A tear slid down the corner of Melody's eyes. "But Mama you said…."

"I know what I said Chile. I'm you Mama. I said what I did because being the stubborn person you were you would prove me wrong. Why would I want you to hold on to me and lose yourself. I had done lived my life and I wanted you to live yours."

"I'm so sorry; so very sorry, Mama. I shouldn't have stayed away for so long."

"You stayed away as long as you needed to."

"You're so brave, Mama. You made me brave too, even when I had to walk alone. I just want to thank you for loving me so much. Daddy, how come you never convince Mama to move?"

"You know your Mama. She said when you came back to see her she would be right here. What if she moved and you couldn't find her?"

Melody's put her arms around her shoulders.

Deloris squeezed her eyes together. She was used to death, but this was hard.

Veronica stood at the door and watched the family's reunion. She didn't feel like thanking God for anything but she needed to for this moment.

"So, what'd you say we have dinner together. Charles has prepared the most scrumptious meal. I will help Melody get ready. Just follow the smell."

"May I help her," Deloris Adams asked.

"Sure, you can, Mama." Melody said.

Deloris helped Melody dress. She tied the scarf over Melody's head where her once thick mane used to be.

"Mama. You know what?"

"What?"

"I still have the brush you used to comb my hair with. Do you remember.?"

The October evening was unseasonably warm, After dinner, Melody joined Veronica on the balcony.

"Veronica Oh, my Veronica" She hugged her friend. "Thank you. How can I ever thank you?"

"For what? We are friends for life and remember what I said. At the dawn of a new day, we'll be together again. Girl, I can't tell you how much I admire you."

"I owe you so much. Thank you. Seeing Mama has completed my journey. I'm gonna be okay." She was tired. Weary.

"Let's make the best of our time together. There has to be a reason for everything, or this life will be too hard to handle. April will be over tomorrow. Let the Trinity give you the strength you need. It will never be goodbye just so long, because Melody Adams, the world has never, and will never, see a woman as classy as you again, and I will never wear another print nightdress as long as I live." The women smiled at each other. They had always understood each other. They were sisters in every aspect of the word. Bound by heritage, achievement, friendship and, above all, love.

"You got that right." Melody, in obvious pain was still trying to make a joke.

When everyone had left, Melody felt her body embraced by the light. Her journey was coming to an end. She could feel it. What a beautiful night and what a beautiful light! How she felt at peace.

Charles eased into the bed next to her. "You did it. You went home. You were so gracious and your parents are amazing."

"How can I ever thank you? You my dear Charles are amazing. You've made my whole life worth living." She fixed her stare on the man whose head was next to hers. "I wanted to live for you. I would have married you. Had your babies. Given you, my soul. I love you, Charles."

"I know that darling. You've given me everything I ever imagined love to be. I yearn for nothing. Nothing at all. I love you, Melody. Always will."

Melody nodded. She understood. "I'm going to leave you soon. Is it okay with you?"

"It will be okay. But take your time, darling. We have so much more to do."

Melody eased her body into his. "Okay, my love." And as the light that came to take her home washed the room in heavenly aura, the beams that beckoned her were warm. Smiling and content she welcomed it. She had loved and had been loved. That was enough.

Rivers of grief welled in Charles Bell, and he was not afraid to let them fall. He felt her body relax into knowingness. He watched as she snuggled closer and into acceptance. "If you want to go, you can, darling. You can leave me whenever you want," he said softly. "I'll find you wherever you go and I will find you in every life." Charles reached into his pocket and took Melody's hand. He wrapped his arms around her and cradled her head. He kissed her cheeks, and then he kissed her lips. "I love you, Melody," he whispered. "You are home now, darling, right here in my arms, right here in my arms. Go on, darling, where you need to. I'll find you; I promise." He slipped a diamond ring on her third finger left hand. "This will help me find you anywhere, anytime. I'm asking you to marry me now and I'll ask you to marry me again when I find you. Don't ever take it off."

Melody touched the ring. "Never. Never." She said as her eyes fixed on the light. She smiled. She squeezed Charles's hand, "I'll wait for you," she said and ever so softly slipped away.

It was one of God's most beautiful days. There wasn't even standing room in the church. All of Chicago, and people who'd never known Melody Adams, came to say goodbye. As the minister said his final sermon, Deloris Adams joined the choir. Then, in the sweetest, angelic, heart-wrenching voice, she sang to her daughter.

"Lay down, my dear child, lay down and take your rest. I'm gonna lay your head upon my savior's breast. I love you so, but Jesus loves you best. I bid you goodnight, goodnight, goodnight."

Charles, Randolph, Courtney, and Sam were pallbearers.

Veronica nodded her head in silent prayer as the casket passed by.

April and Veronica walked solemnly behind the coffin holding each other's hands. Now they were two.

"I wanted to see her," April wailed.

"We were Chicago's brightest stars, Melody." April held her head high as she delivered her speech at the graveside. "You were the brightest and the bravest of us all. You exemplified what it meant to find the person within, to be the best you could have been. You have left us behind, but you will never be forgotten. Through love, we will continue to inspire all to live the motto of the Holy Trinity; the trinity of style, class, and achievement."

"You got that right, girl. You got that right. And we ain't finished yet." Veronica put her arm around April and led her away.

Later, at the wake, Veronica sat quietly beside Charles. "How are you holding up?" She slid a hand over his.

"My only regret," he said, deep sorrow in every word, "is that I never got to teach her to really fly."

"Fly? Oh, Charles believe me. Melody has always flown. And she will continue to fly."

CHAPTER FORTY-SIX

FOUR MONTHS LATER. Charles's parents died four months after Melody, a day after each other. All his friends were by his side. He was lonely but not alone, and he was content to have been loved, not once, not twice, but three times, in a most fulfilling way. Not one day had gone by that he didn't think of Melody. Charles took his place by the open window. Every day at the very second Melody had died, he'd sit by the window, looking out at the light that had carried his love away. And he would remember how she'd held his hand and smiled lovingly at him before fixing her eyes on the light only she could see. Such a peace had come over her face and he saw her smile before the light entered her eyes, closed them forever, and took her on a single ray out of this earth and out of his life. Indeed, the light had embraced her, and no matter how short a period, she had embraced him in her light. He'd find her, of that, he was sure. That she hadn't told him about her beginnings never mattered. Beginnings. Endings. What was it all about? Love is what matters, and those emotions come from anywhere. Charles rose from the window, his hand thrust deep in his pocket. He loved that woman so very much. Just before she'd closed her eyes forever, she had whispered. "The light has come for me." That day a Jaybird landed on his window. "Hello, my love," Charles said.

Back at his desk Charles looked at the incorporation papers, picked up his Waterford and signed boldly. Charles Reginald Bell. It was time to go on with life. The patent papers of his father's invention lay before him. He would pass them on to the world. He would make them live.

The phone trilled softly.

"Charles Bell," he answered.

"Mr. Bell. This is Meredith Charleston. I saw an ad in the paper for a position I'd like to apply for with your new company. I have followed your career since Comtech. Might I send my resume to your HR department?"

"You've got the HR department, Ms. Charleston. My fax number is…"

"I have that number, Sir."

"Very well. I look forward to hearing from you."

July was hot. The garden was in full bloom, and though the city had asked people to water their lawn every other day, that Sunday, April was sneaking in an unauthorized watering. The poor plants needed a drink. She missed Sam. He'd been the one who always made the arrangements for gardening, snow removal, and these sorts of things. It had been almost six months since they had separated. If Melody's life had taught anything it was the fragility and sacredness of love.

"Hi, Mrs. Summers." The mailman eyed her blatant disregard for the city's request, handing her the mail.

"I won't water tomorrow," she promised.

"Have a good day, Ma'am." The mailman retreated.

She rifled through the mail. Her divorce papers should come through any day now, but she wasn't sure if that's what she wanted. She loved Sam and wished she could swallow her pride. How could she take him back and not have him think he could use her as he wished, betray her, and have her run back to his arms when he felt like it? No, she had to be strong. She needed to move on. Then again, she'd so regretted not being by Melody's side when she died. If something happened to Sam, could she live?

The silver Beemer pulled into the driveway. "April." Sam wound down the window. "Do you have a minute?" "Earth Angel" was playing on the stereo, and April felt prickles.

"Sam. I'm on my way out," she said, barely glancing in his direction. He had returned to full "kill-you-on-the-spot" good looks and picture of health.

"This will only take a minute. If you could just spare me a minute." Sam jumped out of the car. A snug pair of washed out jeans hugged his hips, and his gray shirt exposed his muscular chest. A Bull's hat covered his eyes, but she could feel them burning a hole in her heart.

"Don't you make a scene out here?" April hurriedly ushered him into the house.

Sam looked around the house he hadn't seen in over six months. She had gotten rid of everything that had been theirs. And to be honest, he preferred this light décor a lot better. The house was beautiful, light, and airy. He missed his home.

"Why are you here?"

"April," Sam advanced toward her and she stepped back.

"Sam you have got to get a grip. Our marriage is over. The divorce papers will be here any day now, so you can't just drop by when you feel like it. That could be considered stalking!"

"Take me back, April," Sam was on his knees.

"I can't go back, Sam, and there's nothing I can do about the length of time it takes to heal from a betrayal."

"At Melody's funeral I knew I could not live without you. I've changed. Worked out my problems. I don't know what else to say or do to show you how very sorry I am. I've been punished enough. Isn't it time for me to come home? I don't want a divorce. I'll spend the rest of my life making it up to you. If your answer is no, I'll move on one way or the other, but right now, I don't know how."

"Would you like some Clarity tea?" April pulled off her gardening glove and washed her hand under the kitchen sink.

"I'd love that." Sam was hesitant to sit in his own house. "I really need some clarity."

"Well, are you going to drink it standing up?" April motioned him to a chair.

Sam sat at the kitchen table. They used to sit there every morning and have coffee before going their separate ways. He wanted that again.

"I miss you, April. I really do. "Why do you keep saying that? You've always said I wasn't a charm to live with. And I do have to admit, Sam, that to your credit, you didn't bolt. But you hurt me very deeply."

"I know, and I've had a lot of time to think about what I did."

As he liked it, April poured the tea, squeezing lemon and spooning two scoops of sugar into Sam's cup. "What about children. Have you come to terms with that?" April knew Sam wanted more than anything for his lineage to continue.

"I'd be lying if I said I'm over that desire. I'm not. But if you don't want children, I can live with it."

"Sam, to be honest, I have been thinking a lot about us. Having thoughts that keep me up at night. I know I owe us a chance, but I'm scared. When I took the vows of marriage, I meant them, but I'm I will not tolerate infidelity."

"April, if you give me one more chance, I'll show you how much I love you. I will never, never hurt you again." Sam was standing next to her.

"Never say never, Sam."

"Do you mean that I might be able to come home sometime?"

"I didn't say anything about coming home."

"I'll do anything. Anything if you just let me come home. I stay in the guest suite until you're ready to talk."

"There is one thing you'll have to do before we can ever be friends, again, much less come home."

"Anything. What? What can I do?"

"Make peace with my mother. Accept her for who she is. To understand me, you must understand her. She is a part of who I am. I can't let you come home until we are all one."

"I bet your mother really hates me now."

"She knows nothing about Sophie, or even that we've split up. I have learned to lie a lot these past few months. All she knows is that you have been taking many trips."

"I'll try. Believe me, April. I'll really try."

"Good." April smiled. "I'll invite Gabriella and John to dinner on Sunday. Be here at five p.m."

"Sunday. Can't we take this a little slower?"

"No. I'd like to do it Sunday. Monday, who knows, maybe we can go out to dinner and then you can move into the mother-in-law suite."

"I'll be here," Sam said, draining his teacup. "Do you know what the leaves say?" He gave her the cup.

"It says if you do okay on Sunday, we'll have dinner on Monday." April enjoyed watching Sam grovel. She wanted to laugh aloud but kept a somber face.

On Sunday, Sam arrived at five and promptly, at six, the doorbell rang.

"Sam, will you get that, please?"

Sam rolled his eyes.

"Be nice," April admonished.

"Shouldn't you be saying that to your mother?"

"Remember, niceness is the trump card you need."

"Good evening." Gabriella walked past Sam with barely a glance. "John is parking the car. He'll be in momentarily."

"Hi, Mummy." The strain was evident in April's voice. This, frankly, could turn out to be the worst night of her life. "Dinner is ready. As soon as Dad comes in, we can eat. Just help me put things on the table, will you."

Gabriella moved to the China cabinet. "April," her mother pulled plates from the cabinet, "I know what you're trying to do. I don't know what you expect."

"Mother, I expect to feed you, and I will expect a lot of civility from you tonight. It is us, or Sam and I alone. Do you want to lose your daughter?" April said, putting back the Wedgewood her mother was taking out, replacing them with the Lenox. "It matches the floral arrangement." She was glad to see her father coming through the door.

"Hey, Daddy. Don't you look dapper?"

"How else could I look, being married to your mother?"

"Now that's a true statement if ever I heard one."

"What may I get you to drink?" Sam, whose angst was more for her mother than her father, directed his question to John.

"You know, I have wanted one of those great Martinis you make."

"And what about you, Mother?" Sam said to Gabriella.

"Nothing. But let's cut out this nonsense and cut to the chase," Gabriella interjected. Whatever was said about Gabriella, it could never be that she didn't have verve, style, and a way of finding immediate clarity. She didn't appreciate small talk or excuses. "We were not invited here to figure out drinks. We are here because you think I'm a right stick in the mud, and my daughter wants us to get along."

"Mother!"

"April. Why beat around the bush? We are here because you want us to all get along. In my book, understanding begins with honesty."

"You're right," Sam almost hissed but toned it down. "Let me start. I despise your arrogant, superior attitude that makes you think you're better than the rest of us. I despise the amount of control you have over April. But I love your daughter and if getting along with you is what I have to do, I am going to try my hardest…. ."

"I was hoping to get a few martinis under my belt before Mount Vesuvius erupted." John shook his head. "This will be an evening," he raised his glass."

"Sam," Gabriella said. "The world is as you interpret it. If you feel I act superior, you might want to check why you feel inferior. You have no right to impose your views on anyone. I've never tried to impose mine on you. I've simply told my daughter it would have been less of a struggle to marry her own kind. An even yoke, as they say."

"And Mrs. Dixon, what is your daughter's kind?" Sam tried hard not to pull the woman by her ears and throw her out of the house.

"Kinds that would not be bad-tempered for no reason," Gabriella snapped.

"Stop! Please. Mom, Sam. I need you all to be civil. And shut up, damn it. Both of you." April slammed her hand on the table. Sam flinched.

"Mother," April was furious. "We're here to all forgive each other for the big and little hurts. Accept each other where they are. Work out our differences and move on. Sam and I have problems, but we love each other,

Sam crossed his fingers under the table.

and if we can't all get along here, you'll have to be out of our lives. If you force me to choose, Mom I am going to choose Sam. But if we could stop fighting maybe we can start planning a family."

"And who will raise your child if not me?" Gabrille sassed, her eyes crossed at Sam.

"What does that mean, Mom."

It means you'll have babysitters for your child. What else could it mean."

"It's about damn time," John Dixon said. "About damn time."

Sam was beyond words. He couldn't move. Did she say get back together? He wanted to pull his wife into his arms and kiss her for a long time, but he sat still. Did she say baby? He got up from his seat, went to his wife and kissed her, passionately.

"John do you see what I mean?" Gabriella demanded. "Why couldn't he wait until we left."

"He couldn't wait, Mom. We have been separated for six months."

"What do you mean you've been separated?"

"Well, Mom Sam had an affair, and we've been separated for six months."

"Is that so? So how does Sam and I becoming instant buddies going to change his infidelity? Are you really thinking of getting back with him?"

"Gabriella," John Dixon snapped, "No one needs lectures and inquisitions. Have you heard a word April said? I would like it very much if you wouldn't utter one more word about your this and your that. This isn't about you. It is about our daughter and her husband and our future grandchildren. She's pleading for our help, and by God, she's going to get it. We are, as I understand it, starting over from scratch. So dear, every word out of your mouth tonight had better be meaningful for April and Sam. Let's all be honest and open."

"Very well, dear." Gabriella smiled beguilingly. "Let me start by telling April how I coped with your affair."

"Let's do that over dinner, shall we, dear. April, I want to eat. Over dinner, we'll pray for strength. Sam, bring that Martini shaker over here. I'll need a few under my belt before all this affair ruckus begins."

April gagged on her drink, and Sam smiled from ear to ear. This was real. Real. Real.

"Don't forget you're driving," Gabriella said.

"Not if I can help it. Do you see how big this house is? How many bedrooms in this place, Sam?"

"Six."

"There. We can run around and try all five old girl. Remind me why even with all those affairs, I couldn't leave you, hot Mama."

Gabriella almost died. "John, you had only one affair. But I'm happy to remind you whose suspenders hold up your pants. And all five bedrooms will be fine with me."

"Six."

Sam and April burst into gales of laughter.

Three months later.

April made a Joyner-Kersee sprint to the bathroom. Before she could throw the toilet lid up, she was upchucking her dinner. She sat on the floor and heaved until her stomach was empty. Her temples throbbed, and her mouth was bitter with bile. It must have been something she ate at Veronica's dinner party. Brushing her teeth and changing her nightdress, April climbed back into bed and woke up her husband. "I think I have food poisoning."

"Food poisoning? We'd better go to the hospital."

"Nothing they can do."

The next morning the entire scene was repeated. Christ, she should try out for the Olympics. Food poisoning was a bitch. Thank God it only lasts twenty-four hours. That was if it didn't kill her first. Maybe she should call Veronica and see if anyone else had been affected by the dinner.

"Projectile. Uh-huh. What time? Uh-huh. Now when did you say your last period was again?"

"Stop being a baby doctor. I can't be yet. Are you sure no one else is feeling queasy?"

"No. I'm not. Charles hasn't called, so I don't know. Of course, I didn't expect him to. Did you see that, Meredith Charleston? She is stunning. His new comptroller."

"Yes, she was nice too."

"Randolph and I seem to be fine. What about Sam?"

"He seems fine."

"So, when did you say your last period was April?"

"I'm not sure. Two weeks ago. Why?"

"Because last night when you were here, I thought you looked pregnant. I was going to ask, but I figured you'd say something"

"How the hell does someone look pregnant?"

"If you see as many pregnant people as I do, you'd know—something in the face. And if you're so sure you're not pregnant, why don't you just answer my question? When was your last period for real?"

"Fine. I will. Hold on. I'll have to go look at my datebook." April pulled out the calendar she kept on her nightstand, where she wrote down her menstrual cycle every month. "Okay. Let's see. Last month I had a period; oh my, I forgot to write it down. Well, I'll just go back a month. Too much going on with this new company to worry about periods. Now let's see the month before...."

"April, you're six weeks pregnant. Believe me. Come down to my office at lunch. I'll test you."

"Okay, Miss smarty pants. You're going to eat crow."

"And you're going to have a visit from the stork." Veronica chuckled. "Just wait and see. But don't worry, Missy, you have the best doctor in Chicago. I just have one question. Does your company have insurance?"

April arrived at Veronica's, only to find the doctor had an emergency.

"I'm here for a test. A pregnancy test," April said self-consciously.

"The doctor's assistant will be right out."

"What time do you expect Dr. Whittaker back? I'll come back."

"Only if you want to. The nurse's assistant is very capable of helping you."

April sat on the avocado-colored sofa and waited.

"You made it down here fast. "Veronica walked in, looking becoming in green scrubs and paper shoes. "Anybody tested that very pregnant pee yet?"

"No," April said indignantly, "I was waiting."

"Then come on in here, girly, and watch the stick go bluuuueee."

That evening when Sam came home, April had a candlelight dinner ready.

"What are we celebrating?" He kissed her warmly. He was so glad to be home. Never, and he meant it, never again would he take love for granted.

"I'm feeling fine. How about you?"

"Fine too." He looked at her suspiciously. Had April ever cooked since they'd been married? "You look beautiful tonight, dear."

"As I should be."

"And why is that?"

"Because I'm a woman with child."

Sam dropped to his knees. "You mean; you mean, we are pregnant?"

"That's what a woman with child usually means."

Sam jumped up and hoisted April into the air and whirled her. "I can't believe it." He kissed her deeply before putting her back down on the ground. "It's really true?"

"If little blue sticks don't lie. Yes, Sam, it is."

"What? What? Oh, April, is it true?"

"If little blue sticks don't lie." She repeated

Sam pulled her close to him. He kissed her cheeks, neck, arms, lips, and not yet swollen belly, and when he was done, there were tears in his eyes. "Thank you, April," he said earnestly. "Thank you for my eternity."

Sam was more ecstatic as the days went by. He kept rubbing April's belly when there was absolutely nothing to see. "We'll have to hire some help."

I'm only eight weeks pregnant."

"So?"

"You're right. We do need help. I've decided to start the firm after all."

"That's my girl."

"I'm not even going to use Martin's dirt as a competitive advantage. I'll get business, fair and square."

"But April. The entire executive staff is corrupt."

"Yeah. They sure are. I did my part. I sent it to the powers. The truth is going to come out and I have far better things to do than worry about S&G and their shareholders. Like painting rooms and fluffing comforters."

When she was three months pregnant, April started an investment firm. Sam provided many of his entertainment clients as investors. Since his wife owned the company, there was no conflict of interest and if there was, too damn bad. Tell it to the White boys. April even managed to snag five of S&G's most prestigious clients. And as predicted, so it was. The scandal of S&G's mile-deep embezzlement scheme rocked Chicago. The jail was filled with S&G executives. It seems the Kusak cover-up, once exposed, made clients scurry like flies.

"You know what I've been thinking?"

"No, what?" April stroked her husband's head perpetually lying on her stomach. It seemed to have found a permanent home there. "We should take another trip to Jamaica."

"I'm eight months pregnant."

"When the baby is born, I mean."

"Are you sure you can behave yourself this time?"

"I swear on my—well just let's say I swear I will never hurt you again. You're my "Earth Angel." "

"You'd better not stop singing that song." She kissed the top of his head. "Okay," she eased Sam off her stomach and got up to switch on the stereo, flipping the CD to track eight. Deep hypnotic music filled the air, and April's body started swaying in a trance-like manner as though drugged. "Let's get in the mood for Jamaica and let me get this baby started on rhythm. This music is what is called roots music in Jamaica." April danced around the room.

"Until the philosophy that holds one race inferior, and another superior, is finally and permanently discredited and abandoned, and until the color of a man's eye is of no more significance than the color of his eyes, me say war. War in the East….."

"These are the words of Haile Selassie via Jah Rastafari Bob Marley" April was singing and swaying.

"You can dance to roots music? Wait till your mother sees this. She'll disinherit you." Sam laughed and joined his wife, swaying to the hypnotic rhythm. "Roots in a Babylon, man."

Gabriella Dixon was already buying everything made for babies. She bought clothes from websites in France, Spain, Italy, Jamaica, and even a toga from Greece. She was beside herself; though the jury was still out on how she felt about Sam. Like it or not, she had every intention of bringing up the baby the way she did April. Sam would just have to accept that.

Randolph drank from the half-empty glass. He had been signing books for two hours, and the line was still out the door. When he looked up to smile at his next patron, he saw his wife, grinning broadly, a stack of books in her arms. "This one is for Shelly, this one is for April, and this one is for… ."

"Who is this one for now?" He couldn't help laughing.

"I know I'm spending all your profits, but I'm so proud. I want the world to know. But I swear this is my last one."

"Who'd you like me to sign it to?"

"Melody. To Melody Adams with love."

It was Spring.

CHAPTER FORTY-SEVEN

"**A**H, WE'RE ALL brainwashed. What's wrong with good all the time. The world's so banal. So tight assed with a bunch of cock-eyed rules. Me, for one, I'm done. I'm not going to try so hard to fit my square peg into other people's round holes anymore. Where the hell has it gotten me?" Janice a newly appointed EVP's temperature was rising.

"I agree with that. It's hard being everyone's ideal, bending here and bending there. Best be yourself," Veronica agreed, winking at April.

"Success is a trip, eh? I never thought it would be easy, but I never thought it would be this costly either. I'm so sick of these problems." Melanie, Charles's new CFO said.

"Aw-right, now. Who do you know alive that doesn't have problems? I have more problems in my life now than you can imagine. I don't even know how I got there." Veronica smiled. "Dessert, anyone?"

April smiled as the waiter approached the table with perfect timing. The women accepted the menus.

"I'd like the key lime pie," Veronica spoke first.

"And I'd like the Crème Brule." April said."

"Melody would have ordered the chocolate lava cake." Veronica said.

"So, ladies, welcome. This is what the Trinity is about, ladies. Sisterhood. Friendship, support love and cake! We meet every month." April raised a glass: "To Chicago's Trinity, now redefined by us to be four women, screwed up but making waves. May we be masters of our jungle."

"What the hell, JUNGLE!." Veronica made an ape-like face and started singing softly in perfect alto: "In the jungle, the quiet jungle, the lion sleeps tonight." The women looked at each other; their eyes were brimming with laughter. A chorus rang out.

"Ah wimoweh a wimoweh."

Patrons turned to stare, but the women were oblivious.

www.ingramcontent.com/pod-product-compliance
Lightning Source LLC
Chambersburg PA
CBHW070237200726
48293CB00005B/1660